Praise for The Black Knight Chronicles

"Honestly, this is one of the best books that I've read this year and certainly a new series that I will be following from here on out."
—*Black Lagoon Reviews*

"I love this book. It makes me happy in a way that hasn't happened in a long, long time."
—Keryl Raist, Author of *Sylvianna*

"This is another great book in what will hopefully be a large and successful series. I know I will be eagerly awaiting the next installment."
—*Indie Book Blog*

The Black Knight Chronicles, Omnibus Edition

Book One: Hard Day's Knight

Book Two: Back In Black

Book Three: Knight Moves

by

John G. Hartness

Bell Bridge Books

This is a work of fiction. Names, characters, places and incidents are either the products of the author's imagination or are used fictitiously. Any resemblance to actual persons (living or dead), events or locations is entirely coincidental.

Bell Bridge Books
PO BOX 300921
Memphis, TN 38130
Print ISBN: 978-1-61194-201-9

Bell Bridge Books is an Imprint of BelleBooks, Inc.

We at BelleBooks enjoy hearing from readers.
Visit our websites – www.BelleBooks.com and www.BellBridgeBooks.com.

10 9 8 7 6 5 4 3 2 1

Cover design: Debra Dixon
Interior design: Hank Smith
Photo credits:
Christine Griffin

:Lkbo:01:

Table of Contents

Book One: *Hard Day's Knight* 1

Book Two: *Back In Black* 149

Book Three: *Knight Moves* 299

Book 1:

Hard Day's Knight

Dedication

This book is dedicated to some of the fantastic teachers I've had in my life. Thanks for the helping hand and the kick in the butt.

Thanks to:

Marc Powers

Anne Fletcher

Blair Beasley

Ed Haynes

Deborah Hobbs

Kay McSpadden

William Good

Jan West

Durham Smith

Linwood Littlejohn

Billie Hicklin

Betty Dickson

Chapter 1

I hate waking up in an unfamiliar place. I've slept in pretty much the same bed for the past fifteen years, so when I wake up someplace new, it really throws me off. When I wake up tied to a metal folding chair in the center of an abandoned warehouse that reeks of stale cigarette smoke, diesel fuel and axle grease—well, that really starts my night on a sparkling note.

My mood deteriorated further when I heard a voice behind me say, "It's about time you woke up, bloodsucker."

Why do people have to be rude? It's a condition, like freckles. I'm a vampire. Deal with it. We can do without the slurs, thank you very much.

"Go easy on the bloodsucker, pal. I haven't had breakfast," was what I tried to say, but since my mouth was duct-taped shut, I sounded more like a retarded Muppet than a fearsome creature of the night.

My repartee needed work if I hoped to talk my way out of this. Of course, if my mysterious captor had wanted me dead, he'd had all day to make that happen. Instead, I woke up tied to a standard metal folding chair, the kind that gets sacrificed in countless professional wrestling matches. I tested my bonds. I was tied tight, and whatever he had bound me with burned—making him devout and the binding blessed, or the bonds were silver. My money was on silver. The true believers are more the stake-them-in-the-coffins types than the kidnap-them-and-tie-them-to-chairs types.

"Shut up, *bloodsucker*. You, as the one tied to the chair with silver chains, get to sit there and do whatever I say." My captor moved around in front where I could get a good look at him. I knew him, of course. It's never the new guy in town who ties you to a chair. It's always that creepy guy who you've seen lurking around the cemetery for a couple weeks in mid-October, the one that you can't decide if he's there to mourn or for some other reason. And, of course, it's always some other reason.

I'd seen this guy hanging around one of the big oak trees in my cemetery for a couple of weeks, near the freshest grave in the joint. I never paid much attention to his wardrobe until now, figuring it was close to Halloween, so he was just a goth kid getting a jump on the competition, but in retrospect I realized I should have. He wore almost stereotypical vampire-hunter garb. Black jeans, black boots, long black coat, wide-brimmed black hat. Christ, I bet he owned the *Van Helsing* Blu-ray. I swore then that if I ever got the chance, I was eating Hugh Jackman's liver. No, we don't usually eat people, but liver's a good source of blood, and I was pissed. I had been caught and trussed up like a Thanksgiving turkey by a skinny teen who watched too many bad vampire movies.

This kid was white, about sixteen, with mousy brown hair, and he looked like he played too much *Call of Duty* instead of getting a job. His skin was paler than mine, for crying out loud, and I'm dead. His clothes hung loose, like scarecrow garb, on his scrawny frame, and he either had an asthma inhaler in his front pocket or was happy to see me. God, I hoped it was an inhaler.

The kid reached forward and ripped the tape off, taking a layer or two of skin with it.

"OWWW!" I yelled, straining against my bonds. "You little rat bastard, I swear to God I am going to drink you dry and leave your body on the lawn like . . . like an empty bag of flesh!"

Okay, my similes need some work.

"I don't think so, bloodsucker. I think you're going to do anything I tell you to, or I'll leave you tied up there to starve."

He had a point there. It's not like there were very many people who would miss a vampire, and I hadn't yet figured out how to get loose from whatever silver-lined bonds he'd created. Sitting here and starving was entirely possible.

"All right, what do you want?" I asked. Might as well find out right now if he wanted something simple or—

"I want you to turn me," he replied. The look of hope on his face was a little pathetic, really, but there was a determination there that was disturbing. Talking him out of his demand was not going to be easy.

"No." I wanted to get the short and simple part out of the way first, then we could move on to the lengthy explanations.

"Oh, but you will." He leered at me like a bad movie villain.

"Oh, but I won't." I just sat there. I couldn't do anything else, but one thing was certain—I was *not* turning this asshat into a vampire.

"I demand that you turn me. You are at my mercy and must do as I say," the asshat proclaimed. I craned my neck to see if there was an audience behind him. Nope, we were alone and he was performing for the rats in the warehouse.

"Not a chance."

"But . . . but . . . you *have* to."

"Not gonna happen, kid," I repeated.

"Why not?" He deflated like a Macy's parade balloon in a cactus field. Suddenly he wasn't a grandiose vampire hunter, but a scared teenager who'd caught a tiger by his toe and really didn't know what to do with him now.

"Because I don't turn people. Because this life isn't all it's cracked up to be. Because you'd miss all those romantical sunsets you probably write maudlin poetry about. Because it's not fair to the ecosystem to add another predator. Because we don't really sparkle. All of the above. None of the above. Pick a reason, kid, any reason you like. I'm not turning you." I started to look around for another way to get out of this mess, but it didn't look good for our hero. That'd be me since it's my story. Dammit.

For a skinny little gamer-geek, he'd done a good job tying me up. I guess that's another thing we can thank the Internet for—unlimited access to fetish porn has improved the knot-tying ability of men who can't get dates. I couldn't exactly see my hands, but by straining forward, I could see that my ankles were tied to separate legs of the chair with those plastic zip ties you get in the electrical aisle. I could see a silver necklace wound around each tie, and by the way my wrists felt, he'd done the same thing there.

The silver sapped the strength from my arms by contact, and I couldn't get enough leverage with my legs to do anything useful. I looked up to try and Jedi mind trick my kidnapper, when I noticed two things: one—he was wearing polarized sunglasses, which was a neat idea, although ultimately useless against my mental abilities, and two—he was crying.

"You have to turn me!" Tears streamed down his cheeks. "I'm running out of time, and this was the only thing I could think of to fix it!"

I couldn't believe myself. I was actually starting to feel sorry for the guy. "Okay, kid. Why don't you tell me what's wrong, and I'll see if I can help?"

"No one can help, but if I were one of the Undead I could help myself." I swear I could actually hear him capitalize *undead*.

"You know that's kinda my job, right? Helping people that can't help themselves. Kinda like the A-Team, without the Mohawk and the van. Reach into my shirt pocket and grab a business card. I promise not to bite you. The Undead cannot tell a lie." Total bullshit, but I've often found people dumb enough to romanticize the whole vampire thing will believe almost anything.

He reached into my pocket and took out a business card. It had my name, James Black, and cell-phone number under a logo—*Black Knight Investigations, Shedding Light On Your Darkest Problems*. Neither the company name nor the stupid slogan was my idea. And I prefer *Jimmy* to *James*.

"You're a detective?"

I nodded.

"And you think you can help me?"

"I can't really know that until you tell me what your problem is. So, why don't you untie me, and we can talk about this like a pair of reasonable people?" I put a little mojo into my eyes, and he started toward me with a pair of wire cutters in his hand. Then all hell broke loose instead of me.

Chapter 2

There was a huge crash from behind me, and I had a sinking feeling that my cavalry had arrived. I twisted around in my chair to see what was going on and watched as part of the roof came down in a shower of glass from the skylight and rotted wood. A rotund form struck the ground with a bone-jarring thump and lay sprawled on the concrete floor. From the curses emanating from the same general vicinity as the body, my suspicions were confirmed. My partner had arrived to save the day. With his usual subtlety and success rate.

"What the hell?" The kid stared at what had fallen through the roof, my freedom momentarily forgotten. I leaned forward onto my tiptoes and the front two chair legs and turned myself around to watch the floor show provided by my best friend and business partner, Gregory W. Knightwood IV. He's the "Knight" in Black Knight Investigations. Greg looked a little the worse for wear from his fall, but apparently none of the wood he fell on pierced his heart. Otherwise, I'd be looking for someone else to share naming rights with. After a few more seconds of muttered cursing, Greg realized that he had an audience and sprang to his feet, swirling his cape around him dramatically.

At least that was the idea. It's hard to swirl properly when part of the cape is draped over your head, but he gave it a hell of a try. Greg sometimes takes the whole vampire thing a little too much to heart. I was not surprised he'd chosen this moment as one of those times. In addition to the cape, he was dressed all in black spandex, which was not a good look for a guy who topped out at five foot nine and weighed somewhere around two-forty. He had on motorcycle boots, also black, and what looked like an honest-to-God utility belt. It was kinda like a cross between Batman and the Goodyear Blimp. At least Greg wasn't wearing a mask this time.

He fought with the cape for a few more seconds before finally mumbling something rude and tearing it to shreds. He looked at my captor with his most menacing stare and said, "Release my partner, and you might live to see another sunrise."

I thought that was a pretty good line under most circumstances, but Greg didn't know that the kid didn't want to live to see any more sunrises. Needless to say, he was a little taken aback when the kid lunged at him with a cross in hand. Greg stumbled backward a step before his vampire abilities outweighed his natural clumsiness, and he caught himself. Then he reached out, grabbed the cross from the kid and flung it across the room. The kid's eyes widened as he realized what kind of trouble he was in. Greg reached out and grabbed him by the throat, lifting him off the ground with one hand.

At least, he lifted him a couple of inches, because Greg was way shorter than the kid and didn't have the height to properly impress the wannabe vampire. Greg and the kid both seemed to realize this at about the same time, and Greg tossed him across the room in the general direction of his holy symbol. Then he came over to where I was bound and began to free me.

"Nice entrance." I smirked a little.

"You want to stay tied to the chair?"

Good point. I shut up and let him go about the delicate task of unwinding the silver from my wrists and snipping the wire ties. At least the kid had dropped the wire cutters close by so Greg didn't have to use his teeth. He'd freed my right arm when I caught a glimpse of movement out of the corner of my eye. I opened my mouth to warn my partner when he turned on the kid.

Vampires are fast. Like, ridiculously fast. And the first time a mortal gets a real eyeful of how fast we are, it usually freaks the person out. Not this kid, though. He was standing over Greg with a broken piece of lumber, probably what used to be a skylight, and Greg's faster-than-human whirl didn't give him a second's pause. He swung from the heels and cracked the board right over Greg's head with everything he had.

"Ouch," Greg said as he stared at my would-be kidnapper.

"You're still standing." The kid had a good grasp of the obvious, I had to give him that.

"Punk, the only thing you can do with that stick that will bother me is to shove it through my heart. And there's no way I'm just going to stand here and let you do that." Greg reached out and snatched the two-by-four out of the kid's hands. The kid tried to hold onto it, but Greg was way too strong for that. The board clattered end over end across the warehouse, and Greg passed me the clippers. "Why don't you finish the job? I think I need to keep an eye on your friend here to make sure he doesn't do anything else stupid."

I snipped the last plastic tie, shook myself free of the silver chain and stretched my arms and legs. Undead or not, being tied with your arms behind your back was damned uncomfortable. At least I didn't have to worry about him cutting off circulation to my extremities. I stepped to one side and pointed at the chair.

"Sit," I ordered.

"Are you going to turn me now?" the kid asked.

"No, but I am going to get a few answers, and I don't particularly care if you give them to me willingly or if I have to compel you to answer me." I'm not very good at compulsion, but he didn't know that.

"I'll talk, just don't hurt me."

I shook my head. The idiot wanted to be turned into a vampire, and he didn't think that was going to hurt? Kids these days. He sat in the only chair as I looked around for a stool or something and found nothing. Looked like Greg and I would be standing for the interrogation. Greg was poking through the kid's backpack, which was lying in the open trunk of an old sedan. Apparently that's how I'd been brought in, trussed up in the trunk of a Buick. Fantastic.

"Now, what's so awful that you want to be turned into a vampire to get away from it?" I asked.

Greg's head whipped around like it was on a swivel. "He wants *what?*"

"Yeah, apparently young Mister . . ." I paused and looked at the kid.

"Harris. Tommy Harris," he spluttered.

"Apparently young Mister Tommy Harris here wants to become one of the undead. He brought me here to turn him into a bloodsucking demon of the night. I haven't figured out yet if he has an unhealthy affection for the taste of human blood, or just doesn't like going to the beach, but that's why he kidnapped me."

"Wow," Greg said, slamming the trunk of the car and leaning on it. "He's dumber than he looks if he thought he could bully you into turning him. *Isn't he?*" Greg gave me an odd look, like he thought I might have actually turned the punk.

Greg is the only vampire I've created, way back when I was newly turned myself and not completely in control of my powers. Sometimes he picks inopportune times to play that guilt card.

"Yeah, pretty dumb." I decided not to air any dirty laundry in public and turned back to my kidnapper. "Tommy, what's going on that's so bad that you need to become a vampire to be able to deal with it? Maybe we can help. As I was explaining before my partner's unexpected entrance—" Greg sketched a rough salute from the trunk of the car, "—we are private investigators and we're pretty good at what we do. Maybe we can help you."

"I doubt it. I mean, I'm sure you guys are great detectives—"

"We are," Greg interrupted. I shot him a look that said *shut up, doofus* and gestured for Tommy to continue.

"But it's not a mystery you can solve by detecting, And I can't stop it," he finished.

"Can't stop what, exactly?" Greg reached into the top of his right boot and pulled out a blood pack. "Snack?"

"What flavor?" I asked

"O-positive. I didn't know what you'd be in the mood for, what with the whole kidnapping thing." He tossed me the bag, and I ripped it open. As I brought the bag to my mouth, I noticed Tommy looking even paler than before, which was no mean feat.

"What's wrong, kid? Haven't you ever seen one of us eat?" I turned the bag up and started to drink. Nice. This one was fresh, no more than a couple of weeks old, and while the bag smelled faintly of Greg's socks, being in his boot had kept the blood warm. It was smooth, obviously a young donor, without much in the way of contaminants, and the snack sped the healing of the burns the silver necklaces had made on my wrists and ankles.

"No, I haven't seen you . . . eat," Tommy said in a very small voice.

I finished the bag of blood and looked over at him. He looked like what he was, a very scared kid in over his head.

"Well this is a lot cleaner than the old-fashioned way, let me tell you," Greg finished off a blood bag of his own, and I wondered for a minute what flavor his had been. Each blood type had a unique taste, and different donors had their unique qualities, too. Finding a good batch in a blood bank was as likely as stumbling on a really good bottle of Bordeaux at Sam's Club.

Tommy looked a little sick, but he swallowed and went back to his story, careful not to look at either of us. "There's a witch that I pissed off, and now she wants to kill me and my whole family. All I could think of was to get you to turn me into a vampire so that I could kill her before she got to my family."

"Where did you find a witch in Charlotte, North Carolina? And what did you do to piss her off so bad she wants to kill you?" I asked. Our fair city is known for a lot of things—banking, bad basketball teams, good barbecue and car racing. But witchcraft doesn't even make the Department of Tourism's Top Ten list of attractions.

"And more importantly," Greg added, "how did you find out about Jimmy and figure out enough about us to nab him?" Greg hopped off the car trunk and was beside the kid's chair before he could even think about breathing. "Oh yeah, and we can smell it on you if you lie."

That's not exactly true. We can smell fear, and usually people smell a little different when they're lying, but this guy was so terrified already that I didn't think we could scent anything as subtle as a lie through all that fear. But he didn't have to know that.

"Well it all started with a girl," he began slowly.

Doesn't it always start with a girl?

Chapter 3

"She was just this weirdo little kid, all goth and stuff—"

Greg interrupted again. "Wait a minute. I thought goth went out in 1989?"

Tommy blinked before answering. "Uh . . . I wouldn't know. I wasn't born then. I know she wore a lot of black, too much eyeliner, always had on T-shirts with weird bands on them, you know, a freak." He didn't notice that Greg wasn't really listening, but was standing there shaking his head.

"I don't know, Jimmy-boy. I just don't know what's worse. The fact that you got captured by a human, or the fact that you got captured by a human *child*." Greg looked at me disapprovingly.

"Hey!" Tommy exclaimed. "I'm eighteen, you know. I'm no kid. After all, how old are you guys? You can't be more than a couple years older than me."

"None of your business—" I started, as Greg said "Thirty-five."

"Huh?" Tommy looked back and forth between the two of us, confused.

"Remember, kid? Vampires? Creatures of the night? We don't age, moron. We were turned when we were both twenty-two. Yeah, we're older than we look," Greg explained, reclaiming his perch on the trunk of the car.

"Except we're dead." I said, pulling over a stack of pallets and taking a seat. This kid looked like the long-winded type, and even with the blood, I wasn't feeling my best after being bound with silver. I decided I'd rather not stand for his whole monologue. "Anyway, you were saying?"

"Uh . . . yeah. Anyway, she was this weird middle-school kid or goth or whatever, and me and my buddies, well . . . we kinda gave her some crap from time to time. Nothing big, just—"

"Just making her life a living hell for the amusement of you and your idiot friends," Greg said, a grim look on his face. My partner had been heavy all his life, and middle school was particularly rough. An unfortunate side effect of becoming a vampire is your body never changes, no matter how much you eat or work out. Being trapped in an overweight body for eternity will give you sympathy for people who are picked on for being different. His stare never left Tommy's face as he waited for the admission of guilt.

"Um . . . yeah, I guess you could probably say that. But we were just messing with her—a couple of weeks ago—throwing her book bag around, popping her training bra and stuff, when this funky book falls out. It's all leather-bound, and soft, like a journal or something, and has writing on the cover like I've never seen before."

"I pick it up, and make to throw it to my buddy Jamie, and the girl goes nuts on me. She jumps on my back, pulling my hair and hitting me and stuff. She's never done anything like this, so I kinda shove her a little bit, not really even that hard, and she falls right on her butt in this big mud puddle, and the book maybe falls in the mud with her, and then she looks at me, and she curses at me."

He finally looked down, finally had the decency to look a little ashamed of his behavior, or maybe ashamed to have to own up to it to a couple of guys who were old enough to be his dad. But it wasn't enough shame to appease Greg.

"You mean, she called you a jerk, or an asshole, or something like that?" Greg asked. "Because, if you ask me, that was pretty well deserved."

"Nah, man, nothing like that," Tommy replied. "She really cursed me. She looked up at me and said something like 'By All the Dead, I Curse Thee. By All Hallow's Eve shall thee and all thy kin die a bloody death.' And when she said it, I could have sworn her eyes *glowed*, man. And I felt a chill run through me, and I knew she was for real. That's when I knew I had to get some serious firepower."

Tommy came to stand right in front of me and I could see the kid was way more scared of a witch in the future than two vampires in the present—and we could be pretty scary when we needed to. "Will you help me?"

"I don't know, kid."

Greg was less conflicted. "We don't usually go out of our way to defend bullies and kidnappers from justice. Seems to me you might deserve everything you're gonna get."

"I might, man, but my kid sister doesn't!" Tommy crossed to the Buick and grabbed Greg by the shoulders. "You've gotta help her, even if you don't help me. I mean, she's just a little kid. She doesn't deserve anything bad happening to her. If I get punished, that's fine. I screwed with the witch. I deserve to get turned into a frog or whatever. But Amy's only seven. She doesn't deserve to die because I was a jerk."

He was almost in hysterics, and I didn't want to see what would happen if he started crying and got snot all over Greg's costume. Lycra is a great fabric, but it doesn't shed mucus easily. I wish I didn't know that on so many levels. I also wished I didn't know where this was going.

As soon as Tommy mentioned a kid sister, he had Greg hooked. He's a sucker for cases with little kids. It goes back to his baby sister, Emily. That's a long story, and there's no happy ending, either. I was in as soon as he said "witch" because I'd never met a real one before, and I'm a sucker for cases with things I've never seen before.

Chapter 4

The next night a few hours after the sun set we were hanging out on Tommy's front porch waiting for him to finish dinner and lead us to the local witch's house. Or, more to the point, we were sitting on the roof of his porch so as not to scare his parents. I had to be careful to keep my feet from dangling off, and Greg had to be careful not to stray too far from structural support members. I wasn't sure what would have happened if he'd fallen through the roof, what with the rules about being invited in and all.

Falling into an abandoned warehouse was survivable. But an occupied personal dwelling? I didn't know if he would have fallen in and burst into flames, which would have been bad. We decided he should keep to the more solid parts of the roof.

It was about eight when the family fun time broke up, and our client made his way outside to meet us. He muttered some unintelligible collage of "out" and "nowhere" and "nobody" in response to his mother's queries, but eventually he stood on the sidewalk in front of his house looking around.

"Ummm . . . guys?" We let him stand there for a minute feeling nervous, and maybe a little silly, before we jumped down off the roof to flank him. At least I did. Greg, with his typical grace, managed to land half on the sidewalk, half in dog poop.

"Awww, man!" Greg gestured at his shoe. "Do you know how hard it is to get dog crap out of Doc Martens?"

"Bro, I didn't know they still *made* Doc Martens."

"Bite me."

"No thanks, pal. You went stale before the turn of the century."

He flipped me off, and I ignored him. "All right, Tommy, you're going to show us where this witch lives, and we're going to see if we can find anything out about her. If she's really a witch, we should be able to convince her to reverse the curse before anything bad happens to your family."

"How are you going to do that? You never said how you're going to convince her." Tommy was a nice kid, but a little whiny. I didn't need whiny clients. I had a partner for that.

"We can be pretty persuasive when we want to be."

"Remember? Creatures of the night? All that kind of nastiness?" Greg chimed in, having caught up with us after cleaning his boots. I'd talked him out of the spandex uniform for tonight, but he still had on the boots and utility belt. I'd decided to pick my battles on that front. And besides, every once in a while he pulled something useful out of his belt, like a flashlight, or tequila. My only concession to the stereotype was my long black leather coat, but I could get away with it the week before Halloween. Besides, I looked cool.

We walked along in silence for a while. At least, Greg and I tried to walk in silence. Tommy, on the other hand, decided to use this face time with the dark denizens of the night (his words, not mine) to satisfy his curiosity about the finer points of vampirism.

Block One: "Hey guys, is it true that you can't, you know, get it up unless you've fed recently? I mean, it makes sense, it is a blood flow thing." Cue sound effect of crickets chirping. The last thing I'm gonna discuss with a teenage wannabe is my erectile function. Or otherwise.

Block Two: "Hey, um, maybe this is too personal, but are you guys like, dating? I mean, I read somewhere that vampires are all, like bisexual and stuff. And you are always together." He finds it odd that the only two vampires in a city of a million and a half people hang out together a lot. You know, it is perfectly possible for two grown men to be roommates without there being anything out of the ordinary going on. Look at *Sesame Street*. No wait, that's probably not the best example. Just because you pay the bill does not mean you get the personal answers. And, um, *no*.

Block Three: "Um, do vampires poop?" Okay, maybe *this* is the last thing I'm gonna choose to discuss with a teenage wannabe.

Thankfully, the witch only lived about four blocks from Tommy's house. One block farther and we might have had to rip out his throat to stop the interrogation. But he stopped and said, "We're here."

I stared at the typical suburban two-story house—nice wraparound porch, white vinyl siding, bike in the front yard, probably four bedrooms with one converted into an "office" where the dad surfed porn on the Internet while the mom watched *American Idol* in the den. It didn't look much like a haven for evil sorcery. We scouted the outside of the house for a while making sure there wasn't a doghouse or anything else that might screw the pooch on this operation.

Dogs don't like vampires. Cats usually just look at us funny, but they do that to humans, too. Dogs go absolutely nuts when they get near a vampire. They bark, howl, tend to pee all over the place, and depending on the size of the dog we're talking about, either attack or run like hell. Of course it's always the little yippy dogs that attack, and the big dogs with enough sense to run like hell. I've ripped apart my fair share of Chihuahuas in my day. After we made sure that the place was clear of pooches, we reconvened on the sidewalk in front of the house.

"Tommy, this is where you come in," Greg instructed. The kid looked stunned to be called on, like he didn't know whether to run home like he had a hellhound on his trail, or to charge in there and beat the little witch to death with a phonebook.

He took a minute to summon up his courage. "What do I have to do?"

"You've got to convince her to come outside with you to talk," Greg replied.

"Why?"

"Jesus, kid. Not everything you've read is true, but not all of it is wrong, either. We can't go in without being invited. And if she's got any kind of power at all, she'll sense that we're not exactly mailmen. There's no way in hell she'll invite us in. Now, go. Get to convincing." Greg put one hand on Tommy's shoulder and spun him toward the house. He put the other hand in the small of his back and propelled him toward the front door. I hopped up onto the roof of the porch to get a closer sniff of what this chick was and if she was anything out of the ordinary.

Tommy rang the doorbell, and a girl answered right away. I couldn't see her, but I heard her clear as a bell. "I knew you'd be coming. You may not enter, and your friends may not enter, either. Your pitiful life is over, Thomas Harris, and nothing you say to me will change that."

Her voice didn't sound right, like there was something bigger speaking behind her, and I could smell something that definitely wasn't teenage girl floating around. I felt a surge of power and hopped down off the roof just in time to see her try to slam the door in Tommy's face. That's when the kid did something I never figured he'd have the guts to do—he grabbed her. He reached inside and dragged her out onto the porch, slamming the door behind her.

Once she was outside, I figured this would be simple—we'd haul her back to our cemetery, scare the crap out of her, and she'd be begging *please-Mr.-Vampire-don't-eat-me-I'm-still-a-virgin* quicker than you can say garlic mashed potatoes. But as soon as I stepped up onto the porch I realized I was wrong. Again.

Chapter 5

I got to the porch a little before Greg, and we both stopped cold. The girl, who couldn't have been more than fourteen and a hundred pounds soaking wet, had Tommy on his knees. His left arm was hanging loosely down by his side, obviously broken. He wasn't screaming, but it wasn't for lack of trying. The silence had more to do with the fact that she had moved on from his arm and was busy crushing his throat with one hand.

I ran at her. She flicked out her other fist almost faster than I could see, and certainly faster than I could dodge. She caught me square in the solar plexus and doubled me up with one ridiculous punch. Lucky for Tommy she only had two hands, because Greg came at her the same time I did and landed enough of a punch to knock her a step backward, making her let go of Tommy's throat before she could finish strangling him.

"You should not interfere, vampire. There are forces at work beyond your understanding." Again, she used that creepy voice. This chick would have irritated me if I hadn't been scared shitless.

"Well," Greg said in his best placating tone, "we have interfered. Now let's talk about this like rational beings, shall we?"

Greg's always trying to talk his way out of fights. I think it goes back to being the fat kid in school. He couldn't fight, so he tried to talk or joke his way out of getting his ass kicked. I don't know that it's ever worked in all the decades I've known him. Didn't look like it was going to work now either.

The girl looked at him disdainfully, laughed and lunged at him with more of that crazy speed. She started throwing kicks and punches that made Jackie Chan look like a rank amateur, and it took everything Greg had to dodge enough of them to avoid being crushed.

I picked Tommy up over my shoulders and jumped him onto a neighboring roof. "Stay here, and stay quiet. I don't need to explain how you got here to the fire department. I'll come get you after we kick her ass." I made to jump into the scrap, but he grabbed my leg.

"What if you can't beat her?" he asked through a mouthful of blood. I missed the part where she busted his mouth up, but I guessed it could have happened when she switched from breaking his arm to choking him half to death.

"Then you don't have to worry about paying our bill." I jumped off the roof, cleared the front yard in one hop, and joined the rumble, which had moved out into the street. I didn't like the number of porch lights that were flickering on, so I stopped throwing punches long enough to say, "If you want to keep your presence here under the radar for more than the next five minutes, we might want to move this party somewhere more private."

"Or I could just kill you quickly," the girl said, nailing me with an uppercut that sent me flying into the path of an oncoming minivan.

"Or that," I said as the van crashed into my back (or I crashed into its front, whichever way you want to look at it). Greg took a kick to the head that spun him completely around, and she grabbed his head like she was going to twist it completely off his body. That's one of the only surefire ways to kill us, and when I saw what she had in mind, I reached deep down and did the only thing I could think of to save my partner's life.

I picked up that stupid little minivan, and slammed it into the freshman-from-hell with everything I had. Toys, glass, baby seats and a couple of yuppies spilled out onto the pavement, but the girl was finally down. Greg dragged the yuppies over to the sidewalk and dropped his Jedi mind trick on them about hitting a Great Dane and being cut out of the van by firefighters while I used their seatbelts to tie the girl's hands and feet.

There were more porch lights than ever flicking on now, and I could hear sirens coming into the neighborhood. We had to move, and fast, or we were going to have some very uncomfortable questions to answer.

"Grab Tommy and get him to the hospital. I stashed him on a roof," I said to Greg.

"Where are you going with her?" he asked. He was weaving a little back and forth, but he could stand, at least.

"Where else? I gotta take her to Dad's." And I tossed the girl over my shoulder like a rolled-up carpet and took off toward the only place that was safe to interrogate her—St. Patrick's.

Chapter 6

I carried the girl/witch/thing over my shoulder toward St. Patrick's Church, hoping by all I had ever believed in that Dad could contain her. "Dad" is Michael Maloney, the priest at St. Patrick's, and he's one of the best friends a vampire could have. He's also an old friend, the only person from *before* that Greg and I ever associate with. He's been there for us for a long time, and I really hoped that he had enough juice with the Big Guy Upstairs to bind this whatever-she-was long enough to get some answers.

I couldn't go in through the front door. The holy ground thing is true. But there's a corner of the cemetery that sits on unsanctified soil, because the church decided during the Great Depression that it needed a place to bury suicides within the fence. That way the church could keep the funeral revenue. But, since Catholic doctrine wouldn't allow someone who took their own life to be buried on hallowed ground, they bought the property next door, knocked down the non-sanctified house that was there, fenced in the lot and expanded the graveyard. It's really handy to have a place to meet where no one would ever think to look for us, and Greg and I keep a room of sorts in one of the crypts for emergencies. And this was shaping up to be a doozy of an emergency.

I called Dad on my cell when I was close, and he met me at the crypt with a lantern and a battered leather bag. I guessed it was his exorcism tool kit and gave it a wide berth. Mike's never tried to douse us with holy water, but crosses, true believers and vampires don't mix. I steer clear.

"Jimmy, my son, what have you gotten yourself into?" Mike asked as he held the door for me. I dropped my little care package on the floor of the crypt and Mike stood there gaping at the hog-tied teenager in front of him.

"Don't call me your son, *Dad*. And I don't really know what I've gotten into. That's what I've got you for. This little chicklet is way more than she seems. She kicked the crap out of me and Greg both, and if I hadn't dropped a minivan on her head she probably would have killed Greg." That was the moment that my body decided to let all the bruises and exertion catch up with me, and I slid down to sit on the floor of the crypt.

"I don't suppose you've got anything to eat in that bag?" I eyed his satchel hopefully.

Mike shook his head. "Sorry, my—um—Jimmy. I don't exactly keep the red in with the Host."

"It's fine. I'll go out for a snack later. For now, we need to find out what's gotten into this kid. Literally."

Mike's eyes got wide, and he actually inched closer to his bag. "You think she may be possessed?"

"Not my field. But I know she's way stronger than she should be, and she sensed us as vamps from way farther away than even a bloodhound could have."

"Hmmm. Well, extra-dimensional beings would certainly be able to sense the presence of other creatures of their ilk, and demons are reputed to have incredible strength."

"Hey! Go easy on the demon talk, old buddy. Remember, me and my ilk used to slip you *Playboys* in middle school." I'd had issues with religion before I got turned, and since then I've spent most of my nights avoiding religious contemplation.

"No offense meant, James. It's just a term. Now, let me get a closer look at her." He knelt on the floor beside the girl, and only my speed allowed me to grab his shoulders and pull him back intact. The girl lunged at his face, trying for all the world to eat his nose. I yanked him out of the way, and the whatever-she-was laughed the kind of laugh that makes places inside you go very, very cold.

"Come closer, priest. Give us a little kiss," it mocked. Mike grabbed a crucifix from his bag, and thrust it at the girl-thing. It hissed and tried to roll away, but I lost sight of things for a minute. Probably because I was trying to put a sarcophagus between myself and the holy symbol. Mike was the truest type of true believer, and the cross in his hands gave me a monster of a migraine. From the looks of things, whatever was inside the girl liked it even less than I did.

"In the name of God the Father and Jesus Christ his Son on Earth I command you to leave this girl!" When I opened my eyes again, peeking carefully over the big stone coffin I was hiding behind, Mike was standing over the girl, cross in his left hand and a Bible in his right. The cross was glowing with an ethereal light, and it looked like something was floating around the girl. A cloud of what looked like glowing red gnats, buzzing and angry, coalesced around her head. Then I heard the voice again, and not for the first time that night, I got really worried.

"Foolish priest. Do you think that your trappings of faith can save you?" The disembodied voice was all around us, swirling in and out of the cloud like an angry wind. "I see inside your soul, priest. I see your darkest thoughts, your blackest fears, and you are *not* holy."

Mike raised his Bible over his head and pointed the cross at the girl like a conductor's baton. "I am a servant of the Lord God Almighty and by His Grace I am sanctified. You are a beast of Hell and I command you to leave this girl!"

The thing laughed, and I swear the girl's eyes glowed like a cheap *X-Files* effect. "I serve a power older and stronger than your pitiful little carpenter. Your little book means nothing to me, and you cannot command one with power such as mine."

Mike's Bible burst into flames, and he dropped the flaming holy book. He switched into Latin, and since I'm not old enough and certainly not religious enough to have much of a grasp on dead languages, I had no idea what he was saying. But after a couple of seconds of chanting, the cloud-thing screamed in rage and pain, and then flew at Mike like a comic-book bee colony, heading straight for his hand. The crucifix flared into blinding light, first white, then a deep crimson red. The voice sounded everywhere around us, and it began to laugh.

Through that awful cackling, I heard Mike howl in pain. There was one last flash of red light, and a wave of force blew out from Mike and the girl. Like a hurricane, it picked me up and flung me limp into the far wall of the crypt. The last thing I heard before I blacked out was that laugh. And Mike screaming.

Chapter 7

When I woke up, I was alone in the crypt. There was a puddle of melted silver on the floor where I last remembered Mike standing, and the seatbelts I had tied the girl with were lying in a pile in a corner. They'd been cut neatly, not torn, but that was all the info I could glean from my surroundings. I went to the door and eased it open a crack to see the bright sunlight streaming into the crypt from the cemetery.

Crap. I was stuck for a while.

The whole thing about sunlight is real, too. We don't burst into flames immediately, but it doesn't take long for one of us to be reduced to a pile of charcoal briquettes if we come into contact with direct sunlight. I settled down to wait for nightfall and hoped that Mike had recovered enough to go into the church. I decided to check on Greg and Tommy, and reached in my pocket for my cell phone. I pulled out a mangled mass of plastic and computer chips and realized that the phone had been crushed during my fight with the girl-monster. I hoped everyone was okay, because I was trapped until sunset.

After a ridiculously boring day of staring at a sunbeam, I felt more than saw the sun finally dip below the horizon, and I headed out into the cemetery. Mike was hurrying across the sanctified part of the graveyard to meet me.

"Where have you been, dude? I've been stuck in there worried sick all day!" I started to lay into him pretty solid, but then I got a good look at my old friend. He looked his age for probably the first time ever. He had a bandage on his forehead that looked fresh, and his left hand was wrapped heavily all the way from the elbow to the fingers. "Jesus Christ, man, how bad did she get you?"

"Pretty badly, I'm afraid. Not all of us are blessed with eternal youth, James. I recently returned from the hospital with our young guest. She's terribly shaken up. I only got her to sleep in the parish house a few moments ago." He took my elbow and led me further from the church, as though there was someone in there he didn't want to take note of our little chat.

"What? She's in the church?" I was baffled. I would have bet the farm that she was way less welcome on holy ground than me. "And have you heard from Greg? My phone got—"

"Trashed. Again. Here." Greg tossed me a replacement phone as he came out from behind a tree. I looked him up and down, but he didn't seem to be any the worse for wear after getting pummeled last night. As if in answer to my unspoken question, Greg went on. "I'm fine. I had a snack before I went to bed last night. Tommy's arm is a clean break, but she got both the bones so it's gonna be useless for at least a month. They kept him at the hospital for observation. I talked to him while I was on my way over here."

I put the phone in my front pocket this time, since my back pocket didn't seem to be very good for protecting them. "What was that you said about the girl being in the church, Mike? I figured her for a serious bad guy, given what she did to all of us last night."

"What was residing in the girl was, in fact, a very serious bad guy, but the girl herself was guilty of nothing more than curiosity and a desire for a little payback on the kids at school who teased her. I think we can all relate to those sentiments, can't we?"

He raised an eyebrow at Greg and me, and we had the good grace to look sheepish. I'm not sure when my old friend had developed the juice to shame me for my youthful indiscretions, but he certainly had it now. Maybe it came with the first grey hairs. I'd never know.

"She was possessed? By what?" Greg asked.

"Yes, she was possessed. And based on the amount of power she exhibited, we may have a very serious problem. I don't know exactly what type of demon possessed her, but it's incredibly strong. I've never experienced anything like that kind of power. To be able to melt a symbol of the Lord in the hands of a priest . . ." Mike trailed off, and if anything, he looked a little paler. Not as pale as me, but getting there.

"How's the hand?" I didn't like seeing my old friend scared, and wanted to change the subject.

"Mostly second-degree burns. I dropped the crucifix before it completely liquefied, but some of the molten silver landed on my skin. I probably won't have full use of the last two fingers again for a while."

That explained the screaming I'd heard as I passed out. Molten metal eating through your flesh tends to make even vampires scream.

Getting one of my best friends injured and maybe permanently disfigured wasn't making me feel any better, so I switched back to the original problem. "So what do we know?"

"Not much," Mike said. "There are only a few demons that have the kind of power the girl exhibited last night, and all of them are bad news. And if what she said about serving an even more powerful demon is true, then we have to find where the demon went when it left the child, and stop it."

Of course we do. Because we're not vampires, the beasties that give people nightmares and make them think twice about walking down that alley alone, we're detective vampires. We're the good guys. Like Batman, only with dietary restrictions. Sometimes I wondered what it would be like to *eat* people, like a normal vampire. But no, not only do I have a conscience, I have a roommate with a Kal-El complex and a priest for a best friend. If I could find a shrink that kept office hours after sundown, I could spend eternity in therapy.

"What happened to the demon?" I asked.

"When you got it out of the girl it went back to Hell?" Greg asked, a little more hopefully than was reasonable.

Mike wobbled a little. "I have no idea, but I doubt it went anywhere we wanted it to go. I would expect that it found someone close by to inhabit, but the ethereal definitions of close by could mean anywhere in the city."

I led Mike over to sit on a headstone. It was a mark of how much had been taken out of him that he was willing to sit there. Usually that was one of the things Greg and I did to get a rise out of him, sit on grave markers and make fun of the occupants. Mike never disrespected the dead. Greg and I exchanged a worried glance behind Mike's back, and I decided on an impromptu plan.

"All right," I said. "Mike, you stay here and keep an eye on the girl, and when she comes around see what information you can get out of her. Somebody had to help her bring this thing up. No kid has that kind of power. See if you can get the names of who else was in the circle with her that night, and keep her here. The beastie's gotten into her once. That might make her vulnerable to a repeat possession, if there is such a thing."

I motioned to Greg. "We'll split up and keep an eye on Tommy and his family. If getting revenge on him for picking on the girl was part of this creature's contract for getting to this side of Hell, then it may still go after them. I'll take the hospital, and Greg will keep an eye on the sister."

"That sounds good, boys. I think I would do well to do my part from my chair this time. Once I get there." Mike started back toward the church. "Boys?"

"Yeah, Dad?" I answered.

"Be careful. This one is bad. Very, very bad."

Greg and I looked at each other as Mike limped into the church, looking way older than we were supposed to be. We stood there watching our friend's back for a second, then headed off into the night for our respective charges. Good thing I was headed to the hospital. I needed breakfast *bad*.

Chapter 8

It only took me a few minutes to get to the hospital. By bus. I've heard that some of us can take animal forms, but either I haven't figured out how to turn into a bat, I haven't been around long enough, the vampire that made me wasn't strong enough, or something like that. I don't really know. Since I can't fly, I took the bus. And by that I mean I jumped on top of one and hitched a ride to the hospital.

I was out of cash. It wasn't that Greg and I were hurting for money. We did okay with the detecting business and it's not like we had much of a grocery bill, but I was bad about leaving the house without grabbing any cash out of the cookie jar, so I never had any money on me. That meant I rode the top of the bus a lot. It was more fun than mojo-ing the driver out of a free fare.

When I got to the hospital, Tommy had some company that I certainly wasn't interested in seeing—the police. I did a quick one-eighty in the hallway once I saw the guard outside his room and headed back downstairs to swipe a disguise. In general, it's a good idea to avoid masquerading as someone with medical training, because someone always wants you to do something with that training, and that can turn out poorly for you and the patient. So I usually put on my best janitor clothes and grab a bucket. There's never been a hospital that didn't have something that needed to be mopped, and the cleaning staff is usually invisible. Even if someone does notice you, they're just happy to see you working their floor.

I found an unattended supply closet on Tommy's floor and commandeered a bucket and mop. I wheeled my way down the hall to the room next to Tommy's, and headed in to mop and eavesdrop. Fortunately for me, the guy in the room was comatose and didn't care that I was doing a crappy cleaning job. I was able to hear a grumpy-sounding female detective grilling Tommy through the wall.

"Mr. Matthews, how exactly did you break your arm?" she asked.

"Fell off my skateboard." Tommy had the sullen teenager thing down pat, probably because he wasn't acting. He *was* a teenager with a crap attitude toward authority figures and a system full of painkillers.

"That's bull!" I heard her slam something to the floor, and it didn't take a rocket scientist to figure out who was playing the bad cop. If she was playing. "The doctor told us your injuries were consistent with your arm being broken by a very strong person. Now who did it?"

"I told you, I fell off my skateboard." Tommy even managed a little whine at the end. I was impressed. I wasn't anywhere near that good at being a putz when I was a kid.

"And I told you, I know you're lying." I could almost see her leaning toward him. Her voice dropped and became confidential, inviting. "We can't protect you if you don't tell us the truth, Tommy. And you want us to protect you, don't you? I'd hate to have to leave here and take that guard with me. Wouldn't you?"

I certainly wouldn't hate that, but she wasn't asking me.

I heard nothing for a minute, then heard Tommy take a deep breath and say, "Okay, I'll tell you what happened." My heart, if it still beat, would have stopped for a second, and Tommy's next words did nothing to make me feel any better. Before I could reach through the wall and strangle him, he said "I hired a couple of vampire detectives to protect me from a demonic curse, and when we went to confront the witch that cursed me, she broke my arm like a twig."

The silence from the other room was thick, and I leaned my head against the wall berating myself for not eating the kid when I had the chance. After a long minute I heard the woman's voice again, and it was pretty obvious she was not happy with Tommy's answer. She spit out the words like they were bullets. "You little bastard. I have somebody in this town kidnapping little kids, and this girl is the latest. Now, you were seen harassing her at school and the neighbors say a kid matching your description was at her house before she went missing last night."

"You know something about this. If anything happens to that little girl and it turns out you had anything to do with it, I will personally make sure that you do your undergraduate work at the federal penitentiary in Raleigh." With that, I heard her stomp toward the door. Seconds later I felt the wall shake as she slammed the door to Tommy's room.

"Come on, leave the chump here. Anything that's after him can have him," she said to the guard. Without a glance, they passed by the open door of the room I was mopping and headed for the elevator.

The woman led the parade, followed by two uniforms. She was striking more than pretty, a little too sharp in the face for most guys' comfort. Tall, with ass-kicking boots on she was almost six feet, her dark brown curls tied into a messy ponytail. She wore a tailored jacket open to show her badge and gun, and a cross around her neck.

I notice the little things, like crosses. They get to be important. I counted to a hundred twice and then wheeled my bucket into Tommy's room. He was fiddling with the bed when I closed the door behind me and moved a chair under the knob. I didn't need any nurses coming in to take fluids while Tommy and I had a heart-to-heart.

"Holy crap!" Tommy cried. "I almost peed the bed! I thought you guys had left me here to die!"

I crossed the room as quickly as I could, which is pretty damned quick, and put my hand over his mouth. "You want to yell that a little louder? I'm not sure every brat in the nursery heard you," I whispered into his face. His eyes got big as he noticed the pointy teeth, and I backed off a little. "How long were they here? What did they tell you? Start at the beginning and walk me through."

"They were here when I woke up. That chick cop was a real bitch. She was all about wanting to know how my arm got broke, but I didn't tell her anything, I swear." He flopped back onto his pillows looking proud of himself.

"Except the absolute truth, you mean. Good thing for all of us she's a civilian and doesn't believe in anything having to do with our world." Tommy looked a lot less smug, and I cocked an eyebrow at him. "Vamp senses are ridiculously good. I listened through the wall."

I pulled a chair over to the window and looked down. The detective was standing by her car looking up at me. I sat down quickly hoping that she was nearsighted. I knew I'd have to deal with her before this mess was over. She wouldn't see a vampire and think "janitor." Not this one.

"Did she say anything earlier about little kids being kidnapped?"

"Dude, don't you, like, read the paper?" Tommy used the remote to elevate his bed so he could see me better after I took the chair.

"My morning delivery leaves a little to be desired. Enlighten me."

"There's been, like, ten or eleven kids go missing in the last month, dude. There's talk of not letting anybody go out for Halloween unless they catch whoever's taking them."

That would suck. Halloween is one of the best nights of the year. It's like a Vegas buffet, only everyone you nibble on has had so much candy they all taste like dessert. I took the lid off his dinner plate and poked around at the leftovers, hoping for a little Jell-O. "Go on."

"What are you doing? I thought you couldn't eat."

"Old habits. Now about the kids?"

"Oh, yeah. Well, the first couple were no big deal, their parents were all over each other about custody anyway, so most folks figured one or the other was lying and had swiped the kid. But then a pair of twins vanished out of a day care, and people started to get worried. By that time, everybody was making a huge deal about the cops not caring because the first kids were black, and the latest kids were white, and it got to be a whole big thing. The cops made a task force and held press conferences, and made a big news thing out of everything. But while the cops were conferencing, kids kept disappearing. Hey, can you hand me that ginger ale?" He took a drink while I looked at him.

"Is that all?" I asked when he didn't continue.

"What do you mean? I guess. That's what I know, anyway."

Sometimes I wonder if everybody in the world is brutally stupid, or if it's just my clients. "Your demon and this bunch of disappearing kids might be connected."

"No, man. That was, like, a demon or something. This is just some kids going missing. Oh! I get it! You think the demon might be taking the kids, right?"

It's almost cute how excited stupid people get when they figure something out. Like Christmas for morons. "I was thinking that maybe the people calling the demon might have something to do with the vanishing children, yes. How many did you say were gone?"

"I don't know, man. They were all little kids, like middle school. I didn't really pay attention, 'cause I didn't know any of them. But I did kinda know this girl whose little sister got kidnapped. I think they said she was number eight or something like that."

"Does your friend have a name?" I had the beginnings of a plan, but I needed to be able to leave Tommy alone and know he was safe. He was a moron, but he was my moron for the moment.

"Dude, she's not my friend, I barely know her." I motioned for him to go on, because I didn't care. "Janice Reynolds. My buddy Rick used to go out with her or something. Or maybe hooked up with her at a party. I can't remember. But she lives in that new development over by the high school. What are you gonna do?"

He held out his ginger ale and waited. I finally put it back on the tray for him. I hate pretend invalids.

"I'm going to go talk to your friend Janice. But I've got a couple of other stops to make first, and I need to make a little noise so your guard will come back. Try to make this convincing."

"Make what convincing?"

I didn't answer. Instead I put a pillow over his head and counted to twenty. He thrashed around pretty well, but wasn't anywhere near smart enough to press the call button for the nurse. After he passed out, I made sure that he was still breathing, pressed the call button myself and threw the armchair out the window. I figured that would be enough to draw attention even at a hospital, so I wheeled my mop bucket in the opposite direction from where all the people were running and ducked into a stairwell to make good my escape.

Chapter 9

I walked past the crowd of people looking at the armchair that had crushed the hood of a police car in front of the hospital and headed toward the bus stop. The cop car was a nice touch, if I do say so myself. I thought my luck was finally starting to look up as I got to the bus stop, but my phone rang and proved me wrong again.

"Yeah," I said.

"Dude, you gotta get over here!' Greg sounded more than a little freaked out, but he freaks out when he burns a Pop-Tart.

"Slow down. One, where are you? And two, what's up?"

"I'm at Tommy's house, and the cops are here! They're talking to his parents about a string of kidnappings. They think Tommy might be involved, and they're talking about taking him out of the hospital and arresting him!"

Great. "Is there a woman detective there? Tall, ponytail, boots, attitude?"

"Yeah. She's a real ball-buster, man. She's got Tommy's mom in tears and his dad all freaked out about college scholarships and lawyers and that crap."

"Don't sweat it. She'll be leaving any second."

"What are you talking about? Wait, there she goes. How did you . . . ?" Greg trailed off.

"I'll explain later." I looked up and down the street, really wanting a bus to arrive before Detective Kickass got back to the hospital. "Now here's the plan—go knock on the door, and when Tommy's dad answers, mojo him into not seeing you, then deck him. Leave him out cold in the doorway, and then break a couple of windows. Get the hell out of there and meet me at home. We've got work to do."

"What?!?" I held the phone away from my head as Greg freaked out again. I counted to ten, and when he paused for breath, I put the phone back to my head.

"Do it, and meet me at home. I'll see you in half an hour." I hung up, and when I didn't see a bus anywhere, stepped out into the street in front of an oncoming car. The poor banker-type slammed on the brakes, and I pulled him out of the car. He started to say something, but then took a look in my eyes and fell silent, like a rabbit staring at a wolf.

I didn't plan to snack on him, but it had been a long night, and I was still really hungry. And that deer-in-the-headlights look got to me. I grabbed him by the tie and pulled him in. I spoke to him, not really saying words, just noises meant to calm the prey while I sniffed the side of his neck, smelling the fear-sweat and listening to the blood pulse in his carotid.

I took a quick glance around at all the cars in the parking lot, all the people milling around, and decided this would really have to wait. I looked into his eyes and whispered, "Sleep." He sagged like a sack of slightly overweight potatoes, and I tossed him into the passenger seat of his BMW SUV. I hopped in the driver's seat and headed off toward home with a plan in mind and dinner next to me.

I didn't go all the way home, obviously. There are good ideas, and there are bad ideas. And for vampires, leaving a car with your last meal in the front seat parked outside your lair definitely falls into the "bad idea" column. I drove to an alley behind a biker bar called The Thirsty Beaver a couple miles west of our place and got into the back seat behind my meal. He was still out cold, so I grabbed his left hand and brought the wrist to my mouth with little fanfare.

Feeding is a basic need, and not deserving of androgynous and mildly homoerotic adjectives. A man's gotta eat, plain and simple. And what this man has to eat is human blood. I normally would have raided the blood supply at the hospital, but all the police there had made that a little too high profile for my tastes.

I pulled his wrist to my mouth and licked the place at the bottom of his forearm where the veins run closest to the skin. I used the left wrist because between the rapid healing inherent to vampire bites and the fact that this yuppie wore an expensive watch, I figured there were better than even odds that he would never notice he'd been snacked upon. Not that anyone would believe him, but I tried to keep things neat when I could.

My canines extended into razor-sharp points, and I tore as small a hole as I could while still letting the blood flow. It splashed against the back of my throat all hot and coppery, and the thick syrupy liquid went down as smooth as twenty-year-old scotch. And as a matter of fact, I could taste a little hint of scotch. Somebody had been driving while intoxicated—bad boy.

It had been a while since I drank from the source, and it was *good*. Greg doesn't approve, so whenever we're together I drink from the bag, but man, there's nothing like the taste of fresh blood right from the vein. It's hot, with that metallic and salty taste that's like nothing else in the world. We can live on blood bank supplies, but it's the difference between a really good rare filet mignon and a frozen hamburger patty. I drank for a couple of minutes, just a couple of pints, and then leaned back in my seat behind the yuppie, who was still out like a light.

"Was it good for you?" I asked my sleeping dinner. He was as silent as I expected him to be, which was good for both of us. I probably would have flipped out had he woken up at that exact moment, and it's usually not a good idea to be the human trapped in a car with a freaked-out vamp. I took a minute to make sure I hadn't dripped anything on my shirt, steal the snack's wallet and leave him behind the bar. The Beaver had enough hipster traffic that one more SUV wouldn't draw too much attention until closing time, and by then I'd be miles away.

I tossed his wallet minus the cash in a dumpster and headed home. Now I had bus fare to get home on, but since I was close, I took it at a quick jog and was there in fifteen minutes without breaking a sweat. The four-minute mile is a big deal to human runners, but it's pretty much a warm-up pace for dead guys.

Greg was waiting for me when I got home, and he was practically bouncing off the walls. "Apartment" is a generous term for our home, I suppose. We live in the basement of a caretaker's house in a local municipal cemetery. Municipal cemeteries work best for our brand of lurking, because they're not consecrated ground. We can hang out there. Greg and I figure we can cycle through as the "caretaker" every dozen years or so, just to keep the folks that own the cemetery from getting suspicious about the fact that we don't age. We fixed up the basement with a couple of hidden entrances, and outfitted it the way we wanted. The caretaker's cottage is decorated in vintage redneck, so anyone stopping by sees exactly what they expect to see. On they go, and no one gets in our way.

I made up some story for the cemetery owners about being an insomniac writer with an online poker addiction, so they leave me alone when I never go outside in the daytime and am up all night. They don't really care, as long as the graves stay mowed and clean, and I subcontract that work. As long as we don't charge anything for our "maintenance services," they don't charge us anything to live there. It's a pretty sweet deal, if I do say so myself.

"Dude, what the hell took you so long? I've been going nuts here waiting for you!" Greg had an Xbox controller in one hand, but hadn't even bothered to turn on the game. He usually crushes the games, but obviously tonight he was more interested in what I had to tell him.

"Sorry, had to stop for take-out on the way." I sat beside him on the couch and picked up the second controller. "What are we playing?"

Greg was having none of that and grabbed the controller out of my hands. "No frickin' way, man. What is the deal, and what are we going to do about that man-eating woman cop?"

"I don't know what the deal is yet, but I'm starting to get the idea that our little demon chasing Tommy is just the tip of the iceberg. And I'm pretty sure that our distractions will keep the detective out of our hair for a little while. Hopefully she'll be busy chasing after whoever busted up Tommy's house and jumped out the window of his hospital room long enough for us to get to the bottom of all this."

"But I busted up his house, and I guess you broke his hospital window . . ." My partner's book smart, not street smart, but he's damn loyal and has super-powers, so I keep him around. Besides, he's been my best friend since sixth grade. We met getting stuffed into adjacent lockers in gym class. Even then, his was a tight fit.

"You broke the hospital window," Greg repeated as understanding dawned on him.

"Now you get it. So we need to find out everything we can about these kids that have gone missing. Tommy said there were ten or eleven of them, and that's why the cops were after him so quickly. You get online and see what you can dig up, and I'm going to go interview the sister of one of the earlier kidnap victims. Then we crash for a little while and try to catch up with Dad early tomorrow night. Sound good?"

"Works for me. Hey, did you bring any leftovers with you from the hospital? I'm getting a little peckish." Greg headed over to his desk and its brand new MacBook, external monitor setup and a ridiculously large array of external hard drives. Greg's on a mission to collect every vampire movie ever made, so he needs serious storage. He uses more bandwidth in a week than most of Nebraska uses in a year, so it's a damn good thing he figured out how to piggyback onto the network of the bank headquarters down the block.

"Sorry, dude. No leftovers. Not even a drop to spare." And it was true. My donor would probably have felt really crappy when he woke up if I had drunk any more. I wasn't lying to Greg exactly, just avoiding a repeat of the fight we always have when I drink straight from a human.

He barely even looked up from his keyboard as he muttered "Pig" at me. By the time I'd gotten to my closet he had four Firefox windows open with a different Google search running on each one. I swear I think instead of super vamp-speed he got super-fast typing when we got turned.

I went over to my closet and started weapon loading for bear. I usually only carry one good knife, a Marine-issue Ka-Bar tucked into the back of my belt, but this gig had been anything but usual to this point. I put on my shoulder holster and grabbed my Glock 17. I checked that it was loaded with silver bullets, and put a spare magazine of silver ammo in my back pocket. The silver load was for anything supernatural we encountered. I knew how much the touch of silver hurt me, so I figured nothing else in the magical world would like it, either. It meant I had to wear gloves when I loaded my magazines, but I considered that a small price to pay. I loaded the holster with two spare magazines of regular ammunition, and strapped my backup to my right ankle. I carry a Ruger LCP for a backup when I think things could go really bad, and everything I'd seen in this case told me things could go from "peachy" to "holy crap" in the blink of an eye. I put another knife on the other ankle, rolled my jeans down to cover all the hardware, and straightened up, reaching for my black hoodie. Greg had turned away from the computer and was sitting still, staring at me.

"How bad do you think this is going to get?" He suddenly looked as worried as I'd seen him in a long time, and I sat on an arm of the couch and looked at him.

"Bad. I don't know what we're up against, but if what was in that little girl isn't the boss, and I don't think it is, then whatever is running this operation is even meaner."

Greg sat back in the chair and sipped on a juice box. I don't know where he picked up that habit, because all it did was make him pee purple half an hour later, but he was hooked on the silly things. After a long sip, he said, "Then guns and knives aren't going to be a whole lot of help, are they?"

"Probably none at all," I admitted. "But on the off chance that they might be useful, I think I'll bring them along. Besides, the really bad guys use human pawns a lot of the time, and guns and knives work fine against humans. That reminds me." I reached into the floor of the closet and grabbed a couple of spare magazines for my LCP backup pistol. They went into a jacket pocket.

"Man, you can't go killing humans just because they front the bad guys. We have to be sure. What if they got suckered into working for a Big Bad?"

"I know. I know. If I take out any humans, I promise to verify their complete and utter evilness first." I might have grinned a little, but just a little.

"I just meant—"

"I know what you meant. I promise not to kill anyone that doesn't deserve it." I held up one hand, three middle fingers together. "Scout's honor."

"You were never a scout. They wouldn't let you in."

"Objection, your honor! Relevance!" That got a chuckle out of him. "I promise I won't kill anyone who's not a bad guy. We cool?" I started toward the stairs.

"Yeah, yeah. Hey Jimmy?" I stopped, not turning to look at him. I knew what he was about to suggest, because I'd already thought of it. He was right, of course, but I didn't want to think about it.

"Do you think we should talk to Phil?"

"Probably." I still hadn't looked at him. I could feel him looking at the back of my head, and it was a little itchy.

"Then you're going to talk to him now?"

"Only because I have to." I hate dealing with angels. They always make me feel so damn *unclean.*

Chapter 10

I've never been a fan of strip clubs, and I'm even less of a fan of angels, so putting the two together is so far out of my comfort zone it's like dropping Huck Finn into Times Square. I walked across the parking lot into Phil's place, shaking my head, as always, at the blue neon sign flashing "Heaven on Earth" to the passing traffic. I paid the cover, flashed my library card at the bouncer and mojo'd him into thinking it was a driver's license. I'm not terribly photogenic, and I haven't renewed my license since the early nineties. Putting the whammy on people is easier. I took a seat at the bar and tried to order a beer, but a pair of six-inch Lucite platform heels kept getting in the way. I finally waved the girl down to me, slid a dollar in her garter, and she jiggled on down the bar to more interested parties.

A different night, a different case and maybe I wouldn't have waved her off, but this wasn't the time or the place. Especially not the place. Fiction vamps that sparkle and fixate on true love give the rest of us a bad name. I don't sparkle, I'm no more perpetually horny than anyone (or anything) else, and I don't use my vampire powers to get laid. I'm not even particularly angst-ridden, and don't know any vamps that are.

I ordered a Miller Lite and told the bartender I needed to see the boss. He waved a thirty-something woman over who bore all the signs of an ex-dancer who had moved up, or at least sideways, in the world. "I'm Lil, I'm the manager here. What can I do for you?" She slid onto a stool next to me. Dark hair cascaded down her back and she was dressed in black leather from head to toe. Her eyes hinted at some undefined ethnicity I couldn't place.

"I didn't ask for the manager, Miss. I asked for the Boss." I put a little emphasis on the last word, hoping she might pick up on the idea that I knew more than the average lap-dance customer.

"As far as you need to know, kid, I *am* the Boss." She raised me an auditory italics and returned my verbal capitalization with one of her own. When she looked me straight in the eyes, I got a little hint that there was more to her than a fading stripper with aspirations of earning a GED.

"Is there somewhere we can talk?" I asked, looking around at the gyrating bodies. It was loud, but not so loud that I wanted to risk someone overhearing me go into the supernatural aspects of life.

"Follow me." She slid off the stool and walked towards a dark alcove with VIP in pink neon over the doorway. I now understood how the neon industry was staying alive. Apparently it's all being used in strip clubs. I followed her and noticed that the view of Lil from behind was, in a word, incredible. Ex-dancer or not, she still had plenty to show, and the tight black miniskirt she was wearing displayed it very well. Naturally, I thought the most covered woman in the place was hotter than any of the naked ones. I've always been a sucker for a little mystery.

We walked down a black-carpeted hallway with doors on only one side. Each door had a light over it. Some were red, some green, and one was blinking yellow. Before I could ask what the caution light was for, Lil said over her shoulder, "Time's almost up in that one."

I didn't want to think too much about what was going on inside the rooms, and I didn't have to, because past the room with the blinking yellow light Lil opened a door with no light over it. I hadn't even seen the door from the hallway, but when we entered, I realized it led into a spacious office complete with desk, a sofa, a full bar and a bank of monitors that covered the club, the parking lot and all the VIP rooms. She motioned me toward the chair facing the desk as she went over to the bar.

I didn't sit, preferring to lean against the desk and watch her make the drinks. Not only was the view better watching her than the monitors, but it kept her in my line of sight. In my business there are a few ways to get really dead really fast, and turning your back on people you don't know in their lair is near the top of the list.

"Can I get you anything?" she asked as she poured bourbon over ice for herself.

"No thank you."

"Are you sure? We have beer, wine, B-positive, holy water."

I went for my Glock the moment she tossed "holy water" into the list, but instinct kicked in too late. She'd already picked up a small pistol hidden on the bar and pointed it calmly at my heart.

"Don't get frisky, little vampire. It's loaded with silver rounds, and you don't want to know what that will do to you. Now sit down. I'm not going to hurt you. If I wanted to do that, you'd be dead." I didn't take my eyes off the gun until she walked around the desk, sat down, and put it in a drawer. Her left hand was out of sight somewhere under the desk's surface, and I had a sneaking suspicion that the pistol was the least of my worries.

"Okay," I said, sitting, "you know what I am. Is that a problem?"

"Not for me. But you wanted to see the Boss, and he's not a huge fan of vampires. That could be a problem for you." She sipped her bourbon, and it took all I could do not to lean over to look under the desk.

"I'm not a huge fan of angels, but Phil and I have done business before." I shifted in the chair so that, in an emergency, my crossed leg could block most of my center mass from anything but a shotgun blast. I really hoped she didn't have a shotgun. It probably wouldn't kill me, but it would be damned inconvenient. And messy. "He knows me."

"Indeed, I do, James," said a polished voice from behind me. "But I still need to know why you're here."

I jumped almost high enough to touch the ceiling, and when I came down I was standing facing Phil. His manager and her firearm fetish momentarily forgotten, I leaned heavily on the edge of the desk.

"Sweet baby Jesus, Phil. If my heart still beat, I'd have had a heart attack. The whole teleporting thing is one thing, but sneaking up on people is not cool, man."

Phil was dapper, as always, in a black suit tailored to his lean frame. Phil and I were similarly sized, well over six feet tall with broad shoulders and thin builds, but he always looked better than me. It helped that he was a lot more muscular than me, and could afford a tailor.

Girls think angels are dreamy for a reason. He was ridiculously good-looking even to a straight vampire. My hair is kind of mousy brown and sticks out everywhere, but Phil's dark wavy curls always fell perfectly into place. He looked like a print ad for men's hair product, only three-dimensional and annoyingly real.

Phil was right in my face before I stopped babbling. "You know I don't like that name used in my presence." Behind the rage in his eyes I saw something deeper, some kind of regret maybe, something that moved him on a visceral level.

In a rare moment of sanity, I decided not to push. I broke off eye contact and looked down. "Sorry about the J-word."

"Apology accepted." Phil backed off a little and I could breathe again. "Now I owe you an apology of my own for startling you. Please let me offer you a drink. One without a threat. Lilith, would you please provide our guest with a drink?"

He and Lilith shared a look, and I could almost feel the power struggle between them. Just as I was starting to feel uncomfortable, the name hit me.

"Holy crap!" I bounced back to my feet. They both turned to look at me, and I stammered, "Y-you-you're Lilith? *That* Lilith? Like Eve before Eve, but you-wanted-to-be-on-top- and-you-got-banished Lilith?"

She looked at me very coldly, then walked around the desk and stood right in front of me, almost as close as Phil had a moment before. She looked me up and down and said, "That is one version of the story. There are others."

The way she said "others" let me know the story I knew wasn't remotely her version, and that her version probably didn't appear in any of the books I'd ever read, or would ever read. Honestly, I didn't think I was too interested in hearing her version. The look in her eyes promised that if she told me she'd have to kill me.

Breaking the silence, she smoothly asked, "Now, would you like a drink?" She brushed her hair back off her neck and tilted her head to one side in preparation for me to bite her.

Holy crap and sweet baby Jesus.

"Ummm . . . thanks, but no thanks. I've already had dinner tonight." I tried to step back, but my ass was already pressed up against the desk. I had nowhere to go.

"Please, I insist. It is a rare honor my Lord has offered you. If you refuse you dishonor his gift and pass up an opportunity seldom given to one of your kind." She spoke so low it was almost a whisper.

Looking into her eyes I thought for a moment that this must be how a mundane feels when I mojo them. It was almost like my will wasn't my own, except that I knew the choice was mine. The people I whammy don't weigh the consequences of their choices. I did.

I put my lips to her neck and breathed in the scent of her hair, and knew that I would drink. Her hair smelled like everything I missed about being alive, sunsets on the beach, summer afternoons in a park, fresh-cut grass, that intoxicating scent of salt, beer and cocoa butter combined that defines a weekend at the beach. I buried my face in the side of her neck and held my mouth there for a moment, feeling the pulse under my lips.

"You don't have to be gentle," she murmured into my ear. Then a hot spike of pain and pleasure ran down my neck as she bit my earlobe.

Gentle left the building. I sank my teeth into her with no concern for her well-being, because I knew that whatever she was, I certainly couldn't kill her. She put one hand behind my head and held my mouth to her neck, while the other hand wrapped around my waist to rest on the small of my back. Feeding for me has never been a particularly sexy thing. I've never been much for mixing sex and dinner, but Lil was different. The taste of her exploded into my mouth, and I saw colors as my eyes rolled back in my head.

I've drunk from stoners, winos, psychos, schizophrenics and club kids hopped up on everything from acid to ecstasy to the best coke to ever come out of Bolivia. Every substance you can shoot, snort, smoke and swallow makes its way into the blood. But nothing I'd tasted did justice to Lilith's blood. I'm not sure there is a substance that could, and, if there is, I don't think I want to know what it is. Addictions are dangerous.

I took the smallest sip from Lilith, and I thought the top of my head was going to blow off. Every hair on my body stood on end, and spasms went through every muscle.

I stood there with my mouth latched onto her neck twitching like a kid that just peed on an electric fence. The light show going on behind my eyelids was a Pink Floyd wet dream. I drank from her for only a couple of seconds, but I stood there draped over her, gasping and letting her hold me up for several minutes while I came back to earth. It's a good thing Phil didn't have any grudges against me, because if he'd wanted to stake me then and there I couldn't have done anything to stop it. Which is why addictions are dangerous. They lead you to stupid behaviors. I try not to be stupid too often.

After a long moment I got my breath back enough to gasp out, "You're an asshole, Phil."

"You didn't like it?"

I could hear his smirk in the tone of his voice as clearly I could hear the undertone of harp music. "Yeah, I liked it. It was incredible. The best thing I've ever had. And I never want to taste anything even close to that again."

I straightened up and walked on rubbery legs to the bar and poured myself two fingers of a very expensive scotch. The last thing I wanted to do was put anything in my mouth that would erase the taste of Lilith's blood, but I knew that if I didn't start forgetting that taste as fast as I possibly could, I'd keep putting off drinking anything. It wouldn't take long for me to starve out of fear of losing that amazing taste. I slugged back the scotch and poured myself another.

When I felt like I could look him in the eyes, I turned to face Phil. "What's the deal? We've done business before without any of the games. What's different now? Why the snack?"

Phil took a seat behind his desk and gestured toward the chair I'd vacated when he popped in. I sat, and he slid a coaster across to me. I should have known I wouldn't be allowed to do anything so coarse as to put a glass on his desk. He waited for me to arrange my drink, then said, "Things have changed, James. The balance of power in our fair city is in flux, and it is not in my best interest to align myself too closely with either side."

"I don't get it." I figured there was no point in trying to play mind games with an angel, fallen or not. Regardless of our respective brain sizes, I was giving up a few thousand years experience to Zepheril (or Phil when I was being obnoxious, which was always). I went with honest ignorance, which has served me well so far.

"There is a new player in town, James. A player with the potential to shift things significantly to one side or the other. And until I see which way the wind is blowing, I have decided that it would be unwise to make any specific alliances."

"Who? Lilith's new in town, but she's working for you. Who is it?" There was obviously something going on between them, but she looked way too much like she was the slave to his master, at least this week.

I decided I had read that situation right when he leaned back in his chair and laughed. "Oh no, James. Lilith is my servant, at least for the moment. She is here as a result of a wager. A wager that she lost." Lilith didn't look very happy about that. Phil waved her over and gestured imperiously, and Lil sat on his lap like a very sexy and very dangerous kid with Santa at the mall. Only this Santa was a fallen angel, and this kid was older than Eve herself and had more issues than *Reader's Digest*. "I speak of a tectonic shift in the balance of power, a change that may not only herald change for the city of Charlotte, but for the world as a whole."

That didn't sound like anything I was going to like. Still, I had to ask. "Does this power have anything to do with my having to fight a possessed little girl last night and the missing kids all over town?"

"As usual, you have managed to find yourself in the middle of it all. In parlance you might understand—you've brought a knife to a gun fight."

I hate being right.

Chapter 11

I took a minute to digest what Phil had said, and then decided this was going to warrant another drink. I poured my third scotch and returned to my seat. "What kind of power are we talking about, Phil?"

"I don't really know, James. I only know that since the children have begun to disappear I have sensed a power growing in our fair city, and I have watched it with no small interest."

Phil reads too much. I mean, seriously, who talks like that? It irritated me, and that didn't bode well for the rest of my evening. "So you don't know anything that could help me find it, fight it or kill it. Or if you do, you're not going to tell me because you think it's stronger than me, and if I go after it all I'll do is piss it off, and you're afraid if I poke the big scary bear that you'll be facing off with something that you don't want to take on."

"That is a fair summation of the facts, yes." Phil's voice went a little cold, and there was a warning in his eyes that told me not to push this.

I don't like being told what to do. It makes me itchy, and when I get itchy, my mouth runs away from my brain. I knew better than to poke Phil too much, so I turned to Lilith. "What about you, Little Miss Sunshine? Do you know anything about the Big Bad? Or do you think we should sit on our asses and eat popcorn while Rome burns, too?"

Lilith looked at me through half-lidded eyes from her perch on Phil's lap, and I actually blushed. I didn't even know I could blush anymore. I'd assumed vampires didn't have the blood flow to spare. I assumed wrong.

"Little vampire, tread lightly. There are forces at work here that you cannot even imagine. I suggest you go back to your little hole and play your video games. You do not want to be involved in this."

"No, I don't. I definitely don't want to be involved. I'm no hero. I'm just a guy trying to make a living, buy a few video games, and maybe find a nice fresh neck to gnaw on now and then. But like it or not, I am involved. There's a scared kid out there who I promised to help, and as stupid as it sounds, I try to keep my promises." I looked at both of them with as much humility as I could. "Please, tell me what you know, and I'll get out of here and back to trying to save the world without getting my ass kicked too bad."

Lilith chuckled, an earthy laugh that made parts of me tingle that didn't tingle very often since I had become a bloodsucking fiend. I was starting to get a pretty good idea where her powers lay, and I gotta admit, they were impressive.

She got up off Phil's lap and came to sit on mine. She twined herself around me in a remarkable imitation of a wetsuit, and it took everything I had to keep focused. "Little vampire, if you insist on your own self-destruction, you will never be able to taste me again. Is that really what you want?"

"No," I said in a small voice as I watched the gleam in her eyes grow into an inferno. "But it's what I've got to do. Sorry, honey."

Her gaze turned cold, and I could imagine her ripping my heart out with her bare hands and feeding it to me. My newly tingly nether regions stopped tingling.

The moment my body's Fun-O-Meter hit fear instead of interest, she stood up, flounced back over to the corner of Phil's desk, and sat down in a huff. "So be it," she said in a voice like a frosty January window.

Phil leaned forward slowly as if struggling with a decision. Finally, he said, "We are not entirely sure what is coming, but there is a major summoning in process. It requires the exchange of thirteen pure souls for the souls of thirteen of the damned."

"Children would qualify," I said unhappily.

"Whoever is performing this ritual must have some plan for the thirteen damned souls, and it seems to involve Samhain somehow."

"Of course." I chimed in. "It has to be Halloween, which is in a matter of days. Because it's not bad enough that there's a gigantic evil thing about to rise from the Hellmouth and devour us all, there has to be a time limit so we can wrap all this up and go to commercial. I hate Halloween."

Phil just stared at me for a moment.

"Sorry," I said. "But some days it really feels like I'm trapped in an episode of *Buffy the Vampire Slayer.*"

"Your legs aren't that good," Phil said. "May I continue?"

I nodded.

"There have been eleven kidnapping victims to date, and their bodies have been inhabited by the souls of the damned. Until you interfered and released the latest damned soul into the city."

He had me there. I had been the one to ask Father Mike to dispossess the soul with extreme prejudice. "Yeah, that wasn't exactly my best moment. Do you know what happens to that girl now? Last I heard she was a little freaked out, but in decent shape."

Phil steepled his fingers and leaned back. "She will be susceptible to possession unless your friend the priest is able to provide her with some type of shielding. The soul you cast out of her will not be able to return. But she will be more likely to see and hear the presence of souls around her than a normal child."

"And if she continues to dabble in the mystic arts?"

"She will undoubtedly end up dead long before she finishes puberty."

I hate how much that bastard knows about everything. Or maybe it's that I hate having to drag it out of him. He's a bazillion years old, tied to all the bad guys in town and has ridiculously high-speed Internet. The least he could do is not make me beg for scraps. It's a game with him. I'd better know the right questions, or he won't play.

"And the soul?" I asked.

"The soul will look for a host. Typically it will inhabit an empty body, but if one is not available, it will attempt to possess one weaker than itself."

Lilith looked like she might jump into the conversation, but a glance from Phil shut her up. Then we were back to playing Phil's little game. It was time to see if I'd asked enough of the right questions, and if I could be trusted with the answer to the big question. "And how do I stop who—or whatever is behind this whole mess?"

"I don't know. To know that, one would have to uncover exactly who is performing the ritual and what they expect to gain. With that knowledge, then you might be able to stop them."

Phil stood, and gestured toward a door that I was pretty sure hadn't existed until that very moment. "But you will, as I said, have to accomplish that without my help. For I have given you all the aid I am interested in giving you, and now you must go."

One day I'll figure out what powers the fallen have and how much of their power is mojo like mine, but this obviously wasn't going to be that day. I'd pushed as much as I dared. Gotten as much as I could.

Lilith opened the door, and stood very close as I made my exit. "Farewell, little vampire. I do hope you enjoyed my . . . hospitality."

I blushed again as I went through the door and found myself in an alley behind the club. I felt a little dirty, like I'd been caught drinking the Communion wine or something. I hadn't, for once, but my Catholic upbringing always left me a little self-conscious about anything that felt that good.

Chapter 12

I took a moment to regroup, which wasn't easy. I was outside a high-class strip club with a tummy full of immortal hottie blood and a killer buzz. My to-do list now included figuring out what the hell an XYZ ritual was, did, or caused, and of course now I knew that I was on a tight deadline. Halloween was looming just a few days away, and I couldn't exactly go to the cops for help.

Interviewing the family of the victims seemed easier, and probably safer. I decided to do that first. Tommy had given me the address for Janice Reynolds, the older sister of Victim Number Eight, before I left the hospital. I didn't mind the drive. It was all the way south of town in the ritzy Ballantyne area. Ballantyne was a new development built around a golf course nobody could afford to play on and a resort hotel nobody could afford to stay in.

The houses were typical Charlotte pre-recession McMansions with postage-stamp yards and more room in the garage than Greg and I had in our whole basement apartment. The whole neighborhood was pretty boring, except for the token over-decorated holiday house on the corner, with ghosts in the trees and an eight-foot-tall inflatable pumpkin in the front yard. When I found my particular McMansion, I took a quick lap around the house to make sure there was no private security. There were no cops still hanging out, so I knocked on the front door, pointedly ignoring the cardboard Dracula hanging over the peephole.

A fiftyish man answered, and by the way he stood halfway behind the door, I was pretty sure he had a gun in the hand I couldn't see. I didn't blame him. His youngest kid was missing, presumed dead, and the bad guy hadn't been caught. I guess if I was still alive and in his shoes, I'd be a little jumpy, too.

"Mr. Reynolds?" I asked.

"Yes. Can I help you?" He didn't open the door any wider.

I stayed a few feet back from the door on the porch, trying to look as innocent as possible while keeping a little in the shadows just in case this guy was perceptive enough to see through my youthful appearance to the experience behind it. I hoped this would be one of the times that being turned at an early age was an asset. I got mistaken for a high-school kid more often than I enjoyed. Tonight I'd play the high-school kid for all it was worth.

"I'm Tommy Harris. I go to school with Janice, and I wanted to stop by and see how she was doing, what with everything that's happened to you guys and all." I must have nailed my impression of a living high-school senior, because he stepped back and held the door open for me.

"Come on in, son. I'll get Janice."

I stepped across the threshold and felt the familiar tingle that I get whenever I go into someone's home. I've never understood the invitation requirement, but it's as true as sunlight and stakes. We can't enter a private residence unless we're invited, which means Greg and I don't make many house calls. We try to meet our clients in public places so we don't run into any uncomfortable situations. But since Mr. Reynolds had issued the invite, even under false pretense, I was in.

"That's okay, sir. Can I go up?" I could hear the girl open a door upstairs and didn't need her coming down to blow my cover. Dad had tucked his gun away somewhere, but I wasn't certain I could get it away from him before he did enough damage to ruin my night.

"Sure. How did you—"

I left him there asking questions as I took the stairs two at a time. I saw a slim blonde girl at the top of the stairs wearing a pink T-shirt and sweatpants. She took one look at me and got a very confused look on her face.

"You're not—"

I put my hand over her mouth and moved her backward toward her room. I had crossed the last few feet between us with super-human speed, because, well, I'm not human. She hadn't expected that, which actually shut her up a fraction of a second before my hand landed.

"Don't say a word. I'm here to get your sister back," I whispered in her ear as I steered us into her bedroom.

The décor screamed twenty-first-century teen girl chic, with a poster of Lady Gaga over her computer desk and a picture of Edward Cullen over her bed. I have to give Team Edward credit. Despite his sparkling, the Twilight kid has done wonders for vampire public image.

"Can you keep quiet? Because I'd like to let you go, but if you scream, I'm going to have to jump out your window, and I ruin a lot of jackets that way."

She nodded, and I took my hand off her mouth. Of course, she instantly opened her mouth to scream. I grabbed her by the arm and pulled her down to the bed. All the air went out of her in a *whoosh*, and she sat there gasping, eyes wide. I sat in the computer chair and quickly shut down the machine. The last thing I needed was some webcam running or IM client popping up in the middle of our conversation.

"Now will you be quiet? I could have hurt you there, but I didn't. And I won't. My name is Jimmy, and I'm a private investigator. Here's my card. I'm working on the kidnappings, and I'm trying to get as much information as I can to help bring everyone home safely. I'm not a cop, and I don't work for your dad, so nothing you say will get you in any trouble. I just want to help you get your sister back."

"What's in it for you?"

I didn't expect that. "What do you mean?"

"I mean that ever since Lauren went missing we've had private eyes camped out on our front porch, promising to find my sister for money. We've had psychics, drug dealers, snitches, bounty hunters and every other kind of asshole you can think of beating down our door. And now I'm supposed to believe that you want to help because it's the right thing? Bullshit."

This was a cynical kid. I guess I understood where she was coming from, though. I took a deep breath, put on my best I-shouldn't-be-telling-you-this face and gave her my best answer. "I'm not doing this for free. Don't worry, I'm getting paid. By whom is none of your business. Maybe one of the other families is loaded and they want their daughter back. I need to know everything about every abduction to get their kid back, and if I rescue a few extras and get my picture in the paper, all the better. So I get paid, you get your sister back, and everybody's happy. But I can't help your sister if you draw attention to us. Deal?"

She croaked out "Deal," and we bumped fists. I might be old, but I have a television, so I know Howie Mandel's shtick as well as anyone.

"Now, what do you know about who took your sister?"

"N-nothing. She went to school like normal, and never came home."

"She made it to school that day, stayed the whole day, left on time, and never made it home, that's the deal?"

"Yeah, from what we can find out. The cops aren't telling my parents much, and they won't tell me anything. I've had to eavesdrop and snoop around to find out anything at all. It sounds like she left school like every other day, and somewhere between school and here, just vanished. I don't know who would want to steal Lauren. She's just a little kid. She's kind of obnoxious sometimes, but she's a sweet kid, and I don't know why anybody would want to hurt her."

She started to sniffle, and I sat down next to her on the bed. I'm not exactly good with crying girls, so I put one arm around her shoulders and kinda hugged her like that for a minute until she seemed to get herself together.

Sitting there with her reminded me of going to Greg's house for Thanksgiving and hanging out with his baby sister. She was younger than Janice, but she always loved her big brother, and was pretty wild about her "Uncle Jimmy," too. I sat there holding the crying girl and thinking about what I'd lost all those years ago, and it became very important to get her sister back.

"Are you okay?" I asked after a minute. I really hoped she didn't get any snot on my jacket. It was my favorite one.

"I think so."

"I don't think they took your sister for anything she specifically did. I think she was taken for what she is. All the kidnapped children have been around the same age, between nine and thirteen."

"What does that matter?"

"Some religions have something they call the age of innocence, where children are still free from sin. Some folks believe that young kids are inherently innocent, and innocence is valued in some rituals. I don't understand it all, but it's a theory we're working with."

"Do you think my little sister was kidnapped by *Satanists*?!?" Her voice went up a little, and I put my hand over her mouth for a second. I really, really didn't want her dad coming in just then.

She was freaking out, and I was worried that any more noise and he'd do exactly that. Time for Plan B. I had all the information I was going to get from her, anyway.

"Sleep." I made my voice very heavy and looked deep into her eyes as I said it. She shook her head once, as if to shake the cobwebs loose. Then her eyelids fluttered once, twice, and closed. I laid her down on the bed before she could fall off, and made my exit. I closed her door quietly and got almost to the front door before her father's voice stopped me cold.

"Tommy?" he called from the den.

Crap. I held my ground in the entrance hall. "Yes sir?"

"Are you leaving?"

"Yes, sir. I could tell Janice is still really upset about Lauren. I decided to head on home."

"Yeah, there's a lot of that going around. Come in here."

Double crap. I could smell the whiskey from my spot by the front door. He was hammered and his oldest daughter was sleeping off a dose of vamp mojo. His youngest child was missing, and God only knew where his wife was. I owed him the simple courtesy of listening, if nothing else. I might be dead, but I remember how to be a decent human being.

Mr. Reynolds was sitting in a well-worn tan easy chair with a bottle of Wild Turkey on the end table beside him. The Kickin' Chicken was a serious step down from Phil's Glenlivet, but I was pretty sure I was going to find a way to accept a highball glass of rotgut sometime in the next three minutes if it were offered. "Are you all right, Mr. Reynolds?"

"Call me Bob. And no, I'm not. Sit down." He waved towards the couch.

I studied him as I took a seat. I only needed a second for the once over.

He screamed past-his-prime-bank-vice-president, which sounded like half the over-forty population of Charlotte. Thinning hair, going grey at the temples even though he was barely into his fifties Casual clothes for a night at home, a polo shirt and crisp khakis rather than old jeans and a faded T-shirt.

He was pudgy, but looked like he exercised a bit, maybe tennis and golf to try and keep the bulge away. He'd missed a spot while shaving that morning, and that little chink in his armor, coupled with the Wild Turkey, told me he was falling apart fast.

And, why not? He'd had his soul ripped out and stomped on right in front of him.

"Can I do anything to help, sir? Should I maybe call Mrs. Reynolds?" I couldn't stop the question even though the last thing a smart vampire would do is waste time playing nursemaid and/or father confessor.

"You could bring back my baby girl, that would help." His dry laugh was a lot closer to a sob than any sound of mirth. "And as for Mrs. Reynolds, well, I don't know if she'll be any easier to find than Lauren. She said she was going to her mother's, but I haven't heard from her in two days."

"I'm sure she's just trying to get her head on straight, sir."

"Yeah, I'm sure that's what it is."

"Look, Mr. . . . um . . . Bob, I've got to get going. I've got school tomorrow and—"

He cut me off with a wave of his hand. "Don't bother. I know Tommy Harris, and I know you're not him. I suppose you're a reporter or something?"

"No sir, I'm a private investigator. I've been retained by . . ." I trailed off, trying to come up with one of the other victim's names, but it had been a long night. I came up blank.

" . . . one of the other families. I'd hoped that your daughter could remember some additional facts to help my investigation."

"Son, don't bullshit a bullshitter. I'm in sales, and I can smell BS a mile away, and let me tell you, what you're spreading will make the roses grow but it won't help bring my little girl back. Now, I want to tell you one thing. Whatever you want to write about me, go ahead. I'm not the world's best dad, no matter what my coffee mug says, but you write one word about my little girl and I will absolutely destroy you." He leaned forward for emphasis and almost fell out of his chair.

Usually I don't react well to being threatened by anything lower than me on the food chain, but I couldn't help but feel a little sorry for him. I said "Yes, sir. I will keep that in mind," and headed out the front door. I felt an unfamiliar sense of responsibility. These people's pain was real to me now, and I had to do something. So I started walking to where it all began.

Chapter 13

It only took me a few minutes to walk to Lauren's school. Going to the last place she was seen made sense. I could try to pick up any bad vibes, or smells, or even maybe a clue. Ballantyne Elementary School was a sprawling brick building with a cute little portico in front, where parents dropped their kids off when it rained.

I poked around the campus for about half an hour, hoping a heretofore unknown special magic-detecting sense would kick in or that there'd be a huge pentagram drawn on the roof of the building. Instead I found a whole pile of nothing and was about ready to trek back to the main road to hail a cab or unsuspecting solo driver when inspiration struck.

I whipped out the new phone Greg had given me and dialed him up. He answered after the second ring. "Hey, what are you doing, bro?"

"Trying to hack into the police department database to get the case files. Why, what do you need?"

"Two things. I need your super-sniffer, and I need a ride."

"Where are you?"

"Ballantyne Elementary, down south."

"What are you doing, looking for a date?"

"Classy. Just come get me. I'll explain on the way home."

I hung up the phone and sat on the roof of the portico to wait. About twenty minutes passed before headlights turned into the drive. I stood up on the roof and started to wave when I realized that the headlights didn't belong to Greg's car, or to mine. I dropped flat to the roof as a police cruiser pulled into the drive and parked in front of the school.

Great. I'd apparently picked the one school in the district with enough money for motion sensors on the roof. I lay as still as I could while the cop got out of the cruiser and did a lap around the building, shining his flashlight into the windows. I grabbed my phone and shot Greg a quick "stay away, cops are here" text before switching the phone to silent and returning it to my pocket.

After the second lap the cop got back in his car and just sat there. He left the dome light off, but I could see him fingering a picture in his sun visor. He sat there for a long few minutes before driving off. I texted Greg an all clear, and he pulled up in front of the school a couple minutes later.

I waved him up to the roof, and he vaulted to my side in one easy leap.

I'll give him credit, the boy is not the exact image of grace and fashion, but for a chunky nerd vampire, he's handy to have around.

"Give this place a sniff," I said. We all get super-senses, but at different levels. Greg's sniffer is better than mine, I hear better than he does. He's stronger than me, I'm faster than him. And as far as we know, neither of us can turn into bats.

Greg sniffed the air for a minute. "There's something funky in the air, but I don't recognize it. Now tell me again why I had to drive all the way out here to get your sorry butt."

"Because there aren't any buses to Ballantyne at two in the morning, I don't really have the dough for a cab, and I didn't want to steal any more cars this week." I jumped off the roof and walked over to Greg's car. He followed me down and unlocked the car with the remote. Greg loved his classic hot rod, but he loved modern conveniences and gadgets more, so his GTO had keyless entry, remote start, a badass stereo and seat warmers, which are more useful than you'd think for the cold-blooded.

He slid into the driver's seat and started the car. "Fair enough. Hey! What do you mean steal any *more* cars? I thought we agreed that we were the good guys?"

I got in on the passenger side and fastened my seat belt. "Dude, stealing a car and giving it back doesn't make me a bad guy. And I did give it back. That means I borrow cars." I was really hoping he would drop it. He didn't.

"And what about the driver? And don't bother lying, you know you suck at it."

He's right, too. I can't lie worth a crap. Even being immortal and bloodless didn't mean I could spin a solid lie while looking my best friend in the eye. "Fine. I left him asleep in the back seat behind a biker bar on Central Avenue. He might have felt a little out of place when he woke up, but he was safe."

"Asleep? Or drained?" He looked down and not at me. He was really pissed.

"Asleep. I didn't drain him." I wasn't lying. I wasn't going to tell him the whole truth unless he pulled it out of me with a wrecker, but I wasn't going to lie, either.

"But you did feed, didn't you? Don't even answer. I can see it in your face. You look healthier than you have in years. I know you fed on him."

I didn't know what he was talking about, so I flipped down the sun visor on my side and checked myself out in the mirror. He was right. I looked *good*. Well, good for me, anyway. I still had an unruly shock of brown hair hanging in my eyes, and I was still too skinny, but I was a lot less pale than I had been when I woke up that night, and my eyes no longer had the pale, lifeless look that I'd come to equate with my reflection.

Oh yeah, the mirror thing. It's got more to do with silver than with mirrors and souls. Cheap, crappy mirrors like in cars work fine because they don't use silver as a reflective element. Good mirrors sometimes do, and silver doesn't react well to vampires, therefore we don't show up. Same deal with film. Silver nitrate is one of the main developing chemicals, so we'll show up on video or a digital camera, but not on real film. So I could check myself in the car mirror, but not in the mirror in my house.

Flipping up the visor, I said, "You got me. I did feed on the guy, but I didn't drain him, and I didn't really even drink that much. But that's not why I look like this."

I wasn't sure I wanted to tell him about Lilith, and even if I did, I wasn't sure how. He got bent out of shape about me feeding on a human, which is kinda the point of being a vampire. Telling him I'd fed on an immortal hottie would not go over well.

"I was at Phil's. I ate there."

"At Phil's?" He had looked away again, staring long and hard at the road, which meant he was expecting the kind of answer that'd make him mad. I swear, sometimes this partnership is like being married. We fight all the time and neither one of us is getting laid.

"Phil offered. He made it clear that it would be viewed as a serious breach of protocol for me to decline."

"Since when do we care about demonic protocol?"

"Technically, Phil's a fallen angel, which is different from a demon. I think."

"You hope. So, who did you drink from this time?"

Wow, he was going heavy with the guilt trip. He was making it sound like I went around drinking from people willy-nilly. Wrong. I quit doing that years ago, after I got a really embarrassing rash. Bad blood might not kill you, but a vampire can get all sorts of nasty things from it, and some of them take a while for even vampire metabolism to get rid of.

That made me wonder how long the "Lilith effect" would last before I went back to my pasty self.

"Her name was Lilith, and the light's green." I really wanted him paying attention to the road and not to the name of my new acquaintance. I didn't often get what I wanted.

We've read the same comic books, so if I knew Lilith, I was pretty sure he would. And judging by the fact that he pulled into a Burger King parking lot and shut off the car, he did.

"*Lilith?* Like Adam's first wife Lilith? Like the original feminist Lilith? Lilith who was condemned to walk the earth forever spreading lust through the souls of all she touches while unable to ever feel true love?"

Clearly he'd read way more comic books than I had, because the lust stuff was news to me. I sank down as far as the car seat would let me before I answered. "I guess that would be an accurate description."

Greg fumed. I didn't know fuming was audible but Greg managed to fill the car with the sound of it.

He took a deep breath, held it for a long time, let it out very slowly, and counted to twenty. In four languages. Four languages wasn't too bad. Greg was fluent in seven. Anything under five meant he was only moderately pissed. I thought I was maybe going to get out of this relatively unscathed.

"Well?" he finally asked.

"Well what?"

"Was it good?" There was a little longing in his voice, and I hoped that he might finally admit that he missed the taste of live blood.

"Dude, you have no idea. It made me tingle in places I'd forgotten I had places. I saw colors that I don't even have names for. I felt like I could run a marathon at noon in Arizona and not get the least bit crispy. It was amazing." I could have gone on describing the feeling of feeding on Lilith, but the look on Greg's face stopped me. "What's wrong?"

"Listen to me, and listen very carefully." He was scared. "You can never feed from her again. No matter what, no matter who it insults. Legend has it that her kiss, her very touch is so addictive that archbishops have burned their Bibles for a drop of her sweat. You have to stay away from her, or she could take you over completely. And a vampire under the control of a creature like Lilith would not make a pretty picture."

He was right. I didn't use much of my vamp powers in everynight life, but if Lilith was bad juju like Greg thought, then she could wreak some serious havoc if I fell under her control. And Greg was by far the better judge of character between the two of us. I trusted his opinion way more than my own.

"Fine, fine, I'll stay clear of her. You know how I hate going to Phil's anyway. Let's get out of here before some cop rolls up and decides we're making out in the BK parking lot."

"Well was it worth it?" Greg asked quietly.

"What? The blood? It was—"

"No." He cut me off sharply. "Did you get any useful information out of Phil?"

"Kinda. Apparently there's a Big Bad coming to town and if we don't stop it the world might end. Or something like that." I stared out the window, watching the billboards on I-485 roll past and thinking about Lilith. That chick scared me.

"Isn't that on the list of things you should *start* the conversation with?"

"Gimme a break. So I buried the lead. I saw Phil, I drank from an inappropriate woman, and there's a magic something-or-other coming that will destroy the world if we don't stop it. And how was your night, honey?"

I kept looking out the window, but all I could see was a scared little girl and a shattered father that desperately wanted to see his child again.

"I hate you sometimes."

Chapter 14

"So, what's the plan?" Greg asked the second we got back into our apartment.

"I'm still working on that." I admitted, flopping down onto the couch and grabbing the Xbox controller. Hoping to distract him, I tossed him the other controller. "Madden?"

"Sure. I always think better with a little break. Did Phil give you anything we could use?"

I started up the game and picked my team. I always pick the Carolina Panthers, no matter how they did that season. I'm a hometown fan, what can I say? And besides, as long as they have Steve Smith, they'll always make for a fun video game. "He said that Halloween was the big day, that whatever we were up against had to be stopped by then, or not at all."

Greg stared at me with his mouth open while I sacked his virtual quarterback, forced a virtual fumble and sent a virtual Jon Beason to the end zone for a virtual touchdown dance. "You do realize Halloween is this weekend, right?"

"Yeah, I have a pretty good handle on the calendar."

"So what the hell are we doing playing video games?" Greg tossed his control at me and headed over to the computer.

"Really, dude? You don't want to play Madden but you'll go play World of Warcraft?" I was giving him a hard time, but sometimes I did it just because it was easy.

"Bite me. I'm checking email."

"No thanks, I've had my fill of supernatural Scooby Snacks tonight."

He flipped me off, then waved me over to the desk.

"Come here, dude. You gotta see this!"

He was actually bouncing up and down in his chair. I thought we'd broken him of that habit in high school, but obviously not. I leaned over the back of his chair, as much to rescue the furniture from the shock load as anything else.

"What is it, bro?"

"I emailed the guys about the kidnappings to see what they knew, and they've got all the police reports!"

Oh. Crap. "The guys" were a trio of losers that worked in the biggest comic shop in town. They were understandably all over Greg for information on his "ongoing cases" whenever he went in to grab his subscriptions. Every once in a while we used them for daytime legwork or computer help when it was something we couldn't get Dad to do or if the computing was out of Greg's league. They were occasionally useful, but I always had a hard time balancing their annoying tics against the value of their assistance.

"Really? You emailed the Dork Brigade about this case?"

"Man, don't call them that. They're good guys. And Jason hacked into the police database and got us the police reports. So the guys are useful, too."

"And how many free comic books did you get for letting them help?" When he wouldn't answer me, I knew I'd hit home. My partner—the closet Spider-Man junkie.

"Do you want the reports or not?"

I did, so I shut up.

There were ten files, and the girl we'd exorcised the night before was slated to have been number eleven, so we added notes on her and Tommy into the mix and tried to see what patterns emerged. After three hours of taking apart class schedules, church attendance, club memberships and even school bus routes, I lost my patience.

"There's nothing here!" I lay on my back on the floor, surrounded by paper. I looked like I'd been mugged by a shedding yeti, and we had no more ideas than when we started. "What time is it?"

"Seven," he mumbled, still going over attendance records for the fifth victim.

"I'm going to bed. It's been a long night."

I stretched as I stood up, and my thighs threatened to revolt. Vampire or not, you sit cross-legged on the floor for a few hours and even your butt falls asleep. I staggered off to my bedroom and crashed for a few hours while Greg kept going. He's always been better at homework than me.

We do sleep. And we dream, and we don't "die" every morning at sunrise. We can sense the sunrise. It's kinda like our bodies' way of warning us not to go outside for fear of becoming a pile of ash, but I've been known to pull an all-nighter (or in my case an all-dayer, I guess) when I needed to.

Today's sleep wasn't restful, not with visions of scared children running from sexy fallen angels dancing through my head. I got about six hours of fitful sleep and staggered out to the den to find Greg facedown in the scattered mass of case files.

I stepped over him as quietly as I could, opened the fridge and grabbed a bottle of orange juice. I didn't bother getting a glass, just sat on the couch in my boxers and drank straight from the plastic jug. We can drink, too, anything we want. No food, though. The digestive system stops working except for a liquid diet right after we wake up. We don't get any nutrients out of anything we drink except blood, but alcohol still works, only to a lesser degree.

So, I guess that answers Tommy's question about vampire poop. We don't poop, but if we play our cards right, we can pee in some spectacular colors, because what comes in, goes right back out again. You don't want to know how we found this out. Suffice to say that we were young and learning about our new abilities, and leave it at that.

"I don't care if we're dead, that's still gross." Greg's voice came from right behind me, and I jumped sky-high, spilling cold OJ on my lap. That's one of his favorite tricks, but it usually doesn't work on me, what with super-hearing and all. I'd been so wrapped up in the case that I didn't even hear him get up from the desk.

"I might be gross, but you're a dick," I said, looking around for something to dry off with. I gave up on the idea of finding anything lying around the den when I remembered that, yesterday, Greg had been home alone all night, which always led to an almost neurotic level of cleaning. I went into my room and got some fresh boxers and the rest of my clothes.

Greg was sitting up on the floor when I made it back to the den, a look of smug superiority on his face. "What?" I asked.

"What, what?" He kept grinning at me.

"Why are you sitting there grinning like the AV club president who bugged the girls' dressing room?"

"I *am* the AV club president who bugged the girls' dressing room," he reminded me without a hint of embarrassment.

"I remember. And you had that same stupid grin on your face then."

"Well I think I may have found our link between the victims. Career Day." He waved a piece of paper over his head like it was a checkered flag and he was an off-duty Daytona stripper.

I snatched the paper from him and looked at it. There was a column of initials, a column of dates and a column of school names. The school names I recognized, and it didn't take long to figure out that the initials and dates matched up with missing kids.

"Greg, there are only seven names here." I pointed to the paper.

"Yeah?"

"There were eleven victims, dude."

"Yeah, but seven of these schools had a Career Day the week before the kidnappings occurred. There's no way that's not statistically significant."

He had a point. "We need to look into it further."

"Really?"

"Yeah, I think it's a good idea."

Greg looked so happy that I wasn't dismissing his idea out of hand that you'd have thought I gave him an ice cream cone, or a puppy. Or a puppy with ice cream on it.

"Cool. Now what? Where do we start?" Greg asked. He headed to the coat closet and started gearing up—putting on his utility belt, boots, and other combat equipment. I stopped him before he got too far along.

"We start right here. At least until dark, bro. Remember, it's like two in the afternoon."

"Oh yeah. I just got so excited at having a real lead."

"I know, I know," I led him back over to the couch.

"Wanna play *Halo*?" I sat down with the game controller in one hand and my OJ in the other.

"Nah. If we can't go thwart evil, I'm gonna take a nap." My grumpy roommate then tromped off to his room for some shut-eye while I valiantly tried to save the world. Again.

Chapter 15

I finished off season two of *Dexter* on Netflix before Greg woke up. Not long after sunset, I heard the shower come on and a few minutes later, my partner emerged. He was dressed in all black, again, with his combat boots laced tight and his utility belt snug around his ballooning waist. I feel for Greg sometimes. I mean, who knew that turning into vampires wouldn't change our bodies into perfect examples of studliness, and we'd be trapped forever as the dorks we were on the last night of our lives?

The first thing we looked forward to when we got over the shock of being vampires was that now we could exercise all we wanted and build ourselves the buff bodies we'd never had in life. The first thing we realized after that was that no matter how much we exercised, our bodies were never going to change. This was not a welcome realization for either my pudgy best friend or me.

"Really, man. Do you have to wear the utility belt?" I laced up my sneakers and shrugged into my shoulder holster on the way out the door. I hid the firepower under a leather jacket before as we climbed the last steps and walked out into the cemetery.

We opened a tool shed that was really a two-car garage and hopped in Greg's car, a 1967 GTO convertible—black, of course. I always gave Greg a load of crap about his less-than-inconspicuous ride, but he'd had a man-crush on that car since we were alive, so no amount of teasing was going to get him to drive anything else. Besides, I had a blue Camry for when we needed to blend in.

"Where are we headed?" Greg asked as I got into the car.

I pulled out the file folder with all his Career Day notes and started to flip through it. It had been easy to find when he went to bed, because he'd written "CAREER DAY CLUES" on the outside of the folder in purple Sharpie. Sometimes I really thought my partner was secretly an illiterate twelve-year-old girl. I wouldn't have been too surprised to find his notes in a Trapper Keeper covered in unicorn stickers.

"There were three companies that had a table at every event. Bank of America, Joe's World of Tires and the Police Department. Bank of America makes sense, since their corporate headquarters is here. The owner of Joe's World of Tires is on the school board, and I think the cops were just looking for middle-school weed. But we should check them all out regardless."

"Why do we need to check out the cops? They're investigating the crimes. You don't think a cop could have done it, do you?"

My partner has a simple view of the world—police and firemen are good, and bad guys have twirly mustaches and bad French accents. It's charming, really.

"I don't think a cop abducted the kids, but it's possible. Cops are people, so they're suspects. We've got to look at everybody, bro."

"All right, but I don't think it's the cops."

I didn't either, but I could hope. A cop would be easier. I didn't think we were going to find our kidnapper anywhere in this list of companies. I didn't think our bad guy was still capable of "normal." It didn't feel right, if you know what I mean.

"So, where to first?" Greg gingerly backed the car out of the garage. I'm always amazed that he can be incredibly careful with his car but such a spaz on two feet.

"I think we start with the path of least resistance—Joe Arthur, owner of Joe's World of Tires and school board member. We should be able to play the PI card and find out who was representing the World of Tires at the Career Days straight from the source."

I gave him the address, and we headed out to meet the Tire King. I looked out the window and watched the city roll by. A flashing sign for the Morris Costumes Haunted House had me thinking a lot more than I wanted to about ten missing children and the fact that we only had a couple of nights left to stop something from coming to town that even a fallen angel was scared of.

It took us about half an hour to get to Joe Arthur's house, a modest ranch in one of the newer developments out past the university. These little subdivisions popped up all over Charlotte in the late 1990s as the banking boom hit, but now there was a For Sale sign in about every fourth yard.

I noted the bicycle lying beside the driveway. "Looks like Joe's got a kid right in the target age range," I whispered as we walked up to the front door.

"Yep. How do you want to play this? Good cop/bad cop? Two bad cops? Fangs out? Subtle?" He was bouncing up and down on the balls of his feet and shadowboxing his way up to the door. I grabbed the back of his utility belt and dragged him down the steps back to where I stood.

"I thought we'd ask him very nicely to invite us in, then see what he knows about the disappearances." I spoke very low and very slowly, and held one hand on Greg's shoulder to steady him while I tried to rein in his excitement. When you pair his enthusiasm with the fact that we haven't aged in fifteen years, it's easy to forget that he remembers the Reagan administration.

He deflated a little. "Oh."

I shouldered my way past him up the steps, and rang the bell. No one answered, so I rang again. I could hear people walking around inside, but when they didn't respond to the second ring, I knocked on the door. After a couple more minutes, a light flipped on over my head, and the door cracked open.

"Can I help you?" A sliver of a middle-aged woman's face appeared between the door and the jamb, as she looked at me through the security chain. The last time a woman was this unhappy to see me had been my date for the senior prom.

The woman's face was pinched, like she'd been a beautiful girl whose life hadn't worked out as well as she'd hoped, and her eyes darted along the street past me looking for something. I couldn't tell if she was more annoyed at me interrupting her evening, or worried about whatever might be out on the sidewalk at night. I'd seen that look before, on the face of my own mother, and it dredged up some memories that I didn't particularly enjoy.

"Is Mr. Arthur home?" I asked, reaching into my coat pocket for my investigator's license.

"No, he's not," she said, and moved to close the door in my face. I put a hand on the door and held it open. I couldn't go through without an invitation, but I could make sure she didn't close it completely, either.

I held my credentials where she could see them and said, "We're investigating the disappearance of some children. Maybe you've heard about the situation?"

"Yes, yes, I've heard of that. Awful stuff. But I don't see what that has to do with Joe. He's never really hurt anybody." She stopped, eyes round as she realized what she'd implied.

I began to doubt her certainty that Mr. Arthur was harmless. Maybe Greg had found something after all.

"We understand that, ma'am. We're hoping that he could answer a few questions for us about the Career Day events that he attended at several of the schools prior to the disappearances. He may have seen something that could be useful in our investigation. Could we come in and wait for him?" She looked increasingly nervous, and I suddenly became aware of another heartbeat in the house.

"Um . . . no, I'm sorry. I'm alone here, you see, and it wouldn't be proper. You understand? You're welcome to come back later, when my husband is home. Maybe tomorrow afternoon?"

I could hear the heartbeat moving closer to the door but I had no way in without an invitation. A wife-beater or a stone-cold killer could be behind that door, and I still couldn't do anything about it if I couldn't figure out how to get inside. I'm not sure how long I would have stood there if Greg hadn't pulled on my sleeve.

"Come on, James. We'll come back and visit when Mr. Arthur is home. Thanks for your time, ma'am." He led me down the steps by my elbow and steered me toward the car.

"Dude!" I whispered. "What the hell was that about? Something had her wound up—her pulse was up, her skin was flushed, and there was definitely somebody else in that house. I could hear a man's pulse, racing. He was pretty excited, too." I put my elbows on the roof of the car and looked over at where Greg stood by the driver's door.

Usually he was the first one to leap into Super Hero mode. Now, he stood there quietly. I didn't understand. "Why aren't we doing everything we can to get her to let us in so we can help her?"

"Because I don't think she would appreciate our help," he said, with what I guess he meant to be a meaningful glance.

"What are you talking about?" I demanded.

"Let's see—skin flushed, heart racing, doesn't want us in the house, husband not home, someone else in the house with her. Even the man with a thousand strikeouts like you should be able to put those clues together." He smirked at me as realization dawned, and we got in the car.

"I get it." I closed the door. "She's having an affair, and her boyfriend was there. But where does that leave us with the Tire King?"

"Headed to Lucky Strike." Greg put the car in gear and headed towards the big outlet mall north of town.

"Why do you have a sudden urge to go bowling in the middle of an investigation?" Greg didn't really baffle me that often, but this time he had me flummoxed. Admittedly, he often baffled me, but it was usually with his staggering ineptitude with women. I can't understand how anyone can be immortal, live through all these years looking like he's in his twenties, and still have no more game than the dorky kids we were when we were turned.

"While you were trying to get the Real Housewife of Charlotte to let us interrupt date night, I was peeking through the kitchen window checking out the calendar on the fridge. Tonight is Joe Arthur's league night, so he'll be bowling for at least another couple of hours. All we need to do is grab him when he heads for his car, interrogate him, maybe munch on him a little, and find out what he knows."

"*Munch?* Did you, the closest thing to a vegan vampire I've ever met, just suggest that we actually feed from a suspect? Who are you and what did you do with Greg Knightwood?"

"I just thought that, you know, since you were off the wagon, bro, you might want another excuse to behave like an animal."

Now that made more sense. Ticked me off, but made sense. He just wanted to make me feel like a monster again. Whatever. I *am* a monster. And monsters eat. It's what we do.

"No, I think we can do without snacking on the suspects for tonight at least." I leaned back in my seat and contemplated staking my partner while he pulled into the mall's gargantuan parking lot. I couldn't stake him, but I could needle him. "Besides, I'm still full from yesterday."

"Well, if you're sure . . ."

"I'm sure. Park the car."

Lucky Strike is in Concord Mills, the gigantic mall north of town by the speedway. I've never gotten the hang of navigating that place. It's over a mile to walk the entire inside of it, and the mere concept of trying to drive through the parking lot always gives me the heebie-jeebies. Greg pulled up in front of the bowling alley, and we headed in. It made sense that the Tire King would bowl there. It was the closest alley to his neighborhood, and it had a truly excellent beer selection.

"Assuming he's here, do you really want to grab him as he exits?" I asked.

"Nah, I thought we'd flash our badges, ask a few questions about his whereabouts, hint around that his wife is having him investigated for infidelity, and all around ruin his night."

"That sounds a little extreme, doesn't it?" I asked. I liked it, but I wanted Greg to tell me that he'd seen what I saw in the wife's eyes.

"Were you not paying attention back there? That woman had all the classic signs of abuse to go with her affair. If the Tire King's never used her for a punching bag, I'll eat your hat."

Bingo. We were on the same page after all. I knew from the look in her eyes that the wife had been slapped around more than once. If we could get a little payback on Mr. Joe Arthur, upstanding businessman and school board member, I was down with that.

"Fine, but we don't talk about his wife's boy toy unless he's really irritating."

"Nah, if he's really irritating we eat him. We ruin his marriage just for looking at me funny."

"You're wearing a utility belt. Everyone looks at you funny."

"Point," Greg agreed. "All right, we only ruin his marriage if we get something out of it."

"Deal. I'll lead."

"Why do you always lead?"

"I'm taller."

By now we had made it through the parking lot, down the mall and most of the way across the bowling alley, and I recognized Joe Arthur from his commercials. The Tire King was carrying a spare or two of his own, and I don't mean the bowling kind. He was a sixty-something Italian guy with more hair coming out of his ears than he had left on his head. He was about five foot eight which gave me a serious height advantage. I'm a couple inches over six feet. Even Greg had a couple inches on the Rubber Royalty.

He and his league buddies had the least flattering bowling shirts I'd ever seen. I've never met any guy over fifty (and over two-fifty) who can pull off horizontal stripes in turquoise, and these guys were no exception. I wondered if they realized they looked like turquoise Michelin Men.

We waited until Big Joe, as was embroidered on his bowling shirt, got up to bowl. Right in the middle of his backswing, I called out in my loudest voice, "Joe Arthur?" Since I was only about four feet from him, he jumped like a startled, overweight cat and threw a perfect gutter ball.

"Jesus Christ!" He stomped over to me and got as much in my face as he could from his height and bellowed, "What the holy crap do you think you're doing? This is a league game! We're in the running for the championship! What kind of crap was that?"

If the garlic myth had been anything more than urban legend, Joe's breath would have put me down for the count. While my eyes watered, I flashed my badge. "Mr. Arthur, we have a few questions to ask you about some missing children."

The whole trick to flashing a fake badge is to control the flash. You have to open and close the wallet before anyone can get a good look at the contents. I'd actually practiced in front of a mirror when we first opened up shop as detectives. It's embarrassing to admit, but less embarrassing than how I learned to draw from a shoulder holster. Practice paid off, like now. His teammates were nudging each other as if to say, "Look at that. Joe's gone and got himself in trouble." They were focused on Joe, not questioning my ID.

"Mr. Arthur, is there somewhere we could talk?"

"I don't know anything about any missing kids. And I don't feel like talking to you. If you want to talk to me, talk to my lawyer first. And he'll tell you I don't know anything about any missing kids and don't feel like talking to you. Right, Mason?" He pointed over to a scrawny, balding man drinking beer from a plastic cup at a table near their lane. The man, who I assumed was Arthur's lawyer given Arthur's smirk, nodded like his head was spring-loaded and started over to us.

"Now that you've heard from my lawyer, get out of my face and let me finish my game." He turned back to the ball return machine, but I grabbed his wrist and turned him back to face me.

"I asked nicely first, Mr. Arthur. If I have to ask again, it won't be nicely." I spoke very slowly and kept my voice low. I didn't need his buddies seeing me threaten him and wondering what kind of cop would do that. That wouldn't end well for anyone, especially if anyone on the team got suspicious and grew a pair all of a sudden. Arthur looked into my eyes, and I put just enough mojo in them to show him I was not screwing around.

"Now," I told him, "bowl this ball and then come meet us at that table." I gestured to where Greg had settled in at a round plastic table with a pitcher of cheap beer and four plastic cups. "Bring your lawyer if you need to." I let go of his wrist and went over to the table with Greg.

Mason beat his client over to our table and began issuing a list of demands in a nasal, demanding tone that probably had Greg rethinking his stance against drinking from annoying humans. That was my criteria. Since I find pretty much everyone annoying, I drink from whoever I want to. Greg doesn't realize that my list of annoying people is about six billion names longer than his.

At the moment, Mason was top of the list. If I couldn't eat him, then he had to go. I leaned forward looked straight into his eyes and said, "Go to the men's room. Sit in a stall. Fall asleep for two hours. Then go do that thing you've always wanted to do but have been afraid would be too embarrassing."

Mason got up with a decidedly glassy look in his eyes and headed for the crapper.

I leaned back in my chair. "Well, that's one nuisance taken care of."

"You're evil. What do you think he'll do?" Greg asked.

"I don't even want to think about it. But I wouldn't be surprised if it involved anything from playing naked in the pond at Freedom Park to scaling the outside of the Bank of America building."

Joe Arthur, the Tire King himself, joined us at our table after picking up the spare. "Where's Mason?" he asked.

"He went to the can. Something about an upset stomach," I replied. Greg snorted a little beer out of his nose, and I kicked him under the table.

"Fine. You've got me alone. What's this about?" Arthur asked, obviously a man used to being in charge.

I decided to put an end to that as quickly as possible. I reached into the briefcase Greg had brought in from the car and brought out a stack of photographs. Smiling faces began to litter the table in front of us, some of the pictures curling a little as they soaked up spilled beer on the table. I didn't care. I wanted to watch Arthur's face as he realized who these children were. Ten pictures—school pictures, family vacation shots, all pictures of happy kids, beaming into the camera.

"Do you know who these kids are, Mr. Arthur?" I leaned forward, forcing his attention away from the photos and to my eyes. He looked up and I could see that he was shaken. There was something going on with this guy, and I needed to know what it was. He didn't smell like malice, more like mischief, but he was involved in something somehow.

"These are the kids that have gone missing. But I don't know anything about—"

I cut him off before he could go any further. "I know that, Mr. Arthur. You're not a suspect in these disappearances. But you were at seven of these children's schools in the days shortly before they went missing. You were there for Career Day, right?"

"Not all of them. Some of those Career Day things I sent Jake instead."

"Jake?" Greg sat forward. We hadn't heard anything about a Jake before now. "Who's Jake?"

"Jake's the manager of my Pineville store. I sent him to the schools on the south side of town, 'cause they're closer to him. But what's this got to do with me? I don't know anything about any of this stuff."

But he did—I could see it in his eyes, and more importantly, I could smell the little sweat that comes with fear. After a while you figure out what different kinds of fear smell like. For example, innocent oh-crap-I'm-about-to-get-eaten-by-a-vampire fear smells completely different than guilty as sin yeah-I-really-raised-a-super-demon-and-I'm-lying-out-my-butt-about-it fear. Joe's fear was somewhere between I-cheated-on-my-taxes fear and I've-got-corpses-buried-under-my-tomato-plants fear.

I turned the fear smell inside out, but I couldn't quite put my finger on the cause. I was so busy playing "Name That Fear" that I didn't sense a disturbance in the force until I heard Greg whisper "Oh, crap."

Chapter 16

Okay, fine, you got me. I didn't sense a disturbance in the force. But I did notice a silence fall over the bowling alley and smell a wave of fear rippling out from the main entrance. I looked over at the front door and saw the female detective from the night before talking to the shoe rental guy. He pointed to where we were sitting with the Tire King, and she started our way.

"Looks like we might have to come back to this conversation later, Mr. Arthur," I said, getting to my feet and looking for another exit.

"Where do you think you're going?" Arthur asked, getting up himself and blocking my escape route. "You can't come in here and make all these accusations then go running out on me. You sit your skinny ass right back down here and tell me what you think I have to do with those missing kids!"

I leaned down to the Tire King's face, which had gone an interesting splotchy purple color. I looked in his eyes and said, "Sleep."

He passed out cold and fell face-first onto the table, crushing his plastic cup full of Miller with his forehead. I turned him to the side to make sure he wouldn't drown in cheap beer and tried to formulate a plan.

"What are we gonna do?" Greg asked.

"I was really hoping you'd have a plan." My mind worked as fast as it could, which really isn't that fast, all things considered.

"I never have a plan. At least, not one you like."

He had a point there. Greg's plans usually involved some expensive piece of equipment that only existed in comic books, or so many plot twists that by the time he finished explaining the plan, I'd already punched somebody.

"Well, there's a first time for everything. But obviously tonight ain't it." I stood up as the detective got to our table.

The look on her face dispelled any lingering hope that she hadn't noticed me looking out Tommy's hospital-room window. She was tall, and she'd pulled her curly hair back in a severe ponytail. Her blazer was pulled back to reveal an impressive rack, but my attention was drawn to her Smith & Wesson .40 pistol in a shoulder rig. I'll admit it, I have a bit of a thing for women who pack heavier ammo than me.

She snapped her fingers in front of my face and brought me straight out of my happy place and back to the beer-soaked bowling alley. "This would be an excellent time for you to explain to me who you are and why you keep showing up around my investigation."

The look on her face said she was a woman who brooked no BS, but I never let that stop me.

"I'm sorry," I said, holding out my hand and dropping into the hick accent I grew up with. "I think you must have me mistaken for somebody else. I'm Jimmy Black, assistant manager at the Monroe location of Joe's World of Tires. Can I help you with . . . something?" I put a little sleazy twist in there and ogled her chest, trying to make myself look like a slimy tire salesman.

Ogling her chest was not hard to do. More like a job perk.

"Really?" She said, and raised one eyebrow as if she knew something I didn't. "There is no Monroe location of Joe's World of Tires, and you're no more a tire salesman than I am a private investigator. Why don't you cut the crap, Mr. Black and tell me what you and your little friend here are doing screwing up my investigation before I haul you both downtown and book you on obstruction of justice charges."

I knew going legit and getting PI licenses would come back to bite me in the ass. And the irony of that concept is not lost on me. Having failed so miserably with Plan A, I skipped the as-yet-undeveloped Plan B and went straight for the mojo. I looked her in the eyes, which was surprisingly easy since she was almost my height, and said, "These are not the droids you're looking for. Move along."

"Are you on drugs?"

I looked over at Greg, who was as flabbergasted as I was. Mojo didn't fail. This was entirely unexpected. Surprise didn't help me process or communicate. "Huh?"

"You are on drugs. Great, just great. Not only do I have a PI sticking his nose in my case, I have a stoner PI sticking his nose in my case. Get up. You two are coming with me."

I looked at her again, and got serious with the mojo, really tried to supplant her will with mine. "No, we're not. You will leave here and forget you ever saw us. You came in, Joe Arthur was passed out drunk, he has nothing to do with these disappearances and you left. That is all."

She looked back at me just as hard and said "You are a pain in my butt, and you are going to jail for interfering with my investigation."

Since my vampire willpower wasn't working, Greg stepped in for the save. "Sorry to disappoint, but we're not going anywhere with you. I'm sorry we've run into this misunderstanding, but it's not going to happen. Now why don't you get in your car, go back to the station, and forget you ever ran into us this evening."

Greg's best mojo netted equally disappointing results and a disgusted headshake from the officer.

Both of us were seeing this cop in a whole new light. I'd never run into anyone who could shrug off multiple vamp mojo attempts, but this chick evidently had a will of cast iron.

She reached around to her belt and grabbed a radio, clicking it on as she brought it to her lips. "This is Detective Law. I need a wagon at Lucky Strike for two passengers." She put the radio back on her belt and looked at us. "You two are going to spend the night in a holding cell while I figure out exactly what I'm going to charge you with. Unless you have a really good story and start sharing it with me right now."

"Um . . . we were hired by the family of one of the kidnapped girls?" I offered up.

"The Reynolds family?" she asked.

I nodded.

"No, you weren't. They called me as soon as you left there. I left instructions with every family to call me as soon as the vultures, and that means you, started coming around, so that I could run you off. So you came around, they called, and voilà! Here I am, running you off."

"But . . . but . . . ," I spluttered. I'm not proud of it, but splutter was the best I could come up with.

"But how did I find you? Mrs. Arthur also called me, and told me that you had just left her house, and were probably headed here to harass her husband publicly. Looks like she has some shred of marital loyalty left. And here we are."

"And here we are," I muttered. Here I was in the middle of a brightly lit public space with a human that I couldn't put the whammy on.

This was so far outside the norm, I was totally stumped. Greg and I had been bespelling humans for fun and foodstuffs for the better part of two decades, and nothing like this had ever happened before. Primitive survival instincts kicked in. We shared a look that said, "You wanna hit her or you want me to?" and I had just decided to deck the pretty detective in front of about seventy witnesses when her cell phone rang.

She pulled out her phone and pressed a button. "Law"

Thanks to our super-duper hearing, Greg and I had the benefit of following both sides of the conversation.

A disembodied voice said, "Detective, we have another abduction. Marjorie Ryan was last seen leaving a school dance with three of her friends forty-five minutes ago. Her friends all arrived home, but Marjorie did not. We've established a perimeter between the school and the home, and we have a chopper in the air. What's your twenty?"

"Lucky Strike bowling alley. I was about to question a potential suspect. Obviously, he's not our guy. I'm on my way, should be there in fifteen."

I held up my hands and started to back away, saying, "You've obviously got a lot going on, so we'll get out of your way. Good luck catching the bad guys!"

"Don't even think about moving. As a matter of fact, you two are still going downtown, if for nothing else than to keep you out of my hair. No way do I need you mucking around my crime scene and getting in my way. Gimme your right hands." She reached behind her and grabbed a pair of handcuffs.

I shook my head. "Look, Detective. You don't have enough to charge us with anything, and handcuffing us and leaving us here is a bad idea no matter whose police procedure manual you cite." I thought if mojo wasn't working then maybe I could appeal to her sense of reason. "If you think you need to keep an eye on us, take us along. My partner and I have a lot of experience in unusual cases. We could probably be helpful if you'd just let us."

"Okay, maybe you would be useful." She seemed to relent, and reached out to shake my hand. Without thinking, I took her hand, and just like in a thousand bad cop movies, she slapped a cuff on it. Then she reached over to the swivel chair mounted to the scoring station and locked the other cuff around it.

"Now stay put. You," she said to Greg, "give me your keys."

He reached in his pocket and handed her the keys to the Pontiac. "I'm gonna get those back, right?" he asked, looking like a whipped puppy.

"Sure. You can pick them up at the station downtown tomorrow morning. I'll be sure to have them there by nine." With that, she turned and headed for the door. I sat down with my arm twisted uncomfortably behind me and looked over at Greg, who took the other seat.

"This would be a very good time to tell me you have a spare set of car keys," I said, glaring at him.

"Under the back bumper, bro. No worries."

"Good, then I won't have to strangle you in your sleep."

"I don't breathe, so it wouldn't make any difference."

"It would make me feel better."

"Yeah, I can see where you might be a little disgusted with yourself for falling for the old handshake/handcuff switcheroo." He looked unbearably smug sitting there. I hate it when he's got the right answers for things. It messes with the natural order of the universe.

"So, how you planning on getting out of there?"

I stood up and stepped around behind the chair, hiding the handcuff from the rest of the bowling alley with my body. I twisted and pulled, but couldn't get enough leverage to get it off my arm. The cuff groaned a little. I shoved the metal band further up my forearm until it was nice and tight. I flexed one more time, but all I got for my trouble was a red mark around my arm and a couple of stares from a passing waitress.

"Did somebody forget to eat his Wheaties this morning?" Greg asked. "You should be able to snap that like a pretzel."

"Yeah, I know, but I can't get a good angle on the cuff. Time for Plan B." I reached down and grabbed the back of the chair with my free hand. I worked the molded plastic for a minute, couldn't get it to give at all, and finally just ripped the whole seat free of the swivel, which consisted of cheap metal fastenings. I stood there in the middle of the bowling alley with a chair hanging from one wrist. "Let's go," I snarled at Greg, who was having trouble getting to his feet because he was laughing so hard.

I trudged to the front door, pausing long enough to tell the counter guy that the chair in lane nine was busted, and dragged the stupid chair all the way out the mall entrance to the parking lot, attracting more than one strange look on the way. I got to the car and reached under the bumper. I felt around and pulled out one of those magnetic key boxes, and slid it open, only to find a business card for Detective Sabrina Law. She had written a note on the back of the card saying, "Hide it better next time."

Greg made it out to the parking lot in time to laugh some more at the sight of a gangly six-foot-three-inch vampire stomping around the lot cursing inventively and swinging a plastic chair around his head by a handcuff.

"Dude, hold still, let me get you out of that thing," he said when I stopped swearing and flailing.

He reached into a pocket of his utility belt and brought out a small folding saw, the kind they sell at sporting goods stores. I thought of about seventeen wisecracks, but decided I valued emancipation from the bowling alley furniture over a good zinger and held my tongue. His little saw was surprisingly effective, and in a couple of minutes, I was free.

Well, mostly free. I still had a handcuff dangling from my wrist, but there was no longer a giant hunk of molded plastic attached to it. Some nights you can only ask for so much, and this was shaping up to be one of those.

"I don't suppose you have another set of keys in that belt, do you?" I asked hopefully.

"No, but I have the next best thing," Greg replied.

Before I could ask what exactly that was, he reached under my arm, grabbed my Glock and walked over to where a young couple was doing what young couples do in the back lanes of parking lots. Greg tapped on the glass with the pistol, and then put his fist through the back passenger window. He pulled a skinny teenage kid out through the window, pointed the gun at his rapidly shriveling pride and joy, and hinted that the kid should run away. Then he leaned into the back window, smiled at the girl broadly enough to show a lot of fang, and laughed as she beat a hasty retreat out the other door. He tossed a T-shirt at her retreating, and naked, back, and reached into the floor of the backseat for the boy's pants.

"Subtle. That looked like something I would do," I said as I walked around and got into the passenger seat. Greg had retrieved the car keys from the boy's pants by then, settled himself behind the wheel and put the car in gear.

"Sorry," he said without an ounce of remorse. "I was under the impression that we were in a hurry. Problem solved."

He peeled rubber out of the parking lot and handed me back my gun. I tuned the radio to an oldies station and cranked some vintage Springsteen as we headed off to the site of the latest kidnapping. I wasn't sure what our detective friend would think about our appearing at her crime scene, but I wasn't too inclined to care. We only had about forty-eight hours to stop the summoning of a serious metaphysical beastie from taking place, and our Big Bad was now one ankle-biter closer to its quota.

Flying under the radar of the cops was no longer an option.

Chapter 17

Every cop in the greater Charlotte area was camped out in a three-block radius between the latest victim's school and home. It would have been a great time for bank heists, jewelry store capers or just knocking over liquor stores for pocket change.

Greg and I parked the car a couple of blocks outside the ring of flashing blue lights and left the keys in the ignition. I'd rifled through the kid's wallet on the way across town and found twenty-seven bucks and six condoms. The kid was something of an optimist. Or an overachiever.

We circled the perimeter until we found a young, scared-looking cop working a section of sidewalk alone. I walked up to him, smiling my friendliest smile, which is not much more reassuring than Hannibal Lecter after eating bad steak tartare, but I got close enough to see the color of his eyes.

"H-hold it right there," the kid stammered and put his hand on his gun. I hoped he wouldn't shoot himself in the foot before I mojo'd him. "You'll have to go around, sir. Sorry for any inconvenience."

"Me, too, Officer. Now give me your handcuff keys." His eyes went glassy and he reached around to the back of his belt and handed me the keys. I unlocked the cuff around my wrist, relieved to find that my mojo wasn't permanently on the fritz. It simply didn't work on one particular badass Amazon warrior princess cop.

"Thanks, Officer," Greg said politely. "You never saw us."

Then we split up. Greg headed towards the kid's home to see if he could pick up anything there because he's more sensitive to psychic garbage than I am. Psychic anything is right in his wheelhouse.

I concentrated on what I do best—looking for things to hit and annoying pretty women. Toward that end, I headed toward the center of activity in hopes of finding Detective Law. I used her ever-so-helpful business card and my PI credentials to badge my way into the mobile command tent they had set up in the schoolyard, and tapped her on the shoulder.

"Lose these?" I dangled her handcuffs from one finger. The cops around us let out a couple of wolf whistles and I put on my best imitation of a rakish grin.

It probably worked a little, because she stepped in close to me, reclaimed her handcuffs, and whispered in my ear, "I don't know how you got loose, or how you got here, and I don't really care. But you've got about three seconds to get out of my crime scene before I shoot off something you're probably inordinately proud of."

I looked down and saw her Smith & Wesson pointed at Little Jimmy and stepped back quickly.

As much as I usually enjoy banter, we were on a deadline. "This is getting old. Why don't you take me outside?" I turned around and put my hands behind my back, making it easy for her to re-cuff me. I also made sure there was no furniture nearby.

"Oh, I will. Mostly because I don't want everybody to see me beat the crap out of you." She put a hand on my elbow and walked me out of the tent. As soon as we were in some relative shadow, I stopped walking. She had to stop, too, because, despite my skinny frame, she couldn't move me. She looked up, confused.

"You want to take these cuffs off me now," I said.

"I don't think so," she spat.

"It wasn't a question."

She got right up in my face and was about to say something that probably would have accomplished absolutely nothing when I dangled her cuffs in front of her face. It was worth petty larceny to see the look on her face. She got another look entirely as I crushed the handcuffs into a mangled mess of steel and dropped them at her feet.

"Don't bother trying that again." I kept my voice low, and my expression calm. I needed her, and whether she knew it or not, she needed me. She started to go for her gun, but I caught her hand as she was reaching for it. "Don't," I said. "You'll never make the draw, and it wouldn't matter if you did. You know that somewhere in the hindbrain that protects you. Now ignore all this—me, what I am—for a little while. Believe me when I say that if I'd wanted to kill you, I'd have done that already. All I want is to get this kid back home safely. You'll find that I'm happy to take orders, but we need to work together."

"Why should I believe you?" she asked.

"You've already checked us out. You know we weren't anywhere near the crime scenes. Right?"

To her credit, she didn't try to act like she hadn't followed up on us. "Yes. You're apparently just what you say you are—

a couple of low-rent private eyes with no priors. That doesn't explain why I should let you in on a police investigation."

"Looking around this joint, I'd say you've pulled in every resource you can lay your hands on. I'd guess that you're about one missing kid away from calling in a pet psychic to interview the family schnauzer. Just call us consultants."

"I know *how* to get you on the case, asshole. What I don't have yet is a good reason *why* to put you on this case." She crossed her arms in front of her chest, and I looked back at her face, disappointed.

"Because we've proven that you can't get rid of us?" I asked hopefully.

"That may be true, but I don't have to enable you. Now I'm going to go interview the parents. Stay the hell away from them, and stay the hell away from my investigation. I can't keep you off public property, but if I catch you interfering in my investigation again, I can sure as hell put you in the county jail for obstruction of justice."

I stepped back. She stared at me for a minute, and if looks could kill, I'd have been dead all over again.

I looked at her for a long moment and finally nodded. "You win, Detective. We'll stay out of the way." I turned and headed toward the school.

"Hey," she called out after me. "Wait a minute." She took a couple of long strides over to me and leaned in close. "I don't know how you did that little handcuff trick, but it's gonna take a lot more than that to scare me. When I get done with this mess, I am going to find out what your deal is. And if I don't like what I find, you're going to be very unhappy for a very long time."

I looked at her for a minute. "I've been unhappy for longer than you can imagine. Without an end in sight." I turned around and walked off in the direction of the school to see what I could find about a missing little girl.

I kicked myself a little for letting her needle me into that parting shot. I'm not the brooding type, but something in her eyes made me miss being human, just for a minute. I've gone whole years without missing the sun, but right then the prospect of never being able to wake up next to a beautiful woman and watch the sunlight play across her back and legs was enough to make me ache.

I had been lost in my thoughts for a minute or two when I caught a strange scent on the air. I scanned the sidewalk ahead and pulled out my cell and called Greg.

"Yo. Where you at?" I asked.

"God, your grammar gets worse the longer you're dead. I'm on the roof of the school. I found something funny up here. Where are you?"

"About to hop the playground fence over by the swings. Are you where you can see me?"

"Yeah. And fortunately for you I'm the only one who can see you. The cops assigned to the school are all out front and inside. How'd your conversation with the hot cop go?"

"About like all my other conversations with beautiful women," I grumbled.

"That bad, huh? Well, come up here and take a look at this."

"I'll be up in a second." I crossed the playground, trying to figure out what the smell was. It wasn't quite sulfur, but it had a little of that acrid tang to it. I couldn't place where I had smelled it before, so I took a running leap onto the roof and walked over to where Greg was kneeling in front of what looked like a protective circle.

I'm no magician, but I've read a lot of comic books and I know a magic circle when I see one—as long as the circle is drawn by someone with a taste for 1970s Marvel comic villains. This one passed my very limited quality control.

Greg had dabbled in magic when we were in high school, so he had more actual knowledge of the mystical arts than I did. Of course, a retarded orangutan that has walked through a magic shop once has more knowledge of the mystical arts than me. Still, I felt qualified to make this call. "A protective circle?"

"No, it's wrong."

"Nope, pretty sure it's a circle, bro."

"Yes, I know that. But look at these symbols." He pointed to several scribbles and squiggles around the inside of the circle. "These should be on the outside of the circle, so that whatever was summoned into the circle couldn't scratch them out and alter the protection of the circle."

"What if you weren't trying to pull something into the circle?" I asked.

"What do you mean?" Greg looked at me with eyebrows raised.

"Well, couldn't you cast the circle around you, then do a summoning spell so that whatever you summoned couldn't get you before going off to wreak havoc? You'd be safe. It's probably not foolproof or exactly the safest thing in the world, but would it work?"

Greg's sat down on the roof with a *thud*. His eyes got big. "I hadn't even thought about that. That's so awful I didn't think anyone would consider it."

"I think someone did. You don't get eaten, and when you send the *whatever* back to *wherever* all you have to do is erase the circle, right?" I wasn't sure what I was missing, but it looked like it was going to be bad. I hate having smart friends.

"What's so bad about that? Really? You don't get it?" Greg replied. I mentioned I hate having smart friends, right?

He went on. "What's so bad is that once you summon a *whatever* from *wherever* without a circle to bind it, then that whatever is free to do whatever it likes to whoever it wants to do it to, without you being able to banish it to anywhere, much less to wherever it came from in the first place!"

"Not to be the king of understatement or anything, but that doesn't sound good," I said as Greg's explanation began to sink in.

"Yeah. If you hide in a circle and don't bind a demon, for example, into another circle, then that demon is just set . . . free. It can't get you, but it can do anything it wants and you don't have any control over it, except maybe where and when you summon it."

"The timing. The girls," I said in almost a whisper.

"Yeah, the girls," Greg agreed. "Whoever summoned the demon must have waited until they were the only ones left around, then cast the spell."

"But how would they know they were getting the right girl?" I asked.

"I don't think it mattered. I think the summoning party wanted to be sure the demon took an innocent. Which innocent it got was irrelevant."

"So some little—this little girl just drew the short straw?" Even with everything I'd seen, that didn't sit right with me.

"Pretty much." Greg sat there on the roof, looking at the circle and shaking his head. I reached out a hand and pulled him to his feet.

"Come on," I said, walking toward the edge of the roof.

"Wait a sec. I gotta blow this up first." He reached into his utility belt and sprinkled a white substance on the circle. A pale blue smoke hissed up from the roof, and the circle disappeared.

"What was that?" I asked.

"Salt. It's bad juju for magic stuff. Now this circle can't be used again."

"Good deal. Now let's get moving." I resumed walking to the edge of the roof.

"Where are we going?" He asked, falling into step beside me.

"Back to the playground. I smelled something funky, and we might be able to trace this thing by the scent."

"Sometimes I think you only keep me around for my nose," he grumbled.

"And your car. But you've got a better nose than me, so I need you to take a whiff, tell me if it's important, and if it is, you need to track the whatever it is to wherever it went."

"All right, I'll play bloodhound, but if you try to put me in one of those stupid doggy Christmas sweaters again, I'm gonna stake you in your sleep."

Chapter 18

We circled around the playground a couple of times before I caught the scent again. I waved Greg over to where I had smelled it, and he took a deep breath. "Smell that?" I asked.

"Yeah, dude. Smells like vindaloo."

"Good. We know the kind of demon then."

"No, you magic-backward moron. Chicken vindaloo. It's an Indian dish with a lot of curry. Should be pretty easy to follow in this white-bread part of town." Greg took off toward the fence and I followed, trying not to lose him while still keeping an eye peeled for the cops.

Trailing the Big Bad was always so much easier when the Scooby gang on *Buffy* did the trailing. They rarely had cops crawling their turf. Of course, Buffy was usually trying to kill guys like us. I probably shouldn't enjoy the Whedonverse as much as I do.

We hopped the fence and followed the trail of Indian cuisine into a patch of woods separating the school from the neighborhood where Marjorie lived. Our vamp night vision is equal to any human's day sight. Unfortunately, our trail navigation skills were piss-poor. We went stumbling through the woods like a pair of drunken rhinos.

After about ten minutes, Greg held up one hand. Since I was looking at my feet and not at his hand, I walked into his back. Laid him out like a pin at the bowling alley.

"Dammit, Jimmy, would you watch where you're going?" He picked himself up off the ground and brushed twigs and leaves off his knees.

"I was watching where I was going, but I wasn't watching where you were stopping. So why are we stopping?" I helped him up, figuring it was the least I could do.

"I heard something. It sounded like someone trying to be stealthy in the woods."

"So it sounded nothing like us?"

"Not a thing like us. Now shut up and let me try to hear it again."

We heard the exact opposite of someone trying to be stealthy—several loud gunshots came from about a hundred yards in front of us. Greg and I looked at each other and then bolted toward the sound.

That's either brave or stupid for most people, but we aren't people and can't be killed by bullets, unless they manage to completely destroy our hearts or sever our heads. Since those kinds of bullets are pretty rare, running toward the sound of gunshots is generally worse for those doing the shooting than for us.

We hauled ass through the woods, managing to only trip on two or three exposed tree roots in the process, then drew up short at the edge of a clearing. Detective Law was in the clearing, apparently the source of the shots. I say "apparently" because she was no longer holding her gun, and from the looks of her, barely holding on to consciousness. She was lying on the ground in a circle of little girls. None of them looked older than nine, and they were beating the crap out of her.

You didn't have to be the sharpest knife in the drawer to figure out pretty quickly that these were not ordinary little girls. Even the village idiot would have guessed something was amiss when one of them picked Law up and threw her across the clearing at a huge tree. I nodded to Greg, and he jumped over to intercept the flying detective before her head became one with the splinters.

I stepped into the clearing, and tried to buy some time with my wits and humor. God only knew how that was going to go. If I was ever going to be universally funny, it was time for the comedy gene to kick into high gear.

"Now, girls, I don't like curfew any more than you do, but that's no reason to beat up a cop," I said, leaning against a pine tree in what I thought was a jaunty fashion. I felt far less jaunty when a bunch of little girls, all sporting glowing eyes à la *Children of the Corn*, turned to me and started walking in my direction.

I thought for a second about what it had taken to subdue the last one of these possessed super-brats and decided discretion was the better part of valor. I waited until the first couple of them were close enough to almost reach me, and then I jumped straight up into the tree. I cleared a good fifteen feet and swung up onto a branch, looking down to see the girls surrounding the base of the tree like little pigtailed bloodhounds.

"Greg, you got any brilliant ideas? Now would be the time to send 'em my way!" I yelled across the clearing.

"I was thinking 'run like hell' sounds like a plan," he shouted back.

"I don't think that is an option, gentlemen." The woman's voice came out of the darkness on the edge of the clearing. A middle-aged woman with her hair in a bun stepped into the circle of trees and said, "Come to me, my children."

The little girls with the creepy eyes formed a double rank in front of the woman and stood there, so silent that I couldn't tell if they were breathing, even with my heightened senses.

"Okay, lady. We don't have any quarrel with you. Let the kids go and we can all be on our merry way." I tried to hold my voice steady, and really hoped that my coat had enough drape in it to hide the fact that my knees were shaking to a marimba beat. Greg looked up at me from across the clearing and mouthed something at me, but even if I had been able to read lips, he was too far away for me to understand what he wanted.

Any hope of getting out of the woods without a serious fight, and probably a serious beating, went out the window when the bun-head opened her mouth again. "I don't think you're going anywhere, vampire. You got lucky the last time we met, but I don't see any automobiles around for you to hit me with tonight."

Crap. Just crap. In my experience anyone who felt comfortable delivering a monologue before the punching started was strong enough to wreck my day. Plus the middle-aged woman was clearly possessed by the demon that had gotten us into this mess in the first place.

I took stock of the situation from my elevated vantage point in the tree. I was facing a bunch of possessed little girls and what looked like one really pissed-off cafeteria lady. Greg was trying to help Detective Law to her feet, and I had no random automobiles to throw at the rug rats from hell.

I decided to try and talk my way out of trouble. It used to work with principals, so why not crazed cafeteria-lady demons? "What's the plan? You've gotten one step closer to your quota tonight, and then what? You turn in the box tops for an iPod?"

"Fool!" shouted the woman. "Do you have any idea the forces you are tampering with?"

"None whatsoever. Why don't you enlighten me." The longer I kept her talking, the better the chances Greg would think of something brilliant. I hoped. Boy, did I ever hope. I also hoped that this curry-scented psycho had seen all the same movies I had and knew her role was to provide a soliloquy on her plans and motives, giving me enough time to avoid being killed.

"Foolish vampire, the world as you know it is coming to an end. The reign of mankind is over. When I complete my ritual and bring my father forth, all will kneel before the Dark Lord, and Belial shall be favored among all the Host!"

I had no idea what the "Host" was, and the very sound of "Dark Lord" made me more than a little uncomfortable. And she was yelling. In my experience, supernatural bad guys yell right before they hit you very hard, or at least try to kill you in some unpleasant fashion. I thought I'd pre-empt her hitting me and take the fight to the bun-head.

I hopped down from the tree with a nice cape-billowing move and drew my weapons. With a pistol in one hand and a knife in the other I felt marginally better about my chances of surviving the next thirty seconds. All that good feeling evaporated when Detective Law spoke from behind me.

"Drop the gun, Black." I heard her chamber a round, and sighed.

"Greg, why is she pointing a gun at me?" I asked without turning around.

"Because I don't like people threatening the possessed bodies of innocent little old ladies on my shift. Now drop the gun," Detective Law repeated.

"No," I said, never taking my eyes off the little old lady, who was the source of much greater concern than the cop with a gun pointed at my back.

"No?" She sounded surprised.

I suppose people don't typically decline when she points a weapon at them and orders them to disarm, but I didn't have a lot of time for verbal sparring. "No. Greg, get the nice police lady out of here before she gets killed." I raised my pistol and took aim at the bun-lady's head. "Last chance, Mrs. Butterworth. Let the kids go and I won't ventilate your forehead."

Bun-head wasn't impressed. "Your policewoman is right, you won't shoot an innocent body, and you still have too many of your idiotic human ideals."

I hate it when the bad guys have a good read on me. Maybe I should start wearing a mask.

"Children," the bun-lady demon called. "Kill them all." She waved one hand at the three of us, and the entire cast of *Annie* rushed us.

Chapter 19

Most nights I have qualms about hitting kids, but this wasn't one of those nights. I holstered my weapons and kicked the first brat all the way across the clearing, as gently as I possibly could. The second one to get within arm's reach ended up as a projectile, too. The two of them hit trees and slumped to the ground, momentarily stunned. That only left about eight attacking the three of us for the moment, but I had a sneaking suspicion that Detective Law wasn't going to be much use in this fight.

A glance behind me confirmed my suspicions, as several of the brats had her down on the ground and were beating the crap out of her. Again. I couldn't concentrate on her plight for long, though, because there were three of the little ankle-biters swarming me, and the two I'd incapacitated earlier didn't have the courtesy to stay down for long. As much as I hated it, the gloves were going to have to come off.

"I really hope you've got a good idea, bro!" I heard Greg yell from behind me, then I heard a loud *oof!* and a thud that let me know he was off his feet. I jumped back into my tree to get a second's breathing room, only to have company on my branch almost immediately.

"Not fair!" I yelled. "No fair chasing me when I'm trying to figure out how to kick your aaaaa—" I was trying to say something witty (and distracting) when the branch broke and dumped me and the kid who had jumped after me fifteen feet onto the forest floor. I could have been hurt if I'd landed wrong, but at the last minute I twisted and landed on the kid instead.

A remnant of morality twinged, but then I remembered that I *eat people*. It's not like I was interviewing to be her babysitter, and she started it by invading my tree. She puked a little from my having landed on her, and seeing that gave me an idea. It also made me a little nauseous.

I had to get free of the fray for a second to clear my mind. I picked the girl up by her ankles, and twirled in a circle, swinging her like a hammer toss in high-school track and field. After I'd leveled the three other kids surrounding me, I tossed her at the bun-demon and yelled over to Greg.

"Dude!"

"Yeah?" he croaked. He had a kid in each hand by the scruff of the neck, and one was on his back choking him with one hand and hitting him in the head with the other. I would have laughed if I hadn't seen four crumb-snatchers running back toward me full tilt.

"What was that crap earlier about salt breaking spells?"

"Salt—*urk*—disrupts the flow of magical energies. It'll break almost any spell." He managed to throw off all three kids for a second, but then two more dropped on him from a tree.

"Will it screw up stuff like summoning and possession?" I asked, jumping and weaving as the little girls closed on me once again. I needed to end this quick, before I killed a kid or before one of them decided that a broken branch would serve as a stake. Or beat the helpless detective to death.

"I think so!" The response came from under the pile of bodies where Greg was lying.

"This would be a good time for you to—*oof*—tell me you've got more in your utility belt!"

The whole pile of possessed bodies flexed, then flew apart as Greg jumped to his feet. The little rug rats immediately headed back at him, but Greg was ready. He reached into a pouch on his belt and tossed white powder into the faces of the girls attacking him, and they immediately slumped to the ground unconscious. Right at that moment I felt a tremendous pain behind my left knee, and looked down to see one of the brats had actually locked her teeth into my hamstring.

"Oh, that is it!" I bellowed. "Biting is my gig, you little urchin!" I snatched her off my leg and threw her over to Greg. "Salinate this little brat, please!"

"I don't think that's a word, Jimmy."

"I don't have time to call Webster's, man, just make with the salting!"

"Happy to help, bro," he called back.

A few minutes later we were panting in a clearing surrounded by eleven unconscious, salty little girls. Bun-Head was gone. She must have decided that discretion was the better part of whatever and hauled ass out of there once we started dispelling the kids. Apparently, all it took was a good dousing with sodium chloride to toss the demons out and turn them back into normal children.

It was probably going to take a lot more work to get Detective Law back to normal. She was sitting with her back to a tree and her gun in both hands. The slide was back and the gun was obviously empty, but that didn't stop her from pointing the weapon at us and dry firing frantically as we approached.

"*Shhhh* . . . it's okay. We're the good guys. We're not going to hurt you, I promise." I kept my voice low and slowly moved to sit down next to her. All I really had to work with was a little experience working with frightened animals, and reruns of *Dog Whisperer* on Animal Planet. I thought it might be a good idea to get down to her level and look as non-threatening as possible.

That was a little tough, since I was fairly bloody. At least it was all my blood.

After a minute I reached out and very gently took the gun from her hand. She resisted for a second, but eventually let go, and I ejected the magazine and put the empty weapon in my coat pocket. "Are you all right?" I asked.

"I don't think so," she said very quietly.

"I'm not surprised. Most people need a little adjustment period the first time they experience something like this."

She looked over at me, and I could hear shock hovering on the outer edges of her voice. "The first time? Exactly how often does crap like this happen?"

"Unfortunately," Greg said as he slid down to sit on the other side of her, "this sort of thing happens all too often. And we've observed that once the barriers to belief are removed, that you may find yourself seeing more and more of it. You see, our society erects so many roadblocks to any understanding or analysis of the paranormal that it is almost impossible to truly investigate anything that happens outside the ordinary."

Greg had the bit between his teeth. This was his subject, and I didn't have the heart to deny him a good ramble. I'm sure he said a lot more, and I'm sure that it made perfect sense to anyone that would care, but I was most certainly not in that camp, so I did what I'd done for the past two decades whenever Greg started one of his rambles. I had a drink.

Lucky for me, my flask had made it through the fight without any major structural damage. I had a belt of Glenfiddich and passed it over to Detective Law. "Want a belt?"

She took the flask and turned it up for a long slug. "Nice. What is this?"

"Scotch. What were you doing in the woods?"

"The last girl to disappear had her cell phone turned on. I initiated a GPS trace and it led me here. But . . . what was all that?"

"That's a longer story than we have time for. You think you can stand?

"Probably."

"Good, because we should be moving along before your comrades in arms show up."

"Why?" She looked around at the unconscious little girls scattered around the clearing. "We can't leave them lying here."

"If experience serves as any guide, and what good are the bruises if it doesn't, they'll be out for a couple more hours at least. Your people will find them." I got to my feet and brushed the worst of the dirt off my jeans and coat. I reached down and helped her to her feet and returned her sidearm to her. "We, on the other hand, have a different task. In case you hadn't noticed, we're still missing one grumpy old lady."

"Shit. Where did she go?" She put a fresh magazine into the pistol, chambered a round, and holstered her gun.

"If I knew that, I wouldn't be missing her. Now come on, we've gotta go after her, and we don't need to get tangled up in a bunch of—Well, crap, here comes the parade." All hope of getting out of the woods without a few hours of questions evaporated as the bulk of the Charlotte-Mecklenburg Police Department's SWAT team surrounded us, assault rifles at the ready. "I hope you have a foolproof plan for dealing with this."

"I do," she replied. She stepped forward, badge in hand, and yelled "Lower your weapons, boys! Stand down. We've got it under control."

One of the guys in body armor came over, and she huddled together with him for a few seconds. Whatever she was selling, he was buying, because in no time at all he had guys running back through the woods for stretchers and ambulances. Greg elbowed me and motioned to the cops. I gave him my best hell-if-I-know shrug, and we sat down at the base of a couple of huge oaks to wait. Looked like we were going to be stuck in the woods with the cops while our bun-headed magical psychopath got away. Again.

Chapter 20

"Well, Detective, do you believe me now when I say that we can be useful?" I asked as Greg, Detective Law and I sipped coffee at a small table the SWAT boys had set up.

"You've got your moments, I'll give you that. I haven't seen martial arts work like that in a long time, and I sure wouldn't have expected it from you two," she said.

That's a pretty standard coping mechanism for people who see us in action. There are so many kung fu movies out there. They just think we're super black belts or something. I usually don't bother to correct them. This was another one of those times.

"Do you think we can get a handle on some of that reward money?" I asked, as subtle as I knew how to be.

"Maybe. You were actually investigating, and you did help in recovering the kids, so I guess you're entitled." She looked disappointed somehow, and that bothered me a little.

"You know, it's not a big deal, I was just thinking—"

She cut me off with a wave of her hand "No, you're right. You guys deserve some recognition for the work you've done."

That set off an alarm bell or two. The last thing we wanted was recognition. Actually, the last thing we wanted was a nice summer vacation in Phoenix, but recognition from any authority was pretty low on our list of desires, too. Really, I just wanted a few bucks to get the new Madden NFL game. I was really tired of playing Brett Favre in a Packers jersey. While I was mentally kicking myself for opening my big mouth, she walked over to a black guy in a nice suit and gestured toward us.

Greg leaned over to me and asked, "What did you do?"

"Something stupid."

"What else is new? Would you care to be more specific?"

"I mentioned the reward."

"You're an idiot."

"I know. I think we should leave now before we have to fill out forms or answer questions."

"The first girl you talk to in fifteen years, and you run her off because you're a greedy shit. Well done."

"She is not the first girl I talked to. I talked to that girl at Phil's the other night."

"Okay, the first human girl that you weren't simultaneously chatting up and putting a dollar in her garter."

"Point to you. Now let's get out of here."

We double-checked to make sure Detective Law and her boss were looking the other way and slid off into the night. Greg's car was still at the bowling alley, and the keys were still in the pocket of a cop who was not in a mood to look kindly upon me. We improvised and mojo'd a cop into giving us a ride. He pulled up in front of our place, and Greg convinced him that he needed to get to the hospital, ASAP.

"What does he think he's going to the hospital for?" I asked as I unlocked our front door.

"He thinks his appendix has ruptured."

"That's a good one. What if he gets there and he doesn't have his appendix?"

"Then he won't have to worry about that anymore, will he?"

I plopped down on the couch and tossed my shoes across the room. Greg grabbed a blood bag for each of us, and we started to settle in for a marathon *Gears of War* session. All in all, it had been a pretty good night. We rescued the little girls, I talked to a human woman, we beat the baddy, and we made it home before sunrise. Then my cell phone rang, and the night went right to crap all over again.

Chapter 21

The display on my phone read "Father Mike," so I pushed the button and said, "Hi Dad."

"Jimmy, where are you?" He sounded out of breath, and I was a little worried. Mike's pretty unflappable most days (might be something about having vampires for best friends), so anything that had him running around breathless was bound to be worrisome at best and more likely not-good-at-all.

"I'm home. What's up?" I waved for Greg to turn off the TV. I had a bad feeling that we were going to be heading back out. I got off the couch and walked over to my shoes, cradling the phone between my ear and shoulder.

"Is Greg with you?" Mike asked.

I was really starting to worry now. Whenever Mike wanted to make sure we were together, it meant things were not-good-at-all.

"Yeah, he's here. I'll put you on speaker. Done. What's going on?"

"I'm outside. I'll be down in a minute." He hung up on me.

I stood there for a few seconds looking at my phone, wondering what had him so rattled. Then I put my shoes on and got the place ready for visitors. I motioned for Greg to clear away the empty blood bags. Mike knew what our deal was, but we tried not to flaunt our bloodsucking ways in front of him.

I was in the kitchen dumping out half-empty beer bottles when I heard Mike's feet on the stairs. "Want a drink, Dad?" I called out, trying to keep my voice cheerful. I realized cheerful was wasted as soon as I saw how pale he was.

"Scotch," he ordered. "Make it a double. And you'll want one, too, I believe." He sat on the couch and I brought over our drinks.

"Where's mine?" Greg asked from his armchair.

"Still in the bottle, dork. I might have mad vampire skills, but I still only have two hands."

He stomped over to the kitchen and made himself a stout screwdriver. "You never would have survived in the restaurant business."

"Good thing I didn't survive, then," I retorted. "Now, Mike. You look like crap. What's wrong?"

"You really know how to warm a man's heart, Jimmy. But I'm sure I've seen better days. I don't know if you've been outside recently, but it's terrible out there. I think it might be . . . ," he hesitated for a moment and I saw real fear in his eyes. "I think it might be the end times."

"Whoa!" I stood up and went for more scotch. After a brief debate, I came back to the couch with the whole bottle. "Now let's take this from the beginning. What makes you think that this could be the Apocalypse?"

"Oh, Jimmy, I've seen things in my life that no man should see, and you know this."

"Yeah, I know. We're the ones that showed you most of them," Greg piped up. I shot him a dirty look, and he mumbled, "Sorry," and shut up.

Mike continued. "I've seen plenty of terrible things in my time, but nothing compares to what I've seen tonight. The dead are walking, Jimmy! The newly buried dead have risen from their graves and are walking the town. I don't know what to think, but that these are the times of Revelation!" Mike got a look in his eyes that was part fear, part excitement.

I guess this would be like Christmas, the Super Bowl and WrestleMania all rolled into one for a priest.

"Can you give us a few details? What exactly is going on?" Greg asked.

"Three corpses, all dead less than a month, have risen tonight alone." Mike reached for the bottle, and I passed it over. He touched the neck to the rim of his glass, but his hands were shaking and he rerouted the bottle to his mouth. He glanced at me in apology and turned the bottle up. We'd been friends long enough that I didn't begrudge him drinking from the bottle. It's not like I was worried about germs.

"How many dead people are in your cemetery, Mike?" Greg asked.

"Hundreds, I guess, but what does that matter?"

"I'm wondering why only three have risen, is all."

"Well, they were the most recently deceased. And all of their bodies were intact. One man, Alan Rice, who passed away in the same time period, died in a horrible automobile accident. He has yet to rise."

"Or his body wasn't chosen." Greg mused. "Let me make a couple of phone calls." He grabbed his phone and went into his bedroom. I heard one side of the conversations as he made a couple of calls in quick succession, asking the same questions each time.

"All right, I have a theory," he announced, rejoining us and taking a healthy slug of scotch himself, "and if I'm right, we're going to need more booze. And more ammo. And maybe an extra priest."

Mike and I stared at him until he went on.

"I made a couple of phone calls to a friend at the county morgue and a couple of hospitals. These are not guys who get rattled easily, and they've seen enough of our world to believe in the unbelievable."

I raised my hand. "Excuse me, Professor Doofenstein, is there a point coming anytime in the next week?"

Greg shot me the bird and went on. "You're not the only one missing a bunch of dead people, Mike. The morgue has lost four corpses, the hospitals have lost three, and I'd be willing to bet that at least one more church has seen a rash of breakouts from the graveyard tonight. As far as I can tell, there are nearly a dozen dead people that decided to pull a Thriller on us, and they all made that decision about 11:30 P.M."

"That's when the graves at my churchyard began to cast up their dead. How did you know?" Mike asked.

"Because that's when Jimmy and I set eleven angry souls loose on the greater Charlotte area."

Suddenly a very, very bad light came on for me. "Oh crap. The girls," I said in a very small voice.

"Yep, buddy. Free the girls, free what's in the girls," Greg confirmed.

"What girls?" Mike asked.

We told him all about fighting the little kidnapped girls, and the salt, and banishing them. "But we forgot one important thing," I said. "We forgot to send the souls back to wherever they came from."

"So when they got out of the girls, with no unoccupied bodies around, and no spell to bind them into a body, they went looking for bodies that weren't being used and didn't have salt handy," Greg confirmed.

"They inhabited corpses," Mike said.

He looked a little relieved and a little disappointed all at the same time. I suppose that's how it would be for someone who believed they were about to meet their maker and had reason to look forward to the meeting, then found out that they weren't getting that appointment after all.

"Yep, that's what it looks like." Greg looked altogether too pleased with himself for my taste, but I had to admit it was a brilliant bit of logic.

"Now what?" I asked my occasionally brilliant partner.

"I don't know." He sat down on the other side of Mike on the couch.

"We have to return these bodies to their proper rest," Mike said. "We cannot stand by and allow this evil to be perpetrated."

"Yeah, we got that, but it's the 'how' we're a little fuzzy on," I told him.

"Oh." Mike had another belt of scotch. He hadn't quite moved back to drinking from the glass, and I decided to let the stereotype slide for once.

"Let's look at what we know." I started. "One, there are a total of eleven zombies running around the city. Two, if we don't stop them, at some point between now and tomorrow night, these zombies are going to grab a kid and the demon that raised them is going to finish some humongous ritual that will mean very bad things for everyone in Charlotte. Three, the demon, named Belial, has possessed a woman who looks like a retro advertisement for cookware.

"Now let's take a look at what we don't know. We don't know what they're trying to do in the first place. We don't know if the ritual requires a specific site. We don't know where the zombies are now. We don't know which little girl they're going to kidnap to finish their baker's dozen. And we don't know who the crazy lady with the bun is."

"Now that we've established we don't know anything helpful, where do we go from here?" Greg asked.

"I have no idea."

"I do." We both looked at Mike, who looked a little embarrassed. "I have a friend who practices a religion that the Church . . . um . . . frowns upon. She may be able to be of assistance, at least in the matter of the ceremony and those questions."

"Mike, are you consorting with Wiccans again? You keep this up, and I'm going to put a COEXIST bumper sticker on your station wagon."

"Not consorting. Comparing. She's a local high priestess. She's part of a comparative theology breakfast I attend each month. We've gotten to be fairly friendly over the years."

I looked over at Greg and his jaw was as close to the floor as my own. In all the time we've been friends with Mike, and he certainly shows the years a lot more than we do, we never would have believed that our straightlaced buddy would have breakfast every month with a real live witch. Of course, most of his parishioners would have a harder time believing he was drinking scotch in the basement of a halfway house with two vampires, so I suppose that was only fair.

"Do you think you could call her tonight?" Greg asked. "I know it's getting late, but this is pretty important."

"She once told me that I could call her anytime if I had issues that needed her assistance," Mike assured us.

Greg and I exchanged a glance, and I bit back any comments I might have thought about making regarding Mike's vows of celibacy. He went upstairs to get a signal and make the call, which took only a few minutes. He came down the steps holding his cell phone over his head like he was going to spike a football.

"I assume that means she's on her way?" Greg asked.

"Yes, boys, it does. She'll be here in fifteen minutes. I hope you don't mind meeting her here. After all, the whole 'invite me in' thing could become awkward if we went to her apartment."

"Fair enough, I suppose. Greg, you wanna tidy up a bit before we have another guest?" I asked from my seat on the couch.

"Um, no. Those are your socks, bro. You pick up the toxic waste. I'll give the kitchen a lick and a promise, but the footwear funk factory is all you." He headed off to wipe down the counters and put the blood in the crisper so our culinary restrictions wouldn't be immediately apparent while I got to work straightening up the den.

My idea of straightening up was to pour all the half-drunk beers down the sink and put the bottles in the recycling bin. Not much, but it made the den look better. Then I policed any inappropriate magazines and DVDs that Greg might have left lying around, and threw them all in his bedroom. Mike straightened up the video-game equipment, and actually found a scented candle to put out on the coffee table. After about ten minutes, the place smelled significantly less like a locker room, and Mike had ceased to make comments about us having the hygiene of a pack of feral dogs.

I looked around and nodded to my friends. We were ready to welcome a witch into a vampire lair.

Chapter 22

A knock at the top of the stairs announced the arrival of our guest, followed immediately by a trim pair of legs coming into view on the steps. The legs were, as is par for my course, attached to a woman who looked nothing like my mental picture of an overweight gypsy woman with three teeth and a mole on her nose that had its own zip code. Instead, the woman in our living room was medium height, slim, with straight blonde hair that hung halfway down her back. She was younger than I expected and very pretty in a blonde Sandra Bullock kind of way.

She wore Birkenstocks, but they were the closed-toe type and that was her only concession to my mental image of an earth-mother type. She had on jeans that hugged some pretty nice curves, and a bulky tan sweater that looked like it came straight out of an L.L. Bean catalog. "Hello," she said, her warm voice filling the room with a sense of well-being. "I'm Anna. How are you, Mike? You sounded worried on the phone."

"I was worried, my dear, but I feel much better now that you're here." Mike's accent had slipped, and a little of the old South he grew up in had dropped into his words as he gave the pretty witch a brief, and chaste, hug. Good to know my old friend was celibate, but not blind. He turned to us. "These are my friends, Jimmy and Greg."

He pointed to each of us in turn, and I stepped forward to shake her hand. I was surprised when she pulled back, reaching quickly inside her sweater to drop a pentagram necklace out into view. It began to glow, and I took a quick step back. "Hey now, no need to get all magical in my den, lady," I exclaimed.

"I know you, vampire," she said, and when I looked up at her eyes, they were a cold blue, staring right into my soul. If I had one left. The jury's been out on that one for a while.

"Nope, pretty sure we've never met. But if you want to get together sometime for a quick bite, let me know."

I bared a little fang at her, and heard Greg moving up behind me. His pistol cleared the holster and I knew that he had my back. As long as I kept her attention on me, my partner could keep her covered. "Mike, you want to explain to Mrs. Broomstick here that we're the good guys?"

"It's true, Anna. These boys have been friends of mine since before I entered the seminary. I've known them since we were boys in school together, and they're good lads. They have their problems, sure, but good lads nonetheless."

"Mike," the witch said, keeping her voice level and her eyes locked on me, carefully not looking in my eyes, "This good lad, as you call him, is a vampire."

"And you're a witch," I said. "And by the way, you can look me in the eye, our mojo doesn't work with your necklace in the way. Now, can we get past our little stereotypes and species bias and work together to deal with a body-snatching demon and the zombie infestation?"

"What does my necklace have to do with anything?" the witch asked.

"The boys have some issues with religious symbols, holy ground, that sort of thing," Mike said. "I, for one, believe these issues to be more psychological than pathological." Mike was getting on a roll now, so I went to the kitchen for another beer as he explained one of his pet theories of vampirism to his witch friend.

"The discomfort that they experience around objects of faith is dramatically different from the type of pain that is inflicted by sunlight, and the nausea they experience on holy ground is nothing like the barricade they experience when they attempt to enter a dwelling uninvited. So it's long been my theory that there is no reason that Jimmy and Greg can't touch a cross, for example, or enter a church without any ill effects."

"So why do I feel like barfing every time I go visit you at work?" Greg returned to his spot at the computer.

Mike ignored the interruption and went right on. "No reason other than their own subconscious fear that they may have lost their souls when they became vampires, that is. And after these past years of working alongside them, helping people at every opportunity, I can assure you, they have every bit as much of their souls as you or I have."

I went back to my spot on the couch and took a seat. Anna followed me with her eyes, then made her way to the armchair and sat facing me. She wasn't paying any attention to Greg.

"Are we good?" I asked as she got settled. "We wouldn't have called you over here, to our home, unless we thought we could trust you, and unless we needed you. Mike was pretty convincing on the first count, and the situation pretty much covers the second."

"What's the situation?" She pulled a MacBook out of her backpack. "Is there Wi-Fi here?"

"Yes," said Greg from where he suddenly stood right behind her chair. I almost fell off the couch laughing as Anna jumped about eight feet straight up. His vamp-speed from his desk to right behind her got the desired reaction.

"The password is TruBlood. Capital *T*, capital *B*," he said as she glared at him. I shot him a look, too, but that was for picking a dorky password.

When I looked back to Anna, the exasperation on my face was from real irritation. "Seriously? You're just going to Wikipedia 'zombies' or something? Any of us could have taken that brilliant first step." I leaned back on the couch, not just to get further away from her glowing necklace, but also because I think she might have caught me checking her out. She's hot. I'm not *dead*. Well, I am dead, but I'm not dead and blind.

"I'm not just going to Wikipedia it. I have a group of friends I can contact online that may have some firsthand knowledge in the area."

"You know people who have their own pet zombies?" I marveled. "Now that's cool."

She sat there for a few minutes typing and muttering to herself and generally looking way hotter than any woman that had been in our tomb in a decade. Or ever, for that matter. After a couple of "hmmms" and the odd "mmmm-mmmm," I got bored and went to the fridge for a snack. Greg immediately plopped down in my seat on the couch and yelled over to me "You keep eating this late at night, you're gonna get fat."

"We can't get fat, dork. You want anything?"

"Yeah, throw me a bag of B-Neg."

I tossed him the bag and hopped up on the bar that overlooked the living room, my own blood bag in hand.

"Either of the humans want anything to drink?" I asked our guests. "We don't have any food, for obvious reasons, but we've got a couple Cokes—"

"Not so much," Greg corrected.

I tried again, "We *had* a couple Cokes, but we've got beer, ginger ale, and a lot of booze. There might even be some orange juice left."

"Again, not so much," my gluttonous partner added.

"Jesus Christ! Do you ever replace what you drink?"

"Heh heh. Nah, I usually count on the marrow to do that for me." We both laughed, because sophomoric vamp humor never goes out of style. It's like a fart joke, only different.

When I realized we were the only ones amused, I sobered. "Anyway, either of you want a drink?"

Anna and Mike replied in the negative. Greg and I drank our blood in silence while Anna worked. Mike looked a little unhappy about us drinking in front of his friend, but she already knew what we were. No point in hiding it. Besides we weren't slurping.

Cold blood is kinda flat tasting, but it's better than room temperature. Obviously it tastes better at body temp, but I didn't want to offend Greg or Mike by going off to hunt. So it was O-positive flavored with plastic and anticoagulants for me. Yippee.

While Anna was hacking away, I turned to Mike. "Hey, Dad? Did you ever find anything more out from the possessed girl?"

"Oh yes," Mike said. "Michelle was her name. What do you want to know?"

"Well, let's start with how she was planning on cursing Tommy Harris and his whole family into oblivion."

"Oh, that." Mike actually sounded amused. "That was actually a mistake."

"What do you mean, a mistake? She didn't mean to curse him?"

"Oh, no. She definitely meant to curse him, she just didn't know how."

"But she did it. I don't get it."

"The little girl had dabbled in some witchcraft, but was by no means a skilled enough spellcaster to actually make a curse stick."

"You're saying she didn't curse Tommy?"

"Not with anything meaningful, no."

"He was never in any danger?"

"Not until you confronted the possessed child with him in tow, no. She was not focused on him any longer, but then you showed up."

"Great. I love my life. This little girl just happened to be the one possessed, and it really has nothing to do with our case at all?"

"Well, it may certainly be the case that her experimentation with magic made her more attractive to outside influence, but that is generally the case."

"This was all a mistake, and we were never needed in the first place?"

"Basically, yes."

"Story of my life." I went for another drink and sat down on the couch to wait for the hacker witch to finish. I leaned over to Mike and spoke in a low voice.

"What do you think, Dad? Is your witchy woman going to be able to tell us how to send zombies back to Hell?"

"Actually, James, we want to be very careful about that. We only want to send the inhabiting souls back to Hell. The bodies we very much would like to return to their resting places," Mike told me.

"Fair enough, Padre. But I'm not digging. I not ruining this manicure digging graves." I was half joking. I've never had a manicure. But I was serious about the no digging part.

"Well," Anna said, finally looking up from her keyboard and stretching her arms over her head. "You'll have to get your hands dirty if you want this to end. My coven is gathering at the fountain in Marshall Park. If we can get all the zombies there by dawn, we can banish the spirits in a sunrise ceremony."

I choked a little at the s-word, but she didn't even slow down.

"Let's go. Get the zombies, incapacitate them, and drop them at the park with my coven. They can bind the creatures long enough for us to exorcise them, for lack of a better term." She looked apologetically at Mike, who gave a little nod. No one wanted him to think we were stepping on his theological turf, but he wasn't terribly well equipped for this sort of thing, dogma-wise.

"That sounds like a plan," I said. "A crappy one that will probably end up with some of your coven having their brains eaten, but it's the best one we have. Any idea how to find these zombies?"

"I'm on that one," Greg piped up. "I've been following police dispatches on my laptop." That really impressed me, since I thought he'd just been messing around on Facebook the whole time. "It seems like the zombies are all converging on one spot. I don't have enough data yet to figure out exactly where that is, but I think I can use the info I do have to get us within a few blocks."

I raised my hand. "Hey, Professor Pugsley, do I even want to try to understand how you're doing that, or should I wait until you give me the signal and then hit something really hard?"

"Let's all play to our strengths. I'll do the computing, Mike will do the driving, Anna's coven will do the banishing and you do the punching."

"Sounds good to me. Give me a minute to gear up and I'll be right with you." I headed over to the coat closet but stopped cold at Mike's voice.

"No guns."

I turned around almost slowly enough to be a parody of myself, and looked at him. "Why not, exactly? I understood the whole no-killing-the-little-girls rule you came up with, because regardless of my membership in the Walking Dead Society, I'm not a *monster*. But Mike, these guys are already dead. It's not like they're going to get upset about it."

"First, you technically are a monster. There are movies to which I can refer you. Secondly, I cannot allow you to defile the dead in my presence. Even though these may be but empty vessels, I am a man of the cloth and cannot allow you to harm the bodies." He crossed his arms and gave me his best priestly gaze.

The priestly gaze works much better on people who didn't steal licorice from the corner drugstore with you when you were seven. "I won't hold your career decisions against you if you don't hold mine against me. And as much as I love you, Mikey, I'm taking the shotgun for the zombies. Get over it."

"Then I'm not driving."

"Fine, we'll take Greg's car." I caught sight of Greg out of the corner of my eye gesturing wildly at me, but I ignored him. Wish I hadn't. As usual, ignoring him turned out to be a bad idea. Father Mike clued me in.

"Greg's car isn't here. You left it at the bowling alley, where it has doubtless been towed to the police impound lot by now."

Crap. I hate it when other people are right. Because it usually means that I'm wrong. And because it happens so much of the time. Now I had to use non-lethal methods to subdue a dozen dead guys, and I had to figure out how to get Greg's car out of hock without ending up arrested. Again. I might have stomped around the room cursing for a minute or two before I said anything intelligible.

"Fine, you win," I said when I ran out of profanity. "We'll do it your way. I'll leave the shotgun, but can I at least take the cricket bat? I bought it special just in case I ever got the chance to whack a zombie with it."

"And you have the audacity to call me a dork," Greg said from behind me.

"Dude, you still wear Underoos. Your geek-fu is so much stronger than mine, it's ridiculous. You are the Mister Miyagi of geek-fu. You are the geek ninja. You are the first person in history to be granted a P.H.Geek from Oxdork University."

"I get it. Here's your bat." He poked me in the stomach with it as he walked to the stairs. He stopped at the bottom of the stairs and gestured grandly to Anna for her to precede him. "To the car, madam?"

"You first, vampire."

Wow, not only was she a witch, but she was a witch with good taste in men. Greg sagged like a kid who's just dropped his favorite GI Joe down the well. He trudged up the stairs, head hanging low. He was so disappointed that his gallantry went unappreciated that he forgot his cape. I grabbed it to cheer him up, wrapped a few surprises in the black fabric, and followed him up the stairs to load the trunk of Mike's car. According to my best guess, we had a pile of zombies to capture and banish, and only about three hours to do it in.

Chapter 23

Greg's math was better than I'd ever willingly give him credit for—we found the first set of zombies about fifteen minutes after we left our place. The nearest church had lost three corpses, all dead less than a month. They were decidedly gross, even with the whole embalming thing. That process is really only designed to make people look good for a few days. After that, it starts to get very George Romero very quickly. At least they had all their parts. I don't know if I could have dealt with pieces falling off all around me.

Anna had briefed me on her plan on the way, so I had a vague idea what she expected from me. My contribution pretty much boiled down to hitting things. I was okay with that. It had been a rough couple of nights, and I didn't mind the idea of some mindless violence. As the car stopped I took stock of the situation. We had three corpses shambling through a strip-mall parking lot on the east side of town. On the one hand, it being the Saturday night before Halloween made passing them off as drunks pretty easy. On the other hand, they had picked a strip mall with a police substation. That would complicate things a little. We'd have to distract the cops.

Mike and Greg were dispatched to the cop shop with a couple boxes of Krispy Kremes to make sure they got the undivided attention of the constabulary. Then Greg put the mental whammy on them while Anna and I took care of the zombie wrangling. The first one was really easy. We put handcuffs on him, tied his feet together, and that was that. No fight, no attempted eating of brains, nothing.

After the first capture, though, Zombie Number Two apparently got a clue we were going to try and block them from their destination, so he fought back. I had one handcuff on the guy, a middle-aged dude who was a little on the heavy side if I'm being particularly kind, when all hell broke loose. His eyes glowed, and he went from shambling, slow '70s-era zombie to *28 Days Later* butt-kicking monster in a split second.

"Look out!" I yelled to Anna as the dead guy threw a haymaker that would have broken my jaw if it had connected. I got out of the way, and backed into the arms of the third zombie, a woman who was probably attractive in life, at least before she got her face mangled by whatever killed her. She grabbed my arms and the guy zombie put one hand on my throat. He drew back with a huge fist, and I dropped out of the way barely in time to keep him from smashing my face flat. He connected squarely with the woman zombie, and she flew across two parking spaces and fetched up against the side of a Toyota minivan.

"Throw me the bat!" I called as I jumped on the hood of a parked car to avoid the guy's next punch. He jumped right up behind me, but I had the bat by then and clocked him a solid shot to the left temple. I was trying to heed Mike's words about not defiling the corpses, but it was gonna be hard if they were this intent on defiling me first. I heard Anna scream and looked over to see her running toward our car with the female zombie in hot pursuit. They were too far away for me to get there before the zombie closed on Anna, so I threw the bat as hard as I could and got a *thunk* on impact that echoed across the parking lot. The female zombie went down hard, and I looked around to find where the guy I decked had fallen.

Except he hadn't fallen. He was standing right behind me, and as I turned he picked me up over his head like a bad pro wrestling show from the '80s and tossed me about twenty feet. I stopped whistling through the air when I went through the windshield of a parked bakery van. The windshield was now one big popped out sheet of rumpled, shattered safety glass, and I now had a close personal relationship with the gearshift. Slowly, I disentangled myself from it and the front seat. I got out of the van and joined Anna back near our car.

"This is not what I had in mind," she said when I got within earshot.

"Me, neither," I gasped. I was pretty sure I had broken a couple of ribs, and while they would heal quickly, they hurt like the devil right then. "But it's not too far from what I expected. Pop the trunk."

"The trunk, why?" She looked at me in confusion.

"Are you one of those women who will never, no matter how dire the circumstances, do anything unless you understand all the reasons behind it? I just want to know, because if I'm going to die because of someone's ridiculous need for exposition, I'll go flippin' stake myself," I snapped. "Now open the trunk because *that's where all the guns are.*"

"That's all you needed to say," she huffed. But she did reach into her pocket and get out her key fob to pop the trunk. Greg's cape wasn't the only thing I'd tossed into the trunk while everyone else was getting their seatbelts fastened. Mike and Greg came out of the police station, but stutter-stepped when they saw the chaos in the parking lot.

I got to the back of the car and yelled for Greg. "Get over here, bro, I need backup!" He hustled over and I handed him a twelve-gauge and an aluminum baseball bat. "Knees and elbows. We want the demons to stay locked in the bodies but be unable to move."

"Mike won't be happy."

"Mike doesn't get a vote anymore. That was before we realized the zombies can think and react. We have to disable them and get this done in the next couple of hours or we're going to have a bigger mess on our hands than we've ever dreamed of. Imagine these guys wandering through downtown during rush hour. Now, you with me?" I racked a shell into the chamber because Greg always works better with dramatic sound effects.

He took the bait. He cracked his knuckles and said "Let's do this."

I think somewhere deep in his brain my partner has a folder marked "clichés" that he accesses every time we're in trouble. His ability to quote movies in times of extreme stress is impressive, in a sad kinda way.

We came out from behind the car and followed the two unbound zombies, who had abandoned us when we stopped fighting and returned to their original course. They'd managed to navigate more than halfway across the parking lot and almost to the entrance of a fast-food restaurant. The location was problematic. We were about to shoot a couple of walking corpses right in front of PlayLand, but that really couldn't be helped.

I took out the knees on the woman zombie. Greg couldn't shoot a woman, not even a dead one, so I didn't waste time asking him to take her out. Me, I'll open fire pretty quickly on anything, living or dead, that tries to kill me, hurt me or look at me like it might eat my brain. After the knees, I switched to her arms, and broke both at the elbows with my bat. Greg did the same with the guy zombie, and we quickly bound them hand and foot and tossed them over our shoulders. I hoped the spectators in the window chalked it up to a Halloween party gone wild.

We got back to the car and deposited our cargo, but noticed something was missing—the first zombie. I heard a shouted Bible verse from the back of the strip mall. Our broken zombies wouldn't be going anywhere, so we headed off to save the night. When we got to the back of the mall the missing zombie had knocked Anna out cold and was choking Mike against a loading-dock door. We couldn't shoot without hitting Mike, so I tackled the pile of grave dirt while Greg tended to the wounded.

Every year I swear to sign up for a first-aid class that meets at night so I can play medic while Greg plays linebacker. But, once again, I hadn't kept my resolution so I got the dead guy off Mike and beat the crap out of him with my bat.

The problem with beating on zombies is that they don't feel pain, so you have to do real damage. Going after joints is best, but if they're thrashing around trying to kill you, that's pretty hard. I shattered one elbow, but he got a couple of good shots in before I finally connected with a kneecap. With nothing holding his leg upright, he went down like the corpse he was. I took a couple extra minutes to break his other knee and elbow, then hefted him up across my back and took him to where his buddies were writhing around.

You can't really knock a zombie unconscious, so they were groaning and biting and being generally annoying—which is off-putting in a dead person. I walked over to the local supermarket and got a roll of duct tape, and before too long I'd made three silver-taped and very lumpy zombie

Christmas presents. Greg helped Mike and Anna back over to the car, and grinned every second that she allowed him to help her walk. If he got any more excited I was going to put Xanax in his blood bags.

When they arrived we all stood there, panting and bruised—with more than a handful of graveyard dirt and flaky zombie-flesh clinging to our clothes—and took a look at the mess around us. We had managed to break half a dozen cars or so, which I thought was a pretty good record for us. Most of the people parked in the parking lot still had transportation.

Crap. Transportation. I'd stumbled upon a huge hole in our plan. Anna had said she could perform the spell, but even with her whole coven backing her up, it would be a one-time thing. For everything to work we needed all the zombies in one place at one time. Therein lay the rub. We had neglected to address how we were going to carry eleven zombies around until we could banish them. We didn't have a paddy wagon, and we couldn't afford the time to ferry them back and forth to a central collection point after we ran each one to ground.

We needed some way to get these zombies to Marshall Park while simultaneously chasing down the rest of the zombies. And after that fight, we needed all hands on deck to get the job done. None of us had any desire to split up. So I called a cab for our "friends," the zombies.

Even though it was almost Halloween, the deal took a little explaining, a little mojo and a folded hundred-dollar bill, but I got the cabbie to agree to take our three "drunk friends" to the park and deposit them on the sidewalk away from the police station. I told him that me and my fraternity brothers had plenty of partying planned for the night, and if he'd keep his mouth shut and his cell phone on, he could make almost a grand by the time the sun came up. He babbled something about a mother and father and a sick baby, but I didn't really care. I waved half a dozen more pictures of Ben Franklin in his face, and he agreed not to take any fares but my "friends" for the rest of the night. Even after all this time I'm often amazed at what people will believe in the name of cash and a fraternity Halloween party.

Chapter 24

The rest of the zombie encounters went much like the first, with the exception of the car chase. The last dead dude actually made us chase him, in the car, with Greg hanging out the window playing mailbox baseball with his spine. We kept the brain-eater alive, and because Mike had fallen asleep in the backseat long before we got to the last zombie, we didn't get another lecture about defiling the dead.

We tossed Marathon Man in the trunk because I was out of cab fare and I was afraid that even my dreadlocked ganja-befuddled cabbie was starting to think that this was something other than a fraternity stunt.

When we rolled up to join the witches in banishing a passel of angry spirits back to Hell, we had about an hour of night left. Not to mention that a successful banishment would leave us with eleven corpses in Marshall Park, a public space directly across the street from the headquarters of the Charlotte-Mecklenburg Police Department. Of all the places in the greater Charlotte area that I wanted to be when the sun came up, this was nowhere on the list.

We left Mike snoring in the backseat, and I grabbed the dead guy from the trunk. This one was skinny, at least. Some of the zombies we'd bagged that night had been seriously hefty in life, and that made for a slippery, jiggly corpse. If more people toted dead bodies over their shoulders, I'm convinced the obesity epidemic in America would be solved pretty quickly.

There were a dozen witches waiting for us in the dew-covered grass around the fountain in the center of the park. Anna made thirteen. They were arrayed on the concrete steps where countless festival goers and small children have played over the years. I somehow doubted we had the proper city permits for what we were about to do.

Anna explained to us that thirteen was a number of power, like three, seven and nine. I didn't bother to ask more because I really didn't care. I was tired, covered in all kinds of things that flaked off dead people, and had broken and healed ribs twice in one night. Once I even had to heal my arm. That left me hungry, grumpy and smelly—not a good combo for a vampire meeting a dozen witches for the first time. But Anna had carried her weight tonight so I tried. I honestly tried.

"Anna," I aimed to sound cheerful. "Aren't you going to introduce us to your friends?" I made what I hoped was a fang-free and friendly smile all around, but the number of glowing pentacles told me that I wasn't exactly making a harmless impression.

"No, vampire, I am not." Her voice was cold, and I saw Greg's face fall.

I was less surprised to discover we were good enough to hunt zombies with, but not good enough to take home to the coven. Greg falls in love with weather girls, so I wasn't surprised that he'd developed a monster crush on Anna in a few hours. Me, I was just interested in a little nibble, and maybe a little something else. But as hungry as I was, a bite to eat would have been enough.

That wasn't happening. Moving on. "Fair enough, witchy-poo. Where do you want your dead guy so we can finish saving the world?"

She had the good grace to blush a little. "Put him in the circle."

She pointed to where the other ten corpses were arranged carefully in the center of a huge magical circle drawn on the concrete plaza in multicolored chalk, with scribbles and sigils in several languages. I recognized a couple of words of Latin from hanging out with Mike all these years, but just a couple. It wasn't complete. There was about a three-foot opening in the side for me to enter, drop the zombie and exit.

As I got almost to the edge of the circle, something felt out of kilter, and I dropped the corpse on the ground.

"I don't think so," I said. "Your witches can put him in there. I don't want to put his head where his feet should be. I'm all thumbs when it comes to magic, you know." I took a couple of steps away from the circle and turned so that I could see most of the witches and Greg. His face had gone paler than usual at my sudden change of plans.

I caught a glimpse of him taking a position to cover my left, and I concentrated on the witches to my right. Greg and I have been in a lot of tight spots together over the years, and it's nice to have someone you don't have to explain things to when the shit hits the fan. He knew something was up, and went from heartsick to ready to rumble in no time at all.

I didn't actually know if I could be trapped by a circle. Greg and Mike and I have spent a lot of hours researching what made us this way, and we have no idea if we're mystical, extra-dimensional, extra-terrestrial, biological or something even stranger. There's a decent chance the circle wouldn't have bothered me any more than a jail cell made of toilet paper, but I'm never comfortable taking chances that are only decent. I decided to err on the side of caution for a change and not get locked in a magical circle with a dozen zombies on the night before Halloween. Just this once.

Anna spoke from behind me. "Don't you trust us, vampire?"

Her voice had a snide tone to it that I didn't like.

"I don't trust anyone, witchy-poo. It's how I've gone this long without finding splinters in my lungs."

"Well, don't worry, vampire, we won't harm either of you. Tonight."

I didn't like the way she emphasized "tonight," but there wasn't anything I could do about it with sunrise almost over the horizon.

"I'd appreciate it if you didn't harm them, Anna. These boys are under my protection." We all turned at Mike's voice, and I swear my friend looked like he had a glowing halo around him. "I don't think you and yours want to bring down my disappointment, do you?"

When he walked the last few steps to stand next to me I thought the glow might have been nothing more than a street light behind him, but I wasn't sure. It faded as he drew close and whispered, "Thought you'd leave the priest to sleep while all you magical types play in the park, huh? When will you guys ever learn?"

Mike grabbed the zombie by the ankles and started to drag the thing into the circle. The process was made somewhat more difficult by the bandages on his burned hand, but he was strong for a human. The dead guy thrashed around and threatened to scuff the circle, so I grabbed the zombie under its arms and helped Mike carry the animated corpse into the right place in the pattern. I figured the chances of them closing the circle with Mike inside were significantly lower than if I was alone in there, and I knew Greg was keeping a sharp eye out now, so I was willing to help.

Once Mike and I were safely out of the circle, the witches closed it with chalk and mumbling, and then the show started. There was a whole lot of chanting, some smelly stuff thrown into fires at the five points of a pentacle that was scribed within the circle, and a bunch of call-and-response "spellcasting." I was starting to get bored when suddenly the zombies leapt to their feet and rushed at the circle.

They smacked into the magical barrier like it was a wall of glass, and I was exceptionally happy to not be in there with them. They beat on the air, which to them, at least, was very solid, and began to wail. Not the low, guttural kind of moaning that you think of when you think of zombies, but a wail that oscillated like an air-raid siren. It built in volume and pitch until Mike, Greg and I went to our knees with our hands pressed to our heads.

The witches either had earplugs, were deaf, or were protected somehow from the noise, because they kept right on chanting and singing as the keening got louder. Finally, as the zombies literally blew out their voice boxes and their throats exploded with splatters of blood on the air of the magical boundary, silence reigned again. The zombies collapsed to the ground, empty bodies again, and that quiet was the most fantastic thing in the world. I thought for a second that it was all over, that we had sent the souls back where they belonged, but I should have known better.

A new voice came out of the circle, and my blood ran cold as ice.

Chapter 25

"Forgive them Father, for they know not what they do," said the disembodied voice from within the circle. It was a kind voice, a gentle voice, the type of voice that was more soothing than a mother's croon after a nightmare but which also held more strength than a father's sternest lecture. The voice touched a part of me that I thought had died fifteen years ago. Tears rolled down my cheeks at the sound.

I looked over at Mike, and he had the most rapturous look on his face I'd ever seen outside a painting. He stepped towards the circle. He was almost within arm's reach of the boundary when I realized what he was doing. Completely under the spell of the demons in the circle, he was going to break the magical restraints, and all those damned (literally and figuratively) spirits were going to be free again.

I only made it one or two steps before a black blur flew in and knocked Mike sprawling across the grass. The seductive voice turned into a screech of disappointed rage and hurled curses in half a dozen languages at my oldest friend and my partner as they tumbled across the concrete away from the circle. I got a look at a face inside the circle, and if that was what things in Hell looked like, I was glad to be immortal for all intents and purposes.

Greg held Mike down with his considerable bulk and superior strength, and I yelled over at Anna "This would be a great time to wrap this up, lady!"

The witches' chanting grew in volume and intensity, and the light show inside the circle kicked up in earnest. Nearly a dozen angry amorphous, faceless (thankfully) souls whirled and tumbled like psychotic Caspers in a spin cycle, with radiating red, blue and purple lights bouncing around inside the circle like a *Star Wars* rerun on fast-forward. The chanting seemed to last forever, but it must have only been a few minutes, because the sky had barely begun to lighten in the east when suddenly the circle fell dark and silent. All thirteen witches slumped to the ground, unconscious. I looked over at Greg and Mike. They had stopped wrestling around and stood staring at the scene on the plaza.

I walked over to Anna and checked her for a pulse. It was strong, and as I felt the blood pulse through the side of her neck, my stomach gave an embarrassing rumble, testament to the long and painful night that had left me hungry. But you don't snack on witches who'd saved the world. Instead, I shook her gently until she began to stir, and I asked quietly, "Is it done?"

She allowed me to help her stand and walk her over to the edge of the circle. She took off her pentacle and passed it over several of the nearest bodies. When it didn't even flicker, she nodded wearily. I helped her over to a bench, and quickly confirmed that all the other witches were still breathing. I avoided the circle, because even if Anna had broken it by leaning over and swinging her necklace over the dead guys, I didn't want to do anything stupid like scrub out a line with my shoe and end up having to fight all these dead guys again.

Turns out the dead guys weren't my immediate problem. Our little light show had attracted the wrong kind of attention. I heard a gentle "*ahem*" sound and turned. Detective Sabrina Law stood on the edge of the concrete plaza, gun in hand and pointed straight at my heart. Obviously, she hadn't taken our disappearance last night in stride.

I hate mornings.

Chapter 26

"Hi Detective." I reached hard for a pleasant, maybe even respectful tone but was really too tired to pull off anything other than half-dead.

"Hi yourself, Black."

"Please, Sabrina, call me Jimmy."

"No thanks, Black. And my first name is Detective." She holstered her gun and reached behind her for a pair of handcuffs.

I snapped at that point. It had been a ridiculous night. I'd gotten handcuffed to a bowling alley chair, had my ass kicked by possessed middle-school girls, chased zombies all over Charlotte, been tossed through a windshield, narrowly avoided being trapped in a magic circle by a coven of witches and I was not about to be handcuffed again, even if it was by the sexiest cop I'd ever seen.

With less concern than usual for the consequences of my actions, I grabbed the cuffs from her, spun her around and snapped them shut on her wrists. With her hands secured behind her back, I tore off a strip of my T-shirt and balled it into a gag.

I turned her back to face me, looked the very angry detective in the face and said, "We are about to get a lot of things straightened out." With that, I tossed her over my shoulder and started toward Mike's car.

"Mike," I hollered back over my shoulder. "Pop the trunk." He and Greg had started moving about the same time I had, and by the time I got to the car with my kicking bundle of detective, they were close enough to open the trunk. I deposited my cargo, making sure not to drop her head on the jack or tire iron, and tucked her long legs into the trunk.

I leaned down until our faces were inches apart. With fangs on full display, I said, "I'm very sorry you have to ride in the trunk. And I'm very, very sorry about the level of gross going on in said trunk. But you've been a real pain in the butt tonight, and we're going to my place to clear the air. So, I'll be taking this."

I removed her pistol from her side, then grabbed her portable radio. "And this is to make sure you behave on the trip. Oh, and I think I'll take these, too."

Her backup piece was a nice little .38 strapped to one ankle. I also relieved her of her cell phone and her spare handcuff keys. I slammed the trunk shut and got in the passenger seat. It was nice of Greg to read my mood well enough not to make me call shotgun. He got in the backseat and sat there, eyes wide. I told him tackling Mike was a nice save and then stared ahead.

"Let's go home, Mike."

"With her?" he asked.

"Yep. And we should probably not be too concerned about the speed limit or stop lights. The sun's coming up fast, and I'd rather not be a sausage biscuit by the time we get home."

Mike drove like a bat out of hell. He parked his car in back of the cottage, where it would be out of view from the road, and I carried our guest. Then Greg and I hauled ass downstairs before we started to smolder.

"Now here's the deal," I told the detective when I'd dumped her on the couch. "I'm going to take the gag out. Any screaming and I gag you again. We've been through a lot together tonight, and you should know by now that I'm not going to kill you. I'm going to take the handcuffs off, but you can't have any of your guns back until I decide you're not going to do anything irritating like shoot me. Ditto your portable and cell phone. And no one will be tracking you by the GPS in those toys, because I took the battery out of both of them. *Capiche?*"

She nodded and sat there glaring at me, not saying a word even after I took the gag out. I reached around behind her and unfastened the cuffs, and that's when she made her move. She slammed her forehead into my nose hard enough to blur my vision, and shouldered me to the floor as she got off the couch and tried to bolt for the stairs. I grabbed one ankle and pulled her to the floor, and she spun around and kicked me in the side of the head for my troubles. I let go of her leg and lay there for a second as she scrambled to her feet and got into a fighting stance. I thought she was trying to get away, but she just gave herself enough room to maneuver and turned back to kick my ass.

"I don't know who the hell you think you are, but you have messed with the wrong woman, assholes," she said, keeping an eye on both Greg and I.

Greg held up his hands and said, "I'm not the one doing the messing, Detective. That's all my partner's idea."

I'd regained my feet by this point and mimicked Greg's hands-up pose. "We really don't need to do this, Detective. I'm not going to hurt you, and I'm pretty sure you can't hurt either of us."

"Wanna bet?" she growled.

I realized in that moment that there is nothing sexier than a woman who can kick your ass. I shook my head, pushing inappropriate thoughts and images to the rear for the moment, and vamped out on her. I put on a burst of speed and picked up the cuffs from the floor behind her, snapped them back onto her wrists and threw her across the room onto the sofa before she'd even seen me move.

She flopped into a sitting position on the couch and stared at me, eyes a little wild. "How did you do that?"

I crossed the room in less time than it took her to blink and said from the arm of the couch beside her "I have a few talents. Now would you like me to explain them to you?"

She nodded silently.

"Are you sure? We can go a couple more rounds if you'd like, but if our little sparring match goes any further, I'm afraid it will get hard on the furniture. Not to mention you." I hate intimidating women, especially pretty ones, but it had been a *long* night.

"I think I'm good," she said.

"Great. I'm going to let you go now. If you attack me again, I'm going to knock the ever-loving crap out of you and hang you by your ankles from the rafters. Do you understand me?"

She nodded, a bit wary, and I reached behind her back to uncuff her again. This time we made it through without any headbutting or other unpleasantness, so I gave her back her handcuffs and keys.

"What are you?" she asked after a minute.

"Do you really want to get to the tough questions this quickly?" I asked. "How about a beer first? Or something stronger? We have a full bar."

"Of course you do. Beer is good. Light if you have it."

"Greg, a light beer for the lady. And a bourbon for me, if you don't mind."

He fixed the drinks while I kept an eye on our guest. When he delivered the drinks, he plopped down in the room's one armchair. I got off the arm of the sofa and sat beside Detective Law, who slid as far down the couch as she could and still be sitting. Mike came into the room from where he'd been hiding in the safety of the stairs, grabbed a kitchen chair and pulled it over.

When we were all settled in, I looked over at Detective Law and laid it out for her. "We're going to take a huge chance with everything we're telling you tonight. Usually, whenever we get into a jam that we can't talk our way out of immediately, we mojo the person into forgetting they ever met us. But for some reason can't mojo you. We're going to tell you the whole story, with no BS. And when we're done, we'll see how you react. If things go the way I think they will, then we all get to figure out what next to do about all this."

"All what? You mean the kidnapped girls and the pile of dead people in Marshall Park?"

"Yeah, that's the beginning of it. There's a lot more crap going on here, but there are some things you need to understand before we figure out what we're doing next."

I finished my drink in one pull and turned back to Detective Law.

"We're vampires." I waited, but there was no reaction. "Well?"

"Well, what?"

"Well, don't you have anything to say to that?"

"Look, Jim, I've been a detective for the last ten years. This might surprise you, but you're not the first person I've come across that thinks he's a vampire. I figured that out a while ago. The black clothes, the fake fangs, the nighttime-only business hours. Obviously you're part of some type of vampire cult or something."

I sighed and tried again. "You're missing the point. We're not pretend vampires, we're the real deal. We drink blood, we have fangs, we live underground in a cemetery, for crying out loud."

"Sure, and I bet if I look in your crisper I'll find bags of blood from some orderly you bribed at a hospital, right? And you're fast, but you're no Superman. I live in the real world, pal. I deal with real monsters every day. Don't drag me down here and give me some bullshit about things that go bump in the night. I . . . ."

Her voice trailed off to nothing as I pulled her pistol out of my jacket pocket, ejected the magazine, and bent the barrel of her service weapon ninety degrees from normal.

"You wanted Superman?" I asked from my new spot across the room. "Was that strong enough for you?" I was suddenly sitting beside her on the couch again. "And how about fast? Will that do for fast?"

I dropped my fangs into place and leaned in very close to her face. "You're welcome to check and see exactly how real these are if you like, Detective. I could certainly use a snack."

She shook her head, her mouth opening and closing like a flounder on the deck of a fishing boat, so I leaned back to a more acceptable distance, retracting my fangs as I went. "We keep the fangs tucked away until we need them. They make it hard to talk, and they tend to cut our lips if we leave them out all the time."

Mike piped up. "Not to mention the name of the game is for them to blend in."

"We blend as best we can, and, yes, we do indeed bribe a guy at the hospital for our blood supply, but if pressed we can certainly take our meals on the hoof, as it were. Greg pretty much never eats take-out, but every so often I feel the need for a nibble. It reminds me exactly where I stand on the food pyramid—at the absolute top. Now do you believe me?"

She looked from me to Mike and back to me again. She shook herself slightly and refocused on Mike. "But I thought you were a priest? Are you some kind of vampire priest?"

Mike laughed and leaned back in his chair. "I am a priest. A *human* priest. I'm still very much alive, thank you. Jimmy and Greg and I grew up together, and we've been friends for far too long to let a little thing like turning into the living dead get in the way. I trust these boys with my life, and they trust me with their secret. "

She relaxed a little, probably relieved to know that we have a friend that we haven't eaten. "You're really vampires? You and the other one?"

"Yep, Greg. My best friend since junior high and now my undead business partner." I pointed to him and he sketched a rough half bow from where he sat.

"And you really drink blood?"

"Yep."

"And you really can't go out in the sunlight?"

"Poof!" I confirmed.

"Holy symbols?"

"Bad juju for us."

"Stakes?"

"Make us dead as doornails."

"Decapitation?"

"Ruins our night forever."

"Garlic?"

"Total myth. I love Italians."

Law opened and closed her mouth as she realized the distinction I'd just made. I could tell she thought it was funny. Point for me. After a second's pause, she asked, "Running water?"

"I shower every day, so running water is not an issue."

"Silver?"

"Hurts, but doesn't kill. I've never been shot with a silver bullet, and it's not an experiment that I'd care to try."

"How?"

"How what?" I played for time. I figured we'd get to this question eventually. I wasn't really crazy about the answer, but it was going to come out, and I had promised full disclosure.

"How did you two become vampires?"

"That's a long story."

"Well, I have all day. Because I'm not leaving until I'm satisfied you're not as evil as all the stories make you out to be, and I don't think you're going anywhere until sundown."

"All right, but I'm gonna need another drink." I went to get more liquor, and a fresh beer for the lady, and settled in to tell her our story.

Chapter 27

"We were those kids in the corner of the lunchroom, invisible unless you needed someone to pick on. Mike, Greg and I were a modern-day Three Musketeers, tied together by the absence of athletic ability and a remarkable lack of success with women. We made it through high school with slightly more than the normal burdens of angst, self-loathing and wedgies, and off we went to college. Greg and I went to Clemson together. Mike went off to seminary, and we didn't see him again until a whole lot of things had changed."

I looked over at Mike, and he gave me a slight nod. I'd erased some history, especially a big fight the three of us had right before high-school graduation. I'd said some pretty unkind things, including that I never wanted to see him again for the rest of my life. I didn't. I'm not sure that he's ever forgiven me for that. I haven't."

"Greg got a degree in computer engineering, and I managed to flunk, cut, drop and incomplete my way to a BA in English with a minor in psychology." I'd had no idea what I wanted to do except drink beer and play video games, but there's not a degree path in that, so I thought English would be the next best thing.

"One night a few weeks after graduation I met a girl in a bar. Unlike most girls I'd met in college, this one seemed interested. Thanks to my youthful stupidity and tequila, I believed a girl who was *Playboy* hot actually wanted to come back to our apartment with me. Of course, things probably would have worked out very differently if I had looked a gift horse in her mouth, but that would have ruined the story, wouldn't it?"

"I brought her back to the apartment I was sharing with Greg, and we got involved. Then we got very involved. And right as I was about to reach the peak of my involvement—"

"I get it" Detective Law interrupted with a slightly pained expression on her face.

"Sorry. Anyway, just at that special moment, she bit me. And I'm not talking a love nip. I'm talking a fangs-out, attack the carotid, drain you dry kinda bite. So she drained me, in more ways than one, and left me there, on my couch."

"That was cold," Law said.

"Yeah. Stone cold. She left me there, dead and naked from the waist down on my couch, which was how Greg found me a few hours later. And don't think that hasn't made for a few awkward moments in the last fifteen years."

"He found you . . . dead? Alive? Were you a vampire then?"

"I was, and I was *hungry*. Greg got home a couple of hours after she'd killed me, and found my dead, naked body on the couch in front of the television. He tells me that he freaked out a little, checked me for a pulse, and then went to look for the cordless phone to call the police. But the damage was done. When he touched my neck, something inside me snapped awake. I could feel his pulse through his fingertips, and I could almost hear his blood calling to me. I sat up, conscious but not really in control of myself, and when I saw him on the phone, I snuck up behind him and drained him dry in the middle of the efficiency kitchen in our off-campus apartment."

That was a vast oversimplification of things, but she didn't need to know how sweet the blood tasted right from the spring, how amazing and hot and rich it felt as it went down my throat, taking my dead flesh and pouring life into it. It felt like I was forcing his blood down into my desiccated veins, and with every beat of his heart I could feel myself getting stronger, more alive than I had ever been. Everything around me had new color, every sound was crisper, every smell sharper, and the taste was like the most incredible wine and steak and chocolate all rolled into one set of overwhelming sensations.

And as I felt the life drain out of my best friend I didn't care at all about what I was taking away from him, so focused was I on what I was getting out of the exchange. I could hear his heartbeat slowing in my ears, could feel the pulse in his veins getting weaker and weaker with every minute I stayed latched onto him like a pit bull with a T-bone. And I didn't care. I didn't care that I was killing my best friend. I didn't care that I was drinking the life right from his throat like a comic-book monster. All I cared about was how amazing it felt.

"By the time I drank my fill, Greg was dead. I drained him completely, and kept drinking until there wasn't a spare drop lurking in his veins. I really freaked out then, and the only reason I lived through the morning was because I felt too awful about what I'd done to leave Greg's body behind. If I'd run out looking for more food I would have burnt to cinders before I found breakfast."

"I spent the next few hours alternating between freaking out over being a vampire and freaking out over killing my best friend. Every once in a while I'd freak out over how I was going to tell Greg's mom. After a few hours of that, I collapsed on the couch and fell asleep. The combination of dying and coming back to life really took it out of me, I guess. When I woke up it was the next night, and Greg was awake, facedown in the fridge with his head in a bucket of fried chicken."

"Kiss my ass. I was *hungry*," Greg said from his chair. He'd sat through the whole story of his death without saying a word. I knew it still bothered him, but didn't want to try to work group therapy into our confession with the pretty cop-lady.

"I don't remember this asshole killing me, I just remember waking up and being hungrier than I'd ever been before. So I stuck my face in some leftovers and went to town. That turned out to be a really bad choice, since I was no longer able to process solid food.

"Fortunately, I was in the kitchen, so I was able to make it to the sink before the entire contents of my stomach came up in a spectacular mess. That left me hungrier than ever, and I could smell something coming from the living room, and it smelled good. I went in there to see what was for dinner, and the only thing there was Jimmy."

I picked up the thread here. "By now I'd guessed a little about what was going on, and I had opened a vein in my wrist for Greg. He proved my theory right, and latched on like his life depended on it. Greg drank from my arm, and when I started to feel my strength lessen a bit, I pulled him off me. It wasn't easy, but I got him off my arm. A few seconds later, he calmed down, and I explained to him what I thought had happened."

Greg took over again while I went for another round of drinks. "As far as we can tell, the trait of vampirism is only passed on when the donor is drained completely. If the heart doesn't stop, the donor does not become a vampire."

"What about animal blood," she asked. "Does it work?"

"Nope," I answered. "Apparently there are nutrients in human blood that we don't get from animals. Now, we haven't tried gorillas, or animals that genetically close to humans, but after a few experiments with rabbits and cats we gave up on animals. And I wasn't much of a pet guy when I was alive, so being dead has done nothing to increase my desire for a fluffy puppy."

"And for myself," Greg said, "I have all I can handle trying to domesticate Jimmy, so I've never bothered to try to have a pet. But back to the story. In short, I fed from Jimmy, and then we went out to top off the tank, as it were. We didn't drain those first donors completely, more out of satiation than out of any moral compunction against killing them. We just got full. Once we were thinking clearly, we realized that killing a bunch of random people would be a good way to get caught, and that would probably lead to unpleasant things happening in government laboratories, so we went for a more low-profile route."

There was a lot more to those first few nights than Greg was sharing, but even Mike didn't know much about what we did when we first turned, and I was content to keep all that between the two of us. Let's just say we became much more discreet in our later years.

Detective Law finished off her beer and leaned back in her chair. It was a long moment before anyone spoke, and when she did, the rest of us leaned in to hear what she had to say. "So you're vampires. And you're detectives. And you try to help people. But you still drink blood."

"Yeah," I said. "That pretty much covers it, using broad brush strokes."

"Fair enough. And I suppose you can call me Sabrina. After all, I know more about you than I ever really wanted to know, so I suppose we should be on a first-name basis."

"Now you know our story. And while I enjoy your company more than I have that of any living woman in nearly twenty years, I'm tired. And somewhere out there is a crazy bun-headed demon lady with a plan to do something really nasty to the world. And tomorrow night is Halloween, when crazy people tend to do nasty things. I'm going to get some rest, so that when it comes time to punch, stab or shoot something, I'm ready."

Greg yawned and mumbled his agreement, and headed off to his room.

Mike stood and gathered his things. "As much as I like you boys, your housekeeping leaves much to be desired. I think I shall retire to my parish house and get a little shut-eye myself."

"What about me?" Sabrina asked.

"What about you?" I asked right back. "We're getting some sleep. I suggest you do the same. Go home, Sabrina. Get a nap, get some fresh clothes, and meet us back here at sundown. You know we won't be going anywhere until nightfall, so you don't have to worry about us leaving you out."

"Fine, but this is my case. If you try to shut me out of this, I'll show back up here at noon one day and give you a stake dinner you'll never forget. Deal?" She stood and stuck out her hand. I stood up, too, because that's how I was raised.

I took her hand and shook. Her skin was so warm against mine, so alive that for just a minute I really, really missed being alive. "Deal." I stood there and watched her walk up the steps and into the sunlight, and felt the darkness settle into my chest as she closed the door behind her.

I stayed for a minute staring at where she'd been, until Greg came over, gave me an awkward pat on my shoulder, and said, "She's so out of your league it's not even funny. Now go to bed." And I did, feeling more alone than I had in years.

I was gonna have to bite somebody that night. To make me feel better, if nothing else.

Chapter 28

I slept for a long time, almost to dusk, and when I woke up, I felt like I'd barely gotten any rest at all thanks to dreams of Sabrina. Great. I love taking on a huge fight after a crappy day's rest and while I'm carrying around pent-up sexual tension. I should have bitten her and gotten it out of the way. I walked into the living room, and found Greg still sitting at his computer. It wasn't that unusual for me to come out and find him facedown on the keyboard, but this time he was still awake.

"I think I know what the plan is for tonight," he offered as I rummaged in the crisper for breakfast. He'd obviously slept very little, if at all.

"Yeah, dude. We had that covered before we went to bed. We wait here for the hot cop chick, then we find the ugly demon-possessed chick, kick her butt back to Hell, and then hopefully I get to second base with the hot cop chick." I jumped over the back of the sofa and landed with my feet on the coffee table. Sometimes the enhanced agility that came with being undead was handy.

"Don't you think the hot cop chick might have something to say about that?" Sabrina's voice came from the stairs, and not for the first time I wondered why mental telepathy didn't come with all the other fringe vamp benefits.

"Nah," I replied, trying to salvage some measure of my self-respect. "Once we save the world there's no way she'll be able to resist my charms. Breakfast?" I held the blood bag out to her.

"No thanks, I ate on the way over. And I have faith in my ability to resist your charms. And in the necklace my daddy gave me at my first communion." With that, she fished a delicate cross out of her shirt and dangled it from her fingertips.

"That's mean." I leaned back on the sofa and finished my breakfast. "G, what was that about a plan?"

"I think I know what Bun-Head is up to," he said, his tone still flat. I was gonna have to spike his next meal with Red Bull or he'd be useless in the fight to come. Then what he said registered and I was over his shoulder in a matter of seconds.

"Seriously? You've figured out her plan? How?"

"The magic of the interwebs. When you went to bed, I couldn't sleep, and we had no idea what Bun-Head's next step was going to be. So I went back to her first steps to see if I could come up with some other nexus between the abductions. And after a couple of false starts, I came up with the answer—school staff."

"Huh?" I asked. "That doesn't make any sense, bro. Teachers only teach at one school. How could someone work at a dozen different schools?"

"She doesn't. At least not permanently. Our bad guy, or in this case, girl, is a substitute teacher. When I ran the lists of substitute teachers in the system against the abductions, one name popped out as being at each school right around the date of the abductions. Janet Randell. She's been a sub for two years now since losing her job as a teacher's aide to budget cuts. She was at every single school the day of or the day before a kid went missing. So I did a little work to find out where she is today."

"And where is she?" Sabrina asked.

"That's where things got a little tricky. She wasn't working anywhere in the district today. But I knew she would have to be somewhere, at a decent-sized school, since she needed a dozen victims in short order. I widened my search, and found her at Holy Trinity." He leaned back in his chair, arms crossed over his round belly.

"How could she guarantee that she'd be teaching today, much less be at a large enough school to find a dozen likely victims?" Sabrina asked.

I was glad she did the asking. Not only did it save me the trouble, but Greg wouldn't razz *her* for not figuring everything out ahead of time.

"She created a vacancy. The home-ec teacher at Holy Trinity was found dead in her apartment last night. Our Janet killed the teacher and set herself up as the sub on call so she could be close to her victims."

"Nicely done, partner." Had to give him his props. "That gives us a location to start with."

"And end with," he said.

When Sabrina looked a question at us, I said, "Holy Trinity is a pretty tightly wound place, the kind of school that teaches Book Burning 101 and pickets rock concerts. Every Halloween they hold a religious fall carnival to combat the Satanic holiday's influence on our children."

"Lucky for us," Greg added, none too happy, "they'll be hosting this carnival tonight at the school gym."

"Crap." I actually paced a small circle as my brain worked it all out. "There will be hundreds of kids and parents there. If the final summoning needs a sacrificial component, then that would be the perfect place to do it."

I looked up. Both of them were staring at me, slack-jawed. "What? Just because I didn't do the research I can't come up with something more profound than 'Hulk Smash?'"

"Yeah," Greg said. "True enough. We concentrate on the fall carnival, because that's where she'll most likely be. And we go over there, ruin her plans, and save the world from something we don't really understand."

"What if we're wrong?" Sabrina looked from Greg to me, and back again. "I think it sounds like a good plan. And all the logic works. It makes perfect sense. But life isn't always logical and doesn't always make any sense. What if we're wrong? What happens then?"

"Then we all die," a deep voice said quietly before I could answer.

Stunned, we all turned to the stairs. *Phil.* But not my Phil, the one I'd come to know and despise. This was Zepheril, the fallen angel, accompanied by Lilith, the first wife of Adam. Phil had his wings on display, and Lilith had on an outfit that put almost all of her on display.

They looked like extras at a fetish party, only better armed. Phil had black leather pants and a sword belt with a sword on it. Lilith wore thigh-high boots with come-hither heels, a black leather miniskirt and a leather jacket unzipped enough for me to see that the only other thing she had on besides a bra was a shoulder holster. The first guy to build a combo bra/shoulder rig that's comfortable will make a mint.

I blurted, "What the hell are you two doing here?"

Lilith gave me a little smile and came over to me, oozing sex with every step. As she approached, the room suddenly felt really warm, and my jeans suddenly felt very tight. Out of the corner of my eye I could see Greg wiping a bead of sweat off his forehead. Sabrina just looked grumpy.

"Why, we're here to help, little vampire. If tonight goes poorly for you, it could go very, very poorly for us." She spoke into my ears in a low voice, almost a purr, and I remembered the feeling of her blood pulsing through my veins.

Pulling back took almost everything I had. I poured all my reserve strength into looking, very carefully, into her eyes, which seemed about the only safe place I could look. "What do you mean, go poorly for you?"

She chuckled and pulled back from me, giving Sabrina a glance as she crossed back towards the door. "You have no idea what awaits you in the afterlife, little vampire, if you even have one. Zepheril and I, however, know exactly what is waiting for us. And that's why we have no interest in bringing about the end of our lives anytime soon. Because what we have in store is unpleasant beyond your wildest dreams."

Zepheril put a hand on her arm and spoke when she paused. "All that is important is that our interests align with yours for the moment. It is time to go."

"Oh, hell no!" Sabrina said from where she had stationed herself with her back to a wall and a clear line of sight to everyone in the room. "I am not going anywhere with Tinkerboy and his partner, Slinky the Super-Slut. I agreed to work with you two because there's no other way to get this case solved, and I still only halfway believe in vampires. But I am not going into a firefight with a couple of . . . of . . . whatever you are at my side!"

Phil crossed to her quicker than anything I'd ever seen. I mean, he made me look positively glacial. He literally appeared at her side and whispered something in her ear. She pulled back, tears in her eyes, and slapped at him. He caught her wrist and looked deep into her eyes. A long moment passed with them staring at each other. I strained to hear what was said, but it was too low even for my vamp hearing. I looked to Greg and pointed at my ear, but he shook his head. Nothing there, either. After a few more interminable moments, Sabrina sagged a little and Phil let go of her hand.

"Now can we go?" he asked quietly, and for a second Phil didn't look like the self-righteous jerk I'd come to know and half despise. He looked like he must have before he fell, kind, peaceful, caring. I didn't like it, so I was happy when his normal sneer came back.

"Are you okay?" I asked Sabrina.

"No. But let's go. We need to finish the job."

Sabrina shouldered her way past Lilith and hurried up the steps ahead of everyone. I wanted to make some crack to Phil about taking a sword to a gunfight. *Desperately.* But after his little encounter with Sabrina, I knew better than to push my luck by making a joke. Instead, Greg and I followed, stopping at the closet to gear up. I wasn't sure how much good my guns would do in this mess, but it made me feel better to strap them on regardless.

And to make things even more festive, Mike was leaning on the fender of his Lincoln Town Car when we got upstairs. I'd harbored a sliver of hope that we could get rolling before he got here, but I should have known better.

"Going somewhere?" he asked. "I knew you wouldn't be able to come out before nightfall, so I did a little research on our demon, and thought you might like to know exactly what it is that we'll be facing tonight."

"Not we, buddy. You're staying home."

"Not likely, old friend."

"This is not a matter for discussion."

"Then let's not discuss it. I'm going with you, and when you hear what I have to say, you'll agree that you need all the help you can get." Then his mouth dropped open at the sight of Zepheril coming up the stairs.

I had to admit, he made an impressive picture, what with the wings, the sword, the six-pack abs. Mike flapped his mouth open and closed a couple of times then said, "Well maybe you do have enough backup after all."

Zepheril stepped over to the stunned priest and put a hand on his shoulder. "No party is so strong that it cannot be aided by a true man of faith. We would be honored to have you accompany us."

I try not to argue with angels as a rule, even (or maybe especially) fallen ones, so I hopped up on the trunk of Mike's car and asked, "What did you find out?"

He took a deep breath, shook his head, took another deep breath, and finally started to speak. "You told me that the demon identified herself as

Belial. Having certain resources at my disposal that most people do not, I went back to the church and did a little research. Belial is one of the most powerful of the second-tier demons. She is the child of Baal, one of Lucifer's Archdukes. Baal is the ruler of the seventh circle of Hell, which houses the most violent of sinners. All the murderers, rapists, suicides and blasphemers end up in the seventh circle, and Baal has complete dominion over them. That wasn't a dominion that came to him by default. He's earned his place. He is simply the meanest, nastiest demon in all of Hell and there isn't anyone that can challenge him. Not and win."

Phil and Lilith's interest was suddenly clear to me. "And Belial is daddy's little girl?"

"Exactly." Mike reached into his pocket and pulled out a rosary, holding it like a talisman. "Legend has it that she is the offspring of Baal and the Whore of Babylon."

Mike went on. "If Belial brings Baal to Earth, then he would have complete dominion over this realm, just like he does over the seventh circle. Baal is a force of nature, a creature so powerful that even the angels fear his power. If the ritual completes and the sun rises on Baal in this world, then the entire world will belong to him. He will, in effect, create a Hell on Earth."

The wise men of the world are right. Ignorance really is bliss.

Chapter 29

I stood up and started pacing. "All the more reason why you're staying here. I will not be responsible for taking you into a gunfight with a demon."

"Bite me. And I mean that figuratively, of course," Mike replied.

"Seriously, Mike. We can't take you with us. It's too dangerous. I don't know what I'd do if anything happened to you," Greg added.

"Nothing's going to happen to me. And regardless, I'm a grown man. I get to make all kinds of bad decisions for myself. I can drink a little too much, eat too much red meat, and consort with undead creatures if I choose. And really, is this going to be significantly more dangerous than having my two best friends be vampires?"

"Yes. Because we've never wanted to kill you. Strangle you a little, but never really kill you. If what you're saying is true, this demoness is far more dangerous than anything we've ever faced outside of a video game." Greg managed to stay calm, which was more than I could say for myself.

"How do you plan on handling her if she's so . . ." Mike's voice trailed off as he took a good long look at Lilith. "Oh. Now you can consort with demons, but I'm not good enough to come with you?" His voice was cold, and the look he gave me was heavy with disappointment, and something else I couldn't quite figure out. Maybe fear?

"I'm not consorting with them, Mike, I'm using them. They're tools, and like a cheap hammer, they're tools that I don't care about. You, I care about. I don't give a rat's ass if Lilith doesn't make it out of this alive, assuming she's technically alive now, but you're one of my best friends. And I only have two friends, so I can't afford to lose any of you. Please, I'm begging you, don't give me any grief, just stay home."

"No. I'm going with you, and I'm old enough to be stubborn about it. Who's riding with the holy man?" He raised his voice on the last so that everyone else could hear him.

Greg yelled "Shotgun!" and hopped in the passenger seat. I shook my head in defeat and went to get in Sabrina's car. Phil and Lilith started toward Mike's car, but when they saw the look on Mike's face, the fallen angel and his servant changed direction and wordlessly got in the backseat of Sabrina's much smaller sedan. Phil's wings vanished, and I didn't even bother to ask where they went.

"Don't you two have a car?" I asked.

"No," Lilith answered simply.

"Then how did you get here?" I asked. There was silence in the car for a long moment, then I thought about it for a second and got the mental image of Phil carrying Lilith as he flew along Independence Boulevard during rush hour. "I bet that was something for the commuters to see, huh?"

We rode in silence across town to the school and pulled into the far end of the parking lot. Sabrina popped the trunk and pulled out a pair of pistol-grip twelve-gauge shotguns. She handed one to me and started loading oddly colored shells into hers.

"What are those?"

"Bean-bag rounds. Non-lethal, but they'll take almost anyone out of the fight. Plenty here for you, too. Let's try not to kill any civilians if we can help it."

"I don't mind that in concept, but in practice, the civilians are likely to be the only things we *can* kill. I've got a bad feeling about whatever is in there waiting for us."

"Me too." She looked nervous, and I reached out to touch her arm.

"Hey. It'll be fine. We're the good guys." I tried to manage a smile filled with bravado and cocky charm, but I think I looked more like I was about to puke.

I felt more like I was going to puke, for sure. And as our motley crew made our way across the parking lot, I felt worse. The closer we got to the school, the worse I felt. It wasn't nerves, or a bad bag of blood. *Something* was messing with me. I looked around at the rest of the gang and saw that Greg was decidedly green as well. Even Phil and Lilith looked like breakfast wasn't settling well in their stomachs. We were about twenty yards from the entrance to the school gym, when I saw the huge banner across the front of the building proclaiming, "Fall Carnival for Christ!—No HELL-oween here!"

"Ahhh, crap," I said. "We've got a problem." I waved everybody together. Sometime between leaving our place and getting to the school, Phil and Lilith had magicked their outfits into something more early 2000s yuppie than late '80s goth porn. I didn't ask how they managed that trick. I really didn't care right now.

"What's the problem?" Mike asked. "I mean, I certainly don't agree with their odd bias against Halloween, but the rest of our plan seems to be solid."

"Except for one thing—location," I said. I looked around at my queasy partner, and the near-dead-looking Lilith and Phil. Mike and Sabrina looked fine, but that also made perfect sense. "The whole school seems to be consecrated—

holy ground."

"Oh crap," said Greg. I watched the realization creep across the faces of the rest of our group as well.

"What do we do?" Sabrina asked. "How do we get in there and get the job done without our heavy hitters?"

"We just do it, my dear," Mike answered. He reached over and took my shotgun, racked a shell into the chamber and pulled out his crucifix. "You and I go in there and drag our little demoness out into the parking lot where our compatriots can send her back to Hell. And don't forget, I brought a little backup myself. And I daresay he's the heaviest hitter of all."

"I can personally vouch for that." Phil handed Sabrina his pistol. "Silver rounds. I don't know what effect they'll have, but it can't hurt."

He passed a few extra magazines around to the rest of us from his apparently bottomless coat pocket. I didn't question the supply, because I didn't care how he got them or where they came from as long as the rounds gave us an edge in the fight to come.

"Thanks." Sabrina took the gun from Phil, tucked it into the back waistband of her pants and nodded to Mike. "Let's go."

"As they say in the movies, my friends, we'll be back." My old friend looked a dozen years younger as he shouldered the shotgun and headed off to fight a demon in a school gymnasium. If I squinted, I could even make myself ignore the bandages he was sporting on one hand and the limp he had picked up fighting zombies all over town last night.

"Do you think they've got a chance?" I asked Greg.

"I can only hope, bro. For all our sakes."

Chapter 30

I wasn't a patient man. I'm a less patient vampire. I paced the parking lot, growing crankier than hell with each passing moment and no word or indication of what was going on inside. I looked over at where Greg sat on the tailgate of a nearby pickup.

"How long have they been in there?"

He made a show of checking his watch and said, "About three minutes."

"I hate waiting."

"We can see that." Phil was sitting cross-legged on the roof of a minivan, with Lilith beside him.

I started toward the door of the gym, in earnest this time, knowing that forces were in motion against my making it onto consecrated ground. But I'd never tested myself to my limit of endurance. Maybe if a vampire were determined enough, he could make it.

The place pushed back at me, like I was trying to walk through a hard wind. The closer I got, the harder it seemed to push against me, and the sicker I felt. I had gotten almost to the front door when I heard shots ring out from inside. The boom of a twelve-gauge shotgun is unmistakable, and the sound I heard was two of them firing in the kind of rapid succession that would require a fast reload if the job wasn't done.

After about half a dozen shots, the gunshots stopped, and then it got quiet. Too quiet, as the cliché goes. No screams, no running feet, none of the sounds I would expect from a crowded school carnival whose attendees had to contend with a couple of nutjobs unloading a pair of shotguns. The silence reigned for about half a minute, as I kept pushing at the invisible barrier keeping me out. Then a low *whir* reached my ears.

The sound started slow and low, picking up in pitch and intensity, like a jet engine ramping up for takeoff. The noise built for a few seconds, then an explosion from inside sent blinding light out of every window and blasted me back from the doors.

I had almost enough time to gather myself for another assault when the doors of the gym opened up and a stream of people poured out, running like the hounds of hell were on their heels. Which, for all I knew, was true. A couple hundred people ran out into the night, a few of them getting into their cars and careening off down the street, but most just left their cars and ran for home rather than risk the traffic jam in the parking lot.

Phil, Lilith and Greg had pushed their way to my side, and as the stream slowed to a trickle, a familiar figure lurched into view. Mike bounced down the central steps of the building, holding onto the handrail like a sailor on shore leave. Instinctively I broke toward him, expecting the same intense pushback of consecration this close to the building, but there was only a slight roiling in my gut so I kept moving.

I shouted to the others as I ran, "I can make it. Whatever caused the explosion must have weakened the holy hold on the land."

"Mike, are you okay?"

He had a dazed look on his face, and his eyes were out of focus. I had to repeat myself a couple of times to get his attention. When I got through the crush of people, I saw that my friend's hair had gone completely white, like the good guy in a bad horror movie. "Are you okay?" I repeated, and he seemed to come to himself a little.

"What happened? Where's Sabrina? Did you kill the demon?" Greg peppered Mike with questions faster than he could answer. I waved Greg off and then pulled Mike around to the other side of the car.

"She's an innocent, Jimmy." The words were less than a whisper, and I probably wouldn't have understood what he said without my vamp hearing.

"Who's innocent? The teacher? Nah, man, she's the bad guy, I'm pretty sure. What happened in there?" I couldn't follow Mike's line of thought, and I wondered if he'd taken a smack to the head.

"No. Sabrina. *She's* an innocent, Jimmy. In the full meaning of the word. That's how she got caught."

My borrowed blood ran cold as what he said started to sink in. "The demon has Sabrina? Because she's a . . ."

I didn't say "virgin." Just because I'd heard of them didn't mean I necessarily believed in them any more than unicorns. Not grown women virgins. Sabrina was a grown woman. And hot. A hot, adult virgin in today's society? I might be the vampire standing in the parking lot fighting a demon with a fallen angel and an immortal feminist, but pegging Sabrina as a virgin was a leap of logic I'd never have made.

"This is unfortunate." Phil has a talent for understatement. Obviously.

"Yes. Belial has her. Her and a dozen children. We haven't got much time, we have to get in there and stop the ritual before—" He collapsed against a nearby car, coughing. There was a little blood as he coughed, and I wondered what kind of beating he'd taken in there.

"Mike, I wish we could." Greg was starting to freak out, and he always talks really fast when he freaks out. "But it's sacred ground. We can't go in and help. You've got to do it. You're the only one that can save her." That last bit was more like 'theonlyonethatcan*saveher*.'

He hadn't quite lapsed into "Help me Obi-Wan Kenobi, you're our only hope," but we were getting close. Mike tried to stand, but collapsed again.

"Well," I said, letting Mike slide down to a sitting position beside the car. "I guess it's time to test a theory."

Chapter 31

"Oh, *hell* no!" bellowed Greg, as Lilith looked at me and said "What theory, little vampire?"

"Dude, it's the only way," I replied. I looked over at Lilith and said, "Come along, sister, I think you're on this ride, too." I walked towards the entrance, with Greg walking backward in front of me, both hands out.

"You can't go in there, man. We've tried it before, and it doesn't end well. Even if you make it, we can't function on holy ground." He finally got both hands on me and stopped my march to the gym.

"Yeah, but we've never figured out why, have we? Mike has always said that it was our subconscious hang-ups making us sick whenever we went near a church, not anything having to do with our vampirism."

"Are you willing to take that chance?" Greg looked me in the face. "Is she worth it?"

"I don't know, and yes, I'm willing. Now either come with me or get out of the way. And Lilith, get your immortal tookus up here. I need a little pick-me-up." She came up beside me and gave me a sultry gaze. "Hold the smolder, appetizer. I just need the blood."

She pouted a little. "You're no fun when you're being all heroic, little vampire."

"Maybe after I save the world, get the girl and ride off into the sunrise we can play a different game. But for right now, give me your arm, please." She stretched out her wrist to me, and I drank. Not a tentative sip like the last time, but a full gulp of immortal blood. I saw the look on Greg's face, and it mirrored the fear in my gut. I didn't want to end up a slave to an eternal succubus for the rest of my potentially very long life, but I had to get in there and rescue Sabrina. I'd gotten her into this mess, and if it took the end of my free will to get her out of it, well so be it.

The power of ages crashed over me like a wave, and I could feel the sensation of it rolling through me. I could almost feel myself getting taller (the last thing I needed) and stronger (the intended result) and even sexier (a new sensation altogether). I drank for a few seconds, and let her go, feeling more alive than I ever had when I was alive. One step toward the gym and I knew the consecration was weakened. It was now or never.

I looked at Greg and said, "You might want to top off the tank, too, old buddy. I think we're gonna need it. Now is not the time to stand on principle."

Then I pushed past him and headed up the stairs into the church gymnasium to fight the demon that had kidnapped my maybe-someday-if-I-get-really-lucky girlfriend. I wasn't certain which was least likely—besting the demon or winning the girl.

Chapter 32

The gym looked like a cross between *Buffy the Vampire Slayer* (the lame movie, not the badass TV show) and Vacation Bible School. There were prom-style decorations from 1993, glittery letters and bunting strung all around the gym, and cheap poster-board signs over booths with slogans like "Bobbing for Salvation," and "Baptismal Dunking Booth." I couldn't decide whether to laugh or cry at the crazy attempt to de-monsterize Halloween, and felt no small irony that a couple of monsters were crashing the party trying to save the children of parents who would most likely lead the pitchfork party if they knew we existed.

My attention quickly locked on to our friendly neighborhood demon summoning taking place right at center court. The bun-headed lady from the forest was standing in the middle of a glowing circle, and there were a dozen little girls playing ring-around-the-psycho. The kids all faced out, and they all had the same glowing eyeball thing going on as the first bunch we rescued. The kids ranged in age from high-school girls down to one kid that looked barely old enough to go to middle school, but that wasn't the worst part.

No, the worst part was Sabrina. She was floating over the center of the circle, a good ten feet in the air over the bun-headed woman, and it looked like a rope of energy was flowing from each of the kids up to where she floated. As we watched, Bun-head twisted her hand in the air, and Sabrina turned in the air until she was looking straight at us. Her hands extended to the sides and her feet crossed at the ankles in a grotesque mockery of a crucifixion, and the look on her face was pure agony. I took one look at her writhing in pain and launched myself at the witch.

I flew a good twenty feet, landed and took another huge leap, crashing right into the invisible wall of the circle. I slid down to the floor like the coyote in one of those old cartoons, and heard the witch laugh maniacally as I lay crumpled on the hardwood floor. I heard several loud cracks like handclaps and looked up to see Greg shooting at Bun-head and screaming something that I couldn't hear through the ringing in my ears and the chirping of those imaginary birdies that were circling my head. The witch kept laughing as the bullets bounced harmlessly to the ground.

"Did you morons really think you could come in here and stop me that easily?" she asked, as she started to glow herself. The energy from the twelve kids was passing through Sabrina and down into Bun Lady, making her eyes glow and her hair unravel.

"Well, I kinda hoped," I said from where I lay on the floor. "Since our frontal assault didn't work, I don't suppose you have a better idea?" The last was to Greg, who had stopped shooting when it became apparent that he was doing no good.

"I got nothing, bro," he replied.

I tried to come up with something, but between the throbbing in my face from crashing into the circle and the nausea in my gut from being on holy ground, it was getting pretty hard to think.

Bun-head began to chant in some arcane language. The lights coming from the little girls glowed brighter, and Sabrina screamed as the flow of power through her became unbearable.

I beat on the barrier and yelled at Greg for help to get her out of there. "Salt!"

He tossed a fistful at the circle, but it bounced off like everything else we threw at it. "No good!" he said. "The circle is complete and only the caster or someone stronger can break it."

I didn't care about the reasons it wasn't working. I didn't care about anything except that the one living person I'd felt any connection to in a couple decades was on the other side of that magic barrier about to be possessed by a serious bad guy while I was stuck on the outside, unable to do anything about it.

Then Sabrina started to spin, and the light flowing through her started to go supernova. The faster she spun, the brighter she glowed, and the louder she screamed. Bun-head chanted in the unfamiliar language as the ground beneath her began to glow in answer to the light pouring down out of Sabrina. The glowing bands of energy started off white, but shifted to red. Then I noticed the kids in the circle starting to change.

There was no way this was going to end well.

Chapter 33

The only word I have for what the kids turned into was *demon*. I don't know if there's a better word, or if there's some type of hierarchy of Hell that I'm offending with my oversimplification, but when I see a four-foot-tall thing with red skin, horns and a spiky tail where a little girl stood a couple of minutes before, *demon* is the word that leaps to mind, and I don't care what the ACLU has to say about racial profiling.

I was still kneeling on the floor when the herd of demons broke loose from the magical circle and charged me and my partner. I was trying to figure out how to beat the demons without hurting the little kids probably still trapped inside, when Greg stepped up beside me and, without hesitation, shot the nearest monster right between the eyes. It flew backward into the circle and lay still. I tried to process that my partner, the vegan vampire who wouldn't even feed off bunnies, hadn't given a rat's ass whether or not a little girl was still inside the demon.

"I have a few issues left over from being tossed naked into the girl's locker room in sixth grade. I've decided to think of this as therapy." He turned faster than anyone but another vampire could follow and dropped another pair of demon girls before they could close on us.

"Dude! That was almost thirty years ago!" I yelled as I kicked a little girl across the gym.

"Some wounds take a long time to heal, man." He plugged another kid, and I started to worry. This was too easy. The demon children were dying just like any human, only redder, with the pointy extremities I'd expected from evil minions.

Apparently I was right, because that's when three of the demons got to me at the same time. I took one by the throat, and fended another off with the other arm, but the third one jumped on my back and bit the side of my neck.

I hate irony.

I bludgeoned the second kid with the first one, and tossed them both to the far side of the room. The kid-thing on my back was really beginning to annoy me. I reached over my shoulder and grabbed a handful of demon hair. It took a couple of tugs, but the little brat finally came loose from my neck, and I pitched her over to join her friends beneath one of the basketball goals.

I drew my Glock and started plugging away at demon children, who apparently weren't bulletproof, just annoying. For every demon that I managed to kill, an unconscious little girl appeared in its place. I didn't understand the transformation, didn't have time to ask anyone who would know, and frankly didn't care all that much. All I knew was that if I shot them in the head enough times, they stopped trying to gnaw out my spleen. And since I'm uncharacteristically fond of my spleen, shooting them in the face seemed like the best option available.

After a few minutes of shooting, Greg and I were the only monsters left standing, and with the little demon girls taken care of, we returned our attention to Bun-head and whatever hell she was trying to raise.

"Oh crap. This is not good," I muttered when I saw what was going on at center court.

"I think we're gonna need a bigger gun," Greg said.

"What the hell is that?" I asked.

"I think Hell is exactly what that is, bro."

That was a huge beast spinning slowly in the air where Sabrina had been floating barely a minute before. It was at least twelve feet tall, with long curving black horns protruding from a bony forehead that looked like a cross between a wolf and a huge bull's head. The monster had arms the size of pine trees, with foot-long claws at the ends of hands the size of Christmas hams. Its legs were human in shape, but bigger around than my waist. It had bare feet with three claws in front and one backward-facing claw, all razor sharp and shiny in the red light. Its skin was red like the little demons, and it had a double row of teeth that glinted as it smiled down at Bun-head. The demon stopped revolving and floated slowly to the floor directly in front of Bun-Head, then smiled down at her with a hundred pointed teeth.

The voice that came out of the demon made my skin crawl. "You have done well, my daughter. Now shed that weak mortal shell and assume your rightful shape."

As we watched, Bun-Head morphed into a female version of the beast. I could tell it was female because it wasn't terribly modest about hiding the eight teats that hung grotesquely off its chest.

"Dude," I whispered to Greg. "Where's Sabrina?"

"Dude," he answered, "I think the big thing is what Sabrina turned into."

"I was really afraid you were going to say something like that." I looked around for the cavalry I knew wasn't coming, drew my backup piece with my left hand, and stepped in front of the beasties. "Hey, assface!" I yelled.

Both of them turned toward me, and I yelled, "Where's the girl, dental nightmare?"

The big one looked down at me. "More minions? Good? I was looking for a snack. I appreciate the tasty virgins you gathered for me. In thanks for your loyal service, I shall kill you quickly."

The female formerly known as Bun-head whispered something to Baal, and he turned to me and grinned. "Never mind. Belial says that you were no help at all. That means I get to play with you a while before I kill you."

Baal stepped out of the remnants of the circle, and I felt the floor shake with his weight. The glowing magical barrier winked out of existence, and there was nothing standing between me and a monster straight out of my childhood nightmares except about twenty feet of faintly brimstone-scented gymnasium air. Whoever first wrote that high school was hell had no idea just how right they were.

"Greg, you got any bright ideas?" I asked without taking my eyes off the demons in front of me.

"You take the big one, and I'll fight the one with all the boobs?" He sounded about as scared as I felt. Neither of us wanted to show it.

"You only want to fight the chick so you can cop a feel and claim you got to second base."

"Yeah, but that would give me a score in a new decade, so I'd be ahead of you." He fired off a clip at Belial's head and then launched himself at the demon. I was amazed to see that he actually knocked her off her feet. I began to think we might have a shot at surviving this after all.

Then I took stock of Baal. As an opponent he was a couple of feet taller and a couple hundred pounds heavier, with muscles in places I was pretty sure I didn't have places. I hoped Greg had enough sense to run like hell when Baal killed me.

"All right, tall dark and drooling, let's do this." I emptied my backup into his kneecaps, and wasn't surprised when he didn't even flinch. Had to try.

I drew my big knife and jumped at the monster, and a second later found myself looking up at a disco ball hanging from the gym ceiling. "Ooooh. Pretty."

Next I saw a massive clawed foot rushing at my head. I rolled to the side before Baal could stomp my head flatter than a fast-food hamburger. His claws dug deep into the hardwood, and all I could think was *I am not picking up the tab for refinishing that*. I kept rolling and he kept stomping until I finally ran out of floor. I expected to feel my brains squirt out my ears at any moment.

This was where we'd find out if pancaking a vampire head is just as good as a decapitation. His foot came rushing down. I'll admit it—I closed my eyes. I couldn't handle the thought of watching my death come in the form of a size forty-eight bunion.

But no squashing happened, just a huge crash a few feet away and a bellow that literally shook the rafters. A volleyball that had to have been wedged up there for at least five years came down and landed next to me, flat and dusty. I opened my eyes, and when I didn't see a demon getting ready to step on me, I sat up and almost wished I hadn't.

Chapter 34

Greg had beaten Belial down pretty hard, but she was fighting back and they were slugging it out at one end of the gym. But the bigger, better weird show was center court, with a glowing sword in his hands. Baal was down on one knee a quarter of the court away, glaring at Phil with glowing red eyes.

"What are you doing, Zepheril? You're one of us!" shouted the demon, and I could feel the heat from his breath all the way across the gym. I could smell his breath, too. Baal seriously needed to reevaluate his dental-hygiene regimen.

"No matter what I've done, I never have been, and never will be one of you, *demon.*"

The way he said *demon* was like it was the vilest curse he could throw at something. And maybe to him it was. I'd never seen Phil like that—his wings were unfurled to their full width, at least twelve feet tip to tip, and he wore a kind of armor that almost glowed. It looked old, like a flickering light bulb trying to come on that didn't quite have the juice. His sword, which had hung at his side looking normal in my apartment, had grown to about six feet in length, with a huge hilt and a blade that was blinding white to look at.

Baal glared at him, and after a long minute said, "So be it, angel. Prepare to meet your little God again." And he spread wings of his own, gigantic bat wings that I would have sworn weren't there a few minutes ago, and soared towards Phil with his claws out and teeth bared.

Phil flew back at him, and for a few moments all I could see was the flash of the blade and claws, they moved so fast. Then my attention shifted over to the corner of the room where Greg and Belial were still fighting. She was holding Greg up with one hand and beating his face in with the other. I took a running jump and grabbed Belial's arm and spun her around. She dropped Greg and backhanded me. I stumbled backward, but caught myself and spun into her with a right cross that came from my heels.

Maybe the little nibble I had of Lilith did make me stronger, because Belial flew clear across the gym before crashing into the bleachers against the far wall. I shifted my attention to Greg, who was getting to his feet gingerly. He looked like you'd expect a vampire to look after being used as a sparring partner by a demoness—like a bag of crap.

I crossed the gym to within a safe distance of Belial. "Where's Sabrina?"

"You mean the police tramp?" She hissed at me from what looked like a broken jaw.

Good. I hoped it hurt. A lot. "Yeah, her."

"She's gone, vampire. Gone like the idiot woman that drew me to this plane. She was my final sacrifice to bring my father to this world. You've lost, now. Give up. Die like the sheep you are."

"*Baa-Baa*, bitch," I said, and I emptied the clip on my Glock into her face hoping that enough silver bullets in a small space would be enough to send her back to Hell. Finally, after all seventeen rounds lodged in her frontal lobe, she dropped like a rock. "Looks like those silver bullets work after all." I put a fresh clip in the pistol and turned back to where Baal and Phil had been duking it out in the Main Event.

The angel and the demon were breathing heavily, both looking the worse for wear. Phil had blood oozing from a gash on his side, and there was a hole in his shoulder where it looked like Baal had pierced him with a claw. Baal only had one wing left, and it was hanging in tatters. They were circling warily, each probing the other's defenses. Now and then one would take a cautious swipe with claw or sword.

Phil noticed me out of the corner of his eye and nodded to me slightly. I saw him trying to maneuver around so that Baal would be between him and me, so I could get a clear shot, but Baal just stood in the middle of the gym and laughed.

"It will be a cold day below when you can lead me into that trap, Zepheril." The monster chuckled.

"It was worth a try, demon," the angel replied, a wry smile on his lips.

"Why are you helping these mortals, Zepheril? You've always sided with the winners before now. You know that only the strongest survive, so why are you throwing in with these weak sacks of meat?"

"I picked the wrong side once, Baal. If I've been given the opportunity to correct that mistake, I'll not let it go by."

I flashed back to Sunday School and realized they were talking about the war in Heaven, the big one where Lucifer and all his angel buddies were tossed out after trying to lead a revolution.

Then they were at it again. Faster than my eye could follow, Phil went after Baal with the sword. Baal swatted the slash away with one huge forearm, and lashed out at Phil with his razor-sharp claws. Phil ducked under one slashing blow and stabbed at the monster with his sword. Baal actually caught the blade with one hand, but white fire flowed over his clawed fist and the demon yanked his burned hand back.

Phil followed with a slashing overhead blow, but Baal was too fast, dancing backward with a grace belied by his giant size and massive muscles. Baal lunged forward with both arms, stabbing at Phil with his claws, but the angel spread his wings and flew over his attack and slashed at the monster's back. The blade drew a thin line of white fire down the demon's back, and he let out a howl that blew the glass out of backboards all around the gym.

I saw a split-second opening while Phil was clear and the monster was distracted. I took my shot. Squaring my feet, I emptied my last clip of silver ammo into the back of the demon's head, and had the satisfaction of seeing the beast fall face-first onto the gym floor. Phil landed beside the fallen demon and raised his sword high.

"Nooooo!" I screamed and launched myself at the angel, catching him in a tackle worthy of the Pittsburgh Steelers. We tumbled head over heels across the gym as I tried to keep him from killing Baal.

"What are you doing, vampire?" I looked down when we had stopped to find a very pissed-off angel inches away from my face. He stood up, taking me with him, and grabbed me by the shirtfront. "I had him beaten. I've waited centuries to make this right, and *now* you decide to interfere? What the hell are you thinking?"

"Sabrina," I croaked. He had more than a little throat in his grip. "We've got to save Sabrina. You kill Baal's body, what happens to his host?"

"Idiot! His host isn't even on this plane of existence anymore. She's in Hell, you moron! He traded places with her, that's why you could kill all those little girls without murdering a child. Or didn't you think of that?"

"How do you know?" I know Phil had been around since the beginning of time and all, but some things I wasn't quite ready to take on faith. Phil didn't speak, just waved his arm around the gym. I followed his hand and saw a bunch of dazed little girls where demons had been lying, and an unconscious substitute home-ec teacher sprawled on the bleachers where Belial's body had been.

"Oh," I quietly said. "As you were then, back to the killing big demon things."

Unfortunately, Baal was no longer where we'd left him. Why is nothing ever easy?

Chapter 35

Of course the demon wasn't lying where we had left him, all nicely posed for a killing stroke from an angelic sword. Demons aren't exactly renowned for obedience. That's why they're demons and not angels, I suppose. Baal had gotten to his feet and pulled himself back together on the other side of the gym, with his back to a wall. He looked a little the worse for wear, but only a little. I hate fighting things that heal faster than me, so I made a mental note. He definitely had the edge on me in the healing arena.

I took a quick inventory. I had exactly one knife, a .380 pistol with eight rounds of regular ammo, a Glock 17 without a bullet to be had, and a bad attitude. Phil had a really big, magical sword, and Greg had two fists and a concussion. The more I thought about it, the worse our odds looked. I did what I always do in those situations—I stopped thinking before the odds convinced me to stop trying.

I jumped as high into the rafters as I could and yelled out to Greg, "Go low!" He dove at Baal's feet while I dropped from the rafters on his head, hoping to accomplish something besides getting cut in half by Phil's oversized toothpick. Baal was too fast for either of us, though, swatting us both out of the air like mosquitoes. Really big mosquitoes in Greg's case, but you get the idea.

I managed to adjust my course enough to land on a broken basketball backboard, and turned back to the fight to see Phil wading in with his sword. He and Baal were weaving a deadly ballet in the air over the gym floor, Baal's wing and Phil's shoulder healed enough to make the fight too evenly matched again. Thrust, dodge, thrust, slash, duck, repeat. It was almost beautiful to watch, except for our pressing need to help the angel and get Sabrina out of Hell. I made another mental note to ask Mike's Wiccan friend Anna about different planes of existence if I lived long enough to see her again.

I looked frantically around the gym for something heavy enough to hit Baal with, but other than a pile of shattered party decorations and an overturned apple-bobbing tub, there was nothing of any size lying around. Then my eyes lit on the still form of Bun-head, curled in a fetal position beside one set of bleachers. I yelled over to Greg "Make sure big ugly stays off me, I've got an idea!"

"How do you suggest I do that?" he yelled back.

"Keep Phil alive!" I dashed across the gym. Pieces of ceiling fell around us as Baal and Phil's battle raged on. We were going to have to finish this pretty quickly, or there wasn't going to be anything left of the gym.

I got to Bun-head, reached out and shook her shoulder. "Hey, lady. Janet!" I shook her harder, and finally she looked up at me and screamed. I forgot that I had my fangs on display, and that tends to worry humans, even ones that sometimes summon demons. I slapped her across the face, and she stopped screaming long enough to slap me back.

"What in the world is wrong with you, young man?" she asked tartly.

"Wrong with me? Lady, we don't have that much time. Anyway, do you know how to banish this big red bastard?" I pointed over to Baal, and she turned a really gross shade of pale green. I moved back a little, in case she was going to puke, but she got herself under control. Even as I moved back, I realized the irony of not wanting to get a little puke on me when I was covered in demon brains and blood both demonic and vampiric. But we all have our little hang-ups, and one of mine is being puked on.

"How would I know anything about banishing monsters?" She looked more confused than anyone who had caused this much trouble had any right to look.

"You're kidding, right? Lady, you frickin' *summoned* him! I would think that knowing how to put the genie back in the bottle would be one of the first things they teach you in Demon Summoning 101!"

"Demon summoning? What are you talking about young man? And what is wrong with your teeth?"

"We've got way more important things to deal with right now than my teeth. Like the fact that the big red guy over there is Baal, an Archduke of Hell, and that you summoned him, and now I need you to put him back where he came from because there is a very attractive lady cop that is currently hanging out in Hell, where Baal is supposed to be, because when he came here, she had to take his place down *there*. Are you getting this? *Hell*. An innocent woman in Hell."

I was pretty proud of the fact that I hadn't hit her yet, but she was running out of time before I started punching things, and she was the nearest target.

"I did no such thing, young man. I am a Christian! I merely called up the angels to assist me with a certain problem, and nothing more. I would never consort with demons! I won't even speak to agnostics!"

"What 'certain problem' were you calling angels to help you with?"

She didn't answer.

"Cancer? Are you sick? Do you have a sick kid?"

Still nothing.

"Were you praying for peace? Trying to bring soldiers home and bring those families back together?"

Not a peep.

"*Then what the hell was it?*"

"The lottery." She said it so quietly that I almost didn't hear her.

"What?"

"I asked the angels to help me win the lottery. It's up to $165 million, and I could use the money to do so much good."

"I bet you could. If you live long enough to collect and if there are any people left to help."

I couldn't believe it. A string of kidnappings, a zombie infestation, a pile of demon possessions, a parking lot full of trashed cars and a gymnasium that looked like Armageddon was just the opening act, and it was all for money. Root of all evil in-flippin'-deed. "When you called these 'angels' did you use a spell or pray?"

"I found a spell to communicate with celestial bodies. I used that." I heard a huge crash from behind me and chanced a look over my shoulder. Baal had thrown Phil through the DJ setup at the end of the gym and the angel was getting up, scattering CDs, turntables and speakers every which way.

"Well, great job, lady! Look how well that's worked out for everybody!"

"I didn't mean to!" She was almost crying as what she'd done started to sink in. I took a deep breath, looked back at where Greg and Phil were holding their own (barely), and settled myself down.

"I know. And you can make it right. Do you know how to banish this beastie?"

"I have no idea. I don't remember anything since Tuesday night. I was walking home, and all of a sudden I was asleep. I had the most terrible dreams, too."

Crap. Tuesday was when we fought the girl at Tommy's house. When Mike banished Belial, she must have followed the magic back to her summoner and taken her over. Bun-head remembered nothing since Belial took over and started trying to bring Daddy Dearest to Earth in earnest. That meant she wasn't aware when Baal was summoned.

"Stay here, then. And if that thing kills us, start running."

"Where will I go?"

"I don't think I'm going to care very much if I'm dead. If I croak, you're on your own. And maybe even if I don't croak."

I stood up, centered myself and got ready to jump back into the fight. Then, out of the corner of my eye, I caught a glimpse of something shiny. I'll admit that I'm easily distracted by shiny objects, but this time my "attention to detail" paid off.

At one side of the gym there was a little stage set into the wall, and at the front corners of the stage, one on each corner, were two flags. One was the standard American flag with an eagle atop the flagpole, but it was the other flag that caught my eye. I recognized it from playing softball for a Baptist church one summer in high school. It was the Christian flag, a red cross on a field of blue in the top left corner of a white flag. More importantly, the flagpole was eight feet tall and topped with a heavy gold cross. It looked like just the thing to smite an archdemon with. I looked around the gym quickly and saw no better option. It was time to see if this theory about holy objects really held.

I ran across the gym and grabbed the flagpole, pleasantly surprised when it didn't burst into flames at my touch. Okay, maybe vampires aren't all that unholy. What about demons? I yelled over to Greg, "Get high!"

He vaulted about fifteen feet into the air, and I chucked the flagpole at him like a javelin. He harnessed all of his vampire abilities, caught it on the fly, turned a somersault in midair, and dove straight down for Baal, cross first.

Phil saw what we were doing and launched into an all-out attack, thrusting and slashing with renewed fury. I had a brief second to think about how screwed we were if this didn't work, and then Greg was diving into the demon with his Christian flagpole/spear. As the flying vampire got close, the cross atop the flagpole began to glow, eventually bursting into white fire as it touched the demon. Greg buried the cross deep into the meaty part between Baal's head and shoulder, and the demon collapsed to his knees, screaming. Greg landed behind the beast and rolled clear, as Phil moved in for the kill.

He paused for a second, sword raised, and Baal looked him in the eyes. "Why, Zepheril? You could have been the greatest of us all."

Phil looked at him with something like pity and said, "Milton was wrong, Baal. It is infinitely better to serve in Heaven than to rule in Hell. I hope this proves that I've learned that lesson." Then Phil drew back his sword and sliced off the demon's head in the middle of the gym.

Chapter 36

After such a brutal fight, the aftermath was almost anticlimactic. There was no big explosion, no huge lightshow as the demon vanished into sparks, no great gaping maw opening in the earth to suck Baal back into Hell. All in all, it would have been much more impressive if it were designed for the Xbox. But real life, as weird as it is, still isn't a video game.

So the demon disappeared, to be replaced by a screaming Sabrina standing in the gym firing her pistol randomly around her. We all ducked, and she ran out of ammo without shooting anyone on this plane, so all was good.

I waited a minute before I stood up cautiously and said, "Sabrina? Are you okay?"

She looked at me, still holding her pistol, and said in a shaking voice, "Jimmy?"

"Yeah, it's me. Are you okay?" I repeated, more slowly this time.

"I . . . I think so. I mean, I'm back. I'm alive, or at least I think I'm alive."

"Trust me. You're alive. I can smell you."

She wrinkled her nose. "I'm sure I smell like Hell."

"Literally, but it beats being dead and smelling like zombie."

She laughed, which worried me a little. I always worry when a woman laughs at my jokes. When they're laughing *at me*, it's situation normal. But when they're actually laughing at my jokes, I look around for the camera crew.

"So, it was Hell? I didn't imagine that?" Sabrina limped over to one of the tables that had been scattered around for the carnival and sat down.

I followed her and stood beside her. I kept looking around, worried that we weren't quite done fighting for the evening. After all, it wasn't quite midnight, so I figured there was still a chance for everything to go to crap at the witching hour.

"Yes," I said simply. "I'm pretty sure you were in Hell."

"I believe it."

"What was it like?" She hesitated, and I added, "If you can talk about it, I mean."

"Yeah, I think I can. I was surrounded by those psycho little girls from the forest again, and no matter how many of them I killed, more of them kept coming. They swarmed me again and again, and when I finally thought they had killed me, I opened my eyes and I was standing there in the forest again, and they were all coming again. It was like *Zombieland* meets *Groundhog Day*."

She shivered, and I moved beside her and put an arm around her shoulders. "You know, Bill Murray was in both of those movies. It's clear you have a thing for my type."

She elbowed me in the gut, but she laughed a little. That was twice she'd laughed at my jokes. We were gonna need a hospital for her pretty damn quick. She was obviously concussed if she thought I was funny.

Then her smile died. "What happened here?"

I gave her an accounting to the point where Phil cut off Baal's head. When I got to that part, I stopped and yelled across the gym. "Hey, Phil!"

"Yes, James?"

I guess I'd acquitted myself well enough in the fight, I'd been promoted past *little vampire*. "Why did you help us?"

"I told you. Baal was a danger to us all."

"Uh huh. You're a fallen angel, right? Cast out of Heaven for picking the losing side in Lucifer's rebellion? Stuck here on Earth forever because you can't go to Hell and you'll never be allowed back into Heaven?"

"Never is a very long time, Jimmy-lad. And we're not given to see all the way to the end of time." Mike limped into the gym, one arm draped over Lilith's shoulder as she helped him to our table. "Even the worst of sinners is offered redemption, again and again."

Greg and Phil made their way over to us, as did Bun-head, who introduced herself rather shamefacedly as Janet.

"That's a nice fairy tale, Mike. Not necessarily true." I pulled a chair over next to Sabrina, and she didn't pull away. That's always a good sign.

"You made enough peace with your maker to come onto holy ground to fight a demon. Who's to say there's not hope for even a fallen angel?" I shook my head a little, but I generally defer to Mike on spiritual matters. After all, he's the one with the hotline to the Guy Upstairs, not me.

"Hey!" Greg's head snapped up. Even with his vamp healing, he looked rough. His fight with Belial took a toll. Greg had a black eye, which looked about three days old. Split lips were healing, but still seeping a touch. If he felt anything like he looked, then he felt like he'd been killed all over again. His eyes were clear, though, and something had obviously struck him.

"How did you get in here? And what about you?" He asked Phil, and then Lilith. "I thought you couldn't set foot on holy ground without bursting into flames or something."

"That was him. I'm not a fallen anything, little vampire. I can go anywhere I like. I just didn't want to get involved in your little mess." Lilith looked at all of us smugly, obviously pleased she'd been the only one who hadn't been possessed, nearly killed or beaten to a pulp by a demon.

Phil glanced over at Lilith, then sighed and let it pass. "I couldn't set foot on holy ground, but once Baal set the demons free and stepped out of the circle, the gym was no longer sanctified. The very touch of a demon corrupts any place that it alights, and only the holiest of places can withstand that touch. This place was not nearly holy enough to stay sacred with an Archduke of Hell walking around. Rescue became possible."

"And I guess Janet here could come in because she was still a human being, even if there was a demon driving the bus, so to speak. But why was Baal so disappointed in you? The boy was torqued." I wasn't sure he was going to answer me, but he and Mike exchanged a look, and then Phil took a deep breath and started to talk.

Chapter 37

"I suppose after sharing the field of battle, you've earned an explanation," Phil said. "Long ago, in the dawn of mankind, there was a war in Heaven. Lucifer and an army of angels decided that humans were being given too much rein over this world, and that God needed to be deposed. I was one of those angels."

"How'd that work out for you?" I asked. Greg elbowed me in the ribs and I shut up.

"Not well. We were defeated, obviously. The rebels who repented and promised to serve loyally were given their places back in the Host, while those of us who stood by our principles were cast out, forced to live among you worms as a constant reminder of exactly who the favorite children really were. And Lucifer was sent to rule in Hell. He took nine of his closest compatriots with him, and they became the Archdukes. Baal was one of them."

"Wait a minute," I interrupted. "Baal was once an angel?"

"Haven't you been listening?" Phil looked at me like a disappointed teacher, which is a look I was all too familiar with. I love getting put in my place by angels. It's like adding insult to insult somehow.

"Baal joined Lucifer in Hell, and I became one of the Fallen here on Earth. I watched your civilizations, as if the word were even applicable, rise and fall. I watched your societies mature and decay, and over time I came to realize that I had been not only a fool, but a coward as well." The angel stopped and took a breath. I got the feeling he'd been waiting a long time to tell this story, but hadn't had the right audience.

"I couldn't return to Heaven, and I couldn't go to Hell. I was trapped here until I could do something to warrant an audience with the Father again. I had to do something to make him notice me, to remember me, so I could tell Him . . ." Phil's voice trailed off and he blinked rapidly.

"Tell Him what, my son?" Mike asked, and I saw him as his parishioners must see him, as a wise man, a holy man. My oldest living friend almost glowed with an internal peace that made even me want to confess to him.

But we didn't have all night.

"That I'm sorry and I want to come home," Phil said quietly, shoulders tense and head bowed.

"Just ask Him," Mike said so gently I was afraid for a second that Phil was going to cry.

Phil fell to his knees right there in the gym, and Mike joined him. The rest of us followed suit, except for Lilith. Mike looked over at her, and raised an eyebrow.

"I don't kneel. Ever. To anyone. It's my thing." She sat down at the table, leaned back in her chair and propped her spike-heeled boots on the table.

"He knows," Mike said. "He knows." Then he took Phil's hand. "Now, Phil. Ask Him."

Phil looked up and one tear ran slowly down his cheek. He took a deep, shuddering breath and choked out, "Father, may I come home?"

I'd never seen Phil look contrite before. Of course, I'd never seen him cry, or fight a demon before either, so it was another night of firsts for me. Yippee, another learning experience.

"I think," Mike followed the angel's gaze with his own "all you ever had to do was ask." Then Mike put Phil's hands together and raised them straight over his head.

Nothing happened for a moment and then Phil began to glow with an incredibly bright, white light. I could only stand a few seconds of the glare, and even squeezing my eyes shut I knew I'd be seeing spots for a while. When the glow faded, I opened my eyes, and Mike was standing there, with no angel beside him.

Lilith looked around for a minute, and then muttered, "Sonofa*bitch*! He didn't leave me any instructions other than to take care of the club."

"What does that mean?" I asked. She treated me to a look that could kill someone who was actually living.

Lilith took a deep breath and said, "I owed Phil a debt. Since he didn't absolve me of it, I'll have to keep his business operations running until he does, or until the period of my service comes to an end. So I'm stuck here for a while."

"How long?" Greg asked. He kept trying to sneak peeks up her skirt as she leaned back in her chair, but he was about as subtle as a hand grenade.

"Five hundred years, minus time already served," Lilith answered.

"How much time have you served?" I asked.

She shot me another look. "Two weeks."

I looked around at Greg, Mike and Sabrina, and we all burst out laughing. After a few seconds, Lilith got up and left without so much as a good-bye. She did not strike me as a woman who was accustomed to being laughed at, which could go badly for us. Chances were we'd have to deal with her for the next few centuries.

Chapter 38

After our little chuckle, I sat up straight and looked at Janet. "So how do you plan to put all this right, lady?"

"What is there to put right?"

"What is there to—*what is there to put right?* Your little spell goes wonky and a passel of little girls end up kidnapped, a dozen zombies tear up most of Charlotte, a cop—"

"Detective," Sabrina put in.

"—detective gets sent to Hell and we trash an entire private school gymnasium. And all because you wanted to win the *Powerball!* That's what I mean, you nutjob!"

"You're asking for the impossible. I can't possibly do much to change things. But for starters I promise never to do magic again, even the kind that summons angels."

"Demons," I corrected.

"Well, I meant for it to summon angels. That nice man at the Career Day explained it all to me. The spell would summon the angels, who would perform three wishes for me—"

I held up a hand. "Wait a minute. What nice man at Career Day?" I had a sneaking suspicion I knew which "nice man" she was referring to.

"Mr. Arthur. He runs a chain of tire stores. We got to chatting about how school funding kept getting cut, and vocational education was getting hit worst of all, and he gave me a prayer book that he said would summon angels. But it didn't so I must have done it wrong! But I really wanted to help, doesn't that count for anything?"

Everyone around the table yelled in unison "NO!" I made a mental note to have a long conversation with the Tire King about the difference between angels and demons someday very soon.

Janet had the good grace to look ashamed, even if she didn't have a good answer. After a long moment, Greg broke the uncomfortable silence.

"Hey, look. The sun's going to be coming up soon, and this building is no longer what I would consider light-tight, so at least a couple of us would like to get home. The rest of you are welcome to crash at our place if you like, but we need to get going."

"I can't," Janet said. "I have to get home to Mr. Kibble. He must be frantic with worry about me."

"Don't worry. You weren't really invited. And who the hell is Mr. Kibble?" I asked.

"My Pomeranian. He's very high-strung and gets terribly nervous if I don't make it home in time for dinner."

"Whatever. Look, lady, I'm keeping an eye on you, and if I so much as see you buying the wrong color candles near the summer solstice, they'll have to identify you by your dental records. You got me?" I gave her my best intimidating stare, which was helped a little by the blood spattered all over my clothes.

She nodded and scurried out the door before I remembered that she might not have an intact car in the parking lot.

Then I couldn't manage to care. Oh well, now that she wasn't possessed by a demon, I figured the rest of her problems would pale in comparison.

"What about you two?" I asked, looking at Mike and Sabrina.

Mike shook his head, "I've got to get to the church for morning Mass, but I'll swing by later for lunch. I'll drive you, though. My car is still in one piece, and I moved it right up to the gym entrance."

"I'll come hang for a little while, as long as there's no biting while I nap," Sabrina said, standing and holding out a hand to me. I took it and she helped me up. I didn't really need it, but the feeling of her warm hand in mind wasn't something I was likely to pass up.

"No promises on the biting," I said as we started toward the waiting car.

Greg limped past us, leaning on Mike and yelled "Shotgun!" over his shoulder at us. I didn't mind.

"There's just one thing I don't understand," I said in a low voice as Sabrina and I walked down the steps into the parking lot. The eastern sky was barely beginning to lighten from black to deep blue, so it was definitely time to get rolling.

"Just the one thing?" she asked.

I punched her lightly on the arm, and she staggered a few steps sideways. Sometimes I forget that I'm not punching Greg.

"When you were taken, and Mike got thrown out of the gym, he mumbled something about you being an innocent."

"Yeah?" She had that look that women get when I'm about to ask something that'll get me slapped.

"And if I remember right, there were certain criteria for being a sacrifice to raise this demon, and one of them was a very specific brand of innocence."

"Yeah?" she repeated, and unlike Mike, Sabrina had obviously mastered the art of raising only one eyebrow. She was either daring me to go there, or warning me not to go there. *What to do? What to do?*

"So by being part of the sacrifice, does that mean . . ." I trailed off and Sabrina interrupted me.

"Let's put it this way, Jimmy-boy. If you finish the question, you'll never know the answer." She kissed me lightly on the lips, and we got in the car and rode off into the sunrise like good vampire heroes.

Book 2:

Back in Black

Chapter 1

A vampire and a cop walk into a bar . . .

I so wish that was a joke instead of my agenda for the evening, but we really were pulling into a bar parking lot. There were a lot of Harleys lined up out front of the club, and while that's usually a good sign for me, this wasn't my usual hangout. My comfort level was already low—this visit wasn't my idea, and my escort for the evening was Detective Sabrina Law, the exceptionally attractive investigator for the Charlotte-Mecklenburg Police Department who had helped me save the world from plunging into Hell a couple of months ago. And, until today, I hadn't heard from her after our bout of hero-for-hire. Not so much as a peep for eight weeks and four days, not that I was counting.

I looked around the parking lot, taking note of the still-running limo parked at the front door and the *click-click-click* of the cooling Harley engines parked behind it, and pulled my coat tight around me against the January chill. I didn't feel the cold—vampires don't feel cold, but nerves about whatever mess Sabrina had gotten me into were giving me a chill or two. I took a deep breath, held out my arm for my "date," and started across the asphalt toward our oh-so-sleazy destination.

The strip club formerly known as Heaven on Earth had been renamed Fallen Angel's when the last proprietor got his express ticket back to heaven punched. The apostrophe was in the correct place on the sign, but nobody knew that outside a select few supernatural types. Phil, the last owner, had really been a fallen angel, and Lilith, the immortal whatever-she-was who took over Phil's business operations when he left, had a wicked sense of humor. And a wicked sense of everything else.

When Phil had been around, the club had been pretty upscale as strip clubs went. A strict dress code had meant that Greg Knight, my partner in Black Knight Investigations, and I'd had to do laundry whenever we were on surveillance there. Under the previous management there had been more luxury cars in the parking lot than pickup trucks, and the girls had looked like they'd stepped off the pages of *Playboy*. Phil's attention to detail had helped set the tone, garnered the "classy" strip club customers.

More than the name changed when Phil left the place in Lilith's unwilling hands. Apparently the original "other woman" had lost a bet to Phil, chaining her to his business interests for five hundred years. I was around when Lilith figured that out, and she hadn't been happy. So she had surrounded herself with people more to her liking, which meant that Fallen Angel's catered to a slightly different clientele than it had when it was Heaven on Earth.

I looked at the bar and then the woman who'd be going inside with me. *One of these things is not like the other.* Detective Sabrina Law was going to stick out like a banana in a smokehouse, a fact that I tried to impress upon her when she showed up in my bedroom, yanking me from a particularly pleasant and very specific dream featuring her, a case of whipped cream, and three Daleks. Don't ask.

She shook me awake and waved her badge in my face, leaving me no doubt that I'd been talking in my sleep again, and that she'd heard me. She wasn't smiling when she looked down at me and said, "I need to see Lilith. You're going with."

I wasn't really any happier, because my best friend, roommate, fellow vampire and business partner chose that exact moment to barge in without so much as a knock on my suddenly revolving bedroom door.

Greg wore kneepads, a gas mask and an apron that said "Bite the Chef" with little cartoon fangs on a yellow smiley face. He topped off the outfit with elbow-length welder's gloves and thick rubber boots. Greg looked at me, then at Sabrina, held his toilet brush high above his head and announced in a muffled voice, "Bathroom's clean! We got a case! Be ready in a jiff!" Then he turned and waddled off into his bedroom to change out of his haz-mat gear and into his crime-fighting costume. An actual crime-fighting costume.

I watched my portly partner not close the door behind him and looked up at Sabrina. "Since you're obviously not here for a social call, you wanna wait for me in the den? There's beer in the fridge." I grabbed the corner of my sheet and started to sit up to get dressed.

Sabrina's eyes widened, and she turned to the door. "I'll be waiting. Don't screw around, this one's important."

Like the last one wasn't? Like a case where we saved Charlotte from becoming a literal Hell on Earth, wasn't important? I threw on a pair of jeans and a faded X-Men T-shirt, and a few minutes later we were rolling to Fallen Angel's.

Greg and I looked over the crime scene photos on the way to the club, and we agreed with Sabrina's instincts—it looked like there was a supernatural baddy running around Charlotte, and the best place to start looking was with Lilith. I kept trying to talk Sabrina out of coming inside as we pulled into the parking lot, but for a human, she was really, really obstinate.

I was crammed into the backseat of Greg's Pontiac GTO and really looking forward to getting out of the car. "Please don't stare at anyone, or anything. Just keep your eyes on the floor, or on the girls. That's usually safe. This isn't like the clubs you're used to visiting."

"I don't frequent many strip clubs, Jimmy, but I think I can handle myself," she said.

"No, you probably can't. Leave the badge and the guns here. Greg will keep the car running in case we need to make a quick getaway. The back door is to the left-hand side of the stage. It opens right out onto Morehead Street. If things get ugly, we hit the back door running. We'll cross the bridge on Morehead and meet Greg in the Time Warner building parking lot. You good with that, partner?"

Greg nodded. "Got it. I don't like that place."

"I don't either, but we gotta talk to Lilith," I replied. "If everything goes well, we should be out in fifteen minutes."

"And if it doesn't go well?" Greg asked.

"Keep the car running."

Greg shifted into neutral, and Sabrina and I got out of the car. She put her Smith & Wesson .40 service weapon in the glove box, along with a revolver she wore strapped to one ankle. I tossed my Glock 17 into the backseat, then followed it with a Ruger LCP in an ankle holster of my own. I reached under my jacket and stripped off a belt with two daggers in it, then unfastened the Velcro sheaths from my forearms and tossed those knives into the backseat as well.

I turned to see Sabrina staring at me. "What?"

"Nothing." She shook her head and turned to go into the club. We walked across the parking lot, and I watched Greg pull out onto the street. He turned right at the corner and drove a couple of blocks to the cable company parking lot. It was about a quarter-mile sprint from the back door of Fallen Angel's to the car, and I really hoped we wouldn't have to test my legs.

A pair of behemoths that looked like former NFL linebackers flanked the entrance, and one opened the door for Sabrina as we approached. "Serious bouncers," she whispered.

"Those weren't the bouncers," I said. "Those were just the doormen. The bouncers are inside."

We walked down a narrow hallway that was only dark if you were human. I could see the video cameras following our every move, and the two-way mirror along one wall. The hallway opened into a largish reception area with a dark wood desk in the center of the room. A small human woman sat behind it at a computer, a pretty blonde with not quite enough makeup to hide the bruise on her cheek.

Sabrina stiffened at the sight of the girl, and I put a hand on her elbow. I moved past Sabrina and put two twenties on the desk. "James Black and guest. I believe I'm on the approved list."

The girl smiled at me and tapped on the keyboard. "You are, sir. Enjoy your evening."

"Thank you." I stepped past the desk and a huge creature came forward from its hiding spot in the shadows of the room. It was about seven feet tall, looked to weigh about three hundred pounds of solid, blue-skinned muscle and had curling ram horns on top of its nominally human-looking face.

"Spread 'em," the ogre growled.

I held my arms outstretched obligingly, and it patted me down professionally. If the TSA hired ogres to do security, not only would they find anything people tried to smuggle onboard, nobody would ever complain. To their faces, anyway.

Sabrina stepped up and looked at the ogre. "Do you have any female security guards? I'd feel more comfortable with a woman patting me down. You understand, don't you?"

I stared at the floor, giving it everything I had to keep from laughing. The ogre looked down at the smiling detective and growled, "I am female. Now spread 'em."

I failed miserably at holding myself together and cracked up at the expression on Sabrina's face. She gave me a look that would have killed a living man and submitted to the frisking. A few more seconds, and we walked into the main body of the club.

Lilith had spared no expense in redecorating the club into some kind of strange blend between a biker bar and an H.R. Giger painting. The comfy leather couches were still along the walls, and there were several girls in various stages of undress writhing on men in something resembling time to the thumping bassline that pounded through the building. But the nice cabaret tables and chairs scattered throughout the room were gone, replaced by what looked like vintage Waffle House furnishings.

The clientele had taken a marked shift in focus as well. The bankers in suits and businessmen entertaining out-of-town clients were gone, replaced with biker types and burned-out rock n' roll roadies. But the part that had Sabrina's head on a swivel was the collection of monsters on display. There were ogres, a couple of weres of various species, a lizard-thing that I didn't know *what* the hell it was, and half a dozen variations of human magic-users, including a skinny dude sitting in a corner with a leather duster and a glowing staff. I gave him a long look, then turned away before I offended him. He could pull off the leather duster look. I never managed.

Another ogre stood just inside the door, the universal plain black T-shirt of bouncers everywhere stretched across the enormous azure landscape of his chest. He handed me a small sheet of paper.

"House rules," he grumbled.

I looked at the paper. That's exactly what was printed across the top of the page—House Rules. I read through them quickly, just to see if there was something about interrogating the other patrons on there, but they were basic strip club rules. Don't touch the dancers, pay for the dances or have your arms broken, blood rituals limited to the Champagne Room, no dark magic in public areas—the kind of thing you see everywhere. I folded it up and put it in my back pocket.

"Bad idea," the ogre grumbled.

I looked up at him, not understanding.

"Paper's magic. Burns up if you take it out of here. Burn your ass off. Might hurt."

I nodded and pulled the paper out of my pocket.

I handed it to him. "Why not give this to the next guy, then?"

He nodded and put the sheet back in the stack he was holding.

I led Sabrina to the bar that ran along the far wall of the club. The bar was the least populated section of the place, unless you count the strippers taking a break and the token crazy old dude that sits at the end of every strip club bar in America.

There was a brass rail following the curve of the bar up on the ceiling, and a slightly overweight girl was walking around the bar, shaking her shimmy in the zip code of the beat and trying to walk in her ridiculous heels. I did give her credit for her shoes, which spent a lot of time at eye level. I'd never seen stripper shoes with actual fish in them before, but she had a little tiny goldfish swimming around in each heel. She wore a frilly little miniskirt and a lacy white thong, and one garter full of dollar bills.

I motioned for her to come over, and when she knelt in front of me, I slowly slid a five into her garter. She leaned in to give me a kiss, and I shook my head. I leaned up and whispered in her ear, "There's five bucks. Now go away. I want to drink."

Her eyes went wide, then narrowed to slits, and she stood up and flounced over to the crazy old guy and started giving him all her best moves. There were two of them—moves, that is. There was a shimmy, and there was a bounce. Neither of them were terribly impressive, but I'd done my job. She was out of the way.

The music was thankfully a little lower at the bar, so I could almost hear myself think as I leaned across the damp wood surface and ordered two Miller Lites. The bartender was ridiculously hot, as was often the case in clubs of this nature. The women you most want to see naked are not the women who take their clothes off for money. This woman was about five-three, maybe a hundred twenty pounds, with dark brown hair streaked with pink and purple falling straight halfway down her back. Her shredded Metallica T-shirt was cut low enough in the cleavage and high enough around the waist that I wondered if the cuts would meet in the middle and give me a better look at the black bra playing peekaboo with the night air.

I slid the bartender a twenty and she gave me back eight bucks and two beers. I slid that over to her and said, "We need to see Lilith."

"Not for eight bucks."

"The eight bucks was just to get your attention."

"My attention costs more than eight bucks, too." She turned away and took drink orders from a couple of guys at the other end of the bar. Sabrina elbowed me and pointed to a skinny redheaded guy at the end of the bar. The bartender said something to him too quiet for even me to hear, and he vanished down a hallway. A few minutes later she came back to me and gave me and Sabrina a long look.

"What's with the cop?"

"She's with me. We need to see Lilith."

"Lil's not here."

"Bullshit. If she wasn't here you wouldn't have sent a message back to her with the skinny ginger. You would have played dumb and tried to get more money out of me. But she told you to send us back without telling you who we are, and that drives you nuts, because you're used to knowing what's going on, but Lilith doesn't trust her underlings with shit. Now, you want to keep playing games, or do you want to get your head out of your ass and maybe save your job in the process?"

The bartender turned about eight shades of pale, then flushed deep crimson. "I hate vampires. You bastards can hear a fly fart a mile away."

"You don't have to be a vampire, or a detective, to see you sent Ginger back to the back, sweetie," Sabrina said. "Now why don't you go get Lilith like a good girl, and you and I won't have to have a conversation about the vial of coke in your bra."

I followed Sabrina's gaze and noticed a little lump in the bartender's cleavage that I'd completely overlooked before. I was paying attention to other things. Like her eyes.

"Lil will kick my ass if I take strangers back there—"

I cut her off. "I know Lilith. And I've got a pretty good idea what she'll do to you if she ever heard you call her Lil. So be a good girl, get me another beer, on the house, and tell me which one of those dickweeds over there is going to take us back to Lilith."

She reached into the cooler and handed me a brown bottle of beery goodness, then pointed to the little ginger guy.

I walked over to him, Sabrina in tow, and said, "Let's go see the boss lady."

He turned and led us through the Champagne Room, where several dancers were gyrating in g-strings on humans, ogres, a werewolf in half wolf form and a couple of creatures that I didn't recognize. I followed the official etiquette of strip clubs and didn't look too closely at another dude's lap dance. I kept my eyes on our guide, who I quickly realized had hooves instead of feet, and a lot of hair poking out of the legs of his jeans.

"Are you a faun?" I asked when we got through the VIP lounge and he opened an unmarked door to the office area.

He spun around and looked up at me, his face flashing red. "*I* am a satyr. These are deer hooves, you city-bred moron, not goat hooves. And I am not some cuddly little Narnian shithead to be swayed from my queen by an apple-cheeked human girl. Satyrs are loyal."

I made a quick mental note to find out if Narnia was real. If it was, Greg would be thumping around in every closet in North Carolina for the next hundred years. "Yeah, from what I hear satyrs are loyal to whoever can get them laid the most."

"Sounds like human loyalty, then. Come on." The satyr turned and led me down a familiar hallway.

The hall ran behind the real VIP rooms, where things the cops weren't supposed to know about went on. When Phil ran the place, he kept stuff pretty above board. I didn't expect Lilith to follow that tradition. Mr. Tumnus led us to another unmarked door and knocked.

I looked at Sabrina and said, "Please, let me handle this."

Chapter 2

Of course, her only response was to shove me and Mr. Tumnus out of the way and open the door, stepping into Lilith's office without waiting for an invitation. I shook my head and followed, hoping I'd brought enough ammo.

Lilith was sitting behind the desk facing a wall of video screens. From what I could tell, there wasn't an inch of the club except the bathroom stalls that wasn't being constantly recorded. The images flickered on and off the screens almost faster than my eye could follow. Lilith seemed to have no problem following all the action, yet another indication that she wasn't quite human. Well, that and the fact that as Adam's first wife, she was something like eleventy bajillion years old.

She stood up when we stepped through the door and turned to face us. She was dressed in a porno producer's idea of business casual, a black miniskirt that was illegal in at least seven states and three Canadian provinces, a tight white dress shirt unbuttoned to her navel over a lacy black bra that showed through with every breath, and a pair of thick black-rimmed secretary glasses. Her jet-black hair was pulled back into a tight bun with a couple of strands artfully loosened.

Lilith came around the desk and gave me a hug that was as much lap dance as anything going on in the Champagne Room, a full-body hug that oozed her lushness all over my body. I put my arms around her and patted her back awkwardly, trying to minimize contact with the woman who was molding herself to my every angle like spray insulation. When she decided she had me sufficiently off my game, she glided past me and wrapped her arms around Sabrina, burying her fingers in the detective's brown curls and pulling Sabrina's face down to hers.

Sabrina shocked me by grabbing the immortal's bun with one hand and bending her over backward. My brain shut down as she pressed her lips to Lilith's and kissed her thoroughly, wrapping her free arm around the other woman's back and pulling Lilith hard to her. They kissed for a long minute, then Sabrina straightened up, leaving Lilith panting. Sabrina turned and walked to the bar, poured herself two fingers of scotch and took a seat in one of the chairs opposite the desk.

I collapsed into the other one, staring at her.

She gave me a little wink and looked up at Lilith. "Nice to see you again,

Lilith. How've you been?"

The immortal woman straightened and glared at the ginger satyr, who was still standing in the open doorway. "Why are you here, idiot?"

He paled and backed out of the door, pulling it closed behind him.

Lilith walked slowly back to her desk chair and sat, then switched off the monitors with the press of one button and turned to face us. "Lovely to see you again, Detective Law. I'll admit, I didn't expect that level of welcome from you. But I enjoyed it." She almost purred the last bit as she leaned forward on her desk and steepled her fingers.

"Don't get used to it, Lilith. But I knew you'd play games so I thought I'd better make my moves early if I was going to stand a chance."

"And what delicious moves they were, too."

"Thanks."

"Seems to have struck our poor Mr. Black here quite dumb."

"Nah, I'm just wondering when the pillow fight starts. Or if I should be somewhere making Jell-O for you girls to wrestle in." I sipped my beer to hide my shaking hands, and I kept my legs crossed.

"How quaint. I'm sorry, James. That's not on the menu for the evening. But if there was something else you desire of me?" Lilith arched an eyebrow at me, and her hand traced her neck slowly.

I felt my hands shake a little more, and realized that Greg was right, I could never drink from her again. I'd done it twice last fall, once to keep Phil from kicking my ass, and again to fight a demon. But something in her blood was more powerful than any drug I'd ever tasted. There was an old power there, maybe a direct line to the Creator, maybe a crazy old-school sex magic. I wasn't sure which, or if it was both and something else besides, but it gave me a rush like the purest coke I'd ever tried and hooked me faster than a West Virginia high-school kid gets addicted to meth.

Yeah, in the early years I tried every drug I could get my dead hands on. Coke is awesome for vampires—it makes us even faster than we already are, and we can go days without feeding. But the crash is god-awful, and that stuff's expensive. Most addictive substances don't have an effect on us, but Lilith's blood was different. I could hear it beating in her veins, and I *wanted* it, but I knew I couldn't ever drink from her again. If I did, I'd be lost.

Sabrina cleared her throat and I snapped back to reality. She was watching me with concern.

I waved her off, then wiped the sweat off my forehead. "No thanks, Lil. I'll pass on turning into your blood-junkie tonight. We just need information, and figured since you were now providing lap dances to most of the supernatural underworld, this would be a good place to start. Loathe what you've done with the place, by the way. Really ruined a crappy thing Phil had going."

Lilith's eyes narrowed, and a line appeared between her perfectly plucked eyebrows, the only wrinkle on an otherwise flawless face. "That bastard suckered me into five centuries of servitude and then went off to play harps or some other nonsense. And he left me with a money pit of a bar that was hemorrhaging cash. Do you have any idea how hard it is to *lose* money in a strip club? It's almost impossible, but that self-righteous prick was doing it."

"I think nowadays he's a righteous prick, Lil. What with the whole un-fallen angel thing and all." I took a long sip of my beer. Her hypnotic effect on me was lessened by her shrieking like a harpy.

"Screw you, Black. I had to expand our clientele to keep the doors open. And keeping his business operations thriving was part of the bet."

"What did you bet, anyway? What do immortals wager on? The Cubs? Because even taking the ultimate long view, the Cubbies suck," I said.

"Nothing so petty. We wagered on body counts. I took Hussein, he took Pol Pot, and no matter how many sons I tried to add in to the bet, the little Cambodian still outshone my Iraqis by a good twenty percent. So now I'm Phil's bitch for the next half eon. Then he runs off back to Daddy and sticks me here." She knocked back the last of her wine and refilled the glass as Sabrina and I watched her.

Lilith sipped her wine and turned to Sabrina. "So, what was it you wanted?"

I could see Sabrina push aside the concept of wagering on thousands of deaths and try to focus on the task at hand. Finally she killed her scotch, set the glass on Lilith's desk and started. "There's been a series of beatings in the city. I believe something supernatural is behind the attacks. I want to know what you know about them."

"Well, that's direct enough. Who has been attacked?"

"Six young gay men. They were beaten and left for dead in various places around downtown. What's so funny?"

Lilith was laughing quietly, then she gestured behind her at the bank of video monitors. "Should I turn the floor show back on? I think that out of all the places in Charlotte with loud music and alcohol, this is low on the list of must-see venues for the city's gay population. Really, Detective, this is a strip club. Men, straight men, come here to watch beautiful women take their clothes off. It's the last place gay men would be caught dead. Perhaps you should try Scorpio. I understand that's more the core clientele there. Or Chasers, if you could drag your open-minded boyfriend in there." She gestured at me, and I sat up a little straighter.

"I'm open-minded," I protested.

"He's not my boyfriend," Sabrina said in exactly the same tone of voice.

"Really?" Lilith purred at us. "Are you open-minded enough to go to a gay strip club?"

"If I have to for a case, yeah. It's not high on *my* list of Friday night hot spots, but I'll do what I have to do to catch a bad guy," I said, finishing my beer.

"Well, that's where I would start."

"I wish you'd *start* by answering the question," Sabrina said.

"Whatever do you mean, Detective?" Lilith actually managed a surprised and innocent look. I guess with a billion years to practice, she took an acting class once or twice.

"I didn't ask if gay men came to your bar. I asked if you knew anything about monsters beating up people in my city. So let's try this again—what do you know about these attacks?"

"Would you believe me if I said I knew nothing?"

"Probably not." Sabrina said.

"I know nothing, Detective." Lilith leaned back and crossed one leg over another in a slow, sultry motion designed to get every male eye in the room focused on her. It worked.

"Why don't I believe you?" Sabrina asked.

"Native distrust of those more attractive than yourself?" Lilith purred.

"The day I'm worried about competition from someone who watched the signing of the Magna Carta, I'll let you know." Lilith actually flinched, just for a second, then her calm smile returned.

"Very good, Detective. You may be worth my attention after all."

"And you already have mine." Sabrina gave her a little smile of her own. I just leaned back in my chair, trying to stay out of the line of fire.

Lilith put her glass down and leaned forward, her elbows on her desk. "I assure you, Detective, I know nothing about the attacks you're investigating. You have my word."

Sabrina abruptly stood up, and I followed suit, looking from her to Lilith and back again. "Thanks, Lilith. I appreciate the help."

"You owe me one, Detective."

"I'm not going to bring you up to my friends in Vice for all the things I saw in the Champagne Room that are technically illegal in North Carolina. I think that makes us even."

"You know how it is. It's so hard to get good help nowadays. Pan will show you out." She pressed a button under the edge of her desk and turned back to the monitors. She grabbed a remote that would send Greg into paroxysms of geek-joy and ignored us completely.

I took the opportunity to raid her bar for another Miller Lite, then followed the little ginger satyr back out into the main body of the club.

"Don't suppose you want to just hang for a little while and have a couple beers?" I asked Sabrina as we passed through the entrance to the Champagne Room.

She didn't even look back at me, just kept walking toward the door. I killed my beer as I walked, which is my excuse for not seeing the five-foot gargoyle when it stepped directly into my path.

"Oof!" All the breath went out of me in a rush as I almost ran over the little guy. I looked down and there was a gray face glaring up at me. He looked like he'd just flown down off the roof of a building, except there aren't any buildings in Charlotte old enough to have gargoyles. His skin was uniformly gray, with some seriously wicked-looking fangs and claws. His leathery wings stretched out six feet on either side of him, so just stepping around him wasn't an option.

"Sorry, dude. I wasn't paying attention. Totally my fault. I apologize." I tried to step to one side, hoping he'd get the hint and tuck his wings away. He didn't. In fact, he stepped to the side to get right in front of me again.

"What are you doing here, bloodsucker?" His voice sounded like rocks grinding together, and he bared a lot of fang when he talked to me. I decided I didn't like the little dude.

"I'm leaving. Or I would be if you'd get out of the way." Sabrina had stopped a few feet away and had her cell phone out. I really hoped she was calling Greg and wasn't just going to video the beating I was probably about to receive.

"Your kind aren't welcome here. We don't like you, and your Master doesn't like you coming here. Does he know you're here?"

"I don't know what you're babbling about, Rocky. I'm just trying to leave before I break anybody." I let a little menace creep into my voice as I looked down at the grumpy wall ornament.

"You threatening me?" he rumbled.

I sighed. There was no way I was getting out of this without punching something. Which was really just fine with me. That meeting with Lilith had set me a little on edge, and a good scrap seemed like it would be just what I needed. So I never bothered to answer the gargoyle. I just punched him in the nose.

His carved-out-of-stone nose. I heard something *crack* in my fist, and my knuckles split on his rocky visage. I yelled, he laughed, and a stone fist rammed into my stomach in a punch that sent me sprawling. The bouncers didn't budge as several other patrons came over to join in a rousing game of vampire piñata. When I rolled over onto my back I looked up at the gargoyle, a werewolf, what looked like a human except for the pointy ears and a lizard-man.

"This would be a really good time to learn that turning to mist trick I saw on *Buffy*," I said.

Then the kicking started. I actually didn't mind the kicking, because other than the gargoyle, they weren't doing much damage. It hurt, sure, but they were too close to get a good kick in. But after the gargoyle tagged my shins for the third time, I figured they weren't getting tired as fast as I was getting bruised, so it was time for Plan B.

My Plan B was almost exactly like my Plan A in that it involved punching things. Except in Plan B I didn't hit the rock guy in the face with my bare hand. I rolled over a couple of times, and took cover under a cabaret table. Then I came up swinging. I smashed the table into the gargoyle's face, which had a lot better effect than my first punch. He went down in a crash of wings and granite dust.

"That went better," Sabrina said from across the room. She had a were-rat in a headlock and was punching him in the snout. A couple more short jabs, and she dropped the furry bugger on his face, out cold.

I turned my attention back to my mob of supernatural chumps and saw Pointy Ears rushing at me with a knife. I picked him up over my head, threw him at the werewolf, and they collapsed in a tangle of fur and ears. I turned to the lizard dude and got slapped across the face with his tail for my troubles.

"What do you think this is, a Spider-Man movie?" I yelled. I grabbed his tail and pulled, intending to swing him around my head and throw him far, far away, but his tail came off in my hands. I stared at the lizard-man in shock, and he growled at me.

"Do you have any idea how long it takes to grow that back? Or how hard it is to balance without it?"

He came at me, and I decided it was only fair to give him his tail back. So I hit him upside the head with it. A lot. The tail was a good six feet long, and probably two feet around at the base, so when it connected with his face, he stopped cold.

"You hit me!" he said.

"Yeah. That happens in bar fights. Are you new at this?" I reared back and clocked him in the face with his tail again.

"That hurt!"

"That's kinda the point. That whole kicking me while I was down thing didn't tickle, just, you know, FYI."

"Oh. Sorry about that. I thought it was . . . I dunno, part of the show. Like a lap dance, only violent."

"No. This is a fight. A real fight. You're not on *Jackass* or anything like that."

"Oh. Well, what am I supposed to do?"

I sighed, spun him around and shoved him at Sabrina. "Please kick this guy's ass for me."

"Not a problem," she said, planting a foot solidly in the lizard-man's groin. He went down like a sack of potatoes, and I turned away, figuring Sabrina had him handled.

Good thing, since the werewolf and elf (or whatever) had disentangled themselves and were coming at me from opposite sides. They sprang at me, so I sprang straight up. It was like something out of a Saturday morning cartoon. I grabbed a rafter, they smacked into each other and immediately went at each other's throats.

I dropped lightly down to the floor and observed the mess they were making, grabbing bottles off random tables to bash each other with, knocking over chairs, interrupting commerce, the whole nine yards. A couple of ogres were finally moving in their direction when I turned back toward the exit.

And ran straight into a fist of stone. The gargoyle had struggled to his feet and nailed me with an uppercut that almost took my head off. I flew backward a good ten feet to land flat on my back on the stage. A leggy blonde with a huge dragon tattoo on her back was spinning around the pole as I slid underneath her, completely across the stage to land on my hands and knees. I needed about half a second to get my breath back.

Then the gargoyle landed with both feet right on my shoulder blades and drove me into the cheap carpet by the stage. I learned a couple of life lessons in those few seconds. First—gargoyles are really heavy for their size. Must have something to do with being made of rock. Second—strip clubs don't vacuum the floor by the stage nearly as often as you really want them to. I felt every one of my upper ribs crack under the gargoyle's feet, and I screamed like a girl. Fortunately for my manly reputation, I couldn't be heard over the screaming of the actual girls.

The gargoyle hopped off my back, and I rolled over. I looked up at his grinning granite face and found myself laughing.

It had just been that kind of night. I thought I'd be able to help Sabrina with something simple, spend a little time with her and maybe get a kiss out of the deal. Instead I ended up flat on my back with a bunch of broken ribs in the middle of a destroyed strip club with a gargoyle ready to stomp my face flat.

"What are you laughing at, asshole?" He reached down and dragged me to my feet. "Well, at least you'll die happy." He pulled back his fist for one more massive punch, and then his ear disappeared. He dropped me and clapped one hand to the side of his head, then turned to look for the new attacker.

My partner, Greg Knightwood III, stood six feet away holding his favorite pistol, a Beretta Px4 Storm with stainless steel slide. The gun glinted in the flashing lights of the club as he leveled it at the gargoyle's head. "Wanna see what else I can shoot off?"

"My ear! You wrecked my ear! You asshole!"

"You wrecked my partner. I think we're even," Greg said.

An ogre came up behind him and started to reach for the gun. Sabrina, newly rearmed by my partner, pressed her Smith & Wesson to his ear and smiled.

"Now, now. We're leaving. But you lay a hand on my friend, and there will be some new stains on this carpet." She smiled as she said it, and I think that was the part that really worried the ogre. It sure scared the hell out of me. I shook my head and headed for the door, leaning on Greg for support. I hadn't made it three steps when Lilith appeared in front of me.

"Where the hell do you think you're going?" she demanded.

"I think I'm going home. I think I'm going to drink about six pints of blood, then about twelve beers, and then I'm going do like the myths say and sleep the whole goddamn day away because every rib is busted, I think one arm is dislocated and I'm pretty sure I broke about eleven bones in my hand punching that rock-headed son of a bitch back there. Any other questions?"

"Who's going to pay for all these damages? You wrecked my club, Black, and that doesn't come cheap."

I lost it. That's the only way I can explain going off on Lilith like I did, because most days she scares me silly. But I was in pain, a lot of pain, and my night was *not* going the way I'd hoped. I was pretty pissed about it.

"I didn't wreck your club, Lilith. Your asshole patrons wrecked your club. You know, the ones that started a fight with *me*. The fight your bouncers didn't do anything to stop. The fight you watched on your little video monitors until it was over and you could come out and make a scene. I don't know what kind of beef you guys have with vampires around here, and I sure don't know who this Master is y'all keep talking about and I don't give a shit. We're leaving. And if you want to try and stop me, we can find out just how damn immortal you are right here, right now. So, you wanna get outta my way, or you wanna dance?"

Lilith looked up at me, mouth hanging open. I guess it had been a matter of centuries since anyone had really pushed back at her, and she had forgotten how to handle it.

Then in between eyeblinks, she was pressed against me, looking up at me with eyes of fire. "Oh, we'll dance, little vampire. We shall definitely dance. But not now, and not here. You may leave. Unmolested . . . if you like. But you owe me, little vampire. And I always collect on my debts." Lilith gave me a smile that started a fire in my toes and seared me all the way to the top of my head, while simultaneously sending chills down my spine.

I motioned for Greg to help me walk, and we headed for the exit. Greg tossed Sabrina his keys, and she went on ahead of us as he half carried me out of the club.

Once we were out on the sidewalk with no one following us, I said to Greg "Thanks, pal. I don't know what I would have done without you in there."

"Probably died a horrible death. Again."

"Yeah, probably. Hey, how did you know to shoot the gargoyle's ear off to get his attention?" I asked as we walked across the bridge to where Sabrina waited with the car.

Greg didn't answer, and didn't look at me for a long moment.

I pressed. "Come on, buddy. That was really good. I mean it. I just want to know where you learned about gargoyles and how you knew that you could shoot off little parts of it even if you couldn't hurt the body."

"I didn't."

"Didn't what?"

"I didn't know all that about shooting its ears off."

"Then why did you shoot its ear off?"

"I was aiming for the back of its head. But an ogre jostled me, and I missed."

I opened my mouth to freak out on him, but Sabrina rolled up in Greg's car just then. She pulled up alongside us and opened the doors.

"Get in." She said, moving around to the passenger side. I slid into the backseat and lay down as best I could. Greg had a towel behind his seat, because he's a hoopy frood that way, so I tried to put the bloodiest parts of me on the towel to save the upholstery.

"What's up?" Greg asked Sabrina.

"I just got a call while you were in there. There's been another attack. It's just a few blocks away. Let's go."

"What's the rush?" I said as we peeled rubber out of the parking lot.

"The victim. He's my cousin."

Chapter 3

A narrow alley separated the main branch of the public library from the arts center that had once been the First Baptist Church. Now labeled Spirit Square, the old sanctuary was more likely to see an acoustic concert than a choir singing. But tonight it was blue lights instead of bluegrass music as half a dozen police cruisers and a pair of ambulances crowded into the tight space between the buildings.

Greg pulled his car into the small parking lot, and we climbed out and headed into the alley. Sabrina flashed her badge at the uniform guarding the scene, and we were in the middle of a crime scene. Again. But this time we hadn't caused any of the damage.

Sabrina hit the alley and headed straight for a tall black man in an expensive coat. He did not look happy to see us, so I waved Greg over to the side, and we stopped well out of human earshot, which of course was plenty close for us to hear every word.

We picked up the conversation a couple of sentences in, but it was clear that this guy was some kind of boss, and he totally didn't want us to be there.

"I understand your hesitation, sir, but these guys have some resources that we don't have. They have connections within the community to people who are . . . reluctant to speak with the police," Sabrina said to the tall man, who I guessed was her lieutenant.

"I appreciate that, Detective, but it's not your call to make."

"Then whose call is it, sir?" Sabrina was getting upset, and I could tell that her personal relationship with the victim was not going to do her any favors with her boss. "Either I'm the lead on this case or I'm not. And if I am the lead, then my resources are mine to do with as I see fit. If I'd rather hire a couple of investigators outside the department than just line the pockets of the same snitches all over again, I should be allowed the freedom to do that. And if I'm not . . ."

I decided Sabrina shouldn't really give her boss that option, especially judging from the stormy look on his face, so I barged in, feigning ignorance of anything I shouldn't have been able to overhear. "Detective Law? I was able to reschedule our other client. We'd be happy to do whatever we can for you on this case. Oh! Excuse us. Greg and I didn't realize this was a private conversation."

I extended my hand to the man, who looked at it just a second too long before shaking it with his expensive gloved one. "You must be . . . ?"

"I'm Lieutenant Joseph McDaniel. I assume you're the *private investigators* we've heard so much about."

Someday I'll meet someone over the age of twelve who doesn't say "private investigator" like it's a venereal disease, but I doubt they'll work in law enforcement.

"Well, sir, I can't vouch for what you've heard, but we're here to help any way we can." I put on my best aw-shucks face and tried not to look like I could drink every drop of blood in his oversized frame without batting an eye. Not that I thought he'd recognize that look.

"So what can we do to help, Detective?" I didn't put too much extra emphasis on "detective," but I made it pretty plain who we were here for. McDaniel's eyes flashed a little, and I could tell my subtle dig wasn't lost on him.

Sabrina led Greg and me over to one side of the alley as McDaniel made his way back to the main street where all the reporters were waiting. "Here's where it happened, at least the last of it." She indicated a wall of the library with blood smeared at least eight feet off the ground. "It looks like he was held high against the wall somehow and pummeled. The bloodstains and spatters are high."

"Maybe the guy that attacked him moonlights for the Bobcats. But those spots are high even by NBA standards," Greg wisecracked. I kicked him in the shin. "Sorry."

"How is your cousin?" I asked once the boss man was out of earshot.

"They're pretty sure he'll live, but they don't know if there's going to be brain damage. He was beaten so badly I didn't recognize him. They only knew it was Stephen when they looked in his wallet."

Just then a distraught young man ran into the alley and headed straight for the crime scene. He was well dressed, attractive and slender, with perfect hair, and tears were pouring down his face.

He got to the mouth of the alley and froze. "Sabrina?" he asked.

Sabrina turned and stared at him. "I'm sorry, sir. Do I know you?"

"I'm Alex. Alex Glindare. I'm Stephen's husband. You're his cousin Sabrina, right? I recognize you from old family pictures."

Sabrina got that deer-in-headlights look, and her head swiveled from cop to cop trying to see if anyone had heard this little tidbit.

"I gotta take care of this," I muttered to Greg.

"Take care of what?" my socially inept partner asked.

"If her supervisor knows that Sabrina has a personal relationship with one of the victims, she'll be off the case in a heartbeat. I need to quiet this guy down. You see what you can find out from the crime scene guys while I talk to him.

Everything about Alex was the picture of a modern young gay man whose partner just became a statistic. He had on a long dark wool coat over a nice suit, and his shoes probably cost more than my entire ensemble. His wardrobe screamed "bank vice president," but the tears threatening to spill down his cheeks shouted "terrified spouse."

I put an arm around his shoulders and steered him back the way he came. "I'm Jimmy, and I'm a detective. I'm here to help. So you're Stephen's partner?" I didn't bother to add the "private" to the "detective," since the longer he thought I had some official capacity, the more information he was likely to give me.

"Husband. We were married in Boston last year. Where is he?"

"He's at Presbyterian Hospital, probably still in surgery. We can get someone to take you over there as soon as you answer a few questions for us, okay?"

By now I'd gotten him to the back of an ambulance and had him sitting down on the bumper. His eyes darted around the scene, still looking for his partner while the blue and red lights painted lurid shadows down the brick alleyway. I motioned for a paramedic to bring over a cup of coffee and sat there with my arm on his shoulders until he pulled himself a little more together.

After a minute he stopped the worst of his shaking, and I asked, "Are you okay? Can I ask you a couple of questions now?" He nodded, and I went on. "What's your name?" I figured I'd start with some softballs and see how it went from there.

"Alex Glindare."

"Where were you tonight?" I knew this guy could no more cause the kind of carnage I saw in the alley than I could be a Coppertone girl, but the question had to be asked.

"I was working late. I'm in acquisitions for Wells Fargo, and you might have heard that we bought this little bank a while back." He jerked his thumb from one skyscraper to another. I knew something about banks buying each other all over town, but since I'm more of a stuff-cash-in-my-mattress kind of guy, I took him at his word.

"And where was Stephen?"

"He had rehearsal. Down the street. He was going to come meet me at the office when he was done." Alex pointed down Tryon to the Center for Dance, the new headquarters of North Carolina Dance Theatre.

"Do you know when rehearsal was due to be over?" I was trying to keep the questions simple, so he didn't have to push too hard to answer, but still felt like I was giving him some attention. Since I knew he had nothing to do with this, I could only hope that by running interference with the spouse, I was freeing Greg and Sabrina up to do the real investigating.

"He was supposed to finish up around ten, then walk down to meet me. I didn't even look up until after eleven, and when I saw what time it was, I freaked out and started calling him. His phone went straight to voice mail, so I decided to see if he was grabbing a drink at Rock Bottom or Fox & Hound. Then I saw this, and they told me a dancer had been attacked, and . . . we do this all the time, and nothing like this has ever happened."

I gave him a minute to pull himself together before starting in on the more direct questions. "Do you know anyone who would have any reason to hurt Stephen? A jilted former lover, perhaps, someone he beat out for a part in a show, anything like that?"

He took a minute to think about it before answering. I had to give him that. Most spouses in this situation sanctify the injured party, and all of a sudden a wife-beating SOB with a twelve-pack-a-day Miller habit becomes a choirboy who helps little old ladies cross the street.

"No. We've been together for more than five years now, and I'm pretty sure he's never cheated on me, and I've never cheated on him. And as far as competition at work goes, somebody might put Icy Hot in his dance belt, but I can't see a modern dancer beating someone almost to death." He gave me a wry smile. "Stereotypes exist for a reason, Detective. Gay men aren't all sissies, but we're not usually beating people up in alleys, either."

He had a point. I didn't know a whole lot about Charlotte's gay culture, but I couldn't imagine a guy putting another guy in the hospital by beating him with a ballet shoe.

"All right, Mr. Glindare, that's all we need for now. Would you like one of these officers to drive you over to the hospital, or do you think you can make it there safely on your own?"

"I'll be all right. Just, please, catch the bastard that did this to Stephen."

"We'll do everything in our power, sir." I didn't bother to mention that our power included a few things not normally in the police arsenal, but I shook his hand and headed back over to Sabrina and Greg.

Chapter 4

Sabrina and Greg were back at the blood smear with a short balding man with thick glasses who was pointing some kind of laser measuring device at the wall. Just eyeballing it, it looked like somebody had picked the victim up and slammed him against the wall a few times. Only problem with that scenario was that the bloody bricks were eight feet off the ground. So either the attacker brought a ladder to a mugging, or we were playing in the supernatural world again. Sabrina introduced me to the blood spatter expert, whose name I promptly forgot, and motioned me over to the side. Greg stayed behind to geek out over all the buttons and LEDs on the man's toys.

"What did the partner say?" she asked.

"Husband," I replied absently, going through my mental notes to prepare the recap.

"Huh?" Sabrina stopped cold and looked at me for the first time since we got to the alley. Her eyes were tinged with red, and I was pretty sure it wasn't from the wind.

"Husband. They were married out of state last year."

"Okay, what did the husband say?" Her voice was tight and there was a sharp line between her brows that I'd never seen before. I stepped closer, but she backed away, like a skittish animal.

I kept my voice low and even, trying to play it cool. "You okay?"

"No."

"You wanna talk about it?"

"Not really."

"Okay, but I'm here if you change your mind." I held out a handkerchief. "And stop drying your eyes on your scarf, you're getting mascara on it."

"You weren't supposed to notice that."

"I'm a detective, Detective." I gave her a lopsided grin. "I'm supposed to notice things."

She looked at me then, and it might have been my imagination, but I thought that line between her eyebrows might have been a little less deep than a few moments earlier. "Thanks. I appreciate it. Now, what did the partner—husband—say?"

"He doesn't know anything, nobody would want to hurt your cousin, the victim walked alone this way fairly often, blah, blah, blah."

"Kinda what I figured. There's not going to be anything here of any use, either. At least there hasn't been at any of the other scenes."

"So now what?" Not being well versed in police procedure I didn't know if we all had to stand outside for the rest of the night in freezing weather, or just her. Like I said, the cold didn't really bother me and Greg, but with no blood of our own, it took a long time to warm back up after being outside for a while.

"We go to the hospital."

"Good deal, I'm getting a little peckish." Even if my blood hookup didn't work at the hospital, they were good sources of nutrition for so many reasons.

"Oh. I guess I woke you up before breakfast, didn't I? Sorry about that. But you're not going to—"

I cut her off before she had to ask. "I've got a guy who hooks me up out of the blood bank."

"So do you go down there and buy a pint, or what?"

I wasn't sure how much I wanted to get into the details of the bloodthirst with Sabrina, but if it took her mind off her injured cousin, I'd give it a shot. "The human body holds about ten pints of blood. My body doesn't make any blood. I need to replace all ten pints at least every three days, preferably every two. And for me to be at full strength, I need ten pints daily."

"Wow. I had no idea." She looked a little pale as the red and blue flashing lights played across her face.

"Fortunately, most people don't. Now you have some idea why blood banks are always running short, even though they're constantly doing blood drives. It's not just humans and hospitals that are getting that blood. It's vampires too. And some probably aren't as thrifty as me and Greg."

"That must get expensive, and what do you do if your guy takes a vacation? Do you have to go back to . . . you know?"

"Eating on the hoof? Not always. Our guy has a nice little network of assistants and backups, and there are other places to get blood if we really need it. But sometimes, if supply gets tight, we have to hunt. Greg refuses, and he learned some kind of Zen yoga trick that lets him hibernate until the flow is restored, but I'm not against grabbing take-out from time to time."

"I guess it's just a little unnerving hearing you talk about it like that, like it's nothing." She wrapped her arms around herself a little tighter, whether from the chill or the topic I wasn't sure.

I kept my voice soft, "You guys make blood all the time. We don't. It takes you about twenty-four hours to replace a pint of lost plasma, and about a month to replace that many red blood cells. And you'll never miss it. So as long as I'm not drinking more than a pint or two at the most, the worst thing that happens is my donor feels a little woozy when they wake up. I try not to drink from anybody that looks like they're about to drive anywhere. I don't want to cause an accident. And in a few days, they're good as new. But if I don't eat, it's bad for everybody. I will get weak, then I'll get a little nuts, then I'll get really nuts, then I'll turn into a monster. Then I'll eat, with no regard for leaving anything behind, and then we've got a bigger problem."

"A new vampire."

"Yeah, a new vampire. If I go nuts and drain somebody completely, unless I take precautions, they're coming back. And most of the time, we don't want that."

"Most of the time?" She looked at me questioningly.

"Okay, I can't think of a time that I'd want to turn somebody, but it might happen. But yeah, we don't want that. So sometimes I go out for dinner. I don't go after anyone that's been fed on recently, at least as far as I can tell."

"But you guys aren't the only vampires in town, are you?"

"I'm sure we're not. There are too many of all other sorts of critters running around for us to be the only vamps, and you heard the goon in the club tonight talk about vampires and some kind of 'master.' But I don't know any others."

"And don't really want to meet any," Greg said, joining us. "Your Dr. Fishbein was very enlightening, Sabrina. As we suspected, the majority of the attack took place elsewhere, then the victim—"

"Stephen," Sabrina said in a small voice.

Greg toned down the professorial tone a bit and continued.

"Sorry, Stephen was brought here and dumped. But there was an element of the attack that took place in the alley. Apparently his head was held at nearly eight feet off the ground and beaten severely against the wall. I asked Dr. Fishbein to speculate on what could have done such a thing, but he was reluctant to do so." Greg looked a little chastened, like the blood spatter guy had spanked him over something.

"Let me guess," said Sabrina, affecting a hunched posture and nasal quality to her voice "I do not *speculate*, Mr. Knightwood. I leave that to the *detectives*."

Greg looked relieved. "Yes, exactly. I wondered what it was that he has against detectives, but I didn't want to stick my nose in where it didn't belong."

"There's a first," I said.

Sabrina snorted, and I looked over at her. It was good to see her smile again, even for a second. "He's failed his pistol qualifications seven times. It's the only thing keeping him from coming into the department and moving quickly to a gold shield, so he's a little bitter. Don't let him bother you. We've got bigger issues."

"Like what?" Greg asked as Sabrina walked past him to the car.

"We gotta go to the hospital to talk to the victim," I said, following her.
"Oh good," he exclaimed, digging for his car keys. "I'm a little hungry."

Chapter 5

Sabrina got even more withdrawn as we neared the hospital. Greg dropped us off at the front door, then went to try to find parking. Sabrina and I walked in, and the disinfectant smell of the place almost knocked me over. Hospitals weren't my favorite place when I was alive, and having enhanced senses has done nothing to endear them to me, despite the fact the place was now my main grocery store. The smell of fake lemon, ammonia and death permeates every inch of the place, and no matter what time of day or night I arrive, it's always too bright, too loud and too sterile for my taste.

I cracked a couple of lame jokes to try to lighten the mood, but nothing helped the cold shoulder I was getting. Sabrina was obviously worried about her cousin, but I felt like there was something else going on. As we walked past the nurse's station on the way to Stephen's room, I grabbed her arm and pulled her to a stop.

"What's going on?" I asked in a low voice. I didn't want a huge scene if we could avoid one, but I was not going in that room without all the information.

"What do you mean? There's nothing going on, it's just a case." She didn't look me in the eye, which is generally a good idea with vampires, but Sabrina was immune to our mojo somehow.

"Sure," I said, sarcasm dripping from my words, "It's just a case where the victim is your cousin and for some reason your heart is beating twice as fast heading to his hospital room as it was at the very bloody crime scene. So do you want to tell me what you're afraid of, or do you want to keep trying to BS a guy who can hear the very blood in your veins?"

Sabrina looked up and down the hall, and seeing no one, pulled me to a sitting area by the elevators. Greg came off the elevator just then, and I waved him over. She took a deep breath, and then said, "I wasn't telling you everything."

"Wanna move on to the things I didn't already know?" I shot back.

She took another deep breath, dashed a tear away with the back of one hand, and went on. "Stephen isn't just any cousin. He was my best friend growing up. He was like my brother."

I leaned back against the wall. "And you haven't told anybody in the department because . . ."

"Because they'd throw me off this case so fast it would make your head spin, and I'm the only detective that cares enough to actually try to find out who's doing this."

"Not to mention the only one with the appropriate extra-curricular resources to actually get anything done."

"And that."

"What else?" I asked, leaning in to make sure we weren't overheard as a nurse wheeled a cart of expensive-looking equipment past us.

"What do you mean?" Sabrina doesn't do the wide-eyed innocent look very well.

"Really? You're still going to try to lie to someone who can read your blood pressure from ten feet away?" I put a hand on her shoulder and looked in her eyes, no mojo. "Tell me. I'll do anything I can to help. And I won't even be a smart-assed jerk about it, I promise."

"Stephen wasn't exactly the golden child in our family. His parents were—are—very Southern, and very Southern Baptist." She looked from Greg to me to see if we understood what she was saying. Having grown up around here, we got it perfectly.

"So you're saying that he wasn't exactly welcome for Thanksgiving once it became obvious that he wasn't ever going to bring home any grandchildren," I said.

She put her head in her hands and talked to the floor. "Exactly. Stephen came out when we were teenagers, and it didn't go over well at school. He got beat up a lot, but it was even worse at home."

"His parents beat him for being gay?" Greg asked furiously. My partner is a real champion of the downtrodden, having gone through life as an overweight comic book nerd. Now that he's a super-strong, super-fast overweight comic book nerd, he's gotten a little self-righteous about it.

"No," Sabrina said. "They never laid a hand on him. At all. I don't think my uncle even spoke to Stevie for the last two years he lived at home. They just ignored him, pretended like they didn't have a son, and when he turned eighteen, they kicked him out."

"Just like that?" I asked.

"Yeah. He came home from a summer dance clinic to find all his belongings in boxes on the porch and the locks changed."

"That's pretty awful," I said. "But what does that have to do with you?"

"Because he called me that night. When his folks kicked him out, he called his favorite cousin Sabrina to see if he could stay with me, just until he found a place."

"So how long did he stay?" I asked.

"I didn't pick up the phone. I was still in school and needed my dad's money to cover my apartment. I knew if I helped Stevie out, my parents would cut me off. So I didn't answer. I haven't seen him since."

She still hadn't looked up, and I suspected she was afraid of what she'd see on my face.

I reached down and took her hand. "How long has it been?"

"Nine years. We were so close, it felt like I cut off my arm to abandon him like that, but I did it. And now he's lying in there hurt and I'm scared to go see him because . . ." Her words trailed off. She took a deep breath, and shoved her emotions back under control.

"Because you're afraid he'll hate you for leaving him out in the cold." I made my voice a little hard, and it had the desired effect.

Her face snapped up, and she looked at me in a sort of shock.

I went on, "He might, you know. But it's more likely he still loves you and has just been waiting for you to grow up enough to be a part of his life again. Now let's go in there and see what we can do to help him."

"How'd you get so smart all of a sudden?" Sabrina asked as she wiped her eyes and got to her feet.

"He's older than he looks, remember?" Greg chimed in. "You don't live this long without picking up a few things."

"Well, technically, you didn't live all that long." Sabrina laughed a little.

"True, but you can still learn a few things walking around dead. Now let's go have a little family reunion." I took her arm and led her down the hall to her cousin's hospital room.

Chapter 6

Stephen was unconscious, and it was probably for the best. His face looked like something that had been dragged along I-77 behind a truck for a couple of miles, and then beaten with a meat tenderizer. He had tubes coming out of every visible orifice, and three or four bags of different substances dripping into his arms. The beep-beeping of his heart monitor was steady, but I was alarmed to see the respirator pumping away. His skin had a greenish tinge to it, like nothing I'd ever seen before.

Sabrina pulled a chair over to his bedside and sat down in it, taking her cousin's hand.

"Stevie?" she asked in a small voice. I heard a little tremble, and looked up at her. The look on her face was pure murder, and I really didn't want to be the guys that hurt her cousin when she found them.

Greg and I tried very hard to be invisible while she had a moment with her cousin.

"Stevie, baby, it's Sabrina. I'm here now, little buddy. It's gonna be okay. I promise, Stevie, I'm gonna find whoever did this and I'm going to make them pay. Nobody's ever going to hurt my Stevie again, I swear to God." She put her head down on the back of his wrist.

I nodded to Greg that we should give her a minute, and we headed out into the hall.

"Did you smell that?" I asked Greg as soon as the door shut.

"Yeah, that was not the typical hospital disinfectant funk in there. It was some kind of floral smell, but something nasty under it, like decay. I've never smelled anything like it." Greg has the super-sniffer of the group.

We headed down the hall to the waiting room and almost ran face-first into a scowling Alex Glindare.

"Alex," I said when we had all recovered from our near-collision. "What's wrong? I mean, I know what's wrong, but you look pissed. Has something else happened?"

"No, I'm fine," he said in a tone that made it pretty obvious he was anything but fine. "Just a run-in with a busybody nurse. It happens."

"Oh," said Greg. "She didn't want to tell you anything because you're not family in her sense of the word?"

Sometimes my partner is really perceptive, something that's easy to overlook when he wraps himself in black spandex, which happens more often than it should.

"Exactly." Alex took a deep breath, squared his shoulders, and looked down at the floor for just a second. Once he had himself back under control, the questions poured out of him in a rush. "How is he? Is he awake? Did he tell you anything?"

"Whoa, pal. Slow down a little. He's still unconscious. Detective Law is in there with him right now, but I doubt she's learned anything else."

"Detective Law? You mean Sabrina?"

I nodded, just as Sabrina came out around the corner, her hand resting on her gun. I knew she was looking for something to shoot, and I didn't blame her. She drew up short and put on her professional mask when she saw who we were talking to.

Alex cut her off before she could say anything. "You look a lot different than in your ninth-grade yearbook, Detective."

Sabrina smiled a little before saying, "I told Stevie to burn those things. It's a pleasure to meet you, Alex."

"You, too, Cousin Sabrina. I just wish it were under better circumstances."

They stood there staring at each other for a second before I lost all control of my mouth again. "Well are you two going to hug it out so we can get on with the investigation, or would you like to just stand here in the hallway and cast meaningful glances at each other all night?"

Sabrina studiously ignored me while Alex actually laughed. He then looked around guiltily, as if someone might see him laughing and think ill of him for it.

"It's okay, Alex," I said. "You're allowed to laugh when you're supposed to cry. You're Southern, it's the way things are done down here."

He chuckled again and said, "It is indeed, isn't it? Now, what do you know about who beat the hell out of my husband?"

"Right now, nothing," Sabrina said. She made the transition into "cop mode" so quickly it made my head spin. "We found no usable forensic evidence at the scene. The alley just sees too much traffic for us to get anything definite. So now we wait to see when Stevie wakes up and we find out what he can remember. What is it?"

Alex was smiling a little, but his head snapped up at her question. "Oh, sorry. It's just that nobody calls him Stevie anymore. Nobody but me. He always said that there are only two people in the world allowed to call him Stevie. His favorite cousin and me. And here we both are."

Sabrina's eyes clouded over again, and she reached out to take his hand. "Yeah, here we are. And here we'll be until he wakes up. Then we'll go get the son of a bitch that did this and teach him what pain looks like."

"While you two are hanging out here drafting lesson plans on pain, Greg and I will start asking questions," I said.

"Who are you going to ask?" Sabrina prodded.

"We can't reveal our sources, Detective. Isn't that what you keep telling your lieutenant?" Greg replied.

"You guys usually are my sources, you dork."

"Good point, but our issues remain unchanged." My partner put on his best enigmatic smirk, which did more to make him look like he had a sour stomach than a secret, and headed down the hall.

"I have no idea what he's babbling about, but you go wait for your cousin to wake up and we'll see what we can come up with." I turned and started off toward the elevators, where a little kid was staring at Greg's utility belt.

The doors chimed open, and we all got on. The kid's mother pushed the lobby button, while Greg hit the button for the basement, where the blood bank was kept.

As they got off in the lobby, I turned to Greg and said, "Where to now, Caped Crusader?"

He flipped me off as the kid went wide-eyed out the elevator doors.

Chapter 7

The morgue wasn't nearly the creepy, poorly lit place you'd expect based on decades of popular movies and zombie video games, but my impressions of the place could be colored by the fact that I'm dead. It did have a peculiar smell to it, one that kinda lingered on my clothes after a visit. It wasn't just the stink of hospital disinfectant. It was more like formaldehyde with a touch of rot underneath it. Gave me the creeps.

But at least the joint was brightly lit, if with ugly fluorescent lights. Living or dead, or walking dead, no one has ever had their appearance improved by fluorescent lighting.

Greg and I meandered through the hallways between exam rooms and cold storage until we got to Bobby's office. Robert Daniel Reed was not what anyone expected to encounter in a morgue as a medical examiner's assistant. The stereotype of a scrawny little bookworm with visions of defiling corpses flew right out the window when you took a look at Bobby. A former Arena Football League quarterback, he'd migrated from North Georgia when his playing career ended (something about a shot to the knee one night in Birmingham) and tried his hand at entrepreneurial undertaking.

We met Bobby a couple of years ago on a case involving an expensive and prematurely deceased parakeet, and he had become an invaluable resource—a man with an embarrassing bird-related secret in his past and a key to a blood bank. He looked up from what was no doubt a scintillating game of solitaire when we walked in, and his normally cheerful demeanor darkened as soon as he recognized us.

"What do you guys want?" he grumbled, settling all six foot four inches and 260 pounds back into his office chair, which let out a whine of protest.

"I'm hungry, Bobby. What's in the fridge?' Greg walked over to a cooler on the wall.

"Stay out of there, Knightwood, that's a customer."

Greg hastily took his hand off the door handle as Bobby walked over to the wall of slide-out drawers. For a dead guy, Greg has a crazy aversion to corpses. I mean, I'm not a huge fan, but as long as they're lying still, they don't bug me too much. It's when they get up and cause trouble that I have issues.

Bobby reached up and opened a drawer high on the wall, pulling out a sliding steel tray with a pair of Igloo coolers on it. "I keep the stash up here so the boss doesn't get into it."

"Why would that keep him out?" I asked, sitting down at Bobby's computer and updating his Facebook status with stupid movie quotes. That should teach him to leave a window open when there are other people in the room.

"He's five three with lifts in his shoes. He's banned us from ever putting the stiffs in the upper drawers, so I know he can't get into this stuff." Bobby pulled down a cooler and handed it to Greg. "The usual fee?"

"Yeah, here. I put a little extra on here because we're gonna need to fill up before we leave." Greg reached into his utility belt and handed him a thumb drive. Greg's deal with Bobby included not just cash, but cheat codes for the latest Xbox games and some hard-to-find manga.

Bobby stood there looking at us expectantly, and I cocked an eyebrow at him. "You sure you want to watch this? Sometimes people freak out a little."

I wasn't really sure how much Greg had told Bobby about us, so I didn't know if he understood we were the real deal as far as vampires go, or just thought we were humans with a blood fetish. I know, it's gross, but it happens. For that matter, drinking blood grosses *me* out sometimes, and it's how I stay alive.

"Just pretend like I'm not here." Bobby showed no inclination to leave.

I brought a bag up to my lips, grimaced at the cold plastic, and paused as another thought occurred to me. "That's fine, Bobby-boy, but if this shows up on YouTube, my next meal comes straight from the source."

His eyes widened, and he reached over to hit a button on his laptop, apparently turning off the built-in webcam.

Greg and I emptied the cooler, putting away six pints apiece before we ran out of blood, and I felt stronger, faster and even smarter when we were done. Running low on blood always leaves me a little sluggish, but this infusion had me cooking on all eight cylinders again. Even ice-cold and tasting faintly of plastic, a little of the life force of the donor seeped through, and I could smell more sharply, see more clearly and hear more distinctly.

I wiped my mouth with the back of one hand, and then licked the last stray drop from between my fingertips. "Good to the last drop," I murmured, and Greg belched. "You're gross," I chastised my partner.

"It's still funny."

"I didn't say it wasn't funny, just gross. How you doing over there, Bobby?"

Our erstwhile observer had collapsed in his chair and was looking decidedly paler than before we began our meal.

"I-I-I'm okay. I guess. I . . . I . . . just guess I wasn't really sure that you guys were . . ." His voice trailed off, and he looked around, as if to make sure nobody could hear him.

"Vampires?" Greg said from behind him, and giggled as Bobby jumped out of his chair. We're fast, and really quiet when we want to be, and sneaking up on people is one of Greg's favorite and most annoying tricks.

"Yeah. That. So . . . are you guys doing that thing up north?"

Bobby looked at me like I should know what he was talking about, so I played along. "Nah, not this week. We might go back later if the money's right." I had no idea what I had just claimed we did.

"I heard this week's match was really weak. Like the guy didn't even want to be there. Don't know where they get some of these dudes, man. You two would put on a way better show. I hope they call y'all up soon." He made a shadow-boxing motion and gave me two thumbs up.

Boxing? Us? I didn't want to look stupid by asking him to explain now. "Yeah, man. Me too. Hey, if you know anybody who might be able to . . . well, you know, just put a good word in for a loyal customer?" I gave him a business card.

"I'll try. I usually just drive the trucks afterward, you know. But if I get close to the big man I'll try to slip him your card."

"Thanks, Bobby. You rock."

"I know, baby. I know."

"We gotta roll. Later."

"Peace."

I grabbed Greg's elbow and turned him to head out the doors of the morgue and start looking for our gay-basher.

"What was all that about?" Greg asked as we waited for the elevator.

"I have no idea. But it sounds like black market blood isn't the only pie our buddy Bobby has his fingers into, and that might be useful information someday."

Chapter 8

As we drove back to the crime scene, Greg and I started to go over the details of the case. "So what do we know?" I asked, as he turned right onto Hawthorne and put the hospital in the rearview mirror.

"Well, we know that Detective Law has family issues, that some of those issues are currently lying in a hospital bed and that your libido has elected you therapist."

"Bite me," I replied, fiddling with the radio trying in vain to find something other than country music.

"No, thanks, you're stale. But anyway, we know that there have been several of these attacks over the past few months, and the gay community has been up in arms for the police to do more about them. Unfortunately, living as we do in the buckle of the Bible Belt, the police were reluctant to get involved until there had been too many attacks to ignore."

"How do you know so much about this? There hasn't been anything on TV to speak of." I flipped the radio off and stared across the front seat at my partner. "Is there something you've been meaning to tell me?" I teased.

"No, shithead. Popular culture to the contrary, being a vampire is not synonymous with sexual ambiguity. I have not ever been, nor will I ever be attracted to your skinny ass. Or any other part of your undeveloped frame."

"I dunno, Greggy," I needled. "Methinks he doth protest too much."

"Oh, shut up. If I wanted to go after guys, I'd definitely go after better-looking ones than you. But anyway, there's been this invention lately called the Internet. You might have heard of it? I read about the attacks on a couple of city message boards that I monitor."

"What message boards are these, pray tell?" I was beginning to get a sneaking suspicion I knew the answer, but I wanted Greg to admit it.

"Law enforcement message boards. The kinds where people talk about hot spots for crime, places the city can't or won't take care of, that kind of thing. You can find anything on the web if you look hard enough." He looked smug as we pulled into the Spirit Square parking lot and got out of the car.

"Anything except a life, apparently," I muttered as I followed him into the alley.

The crime scene unit had finished up, so we had the run of the place, which was just fine with me. It gave us a chance to use some of our more off-the-record abilities to look over everything. I'd walked the alley a couple of times looking and listening for anything out of the ordinary when I heard Greg give a low whistle. I looked back to see him standing at the top of a concrete staircase leading down to a stage door. He waved me over excitedly, and I headed his way.

"Give this a sniff, dude," he said when I reached him. He pointed at the door.

I leaned over and took a big whiff. My sense of smell is nowhere near as keen as Greg's, but this almost knocked me over. It smelled like rotten food, and blood and serious armpit funk, all overlaid with a coating of cloying floral scent. It was the same as we'd smelled coming off Stephen, only way stronger.

"Ewww. Damn, dude, how about a little warning next time? That is seriously nasty."

"Shut up, you pansy. Have you ever smelled anything like that before?"

"You mean before Stephen's hospital room? No."

"Me neither, but now that I've locked in on it, I can tell it's all over the alley. I think whatever beat up Stephen smelled like this."

"Well, then it oughta be easy to find. Just look for wherever there are a lot of people with sinus trouble, because nobody else could stomach that stench." I saw something fluttering out of the corner of my eye and went back up the stair.

"If you get any of that on your clothes you're totally walking home," Greg yelled after me as I knelt down beside a dumpster and reached under it.

"I'll sit on the roof," I yelled back as I pulled a brightly colored flyer out from under the dumpster. It advertised a drag show at Scorpio, the city's oldest and most famous gay bar. There was a smear of blood across the front of it that told me it had been a lot closer to the fight than it was now, maybe even on Stephen somewhere. I stood up, wiping as much of the alley muck off me as I could. This made the second time tonight that club had come to my attention, and I didn't believe it was coincidence.

I held the flyer out to Greg and said, "Let's get back home and plan our wardrobes."

"For what?" He asked, trying hard to read the flyer and stay downwind of me.

"This show is tomorrow night. We're going clubbing. Now let's get out of here before the sun comes up."

Chapter 9

The next night found me rolling on the floor of my den as Greg trotted out his finest club garb for our investigative trip to the gay bar. I was sporting a patterned T-shirt under a silk blazer with a pair of designer jeans and the only pair of decent shoes I owned, black loafers with buckles. Greg, on the other hand, came out in a pair of black leather pants and a gold mesh shirt that showed far more of my rotund partner than I wanted to know existed.

"Dude," I gasped between howls of laughter, "how many cows had to sacrifice themselves to build those pants? And please don't tell me I'm seeing the sparkle of a belly ring?" I fell off the couch and sat there laughing as Greg stood in the doorway of his room glowering at me.

"Shut up, toothpick. I'm trying to look inconspicuous," he muttered.

"Dude, we're going to a gay bar, not Mardi Gras. You don't have to dress like Captain Jack Sparrow after he slept with a disco ball," I said.

He turned on his heel and went back into his room while I sat there wondering what he would come out with next.

"And since when are you the expert on how to dress for success at a gay bar?" Sabrina asked from the stairs.

I clambered up from the floor and headed over to her. "A guy's gotta eat. How did you get in here? And what are you wearing?" I'd never seen Sabrina in a dress before, and this one didn't leave a whole lot to the imagination. The skirt was short, the top was clingy and red and she had on a pair of heels that I bet were borrowed from a pal in the Vice department.

"One—you're disgusting. Two—you left the door unlocked. And Three—this is called a skirt, and I'm wearing it to the club to keep you two social misfits out of trouble." She went to the fridge and grabbed a beer. "Want one?"

I nodded in the affirmative, and she brought two beers over and set them on the coffee table.

"Judging from Greg's ensemble, it looks like my services will most definitely be needed." She sat down and twisted open a Miller Lite.

"Yeah, we weren't much for the club scene when we were alive, and loud music really plays havoc with our hyper-hearing nowadays, so we don't spend a whole lot of time shaking our groove things." I sat next to her on the couch and propped my feet up. I put my arm along the back of her shoulders, and she didn't shoot me. I took that as a good sign and left my arm there.

"Huh. I hadn't thought about that. How are you going to deal with the noise tonight?" she asked.

"Wax earplugs," I answered. "Greg came up with the idea. They look a little bit like hearing aids but they'll cut enough noise out for us to be able to function. And it's not like I'm looking for a date."

"I thought all of you guys were bi" Sabrina said, looking at me out of the corner of her eye to gauge my reaction.

I didn't give her the satisfaction, just muttered "racist" under my breath and took another sip of my beer. We sat there in easy silence for several seconds. She smelled nice, like lavender with an undertone of spice. I let my hand drop softly onto one shoulder and listened as her heartbeat sped up just a little.

"How's your cousin?" I asked.

"No change. Still unconscious. The doctors don't know why, either. His wounds are pretty bad, but they say he should have woken up by now."

"I'm sorry. We'll find who did this, I promise."

"I know. And thanks. I appreciate everything you're doing."

I tightened my arm around her shoulder in an awkward one-armed hug and just held her. It felt good, then I heard the door to Greg's bedroom creak open, and we jerked apart like guilty teenagers. I smiled at Sabrina, and she gave me a rueful grin in return. I turned to my partner, now resplendent in a flannel shirt and work boots.

"You're a lumberjack and you're okay. Let's go, baby bear," I said, then stood up, and we headed to the car.

We took my car to the club, just in case there was anyone paying attention to the parking lot. Nothing says, "ignore me" like an imported economy car, and we didn't exactly want trumpets announcing our arrival.

The bouncer was wearing a shirt that looked a lot like the one I'd mocked Greg for wearing originally, and he shot me an I-told-you-so look. I didn't bother making any remarks about their respective physiques, just paid the cover and went inside.

It was a good thing Greg had come up with his earplug idea, because I can't stand Lady Gaga at low volume, much less the ridiculous level it was blaring at through the club. The lights were dim everywhere except the dance floor, where the strobes and colored light flashed in time with the music. Everywhere you looked there were ridiculously fit men dancing together, and in the corners of the bar you could see men talking with their heads close together, sometimes holding hands, sometimes just talking. All in all it looked just like a straight dance club only with no women, and I felt just as out of place. Come to think of it, there were never any women in my experience at straight dance clubs either. At least not until they became dinner.

I headed over to the bar and waved the bartender over. He gave me a quick once-over and said "Domestic beer in the bottle?"

"How did you know?"

"It's what all the straight boys drink. It's like a billboard." He smiled and grabbed me three Miller Lites, twisting the tops off into the trash can with a practiced flip of the wrist.

"Who says I'm straight?" I was a little offended that my cover had been blown so quickly.

"Everything about you, sweetie. Don't worry, we don't mind your kind coming in here, just don't start any trouble." He flashed me a smile that I bet got him a lot of second dates, and turned to go down the bar. I waved him over with a couple of twenties, and suddenly his attention was mine and undivided. Some things work with every bartender in the world, no matter the venue, and pictures of Andrew Jackson are a good conversation starter pretty much everywhere.

"Since you know I'm not here looking for a date, I might as well just ask you some questions," I started, but he waved me off right away.

"Sorry, sweetie, not a chance. You've got 'PI' written all over you, and the last thing I need is to end up in some frustrated closet case's divorce hearing."

He started to turn again and I went ahead and brought out the big guns. "I'm investigating the assaults."

He stopped cold and turned back to me. "Really?" He had an eyebrow climbing into his hairline, and I could almost see the wheels turning as he tried to figure out exactly who we were.

"Yeah, really. Our friend in the miniskirt is a CMPD detective, and you were right about my partner and I being private investigators. We're trying to find out more about the victims, and we're starting here."

"Why here? I don't even know a couple of the guys that were beat up, and I know everybody that comes in here more than twice." He looked around and waved the other bartender over. "Come with me. I can't talk to you out here. No. They stay. Just you."

I waved off Sabrina and Greg, and followed him back to the office behind the bar and sat with my back to the door. Not my favorite seating arrangement, but I figured I could out-muscle and out-maneuver anything in a human bar, so I let it slide.

The office was small, but nicely appointed. I was in a nice leather side chair that matched the desk chair pretty perfectly, like it had been part of a set that included the heavy mahogany desk and credenza. Several flat-screen monitors lined the wall to my left, showing various areas of the bar, while certificates and plaques from various charities and arts organizations lined the opposite wall. All in all, it looked a lot like a lawyer's office, if you could ignore the autographed photos of drag queens and Broadway stars that dotted the shelves and walls.

"Alright, what do you want to know?" he asked as he sat behind the desk.

I might not be the sharpest fang in a mouth, but I was starting to get the idea that this guy was more than just a bartender. "Let's start with some introductions. I'm Jimmy. And you are?" I passed him one of my cards, and he tucked it under the corner of a blotter on his desk.

"I'm George. I've been the manager here for the past five years. And I know for a fact that my customers have nothing to do with these attacks."

"And exactly how do you know that?" I asked, turning my chair to at least give myself a little peripheral view of the door.

"Because, like I said out there, some of those guys have never been in here. Or at least have only been in once or twice. They're not regulars, and our regulars are good people. Sure you've got the occasional tweaker and more than the occasional stoner, but most of my boys are just out looking for a good time."

"What if the person doing the attacking was finding his victims here?" I asked. "We don't really think that your establishment has anything to do with the attacks, but a flyer for tonight's drag show was found in the alley at the last attack."

"Well, yeah, it would have been. We papered the hell out of the Spirit Square lot last night. It was kinda our target demographic, you know?"

"No, I don't know. In fact, I have no idea what you're talking about. Help me out a little." I had this sinking feeling in my gut that our best lead so far was going to turn out to be a complete dead end. Sabrina was not going to be happy.

"The play going on at Spirit Square last night?" George went on. "They were doing *Jeffrey*, a total gay comedy. Probably every car in the parking lot belonged to a queen, so I sent one of my bar backs out to put a flyer under all their windshield wipers, so when they came out of the play, they got invited to keep their weekend going here. It's guerilla marketing, baby, the only kind we can afford nowadays. Somebody probably took the flyer off their windshield and tossed it on the ground, then it ended up in the alley."

"Crap. That was our best lead so far."

"Sorry. Wish I could help more, man."

"Yeah, me too. Guess it's time to earn the itty-bitty retainer the CMPD has me on for this case. If you come up with anything else, please let me know." I stood, turning toward the door. I'd just reached my hand out when the door flew open. A twenty-something boy with bleached hair and teeth ran in like the devil himself was outside. Which given my luck, wasn't out of the question.

"George, you gotta come quick. There's this huge guy at the front door and he's fighting with Otto," the boy gasped.

"Otto's a black belt in three different martial arts. I don't think I need to be there to help him." George looked about as concerned as if he'd just been told the floor needed mopping at the end of the night.

"No, you don't understand. He's kicking Otto's ass! We need an ambulance! Call 911, quick!"

The kid was almost hyperventilating, and I shoved past him to get back to the club. I ran past Greg and Sabrina, shouting for them to follow me. We headed to the door at top human speed, still trying to stay under the radar. Any hope of staying incognito flew right out the window when we saw what was waiting for us in the parking lot.

Chapter 10

There was mayhem just outside the front door, and it took me a couple of valuable seconds to figure out exactly what was going on. When I finally got a good look at the scene, I still didn't exactly believe what I was seeing. Otto, the bouncer with Greg's taste in clothing, was bleeding from the nose and mouth and circling a giant on the porch leading to the club's entrance.

Giant is probably a vast oversimplification, but I couldn't come up with a better description for a beast that topped out at about nine feet tall and somewhere in the range of four hundred pounds of solid muscle. This thing had greenish skin, arms bigger around than my waist with claws at the end of each finger and a face that not even a mother could love. Otto was a big dude, and obviously had some hand-to-hand combat chops, because he was still alive, but I knew if we didn't do something fast, that was about to change.

"Do you have a gun hidden somewhere in that outfit?" I asked Sabrina as Greg and I started to fan out and try to flank the giant.

"It's called a handbag, you idiot, and yes," she muttered, knowing she didn't have to speak loudly for me to hear and not wanting to terrify the crowd any more than they already were.

"All right, then get George, the bartender, and tell him what you're going to do." I was moving out of her earshot as I got around behind the beastie.

I saw it freeze and start to sniff the air, and I knew our cover was about to be blown. Vampires have a unique scent, kind of an old blood smell, and creatures that have enhanced senses can pick us out in a heartbeat. That's one reason we don't hunt in the suburbs—too many dogs. This guy obviously had a good sniffer, so our element of surprise was blown. Because it can't ever be easy.

"And what exactly am I going to do?" Sabrina asked.

"Make the crowd ignore this," I yelled as I drew my Glock and leapt for the giant's back.

Greg saw my move and went in from the side at the monster's knees. Otto saw that the cavalry had arrived and launched a flurry of roundhouse kicks at the monster's face to give us a chance to land our best shots.

That didn't go nearly as well as it had in the movie in my mind. The giant took a couple of kicks in the face, but they had about as much effect as peeing on a forest fire. And of course the monster was faster than I expected, so as soon as I landed on its back, it reached over one shoulder and grabbed me by the back of my neck. The thing swept me over its shoulder and right into the path of my flying partner. I crashed into a couple hundred pounds of flying vampire, and my body and my gun flew in opposite directions.

Greg and I thudded to the ground in a tumble of arms, legs and unfortunate wardrobe choices, and I looked up to see a shoe that had to be a size twenty-seven coming down at my head. I flashed back to my fight with Baal a couple of months ago and mentally swore to stop getting stepped on so much.

Greg and I rolled in opposite directions and managed to avoid being stomped into paste. We got up on opposite sides of the creature. I kicked the thing in the knee, and it backhanded me off the porch into the parking lot. I skidded through the gravel for several feet before coming to a halt against a BMW convertible. I struggled to my feet and leaned against a dent in the fender, thinking about all the *Twilight* jokes I was going to have to listen to over that one.

Greg was standing toe-to-toe with the monster, landing huge haymakers on the monster's midsection. I thought I heard a rib crack, and the thing reared back in pain. Then it lashed out with a foot and caught Greg square in the gut. He flew several feet through the air and landed right behind me in the windshield of the Beamer.

I pulled him free of the shattered glass and said, "You okay?"

"No. You?"

"Not really. Let's go."

With that, we ran back at the monster, Greg going low for its knees while I went for a flying clothesline. The thing just jumped straight up into the air, making Greg miss entirely and swatting me out of the air like a wobbly Frisbee. Which is how I landed, too. I got to my feet, wiped a little blood out of my face, and circled around to the monster's side. Greg went in the opposite direction, and to my surprise, Otto the bouncer flew in with a dropkick that rocked the thing back on its heels. He landed in front of the monster in a combat stance, ready to throw down, if a little unsteady on his feet.

"Get out of here," I growled at the bouncer. "You're just gonna get killed."

"Not tonight, friend. But I do appreciate your assistance," the bouncer replied. Then he made an odd gesture with his right hand. Suddenly a gleaming sword with a three-foot blade appeared out of thin air, and Otto launched himself at the giant, sword raised high above his head. He moved almost faster than I could see, and that's really saying something.

"I hate surprises in the middle of a fight," I muttered, dropping to one knee under a backhanded blow from the giant. While I was on one knee I pulled my backup pistol from an ankle holster and emptied the clip into the giant's crotch.

The beast screamed in pain, and Otto's sword flashed down lightning-quick, cleaving the monster's head from its shoulders and splattering greenish-black blood all over Otto, Greg and me. I licked my lips experimentally, but apparently giant blood has no nutritional value, so I was just grossed out.

"Ick," Greg said, wiping giant blood and whatever else out of his eyes.

"Ick indeed," I agreed, looking around for Sabrina.

The porch, which had been crowded with onlookers just seconds before, was curiously empty. Only the four of us and the corpse of a green-blooded behemoth were outside the club. I looked over to where Sabrina was leaning against the closed door of the club and asked, "What did you do?"

She smiled back at me and said, "I held up my badge and gun and shouted 'Raid!' as loud as I could. You'd be amazed how many guys are flushing little baggies of things down the toilet right now. But you probably still want to clean this mess up pretty quickly. And put that away." She pointed at the glowing sword Otto was holding.

He waved it in another curious gesture, and the blade disappeared.

"That was effective. You wanna tell us exactly what the hell is going on here?" I asked the bouncer.

"No, but that probably isn't an option, is it?"

"No. It's not."

"Okay, then. Help me get this mess out of here before anybody notices, then we can go somewhere and I'll explain everything."

"All right. What do you drive, because there's no way this beast is gonna fit in my Camry."

"I've got a truck. I'll bring it around," Otto said as he started off toward the parking lot.

"Way to buck the stereotype," I said to his back as I started picking up arms and legs, trying to figure out how we were going to get the monster into the back of a pickup.

Otto just flipped me off without looking back, then went around the building toward what I assumed was the employee parking lot. He came back a few minutes later in a small panel truck with the club logo painted on the side, and backed it expertly up to the corpse. He jumped out and grabbed the beast under the arms. With a strength that belied his human appearance, he picked up the creature's torso and stood there staring at Greg and me.

"You two going to help me, or do I have to do everything?" he asked.

We each grabbed a thigh and together we wrestled the giant into the truck. Otto tossed the head in beside the body, slammed the door down and said, "I'll take care of this. Meet me at Landmark in two hours." Without looking to see if I had any objections, he got into the driver's seat and pulled out of the parking lot.

"I don't think I want to know what he's going to do with a headless giant in Charlotte at 2 A.M. on a Saturday night," I said as I headed down the hill to my car.

"Yeah," Greg agreed, squelching along beside me, oozing monster blood with every step. "And I don't want to know how much it's going to cost to clean your upholstery after this ride home."

Chapter 11

After a quick trip home to clean up and contemplate burning our clothes, Greg, Sabrina and I headed to The Landmark, a twenty-four-hour restaurant famous for decent food and interesting atmosphere, especially after hours. Greg and I were in our more normal garb, while Sabrina was still in her club wear. I'd offered her some of my clothes, but apparently *Sandman* T-shirts and sweatpants were not her style.

We took a booth in the back and waited for Otto to arrive. He made it there before our drinks did, dressed down in a long-sleeved polo and a baseball cap over his bald pate. He'd obviously taken the time to shower as well, because there wasn't a hint of slimy green blood anywhere on him. The waiter took our orders, and then went off to leave us to our conversation.

"Okay, Otto. Let's start by telling us what that thing was? It looked like a giant with bad hygiene," I started.

"No, that wasn't a giant. It wouldn't have come up to a giant's belt buckle. That was a troll," the bouncer-turned-troll-slayer said matter-of-factly. The waiter paused for a second in delivering our drinks, then shrugged and set the glasses on the table. I guess he'd heard a lot weirder stuff.

"Just once, I'd like to meet a supernatural creature that couldn't spot us from fifty yards away. Just once," Greg muttered from across the booth.

"I pegged you two from a hundred yards away as vampires. It took the other fifty yards to peg you as straight boys," Otto said.

"Anyway," I interrupted, not interested in yet another conversation about the general sexual preferences of vampires, "that doesn't answer the question of what the troll was doing there. Got any ideas, or did you just slice first and ask questions later?"

"I didn't ask. Trolls are ancient enemies of my people. The mere sight of one in my city filled me with an uncontrollable rage, and I attacked. I lost control of myself, bringing shame to my father and my House."

I had no idea what he was talking about. "Who are your people?" I asked, figuring I'd start slow.

"The Fae. Your people call us faeries," he said.

"I know that, but Greg and I, we're a little more progressive than that. We believe in live and let live, don't ask don't tell, whatever two consenting adults do is between them, that whole thing." I trailed off weakly when I saw him looking at me like I was a moron. I get that look often enough to recognize it, unfortunately.

"Not homosexuals, vampire. Faeries. Like in the tales. Except we don't all have wings, and we're not tiny. As you can see." As if to prove a point, he stood up and struck a pose like a Greek statue.

"I get it, I get it. Now sit down," I hissed. He sat, and I leaned forward. "Now, you say you're a real faerie, like faerie godmother faerie?"

"Yes, although I have no intention of singing bibbity-bobbity-boo with you."

"And you guys hate trolls and trolls hate faeries?"

"Yes."

"But how does something like that move around a city unnoticed? It was nine friggin' feet tall if it was an inch. And it was uglier than Greg going through Xbox withdrawal." I knocked back my Coke and motioned to the waiter for another.

"Glamour," Otto said simply.

"Gonna need a little more, babe. I don't think you're hiding that much ugly with Cover Girl concealer," Sabrina said.

"No, human." Otto managed to make "human" sound a lot like "cockroach," but I let it slide. Besides, the term didn't technically apply to me anymore. "Magic. Creatures of the higher realms can easily manipulate what is seen by those from more mundane planes."

"So the troll used magic to hide its true nature until it started fighting you?" I asked, starting to get the picture.

"Yes, then it needed all its resources just to survive. But all those resources weren't quite enough." His face split in a nasty smile, and for a second I was very happy that he hadn't turned that magical sword in my direction.

"This is going to sound like a stupid question, but what is a faerie doing working the door at a gay bar?" I asked. Sometimes I can't believe the words that come out of my own mouth.

"I was sent here to find out who is attacking my people. There have been several attacks on the Fae who live in this city. Our queen sent me here to put a stop to it. Even if they choose to live in this mundane world, her people are still under her protection."

"Your people?" Sabrina asked. "Are you telling me some of the victims of these attacks are faeries?"

"Not some," Otto said. "All of the victims so far have been of the Fae."

"The bloodstains on the wall where Stephen was attacked would be consistent with marks left by a troll attack," Greg observed, moving his waffles around so it looked like he was eating.

"My cousin isn't a faerie, at least not in the literal sense of the word. No offense." She nodded to Otto.

"None taken. But may I ask, what is your cousin's name?"

"Stephen Neal. He's a dancer."

"Hmmm." The faerie looked at Sabrina, then at his drink, then back at Sabrina, then back at his drink.

"It's still full. Now spit it out," Sabrina said, slamming her open hand down on the table.

The faerie looked at her and smiled. "I like you. You are strong for one of the mundane world. You would make a good faerie. Like your cousin. He is not who you think he is. Or what."

Sabrina sat there for a moment staring at Otto, then drained her soda in one long gulp. She waved the waiter over and ordered a screwdriver, light on the OJ, and downed that before responding. We all looked on in silence as she leaned in, took hold of the front of Otto's shirt and pulled him close.

She spoke very slowly and distinctly, as if she were having trouble with the language. "Now. What were you saying about my cousin?"

Otto looked around, made sure that there were no civilians nearby, then pried Sabrina's hand from his shirt. She winced, but let go. "Stephen isn't really your cousin. At least not by any blood relation. He's one of us. Your legends call him a changeling. In certain cases we switch faerie children with human newborns, taking the human child to our lands and leaving the faerie babe to be raised as human."

"Why?" Greg asked.

Sabrina looked stunned, like she didn't know what to say.

Otto fidgeted for a minute, but eventually answered after another glare from Sabrina. "Sometimes it's because the human infant has a condition that could prove fatal without treatments that aren't available in human society, sometimes it's because the family situation of the child is unfavorable, and sometimes . . ." Otto trailed off and I saw Sabrina's eyes go hard.

"Sometimes?" she prodded.

I knew that look, and really hoped Otto wouldn't pick this moment to get stubborn. I wasn't sure the furnishings could survive a clash of wills. And I couldn't afford any more demolished wardrobe tonight.

"Sometimes we need the children to breed with our children to keep a particular line alive. The Fae do not reproduce as quickly as humans do, but we can breed with humans if need be. Our numbers have dwindled in recent centuries, and we occasionally have to resort to extraordinary measures to insure our survival."

"Extraordinary measures?" Sabrina asked.

This conversation was going sideways fast, and I waved the waiter over for our check. I shoved Greg out of the booth to go pay at the counter before my friend and the faerie bouncer redecorated the restaurant in Early Apocalypse.

"Why don't we relocate this conversation somewhere a little more private?" I asked. "We're starting to draw a little attention, and that could be unfortunate for everyone involved."

"Where would you suggest, vampire?" Otto asked.

"Our place, and go easy on the 'vampire' stuff, Tinkerbelle. Some of us try to stay incognito." I got up and headed for the door, Sabrina and Otto followed exchanging glances like two cats that you just know are going to start fighting the second you put the Fancy Feast down. "Greg will ride with you and show you the way," I said to Otto over my shoulder. I led Sabrina out the front door to my car.

The ride to our place was uneventful, mostly because Sabrina sulked the whole way. The way she was acting, you'd think she wanted to tussle with a supernatural beefcake in the middle of a twenty-four-hour diner. We went down the stairs into the apartment (because I hate to think of it as a crypt, regardless of the fact that it sits underneath a cemetery, and besides, crypts don't have high-speed Internet) and got a couple of beers out of the fridge. Then I called in the cavalry, or more specifically, Father Mike. Mike had been running interference at the hospital since we left Stephen there, but I figured his calming influence and priest's collar might be needed.

Greg and Otto got to our place a few minutes after Sabrina and I opened our beers, and we all settled into the living room. Greg pulled a chair over from the computer for himself while Otto sat in the armchair. I stationed myself on the arm of the couch next to where Sabrina sat, putting myself between her and Otto, in hopes that I could calm them down if it all went pear-shaped.

Sabrina took a long pull of her beer and looked over at Otto. "I believe you were about to explain how you kidnap human babies and use them for breeding stock, weren't you?" Her voice could have been coated in honey, except for the obvious razor blade hidden underneath her tone.

"That is a crude way of putting things, but true enough at the root of it all. We did in fact replace your female cousin with a child of our own, the boy that grew up to be your cousin Stephen. No harm has ever been done to the girl, who lives among our people as one of us, and has risen to a certain prominence within our House." Otto paused for a drink, and I took a second to evaluate how Sabrina was handling this news.

She looked shell-shocked, to say the least. "A girl? Stevie was supposed to be a girl?"

"Yes. The child we replaced was a female. We have no real need of human males. It is the gestation cycles of our women that are at issue, not the libido of our men." Otto actually blushed at this, as though this was something not usually discussed in polite company.

Good thing for him he wasn't in polite company.

Of course, this was when Mike made his appearance, which was good, because I needed an excuse to get another drink.

"Hello, boys. What's the emergency?" Mike asked as he came down the stairs and tossed his overcoat on the back of a kitchen chair. I'd given a little thought to a coat rack, but it would just be another thing to not ever get used, kinda like Greg's NordicTrack. I've gotta tell you, that was one disappointed vampire when he realized that no matter how much he worked out, he was never going to burn any fat. Being stuck in the body you died in might be good for Brad Pitt, but when you're an overweight twenty-something, and you're going to be fat for eternity, it just sucks.

I met Mike over by the bar and poured him a double scotch. He took one look at the glass and raised an eyebrow. "That bad?"

I just held out the drink, and he downed it. I poured him another and brought him over to the sofa. He sat next to Sabrina, and I reclaimed my perch on the arm.

I made the requisite introductions and caught Mike up to speed on where we were in the story. It's a credit to how long he's been hanging around with vampires that he barely raised an eyebrow until we got to the changeling bits. Then he stopped me.

"Jimmy, my boy, are you telling me that these . . . faeries . . . steal human girls and use them for brood mares?"

Sometimes I forget that even though Greg and I went to Clemson, Mike actually spent summers on a farm in his youth.

"I think that's about where we had gotten to when you walked in, Padre." Sabrina had managed to stay quiet through my retelling of the night's events, but I could tell she was seething. Part of it was the pulse I could hear pounding in her veins, but mostly it was the I-want-to-eat -someone's-liver tone of voice she was using.

Otto raised a hand to interrupt. "If I may explain?"

I nodded at him, really hoping that he had something good up his sleeve. "The girls are raised as our own, and with the rarity of children in our Houses, they are revered beyond measure. There is good reason every little human girl dreams of being a Faerie Princess, after all." Otto smiled a knowing smile at Sabrina, who bristled at the condescension.

"Some little girls dream of being the ones off slaying dragons, you pointy-eared chauvinist. And regardless, there's a difference between a Faerie Princess and a prostitute. You can't just go around taking little girls and replacing them with faerie boys."

"But what if the little girls would never grow up healthy in your world?" Otto asked mildly.

"What are you talking about?" Sabrina growled.

"Your cousin had a rare genetic disorder called Tay-Sachs disease that would have killed her in childhood had she remained here, probably before she entered kindergarten. By taking her to our lands, we were able to use magic to heal her and allow her to live a normal, if pampered, life."

"Then why didn't you bring her back when she was healed? Why don't you just come over here and heal all the sick babies? Why are you only so magnanimous to the ones you want to squeeze out litters of little faeries for you?" Sabrina wasn't ready to let this one go yet.

"Much faerie magic only exists within the boundaries of our realm. If you bring faerie coin into your world, the gold turns to lead. If you take faerie food out of Faerie, it turns to dust within minutes. And if your cousin were to return to the mundane world, the changes wrought upon her body would immediately reverse, and she would die a horrible, painful death. So she is forced to live in the lands of the Fae and be treated like a precious treasure instead of coming back here to die in agony. Does that sound like a fair enough trade?" Otto leaned back in the chair and sipped his beer while Sabrina tried to process this new information.

"I guess so," she said after a long moment.

She got up from the couch, headed over to the bar and poured herself a stiff drink. She drank down half of her drink and came back to where we were all watching her expectantly. I tensed, ready to throw myself between Sabrina and the faerie if bullets started to fly.

She took a deep breath and said, "Okay, you and Stevie are faeries. You killed a troll at Scorpio because trolls are sworn enemies of faeries, and all the evidence points to a troll attacking Stevie in the alley. Now what?"

"What do you mean, now what?" Otto asked.

"Is that the only troll in Charlotte, or are there more?" Sabrina asked. "And why did a troll beat up my cousin? And why have other gay men been attacked all over town? Are they all faeries? Have all of these been troll attacks? And if so, why? And where do we go to find out?" Her voice had been steadily rising with each question until it was high and thready by the end. I could tell that the night had taken a toll on her, but nothing prepared me for what I heard next.

Otto stood up and put a hand on her shoulder. She looked at him, and the bald faerie said something I thought I'd never hear outside of a Disney movie.

"We must journey to the lands of the Fae."

Chapter 12

The first words out of my mouth were pretty predictable, I suppose. I looked Otto in the eye and said, "Are you out of your addled little mind? There's no such thing as Faerieland, and even if there was, there's no way we're going there. Tell him, Greg."

I looked over at my partner, but he had a look on his face that was somewhere between "kid at Christmas" and "teenager just got to second base."

"I'm up for a trip to Faerieland, bro. Let's roll." He actually bounced off the couch to his feet.

Otto looked down at Sabrina. "We must journey to Faerie to save your cousin. From what Greg told me of his injuries, he has been wounded by a *blanthron*, a spiked glove favored by Trollish gladiators. The spikes are often tipped with venom from the *verdirosa* plant, the Green Rose. It is an extremely dangerous plant that grows only in Faerie."

"And you know all this from Greg talking about Stephen's injuries?" I crossed my arms and stared at the faerie, not buying any of it.

"No, I know this because nothing else in all the realms, magic or mundane, smells like *verdirosa* venom. A floral scent, with a hint of death underneath."

"You win. Whatever beat up Stephen had faerie poison on his fists. Gee, kids! There's a faerie in my living room. First one I've ever met. Guess who's my chief suspect?"

I tried to loom over Otto, but he stood up. He was a lot more buff than me, and having seen him fight, I knew he could probably take me. So I put a Glock in his face to even the odds.

"Sit down, Tink."

Otto sat. "I did not harm Stephen. As a Knight-Mage of House Armelion, I am sworn to protect him. He is my charge, my duty."

"My cousin. My family," Sabrina said from beside me. Her Smith & Wesson service pistol wasn't pointed at Otto, but it was out and ready.

"Can't we all calm down and discuss this logically?" Mike said.

He put a hand on Sabrina's shoulder, pushing her gently back to the sofa. Then he moved in front of me, putting his face in my line of fire. I lowered my gun. This was not the night to be shooting my friends in the face. Not with more appealing targets right there in the room. I sat back down on the arm of the couch.

"Good," Mike said. "Now, let's question our friend Otto, shall we?" He turned to the faerie, put his hand on his cross and rested the other hand on the bald man's forehead and said "Do you swear in the sight of God to tell me the truth?"

"I am of the Fae, minister. I cannot lie. It is not in my nature," Otto replied.

"Yeah, I read that somewhere," Greg said.

"Greg, that was an Alex Craft novel. It wasn't exactly a scholarly work." I pointed to his copy of *Grave Witch* on an end table.

Greg had fallen in love with the author when he saw her picture on a website. I didn't blame him. Blue-haired chicks in corsets are hot. But they are not necessarily reliable primary research sources.

"Regardless, I am incapable of lying directly," Otto said. "Ask me anything, I must tell you the truth or not answer at all."

"Did you harm Stephen Neal?" Mike asked.

"No. From the information Greg gave me, I would guess that he was attacked by a troll wearing poisoned *blanthrons*."

"Will he recover?" Sabrina asked.

"Not without an antivenin prepared from the leaves and roots of the *verdirosa* plant," Otto said.

"Which only grows in Faerieland." I really didn't want to go to Faerieland.

"Correct," Otto replied.

"What happens to Stephen if he doesn't get this antivenin?" Sabrina asked.

"He will die. Depending on the exposure, he has three or four days to live without treatment."

"Crap. Then I guess we go to Faerieland," I said. "Just one question. How do we get there?"

"I am a Knight-Mage of the Fae, and I can grant us passage into the lands of House Armelion," Otto said.

He waved his arms and a brilliant golden glow surrounded him. I turned away from the bright lights, and when I looked back at him he was standing in front of my couch wearing golden chain mail and a helmet. The sword that he conjured up in the troll fight was strapped across his back with the hilt poking over one shoulder, and he looked nothing like the human bouncer that had stood in my den a few seconds before. He looked alien somehow, like his features were just a little too angular, his eyes just a little too blue to be real. And his ears had tapered to distinct points. I also noticed a hint of fang when he spoke, so it looked like Greg and I weren't the only ones vying to be top of the food chain.

"How did you do that?" Sabrina asked, gaping at him.

"My human appearance was a glamour. This is my true self." He smiled, as if he knew how ridiculously good-looking he was, and I started to feel a little self-conscious. I marched over to the coat closet and grabbed my shoulder rig and duster and started arming up.

"Trolls can do that? The glamour thing?" Greg asked.

"Yes," Otto replied. "That is how they manage to pass among humans without notice. They appear to be nothing more than boorish, overweight humans that smell bad."

"So you mean like the typical American," Mike said wryly. I noticed that he was seated at Greg's computer.

"You not coming with us, Dad?" I asked.

"No, Jimmy, I think an excursion to Faerieland might be pushing the bounds of my ordination a little too far. I'll stay here and consult my sources to any information we can find on this side of the veil about trolls and faeries," he answered with a wave to the computer.

"In other words, you're going to hang out with the cute witch that has an unreasoning bias against vampires," Greg observed.

Our priestly friend at least had the good grace to blush slightly. "I will indeed be visiting my Wiccan friend, and you must admit that a human's fear of vampires isn't exactly unreasoning. You do look upon us as a source of nutrition, after all. I'll also stop by the hospital tomorrow morning and see how your cousin is doing, Sabrina."

With that, Mike finished his drink and headed upstairs, moving a little more slowly than I remembered. I looked after him a little worriedly. Mike had taken a couple of tough shots in our last big fight, and my friend's mortality was fresh in my mind. I was honestly a little relieved that he wouldn't be joining us on this trip. I had enough on my plate looking after Sabrina and making sure that Greg didn't fall in love with a faerie girl.

I finished gearing up and walked over to Otto. "All right, Mr. Spock, how do we do this?"

He either ignored or didn't get my Star Trek reference and said, "First, you must all remove anything made of iron or steel that you have on your persons, including your guns."

I held both hands in the air and protested, "Oh hell no. You want me to go into a magical wonderland and meet with fantastical creatures on their home turf, and now you want me to do it unarmed? You gotta be nuts, baldy."

"This is not a point of discussion, vampire. Cold iron is lethal to my people, and to carry it into a meeting is a grave insult. You may bring weapons of bronze, or silver, but no iron or steel can be on your persons." Otto crossed his arms and stared at me stubbornly.

I looked at Sabrina and Greg for support, but all I saw was two people busily divesting themselves of any metal.

"What about zippers?" Greg asked, pointing to the crotch of his jeans.

"Modern jeans use brass or aluminum zippers, so they're fine," Otto replied.

I took a look at Sabrina's nightclub ensemble and figured that wouldn't be the best thing for traipsing around a magical kingdom picking poisonous plants in, so I grabbed a spare pair of sweats for her out of my bedroom, along with the *Sandman* T-shirt she'd declined earlier, and she went into the bathroom to change.

I found a belt that I remembered had a solid titanium Batman belt buckle (don't ask), and loaded a pair of matching silver daggers into it. I poked around my room for a minute and found a tall staff I'd bought at a Ren Faire back before I turned. I slipped on a pair of black leather gloves to let me handle the silver daggers without any adverse effects, and I was ready to rock. Greg found a nightstick and a pair of brass knuckles, and when Sabrina came out of the bathroom I passed her a baseball bat I kept in the closet. All in all we looked like a cross between a demented sports team and the Fellowship of the Ring.

"Okay, Otto, let's go see the faeries," I said when we were all suitably, if ridiculously, attired.

"Before we go," he replied, "I should tell you something of our land. We will attempt to meet with Milandra, the Queen of House Armelion. There may be challenges set for us before we are allowed into her presence, to prove our worth. You must not protest these challenges, or you may be killed outright. Ours is an old society, much older than any human civilization, and our traditions are strong. We are a long-lived people, and change is slow to come to the Fae. We are not like humans, who change with the direction of the wind."

I noticed that Otto's speech had changed as he got closer to going home. He started to sound a lot more like one of Tolkien's elves and less like the bouncer at a gay bar in North Carolina.

"I get it," I said. "Don't piss off the faeries, they'll kick my ass. Now can we move this party along? I'd like to be there and back again before daylight. I didn't pack my sunscreen."

"Very well, vampire. I can see that you will simply have to experience this for yourself. Please remember, stay close to me and try, please try, to keep your mouth shut." With that, he made some kind of hoodoo gesture in the air, and a shimmering portal of light appeared in my living room. "Step through, each of you. I will hold the portal here and follow."

"I just hope that thing doesn't stain my carpet," I said, and stepped through the hole in the air to Faerieland.

Chapter 13

I stepped through the glowing yellow circle and right out the other side. I could tell immediately that I wasn't in Kansas, or North Carolina, anymore. For one thing, the sky was a pale pink with fluffy purple clouds. For another thing, it was daylight, and I wasn't bursting into flames. I got out of the way as Sabrina and Greg came through and looked around. Otto followed close behind them and made some hand gestures that closed the portal behind us.

"It looks like a My Little Pony convention in here," Greg said.

"If anyone would recognize one, it's you." I looked over at Otto. "Why aren't we on fire? It's daylight, and we're outside. We should be crispy critters by now."

Otto looked at me like I was an idiot and said, "You're in the HomeLands, vampire. The sunlight cannot harm you here unless the queen deems it so. Do you understand nothing of your nature?"

"My nature?" I asked. "I'm a vampire. I'm fast, strong, and if I follow a few simple rules I'll never die. I stay out of the sun, avoid big toothpicks and decapitation, and I have a few dietary restrictions. What else is there to understand?"

"I was right. You understand nothing. Let it suffice to say that because you are magical in nature, the light of a magical realm cannot harm you. Anything else is not my place to say. But you should seek some insight into the nature of your existence, vampire. You cannot live forever without sometimes peering inwards."

"Yeah, yeah, 'the unexamined life is not worth living' and all that. But the point is, we're made from magic and the sunlight here won't kill us." I looked around at the foliage in a rainbow of colors. Orange plants, purple grass, blue clover, the whole place was starting to remind me of a bowl of Lucky Charms.

"Correct. A vast oversimplification, but it is correct. Now, we must make our way to the Hall of Queen Milandra." Otto started off down a trail that I hadn't even noticed before, a beaten track of yellow earth between two tall trees that looked like pines, only with pink and green needles.

"How long is that going to take? We're on a little bit of a deadline here," Sabrina reminded him.

"It depends on how long you stand there, and how quickly you start moving," Otto called back to us.

I started after him, struggling through the undergrowth. As I was fighting with one particularly thorny bush, I heard Greg ask, "What's up with the Technicolor foliage? It looks like somebody's TV needs the color calibrated."

"I think it's pretty," Sabrina replied, and looking back at her I saw a strange look on her face. She looked at peace somehow, and younger. It's like I was getting a glimpse of the girl she used to be, before she had to become the tough police detective.

"Our queen has unique tastes in décor, and the realm reflects her desires. Please follow closely. There are things off the paths in Faerie that do not take kindly to visitors," Otto said as he continued to break a trail ahead of us.

He didn't so much cut a path as wave his sword at the undergrowth, and it pulled back enough for us to pass, mostly. Except that the little sticker plants seemed to take a particular glee in poking me in the ass as I walked by. After one particularly sharp jab, I turned around and cut the plant off near the ground with my silver dagger. The stalk hissed and bubbled when I sliced through it with the dagger, and I heard a high-pitched keening wail that sounded as though it came from far away. Otto immediately turned and strode back to where I was standing, sticker plant in hand.

"What are you doing? I told you to stay close," he snapped.

I held the plant up to him and shook it.

He blanched at the sight of it and snatched it away from me. Then he flung the plant into the woods and leaned in close to my face. "Do you *want* to die here, you idiot? Do not attack creatures here. You don't know what they are and you have no idea what they can do to you."

"Otto, it's a plant."

"No, it isn't a plant. That was, for lack of a better word, a finger. A finger of a *terranthyl*, a creature with a plant-like form that attacks by first separating its prey from a group, then dragging the poor creature off into the woods to be devoured. And now you've made it angry. Stay by my side. The *terranthyl* will not attack a Knight-Mage."

I kept close to Otto after that, and tried not to look appetizing. We walked for about three miles before the trees parted and we came into a clearing. Or at least I thought it was a clearing at first. When I continued to look around, I realized that the buildings were so carefully integrated into the forest as to appear that they belonged there. A doorway looked more like a natural crack in a rock face, a chimney looked more like a spire of dead tree and windows just looked like extra knotholes in a tree trunk. The houses were so cleverly disguised that unless you knew what you were looking at, you could walk right through the clearing and never have any idea you'd just passed through the heart of town. Otto led us to the base of an enormous tree that I normally would have called an oak, except I've never seen a pink and purple paisley oak tree before. We walked up a slight ramp that wound around the tree to a crack in the trunk about eight feet off the ground, where he stopped, removed his helmet and knocked.

As we waited, Otto looked at me and said, "Please try to be respectful. Milandra is a kind and gentle queen, but she is the absolute ruler here. Her every whim is answered, not just by we who serve her, but by the very land itself."

"What makes you think I wouldn't be respectful?" I asked, feeling a little insulted. Sabrina glared at me, and I shut up.

After a minute or two of waiting, the door opened, and we stepped into the greatest great hall I'd ever seen. The floor was pink marble, shot through with veins of lavender, pale blue and flecks of white. The ceiling, which must have been thirty feet above us, was painted (or magicked) into looking just like the sky outside, only this was an earthly blue sky with white clouds. There were even birds flying across, which gave me even more reason to believe there was magic involved.

The walls were cut from even more marble, fading slowly from the pink of the floor to the sky blue as they went up. And at the far end of the hall, at least a football field away, stood a twenty-foot dais with a throne on it surrounded by ladies in waiting. A double column of armored knights lined the hall leading to the throne, and every faerie in the honor guard made Otto look like the "before" pic in one of those old Charles Atlas ads from the back of a comic book. They looked at us with undisguised contempt, and I suddenly really, really wanted my guns.

On the throne sat Milandra, and if there was an encyclopedia entry for "regal," she'd be the illustration. Tall, blonde and beautiful, with high cheekbones and delicate features, she was everything Hollywood dreamed of when making a Faerie Queen.

Chapter 14

We got to the foot of the dais, and Otto poked me in the back again. "Kneel," he said, doing so himself.

I went to one knee and out of the corner of my eye saw Sabrina and Greg doing the same.

"Rise, Octavian. And please, introduce us to your guests. Two of the Sanguine and a human? You have selected strange companions, Knight-Mage." Queen Milandra's voiced poured over us like honey, but I could tell that there was a bee sting in there somewhere from the way Otto stiffened.

He bowed his head again and answered, "Your Majesty, may I introduce Detective Sabrina Law, a Peacekeeper of her realm, and her lieutenants, James and Gregory, of the Sanguine."

"It is our pleasure to meet you, Lady Law, and your servants."

I stopped thinking how adorable she was when she got to the bit about servants. I drew in a breath to correct the little Faerie Princess, but Otto shot me another warning look. I shut up, but I was getting a little tired of biting my tongue in the name of interspecies relations.

"Thank you for receiving us, Your Majesty," Sabrina said, stepping forward with a curtsy. She made a warning gesture to me behind her back, and I kept my mouth shut. Now I knew we were in a different dimension, because no way in hell was Sabrina ever going to curtsy to anyone.

"You are welcome here, Lady. Please treat the Great Hall of Armelion as your home for as long as you require our hospitality."

I saw Otto relax when she said that, and I hoped that meant she'd just pledged that no one in her court would try to stake me as long as we were here.

"Many thanks, Your Majesty." Sabrina curtsied again, and I heard Gloria Steinem's ghost screaming in feminist agony somewhere across the dimensional void.

"Octavian, do you pledge the good behavior of our guests and that they mean no harm to our royal person?" the queen asked Otto.

He stood up straighter, if that's possible for someone who was already making a marine at parade rest look like a slinky, and said, "I do, Your Majesty. Upon my honor as Knight-Mage of House Armelion, they shall bring no harm to your person or House."

"Fair enough, Otto, fair enough."

With that, Queen Milandra waved a hand, and the honor guard all disappeared, along with most of the great hall, leaving behind only two guards and a much smaller sitting room. The guards took up positions beside the door, while Greg and I gaped at the new room. I heard tinkling laughter, and spun around to see Milandra sitting, not on a throne, but on what looked like a very comfy armchair, laughing at our confusion.

"Oh, I do love visitors!" She exclaimed with glee. "Especially visitors from the mundane world. Your faces are absolutely priceless." She waved us over to a pair of sofas that had appeared when the room changed. "I prefer to hold audience for friends in my chambers. The great hall is just so drafty this time of year, and no matter how I make the weather outside, it always seems to be chilly in there. I suppose it's all the marble, but I can't remake the great hall, you know."

I sat on the sofa furthest from the queen and closest to the door, not just to keep my escape clear, but also in case something that didn't like me came through the door. Not that I had a lot of hope of taking out anything that could get past the kind of magic Milandra was throwing around, but it made me feel better. "Your Majesty," I began, "We need your help—"

She cut me off with a wave of her hand and turned to Sabrina. "Who let him speak? And why did you let him keep his tongue in the first place? Have you not heard of their powers of persuasion? Or do you just find it exciting to tempt fate?" Her eyes sparkled with the last question, as though tempting fate was one of her favorite pastimes.

"He speaks whenever he pleases, sometimes much to my chagrin. And regardless, his tongue would just grow back if I removed it," Sabrina said, nodding politely to the serving girl who had just brought out a tray of drinks and fruit.

She took a small glass with a pale orange liquid in it, but didn't drink immediately. The queen took a small plate of fruit and a pale lavender drink for herself, then waved over another serving girl, who knelt at Greg's feet, looking up at him with a small smile.

"Do you thirst, vampire? You may drink of Tirina if you wish. But please, leave enough for your friend to share, and do not drain her or I will be very cross." I heard steel in the queen's words, and decided I didn't want to see her cross. Greg looked at Milandra like she was absolutely insane, and started to shake his head.

"Drink, you idiot," I whispered to him. "You don't know when you'll have the chance to feed again, and I doubt there's a blood bank anywhere near here."

"But dude," Greg whispered back plaintively. "I don't do that anymore. I haven't drunk from a person in almost ten years. I can't do it now, in front of people." He got really quiet on the last part, like he was talking about losing his virginity or peeing in public or something.

"You have to, bro. You've gotta keep your strength up, and I know you didn't eat anything before we left the house. Plus, I don't want to piss her off by not accepting." I really didn't want to start some kind of inter-dimensional diplomatic incident by not drinking the girl. Besides, I wanted a snack and had never had faerie for lunch before.

"Your friend is right, vampire. You must drink. I can sense your hunger," Milandra said.

I looked over at the little queen, and she wasn't smiling anymore. She looked at Greg like he was something she wanted to scrape off the bottom of her shoe.

Greg noticed. He stared at the girl's neck for another moment, then took a deep breath and leaned in. He got close enough to brush the faerie girl's neck with his fangs, then pulled back.

"I can't. I *don't* do that." He stood up and turned to me, his jaw set.

"My Lady, are you not in control of your servants? If you would like some assistance in teaching them manners, we would be happy to oblige." The queen's words belied her light tone, and I looked at the guards, trying to decide if I could take them. Maybe, but not Otto.

I put a hand on Greg's shoulder and looked him in the eye. He tried to turn away, but I didn't let him. "Greg, you gotta drink. I know it's a big deal to you, and I'm sorry. *Really* sorry. But either you feed off this girl, or we have to fight our way out of here, and Sabrina's cousin is probably going to die. Now it's up to you."

"I just don't want to lose control again," he whispered.

I looked around, but nobody but me had heard him. "You won't. I won't let you. You'll never be that guy again. I swear it."

There were red-tinged tears in his eyes as he looked up at me. "You promise? This is the last time?"

How could he ask me something like that? I didn't know what was going to happen in the next five minutes, much less the whole future. Well, that wasn't completely true. I knew we were in trouble if Greg didn't sack up. Now. "I promise."

Greg went paler than usual, then turned back to the faerie girl and pressed his mouth to her neck. He went to one knee as the first fresh blood in a decade splashed against his tongue.

I could smell the blood when he broke the skin, and the smell just about drove me nuts. Imagine your mom's fried chicken, with homemade biscuits, gravy and fresh cherry pie for dessert. Well, this faerie's blood smelled like all of that and more, and I could hardly wait for Greg to top off the tank and pass the entree over.

After a long moment, he finished drinking and just knelt there, leaning over the girl with his forehead on her shoulder. I really hoped I wasn't in for a long talk about feelings and other crap when we got home. Greg stood and waved the girl over to me, turning so he didn't have to watch the feeding.

Not being possessed of Greg's moral fortitude, I took a knee instantly and sank my fangs deep into the girl's carotid. The hot blood flooded my mouth, and I saw stars for a second before I got myself under control. Apparently faerie blood is a lot more nourishing than human blood, because I'd drank barely a pint before I felt completely revitalized.

I stood up, giving the girl a kiss on the forehead that left bloody lip prints just below her hairline, and looked around with new eyes at the great hall. Everything had an extra little sparkle, like the first time a nearsighted kid gets new glasses. I could smell a hint of lavender in the air, and I thought I could taste a hint of it, too. I knew it was coming from Sabrina, and I closed my eyes, listening to her heart beat for a long moment, losing myself in its rhythms before I snapped back to the present. I locked eyes with the Faerie Queen, and she smiled a knowing smile at me.

"Did you enjoy your meal, vampire?" she asked with a tilt of her head.

"She was delicious, Your Majesty." I sketched a brief bow, and the girl returned to her serving duties.

"Excellent. Now the rest of us may dine while we discuss what business has brought a Peacekeeper with two assassins to my lands."

She clapped her hands, and an army of serving girls, all looking eerily identical to the faerie Greg and I had just fed from, came in carrying sections of wood that assembled almost by themselves into a huge banquet table. Once the table was in place, Milandra clapped her hands once more, and a feast appeared in the blink of an eye. Fruits in all colors of the rainbow, vegetables that looked like nothing I'd ever seen before, and a roasted flamingo appeared from nowhere. Literally from nowhere. Milandra clapped her hands, and food just *appeared*.

I sipped a nice red wine while the mortal types ate and Otto recapped the troll fight for the queen. I couldn't process most of what was said because I was still hung up on the word "assassins." Apparently here in Faerieland vampires were not uncommon, and we were used as assassins.

Eventually I raised my hand tentatively, and Milandra nodded towards me. "Um . . ." I hate it when I get tongue-tied, but I was really in uncharted waters here. "Your Majesty, we're not assassins. I mean, we are vampires, that's pretty obvious, but we didn't come here to kill anyone." Which might not have technically been true, but since I didn't know who we might have to kill, I figured that bit might best be left unsaid.

"Then why have you come here, mortal?" Milandra turned to Sabrina, who apparently had been elected general when I wasn't looking.

"We are investigating a series of troll attacks in our world. Otto—um—Octavian led us to believe that you may be able to help us find out where the monsters are coming from, and why they are attacking changelings," Sabrina said, with a glance to Otto, who nodded slightly.

Sabrina went on "My . . . a member of my family has been injured, and Octavian tells us he can only be cured by a plant found here in Faerie. He will die within days if we don't get the plant and get back to him."

Otto stood and bowed to the queen. "Your Majesty, if I may?"

She gave him a negligent wave, and he continued. "The changeling Stephen Neal has been poisoned by the *verdirosa* venom. He seems to have been beaten by a troll wearing *blanthrons*."

Milandra sat rigidly in her chair, her face a cold mask. "You are telling me that not only has a troll escaped into the mundane world, in the same city where you are supposedly protecting my changelings, but he has now poisoned one of my subjects using forbidden magics? And you were incapable of stopping this and are now paired with a *human* and her pet *leeches*?"

Otto dropped to one knee at the steel in the queen's voice.

I stood up to protest being called a leech, but Sabrina grabbed my wrist. "Sit down," she whispered.

I looked around, and the two guards were a *lot* closer than they had been just a few seconds before.

Otto spoke, his gaze still focused on his toes. "My Lady, I apologize most sincerely for my failure. The slight was mine entirely. I was investigating the attacks, just as I was ordered. The humans simply stumbled upon an attack more recently than I could, given my limited resources."

This seemed to satisfy the pissed-off little faerie girl, at least enough that some of the fire went out of her gaze. She sipped from a goblet and appeared to contemplate the news Otto had delivered.

After a long few seconds of silence, she looked down the table to where Otto knelt. "Rise, Octavian. I am not wroth with you. Be seated." He did as he was told, and Milandra took another drink, then spoke again. "We in House Armelion have no dealings with trolls, but I may be able to summon their master here for a . . . conversation, if that is what you desire."

Something about her tone made the hair on the back of my neck stand up, and looking over at Otto I could tell that there was something going on here that was most definitely not being said. Sabrina didn't catch whatever warning tone I was hearing, and just replied with "Yes, Your Majesty, we would like that very much."

"We may even be able to provide you with the cure you seek for your cousin. The *verdirosa* is a dangerous plant to find, and even more dangerous to harvest. I believe my apothecary keeps one in his garden for just such an occasion as this. If it is here, you may have it. We will not abandon our people who live across the veil."

"Thank you, your Majesty. Thank you very much," Sabrina said, and I could see the tension flow out of her.

"You are most welcome, human. We could no more abandon our changelings than any of our children. But of course, there is a cost."

The knot building in my stomach reached Gordian proportions, and I knew life had just gotten uglier. Again.

"A cost, Majesty?" Sabrina asked.

"Of course, human," Milandra said. "If it is a boon you seek from the Queen of House Armelion, then it is a boon you shall have." She was smiling way too much for me to feel comfortable, and then she dropped the other shoe. "Once you have completed your quest, of course."

I knew it. Outsmarted by another supernatural chick. The last time this happened, I ended up immortal and with weird dietary restrictions. I just hoped we all survived this one.

Chapter 15

I took a deep breath, stood up, brushed off the knee of my jeans and squared my shoulders, looking right at the Faerie Queen. "All right, Your Majesty, what do need us to do?"

I heard Sabrina gasp a little at my directness, but I figured we were down to the real deal now, so any pretense of formality could go out the window.

Milandra chuckled a little and said, "You are wiser than you appear, vampire, not that that takes much. There is a beast that has been plaguing the western border of my lands for some years now. I would like for you to go there, and bring me its heart as proof of your success. Of course, simply returning alive will be proof enough, as none of the other heroes I have sent on this quest have ever been seen again." There was that little half smile again.

I was really starting to want to smack this chick, magical queen or not. She might look like a storybook picture, with her blonde hair and her fluttery silk gown, but there was steel underneath that porcelain skin.

"Okay, Your Majesty. Would you like to enlighten me as to what kind of creature we'll be fighting, or would you rather we be surprised?" I asked

Greg and Sabrina were on their feet now, Greg shaking his head at me, and Sabrina keeping an eye on the guards just in case they didn't approve of my attitude.

"Oh, I wouldn't dream of having you attempt this quest without proper preparations, vampire. After all, dragon-hunting is not for the faint of heart."

I didn't bother mentioning that my heart didn't really beat anymore, faint or not. I was a little hung up on the casual use of the word "dragon."

"Excuse me, Your Majesty?" Greg asked politely. He even raised his hand. "Did you say 'dragon?'" His voice squeaked a little, and now he sounded like he was almost twelve instead of closing in on forty.

"I did indeed, vampire."

"Does 'dragon' maybe have a different meaning here than it does in our world?" he asked, hopefully.

Milandra cocked her head. "In your world does 'dragon' mean a gigantic winged lizard, roughly the size of a barn, with a twenty-foot long poisonous barbed tail, a head the size of a small bedroom with hundreds of razor-sharp teeth, claws the length of broadswords and just as sharp, with breath of fire?"

"Yes, that's pretty close." Greg said in a very small voice. "Except in our world, these are purely mythical creatures. They don't really exist."

I saw a little glimmer of hope in his face until Milandra spoke again. "You mean fantastical creatures of the imagination, like trolls, vampires and faeries?"

"Yes, Your Majesty, just like that." Greg looked about like I felt, which was kinda like I'd been kicked in the guts by a horse. Or a troll.

"Well, then I assure you, Mr. Knightwood, that this dragon is every bit as mythical as you are. But do not despair, my friends, I would not dream of sending you into battle with such a creature garbed in such inadequate clothing."

With that, she clapped her hands, and Greg and I were suddenly wearing suits of bright metal chain mail, complete with breastplates, arm guards and plates over our shins and thighs. Helmets appeared floating in midair in front of us, open-faced things with silver wings sweeping out from the sides. I grabbed mine and put it on, and looked over at Greg.

"I don't want to think about how much metal went into wrapping your gut, bro," I quipped, and then turned to look at Sabrina, and my mouth dropped open.

She looked like an over-sexed Valkyrie, with her own winged helmet, chain mail and breast plate, but where Greg and I had on chain mail leggings, she had an armored skirt that was slit up way higher than I thought was exactly practical. Her breastplate had some obvious concessions to anatomy, with a couple of vents in interesting places showing a little more flesh than I would have expected. All in all, I was pretty distracted by the image, and I figured any enemy might be as well. I was less sure about what effect her appearance would have on a huge lizard, but at least I'd have some eye candy while I was being chomped to death.

"Um, Your Majesty?" Greg raised his hand again. I'm gonna have to teach him to grow a pair one of these days, but I decided that being on our best behavior here probably wasn't a bad idea.

"Yes, vampire?"

That still bugs me. It's like people think it's a title or something. We have names, after all. We don't go around calling people "human."

"This armor is great and all, but we're going to need some weapons, too. Don't you think?" That's when I noticed that my daggers had gone wherever my clothes had, since they weren't on my belt anymore. Just as well, I doubted a six-inch blade would do much against a dragon anyway.

"Of course, Gregory. Follow me. I will take you to my armory." With that, she turned and headed through a door in the side of the room that I was pretty sure hadn't existed before that second. It reminded me yet again how much I hate magic.

We followed Milandra down a long marbled hallway until she stopped in front of a thick wooden door flanked by two knights holding huge polearms. She gestured to the door, and it opened.

With a wave of one regal hand, Milandra said "You may arm yourselves with anything you find within. Choose carefully, as your lives may depend on the decisions you make here."

I went in first, and my heart sank a little as I looked around. Racks and racks of swords, shields and armor filled the huge room, with dozens of bows, crossbows and spears leaning against a far wall. I looked around the whole room a couple of times, then looked back at Greg and said, "Hey Frodo, you see anything in a 9mm around here?"

Greg stopped waving a battle-axe around and said, "Of course not, dude. We're in the realm of the Fae, a world of magic. There's not going to be a gun shop anywhere to be found."

I passed a crossbow over to Sabrina and said "Too bad for you, chica."

She sighted down the length of the crossbow and set it aside, walking to the wall of bows instead. She picked up a short recurved bow and drew it experimentally. "This works for me. Reminds me of summer camp." She picked up a quiver of nasty-looking barbed arrows and said, "I should probably stay out of range as much as possible, not being gifted with super-strength, speed or healing."

"Good idea." I hefted a huge claymore with one hand. It was a little long, but having vampire strength definitely made me able to swing the six-foot sword one-handed, even if I couldn't exactly bring it back around quickly. After a couple of practice swings I put the oversized toothpick away and picked up a shorter, thinner sword that looked like it was designed for one- or two-handed use. "This seems to suit me just fine." For good measure, I dropped a wicked-looking spiked mace in a hip sheath then slid the sword over one shoulder.

Greg strapped on a pair of broadswords, and we were about to head back out into the hallway when something caught the corner of my eye.

"Hey, Sabrina, try this on," I said as I handed her a battered, plain leather sheath with a thin double-edged long sword in it.

Sabrina belted on the scabbard and drew the sword, slashing the air experimentally a couple of times. The blade had a slight reddish sheen to it, and the hilt fit her hand like it was made for her. "This is perfect, Jimmy. Thanks. I hope I don't get close enough to that beast to need it, but if I do, this will be just the thing."

I ducked out into the hall, almost bowling over Milandra, who stood there waiting for me. Greg and Sabrina chuckled a little and went back to arming themselves, picking out a few daggers and things to round out their arsenal.

When they finished in the armory, they joined Milandra and me in the hallway. The queen handed me a glass globe that seemed full of a bluish smoke and said, "I can use my magic to transport you to the forest where the dragon makes his lair. When you have the creature's heart firmly in your grasp, smash this globe on the ground and stand close together. The globe will return you to my great hall. I wish you luck."

Then, with a wave of her hands and a flash of pink and purple faerie dust (yes, really), we were off to slay a dragon.

Chapter 16

Apparently Faerieland dragons live just like you'd expect them to—in caves deep in dark forests. Because that's exactly where Milandra dropped us, right outside a cave in what looked and felt like a deep forest. The ground was carpeted with thick undergrowth, there was moss hanging from the branches and the mouth of a cave gaped hungrily in front of us.

I stood there for a few seconds getting my bearings (or my courage), then took a deep breath and marched resolutely forward . . . only to trip over Sabrina's outstretched leg and fall flat on my face into a plant that I really hoped wasn't poison ivy or something with fingers. I have no idea if I can still get poison ivy since I'm dead, but I wasn't really interested in finding out. I scrambled back to my feet and whirled to face the grinning cop.

"What the hell was that about?" I demanded.

"Do you have a plan, Brainiac?" she asked.

"Yeah. Go in the cave. Kill dragon. Carve out dragon's heart. Go back to the palace. Get the magic plant from Faerie Queen. Eat another faerie chick. Save your cousin. Make trolls stop beating up gay men in my city. Go home. Drink beer. Did I leave out anything important?"

"Maybe how we're going to accomplish the whole 'kill dragon' step," she said, looking around us as if trying to find something. "Look at the mouth of that cave. Can anything as big as Milandra described get through that opening?"

I had to admit that it looked pretty small for anything dragon-sized. The cave opening was about ten feet tall and maybe a little wider than that. Certainly not as big as I would expect for a dragon's lair. "Okay, you've got a point. So what's your plan, General Patton?"

She waved an arm at the forest around us. "We explore the whole area carefully, make sure there isn't another entrance or escape route for the dragon, and then plan our assault."

I hate it when she's right. I hate it even more because she's *always* right.

"Okay," I said. "That does make a lot of sense. Why don't I go this way, you and Greg go that way, and we'll meet back here in about thirty minutes to make a plan."

"Sounds good to me, but why are you going off alone?" she asked.

"It's not that I'm going off alone, but to be brutally honest, I'm not the most graceful thing in the forest, and neither is Greg. If he and I split up, then anything that hears us will wonder why there are two rampaging elephants rummaging in the forest outside a dragon's lair. Hopefully the noise will be so distracting that any beasties will decide to leave us alone instead of attacking."

"Hey!" Greg protested. "I'm stealthy. Like a ninja." He leaned on the trunk of a tree, which proved to be rotten and toppled over, taking my pudgy vampire ninja to the ground in a crash.

"Yeah, you and Kung Fu Panda, bro."

I headed off into the forest as quietly as possible, which really wasn't that quiet. I'm a city vampire, despite spending my college years at Clemson, which is about as rural a college as you can get and still have big-time football. I don't spend a whole lot of time in the great outdoors, mostly because there's never anybody to eat out there. The wilderness is wild, man. I'll stick to places with delivery.

I wandered around for about ten minutes until I came to what looked like the front of the cave. Now *that* looked like something a dragon could get into. The opening was easily fifty feet wide and thirty feet high. The ground in front of the cave mouth was packed hard and smooth, like something really, really big and heavy used this entrance often. I looked up and saw Greg and Sabrina coming around the other side of the hill.

"I guess this is probably the front porch," I said when they reached me.

"Yep," Sabrina said. "Now what do you think about a frontal assault, Braveheart?"

"Might not be my best idea ever," I admitted. "What does your plan smell like, Sun Tzu?"

"Actually, it's Greg's plan." She waved at my partner, who was bringing up the rear as he fought his way through more of those ass-poking thornbushes. I'd never been so grateful for a long hauberk as when I walked through those woods. And yes, I know what a hauberk is. I played D&D.

"Then we're doomed. I'm pretty sure we don't have the cheat codes for this boss fight, gamer-boy," I said as Greg sat down heavily on a boulder.

"Maybe not, but I've still got a pretty good idea for how to make a dragon trap," he panted.

"I'm all ears, bro," I said.

"No, Jimmy, you're usually all mouth. But I'll take it. I saw this in a movie once, so I know it'll work."

My partner's faith in the world of make-believe is eclipsed only by his encyclopedic knowledge of bad movies. He pulled a dagger from his belt and started to sketch out a diagram in the dirt.

"You and I get up to the top of the cave mouth with our swords. Sabrina goes back around to the back door and sneaks in with her bow. She shoots the dragon in the butt with a few of those nasty arrows, and when it comes running out the front door, we jump on its head and kill it. If we each go for an eye, we should be able to stab straight into the brain and drop the beast without any fuss or bloodshed."

"At least on our part," Sabrina said.

"Yeah, shedding a whole lot of dragon blood is sorta the plan," Greg agreed.

I hated to admit it, but it sounded pretty solid, especially the part where Sabrina stayed back and didn't get in the way of the teeth and claws part of the fight.

"What about the whole fire-breathing thing?" I asked. "Won't the dragon just turn around in the cave and roast Sabrina?"

"I'll have to scout it out. Hopefully there'll be a crevice or a crack in the wall I can hide in." She didn't seem too concerned about going into a cave to shoot a dragon in the ass, so I figured, let her go for it. I was the one volunteering to jump off a cliff onto the same dragon's head, after all, so I didn't have a whole lot of room to talk about good decision making.

"All right, boy genius. Do we do this now, or wait 'til dark?" I asked.

"I don't know. I have no idea if dragons are nocturnal or diurnal," Greg replied.

"Since I have no idea what that second thing means, I guess I don't know either," I said. I'm not really an idiot, but Greg is really well-read and likes to show off in front of girls. I do too, but I do most of my showing off by hitting things very hard.

"Diurnal means that a creature is active during the day," said a new voice directly behind me.

I jumped about eight feet in the air and landed eye to very, *very* large eye with the golden-scaled head of a dragon.

Apparently dragons can move very quietly when they want to. I scrambled backward, and out of the corner of my eye saw Greg and Sabrina doing the same thing. I tried hard to stay directly in the monster's field of vision as they moved out to flank the creature's head.

"Good afternoon, heroes. I am Tivernius. Welcome to my forest. I do wish you would put that away, my dear. I would prefer not to incinerate you quite this close to my home. After all, only we can prevent forest fires."

Sabrina put down the bow and the arrow she had been trying to slowly draw, and Greg and I sheathed our swords.

"Thank you. Now please, come into my home and we can continue this conversation in a more civilized setting. I give you my word that I will bring no harm upon you as long as you do not attack me." With that, the head the size of a Mini Cooper pulled back into the cave on a long, scaly neck.

We stood there for a moment looking at each other until finally Sabrina started walking toward the mouth of the cave. "Where are you going?" I almost shouted.

"I'm going to do as he asked," she said. "If he wanted to kill us, we'd already be dead. He caught us completely flat-footed, and let us off the hook. I'm going to give him the courtesy of a conversation before we fight, at least." With that, she leaned her bow and quiver against the cave mouth and followed the head into the side of the hill.

I looked at Greg, who shrugged back at me and followed her. I waited there for just a moment before I realized that they were in no hurry to come to their senses, and followed my friends into the dragon's lair.

Chapter 17

The passage was long and deceptively winding. We walked for a solid five minutes down the tunnels until the passageway opened into a huge room that made Milandra's great hall look like a college dorm. The ceiling vaulted high above our heads, at least fifty feet into the air, and at a glance, I figured you could have fit a couple of football fields in the room with space left over for at least half a racetrack to boot.

Everywhere around us was opulence decked in gold. The floor was made up of marble slabs set in place and lined with gold. The walls were covered in enormous tapestries in amber, gold and orange hues. The ceiling, almost high enough to have its own weather, was sculpted to look like there was a canopy of trees, all covered in golden leaves.

I was almost disappointed not to see a huge lizard lying sprawled on piles of treasure, but there was no huge pile of booty. No fire-breathing monster running its talons through piles of gemstones, no priceless works of art carelessly piled around the room. There was just a sparsely, expensively decorated hall, with a large table near one wall. Seated at the head of the table was a tall, well-built man who rose when we entered and beckoned us to him.

Something about him looked familiar, but I couldn't put my finger on it. He was dressed entirely in shades of gold, with long blonde hair tied back in a ponytail. He wore golden chain mail, which must have weighed a ton, but he stood and moved with the grace of a ballet dancer. A long sword hung at his belt, and judging by the way his biceps bulged under his armor, he knew how to use the thing. At a glance he looked to be in his late twenties, but something in his eyes made him look far older.

"Come, my guests. Sit, be welcome, and I will have food summoned."

We sat at the table, and our host took his chair at the head of the table. "Welcome. Thank you for agreeing to join us. Now, please, what can I do to help you?"

"I'm sorry if I'm missing something, pal, but wasn't there a dragon in here a few minutes ago?" I asked, sipping from a goblet that appeared in front of me, full of rich red wine. The wine had a coppery tang to it, as though there was a little blood mixed in. I wasn't going to complain, but I had my concerns for Sabrina if we were all drinking from the same carafe.

"I am sorry, my friend. I should have realized that you were not from our land. I am Tivernius. I am the dragon."

I looked sharply at the man and could see just a faint hint of scale at his eyebrows. As I looked closer, I saw that the golden tinge to his complexion was more than just a reflection off his armor, he actually had golden skin. I shook my head and reminded myself that we were in Faerieland, after all.

"Sorry. I thought you'd be bigger." When in doubt, quote *Roadhouse*. It's a philosophy that has served me poorly for many years, but I'm too stubborn to change it.

"We have multiple forms, my vampiric friend, just as you do," Tivernius said.

"Huh?" Greg said. "We don't have multiple forms, we're just vampires."

"Then you have been poorly taught indeed, or are very young for your kind, not to have discovered your other shapes," said the dragon-man, a little surprise coloring his voice. "But it is not for me to teach you. Why are you here? Are you also here for my head, like the others that Fae-witch has sent in the past?"

"Well . . ." I looked for a delicate way to put it and couldn't come up with one. "Milandra did send us, but I'm really hoping that we can come to some type of non-violent agreement." Mostly because I couldn't think of a single way that we could fight this guy in dragon form that didn't end up with my femurs being used for toothpicks. I thought we might have a chance at him in human form, but then I looked at his arms again and that sword, and I wasn't so sure.

"And how do you suppose we do that, vampire? She sent you here, didn't she? And she told you that the only way to get her help is to bring back my head? She's been doing this for months, ever since the last time our negotiations broke off."

"Actually," Sabrina interjected, "we're only supposed to bring back your heart. She didn't say anything about your head."

"Well, isn't that just perfect," the dragon-man fumed. "She refuses to marry me. Then she sends bounty hunters and assassins to rip out my heart. Like she hasn't done a good enough job of that herself." He stood up abruptly, toppled his chair over backward and paced back and forth at the head of the table.

We all jumped to our feet, hands on sword hilts, as I fully expected to be flambéed at any moment.

"Well, maybe . . . nah, I got nothing. Sorry," Greg said after thinking for a minute.

"What were you going to say, vampire?" Tivernius picked up his chair and sat back down. He put his elbows on the table and leaned forward, running fingers through his shoulder-length blonde hair. The dude really did have a serious gold-tone thing going on.

"I was just thinking . . . nah, it just doesn't work out." Greg tried to start again, but gave up.

"Spit it out, bloodsucker. I'm sorry, that was uncalled for. I'm just so frustrated by the whole thing that I don't know what to do." He leaned further forward, his chin in his hands. If I didn't know that he could turn into something big enough to swallow bison whole, I would have thought he was just another schmuck with girl troubles. As it was, he was a schmuck that could level entire city blocks with girl troubles.

"Well, why don't you tell us the story? Maybe we can come up with something to help," Sabrina said. "After all, we're here, and we don't really want to try to carve your heart out, and we're in no hurry for you to barbeque us or whatever, so what harm can come from it?"

"That sounds like a fair idea, young human. Have some more wine." He waved a hand and two carafes appeared. The larger red carafe for Greg and me, and another carafe of white for Sabrina.

"Stay outta the red, Sabrina. Just trust me," I said, filling my glass.

She gave me a look, but didn't say anything.

"It all began at a party," Tivernius began. "I attended a ball in the lands of House Cintharion, a neighboring realm to Armelion. The King of Cintharion was ailing, and he wanted me to meet his daughter, in hopes of building an alliance marriage. But she was a harpy with a terrible disposition and a huge nose, and I wasn't interested. I may weigh seven tons and have scales, but I have my standards. She was a truly unattractive human, not in appearance but demeanor, entitled and possessing a ridiculous sense of self-importance. So I was standing at the bar being miserable, because that is where one stands at a party to be miserable, when Milandra walked in."

"Cue harp music," I muttered, earning myself a sharp look from Sabrina but a chuckle from Tivernius.

"Exactly, vampire. The moment I saw her, I was awestruck by her beauty, her carriage and her very *rightness*. Even at her young age I had never seen anyone so suited to rule. She was not yet queen but already the most regal thing in the room. I introduced myself, and we spent the rest of the night talking about everything under the sun and moon. We connected on a deeper level than I have ever connected with any living being, human, faerie, sanguine or dragon."

"I was in love, if you can imagine. Me, who had seen seventeen centuries without ever giving my heart to another creature, completely smitten in one glance. And by a faerie, one of the most capricious races in all the realms. It was inconceivable, but we continued to correspond, and to build a relationship, and we began making plans to marry."

"Wait a second," I interrupted. "You were going to marry Milandra?"

"Yes, of course," answered the dragon. "We were very much in love."

"But she's a faerie. And you're a lot of things, but faerie isn't on the list."

"Don't be speciesist, vampire. It's petty. Any creature of magic can control his or her form, and we can all intermarry if we choose. And what creature is more magical than a faerie, unless it is a dragon? We are magical, we are immortal, and we were in love. Why should we not marry?"

"You're immortal?" I asked.

"Yes. I can be killed, if anyone is brave enough and skilled enough, but I will never die of natural causes. By the way, you're not."

"I'm not what?" I asked.

"Skilled enough. The three of you never had a chance to kill me. That's why you're down here sitting at my table. I'm as safe from you as I am from old age."

Tivernius leaned back in his chair and sipped his wine while I processed all this. "Okay, so you're in love with Milandra, and she's in love with you. And you guys are planning a wedding. And then suddenly something goes wrong."

"All true," he said.

"So what happened? Why aren't you living over there with Milandra in faerie/dragon bliss or whatever?" Greg asked.

"She became queen. I attended her coronation ball, we danced, we laughed, we kissed. It was glorious." The sappy dragon's voice trailed off into blissful memory. I cleared my throat.

"Then within a matter of days, she turned cold. She would not speak to me, would not return my messages, would not receive my visits. Nothing I did would persuade her to allow me back into her presence, even for a moment so that I might understand what offense I have given."

"So, she dumped you?" Sabrina asked.

"Not only that, but it was then that she started sending these so-called heroes to murder me. Month after month, year after year, fools like you come to my home and attack me without warning. I kill them all, but still more come. I grow weary of this. Perhaps I should let you kill me and end my suffering."

"Okay. That makes it a lot easier on us," I said, standing up.

Sabrina put a hand on my wrist as I reached for my sword. "If you touch that sword I swear to God I will stake you in your sleep," she said through gritted teeth.

"Look, I love a good romance as much as the next guy. Which is to say not at all. But anyway, I don't mind the lovey-dovey crap as long as it doesn't get in the way of the important stuff. Like saving your cousin's life. We're on a deadline, remember?"

"I remember. But I don't think he's just going to let us carve his heart out. Besides, something about this doesn't pass the sniff test." She turned back to the dragon, who was weeping very quietly into his wine. "Tivernius, you said that there was a woman whose father wanted you to marry his daughter before you met Milandra?"

"Yes, Alethea of Cintharion. A terrible woman."

"But socially important?" Sabrina continued.

I looked from cop to dragon and back, starting to follow where she was going.

"Yes, she is now sole ruler of the kingdom, as she has yet to find a man willing to marry her."

"So she was at Milandra's coronation as well?"

"Of course."

"Can faeries glamour each other?"

"Sometimes. If they're very powerful. I fail to see what this has to do with anything."

"You would. You're a man. One with scales and a tail the length of a basketball court, but still a man. Look, Tivernius, I've got an idea. It might not work, and if it doesn't, Milandra will probably kill you herself. But if it does, you get to be with the woman you love. So, you willing to try something a little crazy?"

The dragon stood, a little unsteady from all the wine, and all the whining, and glared at Sabrina. She didn't flinch. I guess after you've been to Hell and Faerieland, one bitchy drunken dragon loses the power to intimidate.

"I would do anything to touch her hand but for one instant, human. Do not toy with me. If you make promises that you cannot keep, the consequences will be dire."

I was pretty familiar with my mouth writing checks that my ass couldn't cash, but it wasn't Sabrina's normal *modus operandi.*

"I can promise that if you will accompany us back to the great hall of Armelion, you will be able to be with your love forever, or at least until somebody kills one of you." Sabrina walked back over to the table, took a last swig of wine, grabbed a big napkin and wrapped a couple of loaves of bread in it. Then she soaked the whole bundle with my leftover red. She looked at me and my flabbergasted partner, laughed a little, and said, "On your feet, Greg. We're blowing this pop stand."

She came to stand with me and Tivernius, Greg hot on her heels. "Now," she said, looking at Tivernius. "When we arrive, stay out of sight. I want to announce you my way, and in my time. Okay?"

"I will do as you ask, just bring me into the presence of my lady once more." Tivernius waved a hand, and with a flash and a disconcerting twist of reality, we were back in Milandra's great hall.

I looked around for the dragon, but could only see Sabrina and Greg.

"We have returned, Your Majesty, and we have with us the heart of the dragon!" Sabrina raised the wine-soaked bundle high in the air, dripping a realistic-looking stream of blood onto the marble floor. Milandra stood, looked at the "blood" spilling onto her stonework, and fell to her knees weeping.

Chapter 18

Sabrina didn't hesitate, just looked at me and Greg, whispered, "Don't say a word," and ran to the distraught monarch's side. I stood right where I was, understanding through years of experience that nothing good would come from me interfering with a woman's plan, much less the plan of an armed woman who knew all the ways to kill me.

Sabrina reached the queen and knelt beside her, bag of bread on the floor just out of Milandra's reach. "What's wrong, Your Majesty? I thought you wanted the monster dead? Have we somehow displeased you?"

Greg whispered "Oscar-worthy" in a tone that only I could hear.

Milandra looked up at Sabrina, and in between sobs managed to say, "I loved him, you idiot human! He betrayed me, and broke my heart, but I loved him. I held out hope for a century that he would return to me, even after his dalliance with that Cintharion bitch, and now he's gone." The queen pulled herself together a little and rose, sniffling.

"Your Majesty, I am sorry," Sabrina said. "I had no idea. What happened? You said you loved him?"

"Yes, human. I loved him. Dragons, like your sanguine and the Fae, have many forms, and his human guise was very pleasing to me. He was my heart's mate, and I was willing to give him anything. Until I saw him kissing Alethea of Cintharion at my coronation ball. To betray my love was bad enough, but to betray me in my very throne room, at my coronation . . . well, it was more than I could bear. I sent many valiant warriors to tear out his heart and bring it back to me, hoping perhaps that Tivernius himself would return to me one day. I would have forgiven him, had he but apologized. It took most of a century, but I realized that my love is stronger than my anger."

Sabrina looked back at us and tilted her head to where Tivernius was hiding behind a column. She whispered "keep him hidden" under her breath so that only a vampire could hear, and I nodded at her.

Tears still streamed down her face, but Milandra was one of those women that could cry in public and still be beautiful. And now her beauty was turning cold as her shock changed to anger. The pink marble floors were slowly turning gray, shot through with veins of black and blood-red. I remembered what Otto said about the very stone reflecting Milandra's moods, and started to worry. The little queen was getting seriously pissed off, and if Sabrina's plan didn't work soon, we were going to have to fight a whole dimension just to stay alive.

"But you're the queen. You can do whatever you want. Your whim commands the clouds in the sky, your slightest wish makes the grass turn pink. If you wanted to marry Tivernius, why not tell him?" Sabrina prodded.

"I couldn't!" the queen almost shouted. "He betrayed me. Humiliated me on my own coronation day. I couldn't grovel to him after that. I would be the laughingstock of all the realms. And now I shall be forever alone."

It was getting dark in the throne room, and I didn't feel good about getting out of there, with or without Stephen's cure.

Milandra collapsed again into sobs, and Sabrina motioned for me to bring Tivernius to her.

I'd figured out where Sabrina was going somewhere between the reveal of the dragon's "heart" and the marble turning black. I got almost all the way to the sobbing queen before saying, "What if you were wrong, Your Majesty? What if you were not betrayed, but merely tricked by Cintharion glamour?"

Silence crashed down around us. The temperature in the throne room dropped thirty degrees and frost filled the veins in the marble. Milandra's eyes went wide, then began to narrow in fury as she caught sight of Tivernius for the first time.

"What is the meaning of this, vampire?" Milandra's eyes bored holes in Tivernius.

I needed to talk fast. "You told us that the Fae have multiple forms. And tons of magic, right?"

"Of course."

"And Tivernius told us that Alethea's father wanted him to marry *her*, not you. Right?"

Tivernius spoke, his gaze locked on Milandra's eyes. "Yes. The horrid woman was always pawing at me like I was her property. She even announced our bethrothal after I told her I would rather die than marry her."

"So it wouldn't take much for a faerie to magic themselves to look like Tivernius and be 'caught' kissing Alethea, would it?" Sabrina asked.

"So you didn't—" Milandra asked, stepping closer to the dragon.

"I could never," Tivernius replied.

He held out his arms, and the two of them collided like clichéd movie lovers running through the surf. He actually picked her up and swung around in a circle before putting her down and laying a kiss on the Faerie Queen that curled *my* toes.

I looked up at Sabrina as they broke apart, and I would almost swear that I saw a glint of a tear in her eye. She caught me looking of course, and shot me the finger, completely shattering the mood.

After the Faerie Queen and the dragon had finished making out in the great hall, Milandra turned back to Sabrina and said, "I owe you a great thanks, human. You have done what hundreds of heroes over a century have failed to do. You have brought me the heart of my dragon." She leaned her head against Tivernius' chest, and I swear I heard Greg sniffle from behind me.

"Yes, I thank you for bringing me to my love," Tivernius said. "And now, Milandra . . ." he looked down into her eyes and took both her small hands in his. Tivernius went to one knee on the marble floor, and looking up at Milandra like she was the only woman in the world, said, "Will you be mine? Will you stand by me until the stars fall from the sky? Will you fight with me and beside me? Will you love me no matter how ridiculous and set in my ways I am? Will you allow me to worship you for the goddess of beauty that you are? Milandra, Queen of House Armelion, will you marry me and become Lady Tivernia?"

Milandra looked down at him and said, "I will love you until the flowers no longer bloom. I will stand beside you until the sun refuses to rise. I will kiss you every day that these lips draw breath. I will be your Lady Tivernia, and you shall be King of the Armelion Fae. From this moment forward may our kingdoms be forever joined."

She reached down and took his face in both her hands and kissed him gently. He pulled her down to sit on his knee and began to kiss her more seriously. After a kiss long enough for me to wonder where their air was coming from, they broke apart to a loud cheer. I spun around and saw that out of nowhere a crowd of faeries and humans several thousand strong had filled the great hall, all cheering and waving small flags with pictures of faeries riding dragons on them.

I don't care how long I live, I'll never get used to magic.

Chapter 19

We toasted the happy couple, listened to the cheering of the crowd, and generally fidgeted around for an hour or so before I finally pulled Otto aside. "Look buddy, I'm all for marital bliss and immortal happiness, but we've kinda got a guy dying back on the other side of the magic portal, remember?"

"Fear not, James. Our queen has sent for the apothecary, who is on his way to you now with the *verdirosa* plant. Once I have it, we can deal with the Unseelie and return to your world to heal your friend."

"That's great, Otto," Sabrina said from beside me. "What's an Unseelie, and when will they get here?"

Milandra joined us then, waving an arm and sending the reveling faeries to who-knows-where. "The Unseelie are sometimes considered the Dark Fae. They are cousins to the faeries you know, but their magic is practiced not to create, but to destroy. They use their martial abilities to enslave, not to protect. They do not typically discuss, preferring to fight. In short, they are the antithesis of everything we strive to be. They keep trolls as bodyguards and servants, while we destroy the loathsome creatures on sight. If there are trolls making their way into the mundane realms, no doubt the Unseelie will know about it."

Apparently the Unseelie were a bit of an unpleasant topic among the Armelion Fae, like *that* uncle at every Southern family reunion.

"As usual, *your highness*, you prove your ignorance with every syllable." An oily voice came from behind me, and I whirled to see a seven-foot tall faerie standing far too close for comfort. Clad all in black, his white hair made a sharp contrast to his ensemble, and his dark eyes scanned the room for threats like a tiger in a cage. He was just as handsome as every faerie I'd seen so far, but his was a cruel kind of handsome, like the chisel-jawed bad guy from every 80s movie.

He carried two long swords with hilts showing signs of use, and a dagger protruded from the top of each knee-high boot. I thought I saw a couple of small blades tucked into his gloves as well, but I couldn't be sure. What I could be sure of was that this dude was bad news, and that he'd somehow gotten close enough to stab me in the back without me ever hearing him enter the room. I pretty much hated him on sight, and by the look he gave me I'd say the feeling was mutual.

"Count Darkoni, you are welcome to my hall and my lands. I pledge you and yours safe passage and lodging as long as you reside here and maintain the peace with my people and other guests." Milandra crossed the room to stand stiffly in front of her throne, hand on the hilt of a sword I'd never seen before. The hilt was plain silver, with a large sapphire set into the pommel, and the scabbard showed signs of plenty of use.

"Fear not, little queen. We shall behave ourselves while we are here. And if we do not, I have no doubt you will enjoy feeding us to your husband. Or is that why I'm here? Do you tire of your pet lizard already? Or did you bring me here to offer me some consolation prize?" He looked Sabrina up and down like a piece of meat, and licked his lips.

She met his eyes without a hint of fear and walked over to the faerie like she was the queen, not Milandra. She reached up and grabbed Darkoni's collar, pulling him down until they were on eye level.

Very slowly she spoke directly into the faerie's face. "Not if you were the last almost-human left in all the worlds. You couldn't handle me, and you certainly don't deserve me." Then she slapped him across the face with a sound like a .22 going off.

Darkoni's hand flashed out, but I was there first. I caught him by the wrist before he could hit Sabrina, and I gave his wrist a good squeeze. When I could hear the bones grind together, I stopped. Darkoni never flinched.

"Don't even think about touching her, Tinkerbelle," I said through gritted teeth.

"Or what? You'll bleed all over me? Thorgun, show our fanged friend here your hand."

The sleazy faerie smiled down at me as I felt the presence of something very large behind me, and a hand very gently covered my head. My whole head, from crown to jaw, fit inside the huge, smelly troll hand that descended from above me. Thorgun didn't speak or even put any pressure on my scalp, he just rested his hand on my head, holding it like I could palm a baseball. I got it. He could squash my head like a grape before I could even think about hurting his boss. I hate melodramatic monsters.

"Now, why don't we all sit down and behave like civilized beings. Even those of us who obviously are not," Darkoni said.

The hand disappeared from my head. I turned around and looked up, way up at his troll bodyguard. He had nothing on Tivernius' dragon size, but at nine and a half feet tall with fingers as big around as my wrists, I didn't want to arm-wrestle him anytime soon. I let go of Darkoni's wrist, after giving it one last squeeze for good measure. Petty, I know, but sometimes that's how I roll.

"What a lovely idea, Count Darkoni," Milandra said, as though nothing out of the ordinary had happened.

She waved her hands and a table appeared with chairs sized for all the occupants, even Thorgun and his twin, who stood on the other side of Darkoni. The Unseelie count had brought a retinue of about half a dozen faeries with him, but the trolls were the real muscle. Both of them made the one we fought outside the bar look like a half-grown kid, and they had hammers hanging over their shoulders with heads bigger than a dishwasher. We took our seats, our team on one side, the Unseelie entourage on the other side, and Milandra got right down to business.

"Count Darkoni, we have called you here to inquire why there have been troll attacks on changelings in the mundane world. Would you care to enlighten us?" the Faerie Queen asked.

When I glanced at her I saw that she had magically changed into her robes of state and crown. Tivernius was decked out, too, and a golden circlet rested on his head to match the silver one on Milandra's brow.

"I would love to, Your Majesty, if I had any inkling of what you are talking about." The Unseelie count had transformed his wardrobe as well, now garbing himself in robes of deepest black velvet with black fur trim. A black circlet capped his brow, with a large red stone in the center. The stone pulsed rhythmically, almost as if it were in time to a heartbeat somewhere. I looked down to see if my clothes were any different, but it was the same armor I'd put on when I crawled out of bed in the morning.

Oh well, can't have everything.

"Please, Your Excellence, do not play ignorant with us. Your kind has long held enmity for the changelings, and you have much truck with the trolls. If you are not behind these attacks, then who?" Milandra seemed almost to be enjoying the jousting with the snotty faerie, but I wasn't sure she was going to get anywhere.

"Of course we loathe the changelings, but it is the human vermin that we would exterminate, not the innocent Fae that *you* cast out like so much unwanted livestock. We are the rightful lords of this realm, and bringing humans here to breed with and create abominations like yourself is an affront to our true heritage."

I took a closer look at Milandra, and for the first time could see that her ears were a little more rounded than the rest of the faeries I'd seen. Must have been a human branch on her family tree somewhere in the past.

"If we wanted to attack anyone, you would be a more likely target than any poor changelings you've cast away into the mundane world like so much rubbish." Darkoni smiled and leaned back in his chair. "I suppose if that is all you have to ask, then we will accept payment for our travels and leave." He reached for a small bag lying on the table beside Milandra's hand, and she clasped her hand over his wrist before he could withdraw.

The Unseelie stood and drew a knife, pointing the tip at Milandra's wrist. "I suggest you release my arm, before you lose your own, Your Majesty."

I whispered from behind him, "I don't think that's a good idea, Excellence."

He turned his head slightly and saw the point of my dagger hovering right beside his eye. Otto and Greg had the trolls covered, and Armelion knights surrounded the rest of Darkoni's entourage.

"This is an outrage, Milandra," Darkoni shouted, veins bulging in his neck. "We have come here in good faith, answered your questions, and now I wish to take my payment and leave. You stretch the boundaries of hospitality to the breaking point, lizard-slut."

"That's it, I'm drinking him." I grabbed his collar and pulled the count's neck around toward my mouth, only to have him twist in my grasp and stab me in the chest with the dagger he'd threatened Milandra with only seconds before. I looked down at the hilt sticking out of my chest, and then I got really mad. Apparently chain mail is only useful against swords and slashing weapons, because the faerie's dagger went through my armor like a hot knife through butter.

"I really, really liked this shirt, you prick," I said, just before I took him by the neck and one wrist and flung Darkoni across the great hall. He crashed into the far wall and slid down like the coyote in a Saturday morning cartoon. I pulled the dagger out of my chest, looked over at Milandra, and said, "Sorry, but he was a real asshole."

"He's also not dead, bro," Greg said from right beside me. I followed his gaze and saw a very angry Unseelie count heading my way with a sword in one hand and a wicked barbed dagger in the other.

"Crap. Sabrina, cover the queen," I yelled as I reached across the table and grabbed Milandra's sword. "Sorry, Majesty, but you need to not be here for this part. Greg, you with me?"

"Right here." My partner, being the smart one of the pair, had not left his sword in his bedroom this morning. Me, being the good-looking one, would be using a sword borrowed from the Faerie Queen in tonight's entertainment. Then with a howl of rage from Darkoni, the great hall erupted in mayhem and bloodshed.

Chapter 20

Greg and I hopped onto the table to get a better view of things, and I ended up eye-to-eye with Thorgun, who was bringing his giant hammer around for a swing at Otto. I waited until he got the hammer up to the top of his swing to slide my sword into the unprotected space under his arm. A gout of greenish-black blood spurted from the wound, and the troll's eyes rolled back in his head. He started to topple forward, right onto Greg and me.

"Split!" I yelled as he fell forward, and the gigantic body came crashing down, tearing the sword from my grasp and turning the heavy wooden table into toothpicks. Greg and I dove in opposite directions, him landing on the back of an Unseelie man-at-arms with an unpleasant crunching sound, while I went headfirst onto the floor.

I'd love to say I rolled to my feet in a smooth motion and came up with a knife in each hand, but the reality of it is that I sprawled on the marble floor like a skinny fish out of water and lay there for a minute cursing about how bad my knee hurt. After a couple seconds' worth of creative profanity, I stood up and looked around for an abandoned weapon. Thorgun's hammer was lying on the ground, but even with my vamp-strength I couldn't swing that behemoth effectively. I snatched up a shattered board and brought it up just in time to block a sword blow from a very angry Count Darkoni, who smiled as he circled me with his sword and dagger.

"I will enjoy bathing in your blood, vampire," he sneered as I tried to parry all his thrusts.

"Well, since I borrow it, you won't technically be bathing in *my* blood," I said as I took a swing at his head. He ducked easily, and I got a slash across the ribs that my armor turned aside. At least my chain mail was good for something.

"No matter, bloodsucker, it won't be inside you any longer, that's all that matters to me." He lunged with the sword, and I batted it aside easily.

Unfortunately I forgot about the knife in his other hand. At least, I forgot about it until he buried it in my thigh. The barbed blade ripped all sorts of useful things when he jerked it out of me, and I screamed as I fell to one knee.

"Now die, fool," he snarled.

I looked up as he raised his sword for one final thrust, and did the only thing I could think of. I bit him on the inside of the thigh.

Darkoni threw his head back and screamed, then stabbed downward with his sword. My armor deflected the worst of the blow, and he dropped the knife to try a second time with both hands. That cost him valuable seconds, though, and as he raised his blade for another thrust I drained more of his lifeblood with every heartbeat. He summoned up all his remaining strength for another downward cut, and I reached out with my left hand and broke his kneecap, knocking him backward and dislodging me from his leg. Arterial blood spurted high into the air, and I crawled up the count's twitching body to get to his throat.

I stopped right before I bit into him again, and looked him in the eyes. "Now who's sending the trolls?"

The count laughed, a wet, dying sound, and spat in my face. "We have no need to kill our own kind, fool. We wish to purge all the realms of inferior beings, like yourself."

"Well, today's purge isn't going so well for you, asshole." With that, I bit deep into his neck and drew the last drops of blood from his body.

I stood up, faerie blood and battle fury roaring in my veins, and took the count's sword from his dead fingers. I quickly cut off his head, just in case faeries could come back as vampires, and looked around at the rest of the fight.

Sabrina had Milandra backed into a corner behind her and was holding off a pair of Unseelie soldiers who looked like they had bad intentions for the Faerie Queen. Tivernius and Otto were duking it out with Thorgun's evil twin, and they seemed to be holding their own. Greg was swashbuckling with two dark faeries, and the knights seemed to have everything else under control. I tossed Darkoni's sword across the room and through the back of one of the soldiers threatening the queen. His partner turned to watch him fall, and Sabrina cut his head half off with her sword.

I ran to pull Milandra's sword out of Thorgun's armpit, and looked around for something else to punch. I froze as a hand wrapped around my ankle, then yanked up abruptly, upending me onto the floor with a crash of chain mail, plates and vampire parts. I rolled over and looked up, trying to see what was after me now.

I lay there, mouth open as I watched Count Darkoni's body reach down, pick up his head, and jam it back onto his shoulders. The count rolled his shoulders like a boxer loosening up before a round, then picked me up and hurled me across the great hall.

I crashed into a wall and slid ten feet to the floor, still staring at the undead Unseelie. The zombie Count didn't seem any the worse for wear from his recent demise, and he stalked across the room towards Milandra with murder in his eyes. I scrambled to my feet, still high on faerie blood, and blocked his path to the Faerie Queen.

"Just out of curiosity, how many times will I have to kill you?" I asked.

Darkoni just grinned and punched me in the chest. I staggered back several steps and looked down at my dented breastplate. The chest was caved in to a point that breathing was nigh-impossible, and I was pretty sure he'd cracked my sternum. I could *feel* the bones knit as the magical blood in my veins kept me going, and I didn't need to breathe except to talk, so I rushed back at the Count.

His eyes widened at my assault, and I noticed for the first time that his eyes had gone completely black. No pupil, no iris, no nothing. Just black. For some reason, that was creepier than the whole screwing his head back on thing. Probably because dead guys walking around had long since lost their ability to impress me.

But he locked those black eyes on me, raised a hand palm-out in my direction, and I froze. It was like invisible bonds wrapped every inch of me, and I couldn't move a muscle. My eyes widened as the dead faerie closed on me, and it smiled at the terror in my eyes.

The Unseelie faerie stretched a hand out to me, and its fingers glowed with a dark aura, almost like it was surrounded by a halo of blackness, if that's even possible. When it pressed a finger to my forehead, the temperature plummeted and everything went away.

I was suddenly alone, floating in a featureless void with no indication of where I was, *what* I was or what was happening. I thought my eyes were open, but the darkness was so complete I couldn't be sure. A voice came from inside me and all around me, a sibilant whisper that penetrated my skull and ran through my brain like rivers of ice.

The voice latched onto my fear, and spun it into a hurricane.

"You're alone, Jimmy, in a pit as black as your name, as black as your heart. No one can find you here, because no one cares enough to look. You're just another parasite, Jimmy, just another leech to be burned off and thrown aside to shrivel and cook in the sun. You're nothing, less than nothing, because at least nothing can survive on its own. You can't even do that, you worthless bloodsucker."

"You're the lowest of the low, Jimmy. You killed your best friend and made him a monster. You watch your only other friend age and waste away, and now you want to spread your filth to that girl? Why would she want a nothing like you? She can have a real man. A man that she can grow old with. A man she can go out in the daytime with. A man who won't try to kill her while she sleeps and turn her into a soulless abomination. You're nothing. You've always been nothing, all the way back to high school."

"But I can make you *something*, Jimmy. I can make you special. I can make you live again. I can make you whole. I can make you into something she can love. Something she can touch. Something she won't be afraid of. Just say yes, Jimmy. Just let me in, and I"ll make you a real boy."

The voice wrapped around my head and my heart, poking at all my soft spots. I didn't know what it wanted, then I did. Then I knew.

I spoke. "Come here," I whispered.

I could feel it, the *presence* that had been riding along with Count Darkoni. The nasty hitchhiker that wanted to piggyback on my soul for a little while.

"I'm here, Jimmy. Are you ready?"

"I'm ready," I whispered back.

"Say the word, and I'll make you magic."

"Here's a couple of words. Go. Fuck. Yourself." I opened my eyes and I was back in the great hall, half a second after the dead faerie had mojo'd me. I stepped forward, Milandra's sword flashing across the distance between us, and I sliced the count's head cleanly from his shoulders again.

This time, instead of a simple collapse, a black mass rose out of the body with a shriek, spinning faster and faster in a whirlwind toward the high vaulted ceiling, finally disappearing with a flash of crimson light. The body itself crumpled to the floor and dissolved into a steaming pile of dust.

I looked around at where my friends and Milandra's people seemed to have the battle well in hand, and took the opportunity to crawl under the huge table and pass out.

I woke to Greg's toe prodding me in my ribs, none too gently I might add. I looked up at him and felt an indescribable warmth flood through me. I scrambled to my feet and pulled him to me in a tight hug. It wasn't even one of the one-armed bro-hugs that we usually do, it was a full-on hug with my arms wrapped all the way around his pudgy body.

"Thank God you're still alive," I said.

Greg patted me on the back awkwardly and slithered out of my grasp. "Yeah, you too, pal. Really. Glad you're not deader. Now . . . uh, let's just . . . not hug anymore, okay?"

"Yeah, fine. Okay. No more hugging." I looked around, and Sabrina, Milandra, Otto and Tivernius were all looking at me strangely. They kept their distance, as though I might have come down with some kind of weird disease that's spread by hugging.

I held Milandra's sword out to her, hilt-first. "I think this is yours, Your Majesty. Sorry about kinda stealing it."

She held up a hand, then unfastened her sword belt and passed that over to me. "I think you may need it more than I do, James. Especially if what I suspect happened near the end of the battle is true."

"Yeah, dude," Greg said, "what happened to you? I finished off my guys, then helped Otto and Ty take out the last troll, and when we turned around you were out like a light under the table."

"Didn't you see what happened with the Count?" I asked. Greg shook his head, and I looked around at the rest of them.

"I believe I understand what you saw, but I would like to hear you describe everything in your own words," Milandra said.

She waved a hand, and comfortable chairs and drinks appeared. I had to admit, I might not love magic, but I could get used to some of the perks.

I described everything that happened from the time I killed the Count to the time I killed him again, then told them all about the black cloud thing, the void and the whispers. I didn't mention exactly *what* the voice was whispering, preferring to get out of the encounter with a sliver of dignity.

"So, Your Majesty. What was that thing, and how did I run it off?" I asked when I was finished.

"*Sluagh*," she said, and Tivernius' eyes went wide.

"Bless you," I said. Nobody laughed. "Okay, fine. What's a *sluagh*?"

Milandra actually shivered at the word. "The *sluagh* are souls. In a vast oversimplification, they are the vilest souls to ever walk the earth. Far too foul for Heaven, these creatures are rejected by all the Hells as incapable of redemption. They can touch all realms, but are of none. They wander between the worlds wreaking havoc as they see fit. They can only be slain by weapons of powerful magic, that's why when you slew Darkoni with his sword, the *sluagh* inside him was able to continue manipulating his body as it searched for another host."

"Another host?" I asked.

"You damaged the host body, James. It needed to find another one to inhabit. But it can only bond with a willing inhabitant. When you rejected it, the spirit needed to find another host. Then you struck it with my sword, and that was enough to kill both host and spirit."

"You're telling me your sword is magical, and that I just killed a spirit-creature that's too evil for Hell?" I asked.

"In a nutshell, yes," Milandra replied.

"Shit." I trend toward the profane when truly shocked. "But if I killed it, why do you want me to keep your sword?"

"I have a feeling you're going to need it more than I will. After all, if there was a *sluagh* controlling a pack of trolls here in Faerie, perhaps there is another one commanding the beasts in your realm. If nothing else, think of it as a gift from a grateful wedded couple, with no obligations."

"Thanks, Your Majesty. I'll try not to kill anything inappropriate with it," I said.

"I hate to be the one to break up the party, but can we get home soon? I do still have a cousin dying there," Sabrina said.

"Of course, my dear. Otto will travel with you to administer the cure. He knows how to properly prepare the *verdirosa* so as not to kill anyone who touches it."

"Well that's handy," I said.

Milandra stood and waved her hands in a big circle. A shimmering circle appeared in the hall, and Sabrina stepped through it. Greg followed, and I started toward it.

Milandra held up a hand. "Be careful, James. I feel there may be something larger at work here. In all my years I have never heard of a *sluagh* attacking Faerie. If someone is commanding these creatures, they may be more powerful than we can comprehend."

"Yeah, I'm out of my league. I know. Again," I said as I stepped through the portal.

Chapter 21

We stepped through a glowing golden portal and were suddenly back in my less-than-glowing apartment. No more pink sky, no more Technicolor foliage, just some stains of indeterminate origin on the carpet and a couple of discarded *Magic: The Gathering* card wrappers under the coffee table. Sabrina took one look around, then grabbed her cell phone. I don't have any idea where she hid it under the fanboy's wet dream of armor she wore, but she pulled out the device and breathed a sigh of relief.

"Okay, it seems like it's the same day we left, and according to this . . . that can't be right." She shook the phone, then stared at the entertainment center for a minute, then opened up my laptop and looked at the screen.

"You want to tell me what you're doing, or should I just ask for the warrant, Detective?" I asked, closing the lid on my laptop. I had no recollection of the last thing I'd been surfing, but I was pretty sure it was nothing that I wanted Sabrina to see.

"According to my watch, we've only been gone four hours," she replied.

"Time moves differently in Faerie, Detective. And Her Majesty is the ultimate ruler of the land. She created this portal to bring us back very shortly after we left, so I would have plenty of time to deliver the cure to your cousin."

I turned, and there was a giant bald faerie in my den. Again.

"Hi, Otto. Want a beer?" I asked, heading for the fridge.

"No thank you, James. I would like to deliver the *verdirosa* plant as quickly as possible. It decays rapidly and begins to lose effectiveness soon after it leaves Faerie."

"Then we should roll. I'll drive." Sabrina headed up the stairs grabbing her car keys off the bar as she passed. I didn't move, enjoying the thought that she had a place where she always put her keys in my place, and wondering how far up the stairs she'd get before she realized she was still dressed like She-Ra.

She made it almost to the top, then her chain mail skirt got tangled in her feet, and she turned around. "Would you have let me get to the car in this outfit?" she asked me.

"The car? Oh, yeah. But I would have stopped you before you pulled out onto the street." I went to my bedroom, deposited Milandra's sword in a corner, threw on some clothes that didn't look like they came out of *Lord of the Rings Part IV*, and brought out some sweats and a T-shirt for Sabrina. She went into my room to change, and two minutes later we were ready. Otto, of course, just waved his hands and was dressed like a normal, if slightly more fashionable than usual, Charlottean.

Ten minutes later we were all headed for the hospital. Sabrina led the way in her car, lights flashing as she ran red lights and weaved through traffic with abandon. I tucked right onto her back bumper and enjoyed watching Greg hyperventilate in the passenger seat. For a dude with a muscle car, he panicked at the least bit of NASCAR influence on my driving.

"You know the magical plant is in the car ahead of us, right?" he said through gritted teeth.

"Yeah, so?"

"So why are you driving like a bat out of hell?"

"No puns, etc. etc. Because it's 6:45, dude. And I'd like to be inside the hospital before sunrise."

"Sonofabitch," my partner muttered. "Are we gonna have to hang out in the waiting room all day again?"

"I think we can get somebody to drive us home in the trunk if we need to. Hey, maybe we'll get lucky and it'll snow," I said without much hope. Charlotte, NC, has never been known for its snowfall, even in January. But we might luck out and get a really crappy, rainy, overcast day, and then we'd only get nasty sunburn, not charcoal briquet level sunburn.

We pulled into the hospital parking lot, and Sabrina threw a CMPD placard on her dash. I reached across Greg to pop the glove box, and pulled out a small 'Clergy' placard and placed it on the dash of my car.

"Where did you get that?" Greg asked, his eyes wide.

"Stole it from Mike. Come on." I opened the door and got out.

"I am not misusing a clergy sign to get a better parking place. That's so wrong it's out of bounds even for you," Greg said, getting out of the car and slamming his own door.

"Dude, we eat people. We're not friggin' pantheons of morality, okay. Remember, *vampires*. Nosferatu, Lestat, Dracula, the scary one, not like the goofy dude in that episode of *Buffy*."

"But we're not like that. And I don't eat people."

"Tell that to the faerie chick you nibbled on yesterday."

As soon as I said it, I wanted the words back. Greg's head snapped back like I'd slapped him, and I felt like the world's biggest asshole.

After a second or two of cold silence, I said "Look, man, I'm sorry. I didn't mean anything by it. I know that shit was really hard for you, and I hate that you had to do it. But you had to, and you did, and now it's over."

"It's not over. I can still taste her. And I can smell the blood from every human in a hundred yards. And it smells *good*. I don't know how you think you can control it, but you can't. I can't." He didn't look at me for a long few seconds, and when he did, I stepped back a little from the look in his eyes.

"You go ahead, Jimmy. I'll park the car and meet you up there."

"You sure? I'll go with you to park—"

"Go." The word came from somewhere deep inside him, and I remembered the last time I'd heard Greg sound like that. He had been kneeling over the body of a teenage girl, her throat ripped out and her life's blood staining the front of his T-shirt. I'd almost lost him that night to the animal that lives inside of us, and I didn't know if I could pull him back from the edge again.

After a long moment, I tossed him the keys. "Don't scratch the paint."

That worked. He laughed, and the monster was buried again. Greg, the real Greg, gave me the finger and said "I couldn't find a new place to dent this heap of crap if I tried."

While Greg parked the car, I headed up to see Stephen. Sabrina was standing in the sterile hallway outside his room with Mike. Mike took one look at me and burst out laughing. I glanced over at Sabrina, who was trying hard to restrain herself from doing the same thing.

"What? Did I put my shirt on backward again?" I checked my fly, and Jimmy Jr. was safely tucked away. Then I got a good look at my arm. "No," I whispered, the mere thought of this horror chilling me to the bone. I turned and ran down the hall past the elevators and the waiting area to the public restrooms.

I flung open the door and skidded to a halt in front of the wall of mirrors. Fortunately for me, the hospital went cheap on their mirrors and didn't use real silver backing. Vampires don't reflect in those since the silver screws with our magic. But cheap mirrors, no problem. So I could see exactly what had my friends in hysterics. I was *sparkling*.

Not only was I sparkling, but I was sparkling in colors. Milandra obviously had a sense of humor, since she returned me to the real world with a shower of pink and purple sparkles trailing from my hair. I looked like I'd run naked through a gay glitter factory. I turned on the water and started frantically pulling paper towels from the dispenser and scrubbing myself, but the sparkles were stuck to me with some kind of magic. I was just going to have to look like a cross-dressing stripper, or a teenaged girl's makeup set exploded all over me, until it wore off.

I trudged back to where Mike and Sabrina stood. I stopped in the hallway and did my best runway turn for them. "I sparkle. I get it. It's funny. Pretty soon I'll get angsty and use more hair product. But for now, how's Stephen?"

Mike spoke up. "Your faerie friend is in there with him now. He refused to allow us into the room as he administered his treatment, saying that it could be dangerous to humans. To his credit, Mr. Neal's partner refused to leave. Mr. Glindare made it very clear that he would not be leaving his partner's side for any reason."

"Husband," I corrected.

"You'll have to forgive me if I stick with 'partner,' James. I'm as progressive as I can be, within the limits of Church doctrine. And until the Church recognizes their union, I'm afraid 'partner' is as far as I can go."

I decided not to get in a conversation about separation of church and state with one of my oldest friends in the middle of the lemon-scented hallway of a hospital, so I let it go. Otto came out of the room then, and the scent of the *verdirosa* followed him in a cloud, mixed with something new, something sweeter and a little hint of faerie blood. Otto looked more tired than he had after our fight with the Unseelie, but he smiled as he looked at Sabrina.

"He will heal," Otto said.

Sabrina sagged against me in relief. I wrapped my arms around her instinctively, then tightened them a little when I realized what we'd done. She pulled back, wiping her eyes with the heel of her hand and giving one of those embarrassed little chuckles that people do when they let you see more than they wanted to. But I heard her heart beat, and I heard it speed up a little when I pulled her close, and the sound made me warm, even though the January chill still lingered on my skin.

"Thanks, Otto. That's awesome. Is he awake? Can we go in?" I asked.

Otto waved us on, then turned to leave.

Sabrina stopped him. "Thank you. Really. If you ever need anything, I owe you one."

Otto smiled down at her. "You owe no debt to me, Defender. I did as my queen ordered, and gladly. I provided aid to one of my own, and in doing so brought succor to a friend of my House. But should I require your assistance in the future, I shall call."

"Do that, Otto. We'll be there," I said, holding out my hand.

He smiled, shook my hand, then Sabrina's, then stepped through a glowing portal and vanished.

"I will never get used to that," I said, turning to Stephen's door.

"Wait," Sabrina said. There was a tentative quiver in her voice, completely out of character with the woman who was willing to shoot a dragon in the ass for her cousin. But I guess family can get you where monsters can't touch.

"It'll be fine," I whispered to her. "He still loves you, or he wouldn't have told his husband about you."

She looked at me nervously, then nodded once and put her hand on the door.

"Come on in, cuz. I know you're standing out there getting all worked up for nothing. And bring your pet vampire in, too."

Stephen's voice sounded strong, but if he called me a pet again I might see what I could do about that.

We walked in and Sabrina's cousin was sitting up in bed, looking very little like someone who'd been beaten nearly to death less than forty-eight hours earlier. Mike followed us in, nodding pleasantly to a very confused-looking Alex.

"Ummm, Stephen, did you just call him a . . . ?" Alex trailed off as he looked over at me, seeing nothing about me that screamed "vampire." After all, the traditional mythology does not include skinny, six foot four inch vampires with pointy noses and brown hair that shoots out in every direction out from under a purple Clemson Tigers baseball cap.

I nodded to him, and held out my hand. "Mr. Glindare, good to see you again. I suppose you must be Stephen."

We shook hands, and he looked past me to Sabrina. She stood in the doorway, showing nerves you wouldn't expect from a woman who's traveled to Hell and back for a case, literally.

"You two want a moment alone? A pair of boxing gloves? Dr. Phil?" I asked.

Stephen struggled to a more upright position and held out his arms. Sabrina rushed into his embrace, and you could almost watch a decade of distance vanish in an instant.

"This would be when I say something like 'don't worry, they're cousins,'" I said to Alex.

"Funny, I was thinking I should say the same thing to you." He grinned up at me.

I looked around for a chair. Finding none, I sat on the edge of the bed at Stephen's feet. "Now," I began, "I hate to break up the touching reunion scene, but I'd like to make sure that there's not another one of these things coming back to finish the job. You know it was a troll that attacked you, right?"

"Actually, I had no idea what it was. I was walking to meet Alex after rehearsal, and something grabbed me and pulled me into the alley. It muttered something about me being the next contestant, or something like that, and to come along quietly."

He took a deep breath, and Alex reached over and patted his leg. "It's okay, babe. Take your time."

Stephen continued. "I grabbed my cell phone to call Alex, and the thing just swatted it out of my hand. It punched me in the face, and knocked me cold. The next thing I knew I woke up in a locker room, wearing a pair of shorts and nothing else. Another . . . troll, I guess, was in the room with me, and he shook my hand and told me he was about to kill me. I told him I didn't want any trouble, and he said it was nothing personal, that's just how the fight was scheduled—to the death. Then a door opened, and he walked out of the room. There were all these people out there, and they were all cheering, and screaming for him, and for me."

Stephen looked around, then went on. "Then the door opened again, and two other trolls came in. They dragged me out into this cage, put a sword in my hand, and told me to fight. I threw the sword down, and they put it back in my hand. They told me I could either fight and die, or just die. They left, and the first troll came after me. He had on these huge metal gloves with spikes on them, and I—" He took a sip of water, trying to pull himself together.

"I couldn't do anything against him. I've taken some judo and tae kwon do classes, but this guy was huge, and fast, and I'd been knocked out. He beat the hell out of me. The last thing I remember is him catching me with an uppercut and hearing my jaw crack. After that, it was all black. Then I woke up here, with a bald faerie feeding me magical guacamole."

"Yeah, about that . . ." Alex said, looking from me, to Sabrina, to his husband. I held up both hands and stood, not wanting to get involved in family drama.

Stephen blushed. "Yeah, so . . . Honey, I'm a faerie! That's a lot easier to say when you've been called one your whole life. I'm sorry I didn't tell you, Alex. I just found out about this a couple weeks ago. Up until then I just thought I was, you know, talented."

"Being one of the Fae has nothing to do with your ability at dance, Stephen, just like the fact that I'm a vampire has nothing to do with my rapier-like wit." I paused to glare at Mike, who was suddenly afflicted with a coughing fit. "It just means you're a bit faster, more agile and stronger than a human. And it means you'll probably live forever. Unless that only counts in Faerieland. Then forget I said anything." I threw that last bit in because his husband was right there, and I didn't want to have to watch while they sorted through the whole immortality thing.

"So now where are we?" Sabrina asked. "Instead of a series of random beatings, we've got some kind of underground fight club going on with trolls and faeries, and no idea where to find out more about it."

"Oh, I think I've got a pretty good idea," I said, heading toward the door. "I've got something I want to look into. Sabrina, can you stay here and play catch-up with your cousin for a while? I want to make sure somebody is here in case someone, or something, tries to get at him again. Can you meet us at our place with the case files on all the attacks tomorrow night? I want to look at all the data and start to re-interview the other victims. Maybe one of them remembers something."

"I can do you one better," she said, reaching into her purse and pulling out a USB memory stick. "I've got all of the case files with me, so you guys can start tonight while I hang here with my cousin."

I took the memory stick and tucked it away in my pocket.

"That's great. Mike, can you get in touch with your witch friend and see what she knows about trolls and faeries? Maybe there's some kind of secret Wiccan database that she can tap into. I'll get Greg and we'll look into my lead. Stephen, if you think of anything, give us a call. Sabrina, if anything bad happens, call me immediately. Please do not try to stop a troll on your own." I started out the door and stopped when I realized everybody was still staring at me.

"What?" I asked.

"I think we're all waiting for you clap your hands and yell 'Break!' coach," Sabrina said with a smirk.

"Oh, shut up. And be careful," I said on my way out the door.

"Aye, Aye, Cap'n," Sabrina said to my back as I headed down the hall. "Oh, and one other thing," she yelled. "Take a shower, you sparkle!"

Chapter 22

I caught up with Greg as he got out of the elevator, holding a Styrofoam cooler. I grabbed him by the elbow, spun him around and pressed the button to take us back down to the morgue.

"Where are we going? I stopped off at Bobby's already for extra blood," Greg said as the doors slid shut.

I raised an eyebrow at him.

"This seems like a tough job, and I don't want us to run out. And I thought Sabrina might have some family crap to deal with. Just trying to be helpful."

Every once in a while, like once a decade or so, Greg surprises me with his observations.

"Fair enough," I said. "And thanks. We're going back to see Bobby. He knows more about these attacks than he told us."

The doors slid open, and we walked down the hallway. Greg kept trying to say something as we walked, but I just held up a hand. Bobby knew what was going on, and he hadn't bothered to tell me. I was pissed, to say the least.

I barged through the doors of the morgue right in the middle of an autopsy. Bobby was elbows-deep in a dead guy's midsection, and I skidded to a halt right inside the door. The smell was almost enough to knock me over, the scent of blood and decay and disinfectant making my eyes water.

"Jesus Christ, Bobby. How do you work in that stench?"

Bobby reached up and clicked off a recorder. "I'm human, Jimmy. And I put Vick's VapoRub on my upper lip for the bad ones. This is a bad one. The jar's on the counter."

I opened the jar and smeared some of the ointment on my lip. I held it out to Greg, then realized that he wasn't with me. My partner, knowing what was going on, had stopped outside the swinging doors to the autopsy room. He waved at me. I mouthed *Asshole* back at him. He waved again.

"What happened to him?" I looked at the corpse. It had been lying around for a few days getting smelly. Bobby had the midsection cut open and the front of the ribcage out.

"I think a heart attack. His mailman found him today. The mail had been stacking up for about four days, and that fits with a rough time of death. Poor dude lay there all alone, nobody to miss him but his cat."

"How do you know he had a cat?" I asked. I almost told Bobby not to answer that question, but my morbid curiosity got the better of me. Again.

"There are injuries to the soft tissues of the face consistent with a house cat," he said in his most clinical voice.

"You mean his cat ate his face?" I moved around to the head of the body. Sure enough, his eyes, lips and part of his nose were gone. There were little bite marks on his cheeks, and his earlobes looked chewed.

"Damn, dude. That's nasty," I said.

"This from the guy that drinks blood to stay alive," Bobby said.

"That's what I'm saying. My bar is pretty high, and that's nasty even to me. But I didn't come down here to talk about eating faces."

"Yeah, what's up? Greg was just here and I gave him a special deal on some extra B-negative we got in. Private donor, with instructions that his blood only be used for his transfusions. Then he died of pneumonia. Ironic, huh?"

"I guess. Tell me what you know about the faerie fights."

"The what? Oh! You mean the thing? Yeah, well, you know all about it, you said so."

"I don't know anything about it. I was lying."

"You lied to me? That ain't cool, man."

"Hello? Vampire? Bloodsucking soulless demon, remember? I lied. Now I'm not. So tell me what I want to know."

"I can't, Jimmy. They'd sic their trolls on me if I talked, and you saw what they can do to a faerie. I don't even want to think what they'd do to a human. Besides, I don't know anything. I just go to the fights, put a little money down, watch the show, you know? It's not like they're people. They're monsters."

"Like us?" Greg asked.

He'd finally braved the funk in favor of knowing what the hell was going on. I swear, curiosity might turn out to be lethal to vampires, too.

"Nah, you guys are cool. But I don't know these guys. I mean, look, I'll tell you what I can." Beads of sweat had popped out on Bobby's forehead. Even though he was a big guy, and a former professional athlete, he knew he didn't want to find out just how strong a pissed-off vampire is.

"Let's start with where the fights happen," I said.

"They move, man. I get a text with a date, and if I want to go to the fight that night, I reply 'yes.' Then I get a text with an address and a time. Never more than an hour's notice, and so far it's never been the same place twice."

"When's the next fight?" Greg asked.

"Tomorrow night. I didn't reply, 'cause I got a date with a good-looking lady, you know?"

"Reply. Tell them yes. Then when you get the location, you call me. Immediately." I leaned in and showed a little fang to drive my point home.

Pun completely intended. Bobby nodded frantically, then pulled out his cell phone.

He sent off the text and looked up at me. "You gonna head out now and go do some investigating or something?"

"Not yet, Bobby. First you're going to tell me everything you know about the fights. And I mean everything."

"Okay, just . . . back up a little, would you? You're kinda crowding me a little."

"It's intentional." I loomed a little more, then backed off and sat on a rolling stool. "Speak."

"Well, as far as I can tell the fights have been going on for a couple months. They started off slow, like boxing matches, or something. But as the crowds got bigger, the fights got rougher, nastier. They had a first blood match, where the winner is the guy who makes his opponent bleed first. Then they built the cage, and it went no-holds-barred. Whatever the fighters wanted to use, they could use. That last fight, with the faerie dude? It was a damn bloodbath. That troll had lost his last two fights, but he was jacked up and ready to go. He lit into the faerie like a pit bull on a steak, then he broke out this funky spiked glove and just beat the hell out of him."

"The faerie just stood there, taking it as long as he could, but he was crushed, man. And the faerie that runs the place was *pissed*. You could tell he wanted a better fight, and the crowd did too. So after the troll pounded the faerie into paste for a little while, they did a troll match. That was a lot better."

"You know that faerie was our friend's cousin, right? And that those gloves were poisoned and almost killed him, right? And that I'm gonna—"

Greg grabbed me and pulled me back before I broke any parts of Bobby that might be useful later. Like everything.

"I'm sorry, man. I didn't even think about it like that," Bobby said.

"It's cool. Just call me with the address the second that text comes in."

"Sure, man. Sure. But what are you gonna do?" Bobby looked back and forth from me to Greg.

"We're gonna do what we do, Bob. We're gonna be monsters." I let go of his collar, and he slumped backward against the corpse. "Be careful. You've got an elbow in that guy's intestines."

Chapter 23

Fortunately for us, the day turned out to be severely overcast, so Greg and I weren't trapped in the hospital until nightfall. It was still a little unnerving to be driving during the day, so I was grateful to get home after our little chat with Bobby.

I clumped down the stairs to our apartment, tired but energized to finally be making some progress. I hung my coat and guns in the closet and headed to the fridge, even though I smelled Mike hiding in the corner.

"O, B or A?" I asked Greg.

"One of each." He said as he fired up the computer. I tossed his bags of blood on the coffee table and bit into a bag of B-negative. The cold blood wasn't terribly appealing, what with the anticoagulants and plastic taste, but I needed to fill the void. I polished off the first bag and let out a contented sigh.

"Well, Mike, you gonna say something or just lie there on my couch all night?" I said to the priest.

"You knew?" he asked, impressed.

"I'm hungry. I smelled you from the top of the stairs. Been biting your nails to the quick again?"

"An old habit I revert to in times of stress," he answered.

"And this case has you stressed? That's sweet," I said.

"I do have other things in my life, James. As much as it may amaze you, I do not live solely to be your daytime errand boy." There was an odd note in Mike's voice, but he waved aside my concerned look. "Don't listen to me. I'm just a grouchy human up past my bedtime. But I am a grouchy human with information."

"Bedtime? It's not even noon," I said.

"Yes, but I haven't been to bed, Jimmy. I was planning on getting some sleep after I knew Stephen would heal, but *somebody* needed me to talk to Anna and her coven." Mike walked over to the bar and poured himself a scotch. That was one I'd never seen before—Mike drinking before noon. But I guess if you haven't slept in a couple of days, afternoon is relative.

"Sorry about that, pal. Sometimes I forget you're human."

"I'm not sure how to take that, but I'll assume it was meant as a compliment."

"It was, and besides, Anna hates me. So did you see her?"

"No. There is this remarkable invention, Jimmy. It's called a telephone. You can use it to speak to people without showing up at their place of business looking like a disheveled wino."

I gave Mike a closer look, and he did have about three days' worth of beard going, and there was more white in it than I had ever seen before. He'd lost weight, too, and it didn't look like the healthy kind. I opened my mouth to ask him about it, but he spoke first.

"Anna and her friends have noticed an increase in magical energy in recent weeks, much of it centered north of Uptown."

"There is a disturbance in the Force," I intoned gravely. Mike glared at me so I shut up. At least Greg laughed.

"Anyway," Mike went on, "according to the witches, there has been a great deal of powerful magic in use, and by several powerful practitioners. They fear that something dangerous may be on the horizon."

I raised my hand, and Mike looked over at me. "Are we talking about slip-on-a-crack-break-your-mother's-back kind of dangerous, or raising-a-demon-to-take-over-the-world kind of dangerous?"

"They couldn't tell me," Mike said ruefully. "I think they were a little embarrassed that they didn't really understand the nature of the forces at play. Anna thinks it feels potentially very bad, but couldn't say why, and no one else sensed that much."

"That's it? There was a big pile of magic being tossed around somewhere north of downtown?" I asked.

"Uptown," Mike corrected automatically.

"You realize that those are ridiculous arbitrary labels for the same piece of real estate, right?"

The whole uptown/downtown thing always bugged me. People who grew up here, like me, called the center of town "downtown," because that's what you always call the center of town. But a few years ago, the rich folks in the middle of the city decided that it should be called "uptown." So now there's all this confusion about what to call an area of like eight square blocks. But this is the same town where you can stand at the intersection of Queens Road and Queens Road, so what do you expect?

"No matter what you call the neighborhood, the disturbance seems to emanate from the industrial district between downtown and the arts district on North Davidson Street. But it moves around some." Mike rattled his glass and looked at me meaningfully.

I motioned for Greg to fix him another scotch. "All righty, then. There's a gallery crawl tomorrow night, so let's go out among the hippies and freaks to see if we can turn over a rock and find a troll underneath," I said. "If there's something going on up there that needs juice, there will be plenty of souls running around to siphon off of."

"Good idea," said Mike. Before I could find the sarcasm in his apparently sincere comment, his phone rang.

"This is Michael," he answered .

As soon as I heard the voice on the other end, I was on my way to the closet to grab my guns and coat. I put the Glock in my shoulder rig and strapped my Ruger LCP to an ankle holster. As I was pulling on my coat, I tried to listen to the conversation between Mike and Sabrina.

"He . . . it's back!" I heard Sabrina through the phone.

Greg bolted for his room to gear up as well, while Mike talked to Sabrina.

"It's beating the hell out of the cop in the hallway, and then it's coming in here for Stephen! Get away from him, you son of a bitch! No, Alex!" I heard a series of gunshots, then nothing.

I bolted for the stairs, yelling back at Mike, "Wait for us here. Tell her we're on our way."

We dashed up the stairs and jumped in Greg's car. He jammed the hot rod into gear and tore out of the cemetery parking lot like a bat out of hell. I just hoped we weren't too late for Stephen. Or Sabrina.

Chapter 24

We beat the cops to the scene, and didn't bother parking. We just pulled up to the curb and ran for the stairs. I was out of the car before it stopped—rolling awkwardly toward the building—and springing up at a dead run. And when we run, we *move*. I didn't really stop for the door, just ripped it out of the frame and ran up the three flights of stairs to Stephen's floor. I was about to rip that door off the hinges, too, when Greg grabbed my arm.

"What?" I snarled at him. My fangs were fully out, and I was in full-on attack mode. Greg pulled back a hair, but he held fast to my arm.

"Chill for a second. We don't know what we're getting into out there," he said.

"There's a troll out there, and it's come for Stephen. Sabrina's in there. I don't want it to get either of them, so I'm going to stop it," I said and tried to turn back to the door.

Greg held me still without a problem. Truth be told, he's a lot stronger than me, and I'm really strong. We've never known why some of our powers are stronger in one of us than the other, but that's the way it is.

"Dude," he said firmly. "You need to chill for a second. She's a trained professional, she can take care of herself. What if there are already cops out there? You go out there all vamped, and we've got way bigger problems than just a troll. And all you brought was guns? You know you can't take a troll out with bullets. I grabbed this for you." He handed me the sword I'd brought back from Faerieland, the one Milandra thought I might need.

"Thanks. All right, I'll go out—" Just then a huge crash from the hall shook the entire building, and we heard an enormous bellow of rage from the other side of the door. "Screw that, I'm going troll-hunting!" I flung the door open and found myself face to face with . . . Stephen.

But this was Stephen as I'd never seen him, and I was pretty sure Sabrina hadn't either. He had dropped whatever illusion kept him looking human, and he was a big dude. Stephen in faerie-form stood at least six foot eight inches and was cut like a professional wrestler. And I don't mean Dusty Rhodes. Homeboy was ripped, and he was covered in blood that didn't look like it was his. His back was to us, and I could see that he never learned that you could wear boxers under a hospital gown. But that wasn't what stopped me cold. That was the sight of Sabrina unconscious in the hallway with a nine-foot-tall troll barreling toward her at a dead run with murder in its eyes and green stuff dripping from its teeth.

I shoved Stephen to the side, and launched myself at the troll, sword outstretched. I crashed into the monster and buried my blade into its gut to the hilt. I saw about a foot of steel come out of the thing's back, but that didn't stop the troll from wrapping one enormous hand around my throat and punching me in the head with the other fist.

I felt knuckles the size of golf balls crunch into my head and my vision swam black. It pulled the fist back again, and I kicked out, catching the monster in the throat with one foot. It shook its head in sudden pain, and I took the opportunity to puke in its eyes and pull my sword from its belly.

It dropped me to wipe the blood out of its vision, and Greg came in from the other side. He buried a silver dagger in the troll's back, and the beast caught him in the face with a backward-thrown elbow. Greg crashed into the opposite wall, and I saw him sink through the drywall.

The troll caught sight of Stephen again, and started down the hall towards him. "Stephen! Get to the roof! We need room to maneuver!" We also needed a few seconds' breather, and I hoped he could outrun the massive creature long enough for Greg and me to recover our balance.

"Come on, partner, we aren't dead yet," I said as I pulled him out of the wall.

"Actually, we are," he said with a sickly grin. He pointed to the puddle on the floor. "You puked first."

"Strategy. I blinded him with my stomach acid," I said as we staggered to the stairwell. I heard the door to the roof bang open four floors above me. "We gotta hurry. Stephen can't hold that thing for long."

"We don't make stomach acid," Greg said, as we dashed up the stairs. Always gotta have the last word, that's my partner.

We reached the roof a few seconds later, and froze at what we saw. Stephen was there, and he was putting on a demonstration of the uncanny agility of the Fair Folk. I suddenly understood why legend had given them wings—Stephen looked like he was flying as he jumped and somersaulted over the swinging fists of the troll. The monster kept throwing punches, and Stephen kept dodging with a grace that was, well, otherworldly. No wonder the dance company kept him around.

"I bet he's amazing in Swan Lake," Greg murmured, just as awed as I was.

"What do you know from Swan Lake?"

"I'm cultured. But that's not the point. Let's go kick some troll ass."

I nodded at him, and then yelled out to Stephen. "Hey, Baryshnikov! Get over here, and bring your ugly friend!"

The faerie changed direction in midair and landed just in front of us, facing the troll. Greg and I spread out a few feet to either side of him, making a triangle facing the troll, who was readying for another charge. From thirty feet away, the monster bellowed a challenge, or at least what I thought was a really bad insult in Trollish. I bared my fangs and shrieked a scream that came from somewhere around my navel, and all of us rushed forward. Seconds before the inevitable collision, inspiration struck me and I knew how we could kill this thing and not get any more hammered than we already were.

"Go for the knees," I yelled at Greg, and we both dove under the troll's outstretched arms and rolled past the monster.

I lashed out with Milandra's sword and cut the monster's right leg nearly in two, while Greg spun around and shot out the troll's left kneecap. The troll flopped on its belly and slid halfway to Stephen, who looked around for anything to hit the thing with. I threw him my sword, and he cut off the troll's head, splattering even more green-black blood all over the roof. Stephen looked down at the headless monster lying in front of him, and promptly vomited all over its corpse.

"Feel better?" Greg asked me. "Now you're not the only one that puked."

"I told you, that was part of the plan," I protested, and then headed back to where the faerie was standing holding the queen's borrowed sword. When I got to him, I took the blade out of his hand, noticing as I did that the flesh of his fingers was blistered from touching the steel.

Just then, Sabrina burst onto the roof with a shotgun in hand, yelling, "Nobody move!" She saw us standing there, and then rushed over to wrap her arms around Stephen's waist. "Are you okay, Stevie? Did it hurt you? Where's Alex? Is he okay?"

"Alex is fine. I got him to hide in the bathroom when you ran out in the hall after the troll, then I led the thing away from my room so he couldn't get hurt. You guys got here just in time. I don't know how much longer I could have held out against it." The air around him shimmered for a second, and when it cleared he was in his human form again.

"I'm just glad you're both all right." Sabrina hugged him again, and then looked over at me. "What about you?"

"We're all right. A little battered, but nothing a little midnight snack won't cure. What about you? That looks like a nasty bruise." I reached out and gently brushed my fingers against a lump rising on her forehead.

Sabrina looked away quickly. "It's nothing. Just a lump."

"Well, make sure you get that looked at. We'd hate to have to break in another police department resource. Right, Greg?"

I turned to my partner, but he wasn't here. I looked around, and found him searching the troll's body. Greg reached into the dead troll's coat pocket and pulled out a cell phone and a business card.

He held up the phone. "That was nasty. But I bet this is going to be very useful indeed." Then he looked at the card. "Whoa." He passed it to me.

It was one of mine. Now that was weird. And disturbing. I don't give out many of the things, because of the stupid slogan Greg put on them. "Shedding light on your darkest problems." Bleh. But that narrowed the list of people he could have gotten the card from down considerably.

Sabrina walked over to him and held out her hand. "That's evidence, Knightwood. Hand it over."

Greg snatched back the card and slipped both items into his pants pocket. "No way. This is evidence, all right, but you guys can't fight this. If your people go looking into whatever is on the other end of this phone, a lot of them are going to end up hurt or dead. So we'll hang on to the phone, and we'll make the body disappear. And you'll figure out how to write this up in a way that doesn't mention faeries, vampires or trolls. Because that's what we do. Right?"

Sabrina stared at him for a minute, and I could almost see the wheels turning as she tried to come up with a way to follow police procedure and still do the right thing. Finally she said, "Right. I hate it, but you're right." She looked over at me. "When did he get to be the smart one?"

"As much as I hate to admit it, he's always been the smart one," I said.

"Fair enough, but I've got some questions about this troll attack, and we need to get Stephen back to his room." Sabrina took her cousin by the arm and led him through the destroyed stairwell door and down into the hospital.

We rescued Alex from the bathroom, and after convincing him that Stephen was fine, and swiping a couple of chairs from a comatose patient across the hall, we were all crowded into Stephen's room. Alex and Stephen sat on the bed, with Sabrina seated next to them.

Greg wedged a chair under the door, and he and I sat across the bed from Sabrina, who kept eyeballing Greg's jacket pocket like she really wanted that phone back. I scooted forward in my brown pleather hospital chair and moved to cut that off before she got rolling.

"We're all here, Sabrina. What were those questions you wanted to ask?"

"There are a few. Let's start with where did the troll come from?"

"That's an easy one," I replied. "What is Faerieland, Alex? Can I have silly questions for four hundred?"

"No, asshole. Why did it come here specifically? It seems pretty obvious that it was after Stevie, but why?"

"Maybe he was here to make sure Stephen was dead, or dying," I said. "Can you walk us through what happened when the troll first got to the hospital? I'm guessing it didn't just show up all green and rampaging. So what happened before you called us?"

"He looked human when we first saw him," Alex said.

"Yeah, he was dressed like an orderly, or a nurse. I can't tell. He was wearing scrubs," Sabrina agreed.

"He came into my room, and seemed surprised when he saw that I was awake. When I looked at him, I could see through his glamour. It was like there were two of him. One was the orderly, and that looked fake, like a ghost image. And then I could see the troll underneath that, and I freaked out," Stephen said.

"And when Stephen freaked out, the troll dropped the illusion, and all hell broke loose," Sabrina said.

"That's when some of us got thrown into bathrooms for our own safety," added a bitter-sounding Alex.

"I said I was sorry about that," Sabrina said in her least sorry voice.

"Okay, so what does that tell us?" I asked.

"It seems that the troll didn't expect Stephen to be awake, and when he was, he had to switch to Plan B in a hurry," Sabrina said.

"His Plan B sounds a lot like mine," I muttered.

"You mean 'punch something a lot?'" Greg asked.

"Yep, that pretty much defines my Plan B. And my Plan A, come to think of it," I agreed.

"But what does that tell us? And why did they come after Stevie and none of the other victims?" Sabrina asked.

"How do we know they didn't?" I felt a lump the size and shape of a brick settle in my stomach as a bunch of pieces started to fall into place.

"What do you mean?" Stephen asked.

"We don't know that they didn't go after the other victims, too, do we?" My eyes got wide as I listened to the words coming out of my mouth. "Oh shit."

"That doesn't sound good," Greg said.

"It's not. Whoever sent the troll here wanted to tie up Stephen as a loose end," Sabrina said.

I was still sitting there with my mouth flapping in the breeze as I realized what a hornet's nest we'd stirred up this time. "That means they'll be going after all their other loose ends, too."

"Oh shit," Greg said, realization dawning in his face.

"Yeah," I said. "And I bet if you give that card a good sniff it's going to smell like domestic beer and expensive cologne," I said.

"Why?" Alex asked, looking lost. "What's going on? And is anyone else going to come after Stevie?"

"Yes. They will come after Stephen again. And you too, now that you know about the trolls. The card will smell like beer because Jimmy gave it to the bartender at Scorpio, George. So since we talked to George, and we're involved in this mess, George is hopefully being held hostage until he's forced to fight in their next cage match."

"Why is that hopeful?" Stephen asked.

"Because that means they haven't killed him yet," I said. "Now if you'll excuse me, I've got to go find all the other victims and get them out of harm's way. If I'm not too late. Sabrina, I'm going to need you with me for the official authority. Greg—"

"Stay here and make sure that anything coming in the room with ill intent ends up with a bad case of the dead." My partner already had his pistol out and was checking the magazine.

"Detective," I said, holding the door for Sabrina. "We've got a town full of faeries to rescue."

We started at Scorpio, but before we got there Sabrina got a call telling us what we feared—the place had been trashed and George was missing. We pulled into the parking lot, and she badged us past the uniforms at the door. I looked around for Otto, but he was nowhere in sight. The club looked different with the fluorescent lights on, smaller and dingy instead of dark and mysterious. The carpet was threadbare, and the bar needed a good coat of varnish. None of this was noticeable when the dance floor was jumping, but in the midday cleaning lights, the whole vibe seemed a little sad.

I took off my shades gratefully as we walked past the vestibule and away from the daylight.

"You okay?" Sabrina asked.

"I'll live, but it's not exactly comfortable. Even with the cloud cover, I'm getting a nice sunburn. And it's hell on my eyes. My pupils are permanently dilated, so I can see in pitch darkness, but even the dim light out there hurts like a mother."

"Sorry."

"Can't be helped. Looks like they took out the front doors and surprised George behind the bar." There was a splatter of greenish-black fluid along the floor that I recognized as troll blood. That one was going to give the crime scene boys fits. Bar stools and bottles were strewn all over, George must have put up a good fight.

I spotted a few small holes in the bar top and pointed them out to Sabrina. She flagged them for the evidence guys and then dug into one of the holes with her pocketknife. A little fishing around, and she dug out a misshapen lead ball.

She held it out to me. "Shotgun."

"Yeah, I smelled gun oil on George last time we were here. He probably kept a twelve-gauge behind the bar." I hopped over and knelt down, coming up with a cut-down pump shotgun. I held it out to Sabrina.

She turned it and the pellet over to the crime scene guys and we moved into the office. A uniformed patrolman was already there, checking the surveillance tapes. I didn't expect him to find anything, since magical disguises play havoc with technology, and I was right. Just about the time two large shapes appeared on the tape, it started to static up. The best we got was that there were two big guys, and after some flashes that I took to be George shooting at them, the two big shapes carried a smaller shape out. Then the tape returned to normal.

"Weird. That's gotta be the attack, but it's like the attackers were tampering with the video somehow," the uniform said.

"Yeah. Weird," I agreed.

I motioned for Sabrina to follow me out, and we walked back into the main part of the bar. "We're not going to find anything here."

"No," she agreed. "These guys have been doing this for too long without notice to get caught by something as simple as a cheap surveillance system. We need to check on the other past competitors. If they're tying up loose ends, then anyone involved is in danger."

"I assume you have the addresses?" I asked.

"Yeah. I'll send uniforms to most of them, but this one is close. You drive. I'll call in cars for the other victims on the way."

"Where are we going?" I asked, opening the door to her car.

"The Arlington. You can find it?"

"Wish I could miss it." I slid behind the wheel and headed back toward downtown.

The Arlington caused quite the stir when it was added to Charlotte's skyline. In a city not known for terribly interesting architecture, a high-rise condo building with hot pink reflective glass in the middle of South End raised as much blood pressure as it did eyebrows. I'd never been inside one of the condos, and I didn't know anyone who could afford one. But apparently one of our victims was doing well for himself.

I took Freedom Drive to Morehead, then hung a left on South Boulevard to get to the fuchsia eyesore. The doorman came out waving his arms wildly and stretching his coat buttons to the breaking point when I parked right in front of the building, but one look at the gun in my hand and the badge in Sabrina's silenced any protests he had.

We took the elevator to the twelfth floor and knocked on the door of Benjamin Overcash, age twenty-six. Nobody answered. I checked the knob. "Locked." I whispered to Sabrina. "Do you have one of those cool lockpick kits like cops on TV?"

"No. Breaking and entering is still illegal on this side of reality." She pounded on the door. "Charlotte-Mecklenburg Police! Mr. Overcash, are you there?"

"Do you always have to say 'Charlotte-Mecklenburg Police' like that? Isn't that a mouthful?" I asked. "You ready for me to kick it down yet?"

"No. And yes. I mean, no, don't kick the door down. And yes, I announce myself properly every time. At least the first time." She banged on the door again. "Mr. Overcash! We believe you might be in danger. We want to help you. Please open the door."

From the other side of the door I heard a little dog barking.

"Well, he's either home or he's been taken, too. No way a man leaves his dog behind," I said.

"Does that apply to yippy little dogs, too?" Sabrina asked.

"Of course."

"That sounds like a dog crying for help to me, then. Kick it down."

I looked at her. "One day we're going to have a talk about exigent circumstances and just kicking in doors for the hell of it. For the record, I prefer to kick the doors in for the hell of it." So I kicked the door in.

And found myself staring down the barrel of a revolver held by a very angry-looking man holding a very small dog. He was a trim white guy with short blonde hair, khakis and a pale purple polo shirt. He looked just like every other off-duty bank drone in Charlotte. I peeked around the side of his head to see if I could spot the pointy ears, but his glamour was locked down tight.

"What the hell are you doing?" he asked.

"Would you believe me if I told you we were rescuing you?" I asked, snatching the gun away from him. He didn't look like he wanted to shoot me, and I didn't want him to screw up and disappoint himself.

"Most people who want to rescue me don't kick my door in," he said, backing away and pulling out a cell phone. "I'm calling the police!"

"We are the police," Sabrina said, holding up her badge. "Well, I am, anyway. This is James Black, he's assisting the department with our investigation into the attack you experienced earlier this month. Now please put the phone down and come with us. It's not safe here."

"Obviously not, with you barging in here like that. And I'm not going anywhere with you, especially now that my door has been destroyed!"

He was starting to vibrate, he was so pissed. I would have normally found it amusing, but George was missing, and I felt responsible. It was my business card that brought the trolls to him, after all.

"Cut the shit, pal. We know you're a faerie, and that it's not just a slur. We know about the fights, and the people that run them know we know. And they're tying up loose ends. Permanently," I said, stepping all the way into the apartment and closing the door behind me.

Overcash turned as pale as a vampire as he processed what I was saying. He stood stock still for about ten seconds, then thrust the dog into my arms and said, "Hold Phoebe." Then he turned and sprinted into what I assumed was a bedroom. He came back seconds later with a duffel bag in his hand and a backpack across his shoulders. He took the dog from me, took a look back into his apartment, then sketched a circle in the air between us. A glowing portal opened up, he stepped through, and Benjamin Overcash, age twenty-six, was gone.

"Is there anybody in the world except me that can't cast spells?" I asked Sabrina.

"I'm still just a lowly human. You're not completely outclassed by the cosmos yet," Sabrina said. "On the bright side, I don't think we need to worry about Mr. Overcash's safety."

"True enough. But he didn't give us any information we could use. Where are we headed next?"

I pulled the door closed as we left the apartment and headed for the elevator. Sabrina started calling the uniforms she'd assigned to the other victims. Just as we got in the elevator, my pocket buzzed.

My cell was thankfully intact after my trip across dimensions, and I read the screen. "Well, shit. You can hang up now," I said to Sabrina.

"Why, what's up?"

"Just got a text from Greg. Bobby called him to say that the announcement for tonight's bout just went out. No location, but on the card is a twenty-person battle royal featuring all their former competitors plus a host of special guest combatants."

"Son of a bitch."

"Yeah. So it sounds like they've gotten their hands on most of the victims already."

"And I can just guess who they want for their special guest fighters," Sabrina said as we got out of the elevator.

"Well let's get everybody together at our place and figure out how to ruin their plans."

"You drive, I'll gather the troops," she said, throwing me the keys.

Chapter 25

Two hours later there were six of us crowded into our increasingly cramped living room, sitting around the coffee table drinking the last of the coffee and watching Greg try to hack the encryption on the troll's smartphone. Who gives a troll a four-hundred-dollar phone, anyway?

"You got anything?" I asked again.

Greg had been trying every trick in his MacBook to break into the troll's phone, but couldn't come up with the password. "No. Still. And the more times you ask, the less likely I am to be able to concentrate on this and actually do anything," he snapped.

"Sorry. Sounds like Mr. GrumpyPants got up on the wrong side of the coffin tonight," I muttered.

"You don't really sleep in coffins, do you?" Stephen asked, a little confused.

"Seriously? Dude, are you really six inches tall with wings and a tiara?" He ought to know better.

"Well, I do have a tiara, but that's a long story," he joked.

"I got it!" Greg suddenly shouted.

"Got what?" I asked.

"The password. I got it. Sorry it took so long, but there are a *lot* of random five-digit numbers. Now all we have to do is look at his inbox and see who the last few text messages are from, and we should be able to go from there."

Greg pressed a few more buttons, plugged in another cable that I didn't recognize and a list of text messages popped up on the TV.

"Who has he been texting?" Sabrina asked.

"Well, there have been seven text messages since we killed him, all escalating in intensity. The last one reads 'Where r u? Got to go tonight! Must have package. Contact me immediately.'"

"Awesome. That fits with my plan perfectly," I said.

"You want to share with the rest of the class?" Sabrina asked.

"Yeah. We pretend to be the troll and find out where he was supposed to take Stephen. Then we show up instead and bust the bad guys," I said.

Greg nodded and started typing on the phone's small keypad, sending a reply to the phantom boss.

"Wait a sec." I handed him my cell. "Use this one. Tell him the troll's old phone was wrecked in the fight and he just got a replacement."

"Good idea," Greg said. He took my phone and started typing. "Sorry 4 delay," he wrote. "Trouble @ hospital. Phone busted, just got new 1. Got package, send delivery address."

"What do you mean? Sent yesterday!" was the immediate reply.

"Phone wrecked. Need address," Greg typed after a second.

"I thought that's what you had Bobby for." Mike said.

"Bobby never gets the location until an hour before the show. If we can get there earlier, there should be less chance of civilians getting hurt."

A reply flashed on the screen. "1431 Toal. Be there by 11, show starts @ midnite."

I looked at the clock—7 P.M. "Okay," I said. "We've got four hours to get there, recon the place where the 'show' is supposed to take place, figure out what the 'show' is, and ruin everybody's entertainment for the evening."

"Well, I can help with some of that before we leave," Greg said, typing more on his laptop. A new screen popped onto the TV with an aerial view of the address from the text message. "It's not exactly NSA-quality stuff, but Internet maps and satellite views will at least give us an idea of cover and entrances and exits before we get there."

"And keep us from getting a nasty surprise," I finished his sentence.

"Exactly." Greg said. "Now, it looks like this street makes a loop, and the warehouse in question is set a little back from the main road. We have loading dock doors on the right-hand side, and office doors on the front of the building. I don't have a decent view of the back of the warehouse, but let's assume that the traffic is going to be coming in from the loading dock."

"Why would you assume that?" Mike asked.

"Because it's hard to carry an unconscious person through a single door. Don't ask me how I know that," I replied.

"Right," Greg agreed.

I stepped in and grabbed the mouse, using it as a pointer. "If we park here and here," I indicated a couple of buildings around the corner from our target, "then Mike and Alex can keep the exits to the office park covered in case there are runners. Stephen and I will go in from the loading dock, while Sabrina and Greg slip in from the front entrance."

"Why am I going in the back way?" Sabrina asked.

Greg spoke up with a grin. "Because Jimmy and Stephen are better suited to a frontal assault. You're not as fast or as strong as either of them, so you should try for the sneak attack. I'm not the most stealthy, obviously, but I can keep my mouth shut, and Jimmy can't, so he has to go in guns blazing."

I didn't dignify my partner's insult with a response. Besides, he was right.

"Okay, everybody make sure you're armed enough." I stood up and lifted the lid off the coffee table.

Under the tabletop was a cleverly disguised gun safe, with room for half a dozen shotguns and rifles, plus a dozen or so handguns. I went to the coat closet and put my guns back on, double-checking my ammo situation. I hadn't fired a shot in last night's encounter, but it's always worth another peek before you leave the house under-armed. Greg had a Glock identical to mine in a shoulder holster and a Mossberg shotgun. Sabrina had her department-issued Smith & Wesson .40 in a shoulder rig, and I saw her pick up a Glock 19 from the case and clip that onto her belt as a backup.

"I don't really know much about guns," Stephen said tentatively, obviously unnerved by the amount of ammo and gun oil floating around the room.

I handed him a belt with a couple of long daggers in it and said, "Use these for anything close. Grab that shotgun and point it in the general direction of anything you want dead. The buckshot will take care of the rest."

He still looked a little shaky, but better nervous than dead. Mike, as usual, declined the use of a gun, but Alex picked up a .38 revolver, checked the cylinder expertly, and tossed a couple of speed loaders in his jacket pocket.

I raised an eyebrow, and Alex laughed at me. "Remember, Mr. Black, faerie, not pansy. I know my way around a pistol."

"Noted." I chuckled. All geared up, we split into separate cars and headed out for a little party crashing. Just before I walked upstairs, I reached back into the closet and grabbed Milandra's sword. It had come in handy once already. No sense in leaving it behind.

Chapter 26

We got to the meeting place and split up according to the plan. Stephen and I got into Greg's car and rolled slowly into the parking lot, while Sabrina and Greg went in the front door on foot. Not for the first time, I wished for those snazzy in-ear two-way radios that you see on all the cop shows, but as it was, we just made sure our cell phones all showed roughly the same time, and went for it.

The big roll-up door at the loading dock was open, with a pair of trolls flanking the opening. These guys were decked out in full leather armor, with chain mail pieces, helmets, giant battle-axes and war paint. It looked like some comic book version of what a troll warrior was supposed to look like. They would have seemed ridiculous if they weren't nine feet tall with axes that gleamed in the streetlights.

I got out of the car and walked up to the steps beside the dock, Stephen in tow. The smarter-looking of the two trolls (and let me tell you, that's a race to the bottom if I've ever seen one) held out a hand and reached behind his back. I tensed and put a hand on my Glock, but relaxed when he brought out an iPad.

"Are you on the list?" he rumbled. In his giant mitt, the iPad looked like a Barbie phone, but he managed to scroll down a list of members or something.

"Probably not. I brought the faerie you've been looking for." I gestured back at Stephen, who did that shimmer thing and revealed his true form. "Let me talk to your boss."

"No way, vamp. Give us the faerie, and we won't crush your head. But you don't get to see the boss."

The dimmer-witted troll was looking very confused by all this talking, and he started forward, axe in hand. His partner waved him back and said, "Gorton wants to smash you. Give me the faerie, and I won't let him."

"As much as I appreciate you looking out for my well-being, I think I'll pass. Now call your boss and I won't blow off anything you're fond of." I pulled my Glock and pointed it at an area just south of his belt buckle.

He got the point, but his friend Gorton didn't. As soon as he saw the gun, he raised the axe and charged. Stephen suddenly got over his fear of firearms and put five shells of double-ought buckshot in the troll's chest. It went down in a spray of green flesh and black blood, axe clattering across the pavement. That wouldn't kill a troll, no matter how much I wished it would, but he'd be out of the fight.

"Now," I said, keeping the Glock trained on the other troll's most prized possession. "About that whole 'seeing the boss' thing?"

He looked over at Gorton, then back at the pair of us, and motioned for us to follow him into the warehouse. Since no one else had come running when Stephen went all Rambo on the troll, I figured Sabrina and Greg had taken care of the other guards. I nodded to Stephen, who had finished reloading, and we walked into the dark warehouse after the troll.

I paused just outside the door to listen for heartbeats, breathing, guns cocking—anything that would give away that somebody on the other side of the door was going to put a couple rounds in my head as soon as I crossed the threshold, but I heard nothing. Our guide led us through a maze of shelving to a big open area where a cage had been set up with bleachers and lights all around it. I looked around in confusion, trying to reconcile the arena-sized interior of the building with the warehouse-sized exterior.

Stephen saw my puzzlement and chuckled. "Magic, Jimmy. The building is bigger on the inside than on the outside."

"How?" I asked. "That doesn't make any sense."

"I did mention magic, didn't I? It never makes any sense except to the spell caster, and they're all a little bit crazy. Keep your eyes open. This is going too well."

"That's what I was thinking. I hope the others are okay." Just then the troll reached the far wall of the open area, and knocked on a door. The door clicked open, and he gestured for us to go inside.

"Boss is in there. I gotta go help Gorton pick buckshot out of his lung. That wasn't very nice, shooting him." He looked at Stephen reproachfully.

"It wasn't very nice of him to try to cut me in half," Stephen replied calmly.

"He's not very smart. He saw guns and got angry. It happens." The troll shrugged a shoulder the size of a VW bug and walked past us back the way we came.

I looked at Stephen, who looked back at me and shrugged himself. That seemed to just about cover the situation, so I shrugged back at him, and walked in the door.

We stepped into an office that looked nothing like anything I expected. It looked more like a cross between a library and an armory, with melee weapons of all shapes and sizes on stands and on hangers all over one wall, all showing signs of heavy use. Two walls were taken over by floor-to-ceiling bookshelves, filled with old, leather-bound books. The books also showed signs of heavy use, and the room even had one of those rolling ladders on a track circling three walls to provide access to the upper shelves and the highest weapons.

The fourth wall was taken up by a bank of flat-screen televisions, some showing news feeds, some showing movies, and several showing closed-circuit security camera feeds from around the building. I pointed to one screen that showed Gorton lying on the loading dock while his compatriot picked buckshot out of him with a pocketknife. Of course, a troll's pocketknife would be a human short sword, so it wasn't a simple operation. Somehow I still couldn't find it in myself to feel bad for the guy. Especially since another screen showed half a dozen terrified men in their twenties crammed into a cage half-naked and dressed like extras in *Spartacus*.

Seated in one luxurious chair in front of the bank of television screens was the last thing I would have expected. Sipping on amber liquid from a crystal glass was a faerie. He wasn't nearly as good-looking as the other faeries I had met. He had pinched features, beady dark eyes, and slightly greasy hair pulled back into a tight ponytail, but he was unmistakably a faerie. The chiseled jawline, ridiculously high cheekbones and angular slant of the eyes would have been clues even if I hadn't seen the pointed ears right away. He looked a lot like someone took everything that made the Fae so annoyingly attractive, and then dropped those features on a third-string mobster. *Great*, I thought. *We get to bring down the Joe Pesci of the faerie world.*

I didn't say anything, and neither did Stephen. I just walked over to the wet bar behind his little seating area, poured myself a drink, and took a seat. Stephen passed on the drink, but sat in a chair off to one side.

After a long few moments, our host finally looked over at us and said, "You two have cost me a great deal of money, and two trolls. That bill will have to be settled." He looked at me and his dark eyes glittered. "I have heard of you, vampire. I am not impressed."

"Sorry to disappoint. If I'd known I was meeting fans today, I would have put on clean socks." I finished my drink. "Nice scotch. Now, time to shut down your little fight club."

"Or?" One greasy Fae eyebrow shooting north almost to his receding hairline.

I've always wanted to be able to do that, but regardless of the hours spent practicing in the mirror, I can never get only one eyebrow to go up. So instead of looking bemused, or sardonic, or some other fifty-cent word, I just end up looking surprised.

"There's no 'or,'" Stephen answered while I was contemplating eyebrows. "Just stop. Simple as that."

"Well, my dear ballerina, I fear there is nothing simple about it. You see, gentlemen, I make a great deal of money from our little enterprise here, and as I rather like money, and what it can buy me, I doubt I'll just decide to stop out of the goodness of my heart. Besides, I enjoy it." He leaned back in his chair, and picked up a remote control. "Take a look. You might find yourself hooked."

He pressed a few buttons on the remote, and the lights in the room dimmed. A projection screen lowered from the ceiling, and images flickered to life.

We sat there as a greatest hits montage of faerie/troll combat rolled across the screen. I recognized all the beating victims in one state of combat or another, from standing triumphant over a fallen troll to bouncing off the canvas with blood oozing from eyes, ears and mouth. In every shot one thing was constant—the crowd was going absolutely nuts. No matter who won, the crowd screamed with a frenzy that one usually only sees at NASCAR crashes.

Our host spun his chair back around and looked levelly at us. "As you can well imagine, there is a significant amount of money wagered on these events. And no matter who wins the fight, the real winner is always the house. As I am the house, I do not intend to give up that revenue stream. So it seems we are at an impasse. And if you are not here to fight in tonight's event, it seems I must recruit another combatant."

"Like your monster tried to 'recruit' me?" Stephen spat.

"Precisely. Given our kind's recuperative capabilities, had you been a little less resistant, we could have knocked you unconscious, brought you here and put you through a full bout without anyone ever being the wiser. Now look at all the problems you have created." He put down his glass and steepled his fingers. "What could I ever do to convince you that it would be in your best interests to participate in tonight's event? Oh, I have an idea."

I didn't like the sound of that. I hate it when the bad guys have ideas. I hate it even more when they smile about those ideas. Our nameless little friend picked up his remote again, and the screen withdrew back into the ceiling. On the center monitor was exactly what I was afraid I'd see—an image of a troll carrying an unconscious Sabrina in through the loading dock door.

Our host looked up at us, wearing a smile colder than the winter wind outside, and gestured to the weapons lining the walls. "Choose your weapons, gentlemen."

Chapter 27

Stephen drew both daggers and started for the faerie behind the desk, but I held him back. "I don't think that's going to do your cousin any favors."

"Quite correct, Mr. Black. What *has* this world come to when a bloodsucking fiend is the voice of reason? Now, Stephen, our bout begins in just a few hours, so I suggest you go to the locker room and join your compatriots. I have something very special planned for tonight's event. Have you ever seen a *real* battle royal, gentlemen? Not the silly things on your wrestling programs, but a real fight to the death? I think in this case it will be more like twenty men and trolls enter, no one leaves. How does that sound?" He leaned back and smiled again, reaching for his glass.

His hand never got there. He froze as an enormous crash echoed through the warehouse. Gunshots and screams rattled the walls as the cavalry appeared on the monitor. Greg was a blur on the screen, blasting his way through a horde of trolls on his way to rescue Sabrina, who had "suddenly" regained consciousness and was steadily shooting holes in the trolls nearest her.

Our oily friend reached into his pocket, but I was behind the desk with one hand on his wrist and the other lifting him by his throat before he could withdraw his hand.

"Take your hand out of your pocket. Very slowly. And if it's not empty, I'm going to rip it off and drink you dry from the shoulder."

He looked down at me, and I don't know if it was the fangs or the look in my eye that convinced him, but he complied. I was a little disappointed, having developed a taste for faerie blood over in Never-Never Land. I looked back at the monitors, then at Stephen. "Go ahead, kick a little troll booty of your own. No point letting the cop and the bloodsucker have all the fun."

He ran out to join the fray like a kid running into the living room on Christmas morning. I wondered for a second how his new bloodthirst was going to go over with the other guys in *Nutcracker*, then turned my attention to the matters at hand.

I dropped the faerie into his chair and sat on the edge of his desk. "So your guys fell for the noisy decoy and missed the stealthy fat vampire. I think you need to buy a better class of henchman next time. But now that we're alone, I don't have to be nice."

"I wasn't aware that you were on your best behavior when you threatened to rip my arm off." He rubbed his throat.

"If I wasn't on my best behavior, I wouldn't have given you the option to keep the arm." I knocked back the last swallow of his scotch, then continued. "What's your name?"

"Not that I owe you anything, vampire, but I am called Leonard."

"Okay, Lenny, who's your boss?"

"I am."

"You know I can hear your heartbeat, right? I know when you're lying." I leaned in like I was listening close. "Yup, big old fibber. Now let's try this again." I punched him in the chest, cracking a couple of ribs in the process. "Who. Is. The. Boss?"

He coughed hard, and rubbed his chest where I'd just left a handprint as a souvenir. "I run the show here."

"That's not what I'm asking," I said, as I backhanded him, hard. Both lips split and a thin line of blood arced out to splatter on the desk blotter. "I'm going to run short on time soon, because my friends don't approve of me beating people up. So stop dancing around, and just tell me what I want to know."

This time I punched downward, breaking his nose and sliding it sideways across his face. Blood poured down the front of his shirt, and I was really starting to have trouble not eating him when I heard him mumble something.

"What?" I said, yanking his head up.

He grinned at me, his face a mask of blood.

"What's so funny?"

Unable to talk, he stretched out a hand and pointed behind me. I turned, and let his head drop as I caught sight of the monitors. The fighting was all over, with Stephen joining Greg and Sabrina in high-fives and touchdown dances with unconscious and wounded trolls scattered all around them.

But of course that wasn't the only thing on the monitors, and it wasn't the most important thing, either. In the center monitor, coming through the front door, was a pair of faeries that looked like stereotypical martial arts movie bad guys. They had the long ponytails, long coats, no shirts, and most importantly, they had pistols pointed at Alex and Mike's backs.

"Crap." I let go of Lenny's ponytail.

His head bobbed loosely for a second before he regained control of himself and stood up. He was recovering pretty quickly—I guess faeries do heal fast.

"Crap, indeed, vampire." He turned his head to the side and spit a gobbet of blood onto the floor. "Now I'm going to have to clean the carpets. Do you know how hard it is to get blood out of carpets?"

"You should ScotchGard. And yeah, I know exactly how hard it is to get blood out of carpets. Try hardwood sometime. You never get everything out of the cracks." I got a smile out of him with that at least.

Then I realized that he wasn't smiling because I was funny, he was smiling because he had a very large pistol pointed at my chest.

"Have you ever wondered whether anything other than a wooden stake through the heart could kill you, vampire?" he asked with a nasty grin.

Then he shot me in the left leg, and I went down like a scrawny sack of potatoes. I lay writhing on his floor for a minute before I looked up at him and said, "This isn't going to help with your cleaning bill."

"I'm pretty sure they'll give me a rate just to do the whole room." Still smiling, he shot my other leg, this time through the calf, because I was hunched over my thighs.

It felt a lot like I'd imagined getting shot would feel. In other words it hurt. *A whole lot.* It felt a little bit like getting smashed in the leg with a hammer, if the hammer drove a burning coal all the way through my leg.

Lenny used one foot to roll me over so I was lying flat on my back. He put his boot on my right shoulder to hold me in place, and then sighted along the barrel.

"Now," he said, "I asked you if you'd ever wondered whether anything other than a wooden stake through the heart could kill you. I mean, legends are old, and there probably weren't guns when the legends first came about. So maybe we just need to conduct a scientific experiment. I know! I'll shoot you, right through the heart, and if you heal, then it will take a wooden stake. If you die, then the legends are wrong."

He stretched out his arm, and I thought about how many vampire legends were wrong—garlic, holy water, churches—all that stuff dead wrong. Sunlight did in fact burn like a champ, but we'd never experimented with the stake or fire thing. Same with decapitation—we just figured those killed pretty much anything, so no reason to think we were exempt. Now it looked like I was going to find out the hard way.

The greasy little faerie reached up, crunched his nose back into place, spat another big glob of blood onto my shirt and then shot me right through the heart.

Chapter 28

I woke up hanging from the ceiling of the warehouse, hurting in places I wasn't even really sure were places. The room was dimly lit, and smelled like old blood and rust. I tried to look around, but moving my head made me want to puke, and I thought that barfing while swinging from my wrists might be a bad idea. And it certainly wasn't going to do any favors for my poor wardrobe, which was already blood-soaked and perforated.

When I was finally able to lift my head, I saw Greg hanging opposite me, with Stephen also swinging from the rafters across the room. Sabrina and Mike were tied back to back on the floor, and Alex was tied to a folding chair. All of them looked to be in some state of disrepair, and I had a brief flash of fierce pride in my friends knowing that we didn't go down easy.

I heard the rumble of a crowd outside the room we were in and knew we were still backstage at fight night. We weren't in the room I'd seen on the monitors with the other faeries in it, so we still had to find and free them as well as ourselves.

"Good, he's awake," Greg said. "This would be a good time to tell me you have a plan." He looked like someone had taken a baseball bat to his face, with one eye swollen shut. His mouth wasn't really working all that well, so he was a little hard to understand.

Before I could come up with something witty to say, Mike looked up at me and said "I'm sorry, James. I blew the whole operation. They appeared out of nowhere, and I couldn't fight them. I ruined everything. I'm sorry."

Mike actually looked in the best shape of all of us, even though his face was red from shame. It looked like the bad guys hadn't wasted much energy on the humans, concentrating the beatings on Greg and me. Even Stephen looked pretty fresh, although his lip was swollen and there was a splash of blood down the front of his shirt. Sabrina was sporting the beginnings of a black eye, but otherwise just looked really mad.

"Don't sweat it, Dad. I shouldn't have had you stationary. It was dumb on my part. You and Alex should have been circling the business park, not sitting still."

"But another vampire would have heard them coming," he said.

"Yeah, but I'm kinda short on vampire friends, so I gotta go slumming with humans." I laughed at my own joke, and the laugh started a coughing fit. The coughing fit racked my chest until after about half a minute of coughing and spitting up blood I heard the plink of a piece of bullet bounce off the concrete floor. "That's better. Lead tickles when it comes up, did you know that?" I asked no one in particular.

Lenny stepped out of the shadows and responded, "I've heard something about that. Well, vampire, now you know that getting shot in the heart won't kill you."

"Now it's time to find out if the same is true for greasy faeries," I said, spitting a gob of blood on his expensive Italian loafers.

He calmly pulled a handkerchief out of his breast pocket, wiped off his shoe, and then kicked me square in the balls. My vision went white from the pain and I tried my best to curl up into a ball, which is really hard when you're hanging from your wrists with your feet dangling six inches off the floor. Who would have thought the little chump could kick so high?

"I think we're past insults, don't you?" he said when I was able to focus my eyes on his face again.

"Not at all. You're still ugly and your mother dresses you funny."

Sabrina cut in before I could speak. "You know I'm a cop, and you know that this place will be crawling with police in a matter of minutes. If you're lucky, they'll just put you behind bars. It'll go easier on you if you surrender now."

"It'll go easier on you if you just keep your stupid whore mouth shut like cattle should, you human trash." Lenny was in front of Sabrina before I saw him move, and he had a knife tracing a thin line of red along her stomach.

She didn't make a sound, just gritted her teeth against the pain and closed her eyes tight. I thrashed against my bonds, rage blinding me to my pain for a moment.

"Come here you little shit, I dare you. Come on, greaseball. Try that shit with someone as strong as you!" I bellowed, then Lenny was back at me, jabbing the knife into my guts and twisting.

The last thing I heard before I passed out was a cold voice whispering, "There is no one as strong as me, little vampire. No one."

When I came to again, the smarmy little faerie was still there, grinning like a cat with a spare canary.

"Now would you like to hear my proposition, or should we just trade barbs and torture all night?" Lenny asked.

"Which one is going to hurt more?" I asked.

"Well, one has the potential for great pain, while the other has the certainty."

"Then why don't we go for 'potential' for a change? I'd hate for you to get bored with torturing me."

"Oh, don't give up on my account. I have a great deal of patience when it comes to torture."

"Oh good lord, will you can the witty repartee and move on to the monologue already," Greg yelled.

I closed my eyes as Lenny crossed the floor to face my bleeding partner.

"I'm sorry, vampire, I don't think anyone was talking to you."

"Oh, come on. We've all read the comic books. This is the point where you tell us your diabolical plan for world domination, so we can come up with some clever and unexpected way to stop you." Greg looked down at the greasy faerie. "It's a formula thing, just go with it."

"Well, Mr. Knightwood, I hate to disappoint, but I have no aspirations to rule the world. I just want to make a lot of money. And you fine people are going to help me."

"I doubt it, assclown," Sabrina said.

"Detective Law, didn't anyone ever teach you to shut up when the more evolved species are speaking? It's better for your health and you might learn something."

Lenny took two long steps to where Sabrina and Mike were sitting and slapped her hard across the mouth. She rocked back and I saw blood coming from her split lip.

"You done beating up humans and defenseless vampires, or are you going to prove your sexual inadequacies a little more fully before you make your offer?" I said. I didn't really *want* to get kicked in the balls again, but better me than Sabrina or Mike.

He turned to me, glaring. "Here is what's going to happen, Mr. Black. My card starts in thirty minutes. I have a few warm-up matches, some troll on troll violence, a few faerie volunteers, that sort of thing. Then, just as the crowd is building to a fever pitch, you are going to go out there and fight a troll in a cage match to the death. These people have never seen a vampire before, so I can substitute that as a main event and not have to refund anything.

"If you win, everyone here goes free. All the faeries, all your stupid human friends, everyone. If you lose, well, you won't care very much in that case, now will you?"

"What about your battle royal? Why would you keep your word if Jimmy wins?" Greg asked.

"You mean when I win, right partner?" I asked through a mouthful of blood.

"Sure, whatever. But why should we trust the ugly fairie?" Greg asked.

"Because you have no choice," Lenny said. "You're my captives, and if I want to kill you, I can. But I'd rather see you fight. I make more money that way. And you bleed longer. Now, what's it going to be, vampire? Are you going to play the lone hero, or do I start killing the humans?"

Chapter 29

The crowd was rabid as I walked to the ring. The spells cast to make the warehouse bigger on the inside than the outside were in full effect here. There was a whole damn arena set up. There was a lighting rig worthy of ESPN, aluminum bleachers like you see at every high-school football field in America and a round cage with eight-foot chain link walls, just like on TV. Except on TV the metal poles holding the cage together were covered in padding with sponsors' logos on them, not barbed wire.

I was dressed in clean clothes that Lenny had brought over from our place. Too bad faeries don't have the same breaking and entering restrictions as vampires. He had taken the time to feed me, and since he'd ordered his faerie ninja bodyguards to let me drink from them, my wounds had pretty much healed.

I looked across the ring, and standing there with a battle-axe in each hand was my old friend Gorton the troll. He looked pretty healed, too, and pretty grumpy with me. I was unarmed, except for my teeth and my wits, which basically meant that I was unarmed.

Lenny walked into the center of the ring, and a microphone descended from the rafters. "Ladies and Gentlemen, welcome to Fright Night Fight Night!"

The crowd actually cheered for this crap, proving that there really is no relation between taste and cash.

"We have a very special treat for you tonight, a battle of legendary enemies, creatures whose races have hated each other since before the dawn of human history. The hatred that these monsters bear for each other makes Jon Stewart and Pat Robertson look like bosom buddies!"

The crowd laughed again, and I looked over at Gorton, trying to see if he had any deep-seated hatred I hadn't noticed in our first meeting. He just looked back at me as if to say *what can you do, he's got the microphone and is nuts besides.* I turned my attention back to the faerie with the microphone, thinking how much I'd rather have him locked in the cage with me than the troll.

Lenny went on. "In this corner, we have your champion, the hero of the cage, the Green Machine—Gorton the Troll!"

Gorton raised his arms above his head and played to the crowd. I could see a line of people building at what I assumed were betting windows in the back of the room.

Lenny turned to me and said, "And in this corner, hailing from right here in Charlotte, NC—the bloodsucking demon of the night, the Vampire!"

Great, I didn't even rate a name. Asshole.

"You know the rules, ladies and gentlemen. There aren't any. You have thirty seconds to place your bets, either in person or online. Wave to our audience at home, fighters." Lenny waved at the ceiling, and I noticed cameras mounted above the ring for the first time. The son of a bitch was *streaming* this?

"The betting is now closed. Let's get ready for Friday Night Fights!"

The crowd actually chanted the last bit along with him, and Lenny turned around in a slow circle, basking in their cheers. I couldn't figure out what it was—the ponytail? The earrings? The fact that the whole crowd was plastered? He wasn't any funnier than me, and I had the whole vampire chic thing on my side, but he had these folks eating out of his hand.

I looked across at Gorton, and he actually mouthed *sorry* at me. I was going to feel bad about killing him, even if he was a troll. Of course, I'd feel even worse if he managed to kill me. But since I'd technically been dead for most of two decades, I didn't mind all that much.

Gorton took a step forward, and I suddenly noticed that Lenny wasn't talking anymore. As a matter of fact, he wasn't even in the ring. I was now locked in a cage with a troll who wanted to cut my head off, and a whole bunch of people just outside that had serious cash on him doing just that. Even if I beat Gorton, I might not make it out of this alive.

I didn't have a whole lot of time to contemplate my eventual escape, because Gorton charged me, twirling his battle-axes like a Bruce Lee villain. Except they usually had nunchuks. And except that Bruce Lee could usually beat them. And except that was in the movies, and this was frighteningly real. Okay, now that I think about it, it was nothing like a Bruce Lee movie, but in the heat of the moment, that's what came into my head.

Gorton came at me in a dead run, and I sprinted away from him, running in circles around the cage while I frantically tried to think of a plan. I'm sure I looked like Andy Kaufman in a wrestling ring, but I had no idea how I was going to go toe-to-toe with a nine-foot troll and live, especially since he had two battle-axes and I just had me.

Then it came to me—I had *me*. I was a lot faster and at least marginally smarter than the troll, so that's what I had to work with. I stopped abruptly, dove backward toward Gorton and flipped over his back.

He almost turned himself inside out trying to reverse his run and get turned around to face me, and that's when I was able to snatch one axe out of his hand and fling it outside the cage. I heard a few shrieks from the crowd as the six-foot axe cleaved a bleacher, but they weren't high on the list of things I was worrying about. I guessed the people scrambling out of the way had bet on the troll.

One axe out of the way, I squared off against Gorton, who had regained his balance and was facing me head-on. He feinted once at my head, and then made a huge upward sweep at my face as I ducked. If I'd been human, that would have split my head open from jaw to eyebrows, but I left human behind a long time ago. I pulled my head back in the nick of time, and lashed out with a kick at Gorton's knee. My foot connected solidly, and I heard something go crunch. The troll didn't fall, though, just shifted his weight and brought the axe back around.

I gotta get a book on monster anatomy, I thought as I skipped sideways to avoid a huge over-handed slash that tore the canvas and splintered the wooden floor underneath.

"Careful, there, Gortie. If you break the cage it's gonna come out of your pay." I kept dodging, hoping I could rope-a-dope long enough to get a good shot in.

"What pay, vampire?" The troll asked as he slashed at my head again.

I ducked easily and rolled forward under his arm, forcing him to stop hacking at me for a minute to untangle his feet again. "You mean you're letting the faerie make all the money? That's generous of you."

"What do I need money for? He gives me blades and things to hit. That's all I need." He raised the axe over his head and charged again.

I slid sideways and gave him a couple of quick punches to where a human's kidneys would be. By the grunt he gave, I hit something uncomfortable at least.

"Don't you want more out of life? A little piece of land with a house, a yard and a Mrs. Troll in the kitchen?" I ducked another attack and this time threw a knee at the big muscle in the troll's thigh.

He yelped and backhanded me across the cage. I slid across the canvas all the way into the chicken wire walls twenty feet away, and heard people outside yelling for my blood.

"You ever *seen* a lady troll, vampire? If so, you know why I never want to get married." He came at me again, axe slashing the air at waist height.

He made a nasty sideways stroke, and I decided to do the last thing he expected. I stepped inside the axe strike, blocking his arms with my body. His elbow caught me in the midsection, but I was able to reach out and land a punch right on the tip of his bulbous nose.

I don't care how big you are, a shot to the nose is the great equalizer. Your eyes get blurry and there's nothing you can do about it for a couple of seconds. And a couple of seconds was all I needed. As Gorton reached up to grab at his face with one hand, I took his other wrist, the one closest to me, in one hand and put the other hand on his bicep. I put all my strength in one huge move, and slammed his outstretched arm across my upraised knee with a sickening pop that sounded like a huge balloon exploding. Gorton's elbow snapped like kindling, and his axe went clattering to the floor.

I held onto his wrist and pulled him around, muscles straining against his huge bulk. He overbalanced easily, going head over heels in a move I couldn't replicate if I tried it in the gym a thousand times. The troll landed flat on his back with his arms and legs splayed out wide. I picked up the axe and raised it high over my head. I looked down and saw the troll close his eyes as I brought the massive blade crashing down.

Then his eyes flew open as the splinters scratched his face when I buried the axe in the floor beside his head.

"Don't move," I whispered to the troll. Then I jumped from the middle of the ring to the upper corner of the cage, balancing precariously on the upper rails of the chain link.

"I win, Lenny, and the troll lives!" I shouted. "Now open the door. I'm hungry, and I don't really care if I eat you or one of your patrons."

I looked down at a balding man in a suit that cost more than my first car. He had a woman on each arm, obviously rentals or just run-of-the-mill gold diggers, and a Tag Heuer watch that kinda caught my eye. I bared my fangs at him, and he fainted dead away. The girls ran off, and I jumped out of the cage to land beside the fainted wuss.

"Nice watch. Thanks," I said, slipping it onto my wrist.

"That's not very nice, Mr. Black." Lenny's voice came from right behind me, and I turned to see him pointing a revolver at my head. It looked like a .357, but it was hard to tell with it pressed up against my nose.

"I'm not a very nice person, Lenny." I reached up and pushed the barrel of the gun aside. "Now open the doors. I won. My friends and I are leaving." I looked at him and put a little mojo into my voice, but it had no effect on the faerie.

"You cannot bespell our kind, you idiotic little vampire." Something in the way he said that sounded familiar, but I couldn't quite put my finger on it. "You did not win, you forfeited. That was a death match you just ruined. You don't get to change the rules. My house, my rules. And you are most certainly not leaving. I promised these people blood, and blood they shall have."

He clapped his hands, and a small army of trolls stepped forward out of the shadows. One held each of my friends and the earlier beating victims, and the ones that weren't holding prisoners held nasty-looking axes, swords and short spears with barbed points that looked like they could do really unpleasant things to people. I was happy to see that George looked like he'd held up well through the whole kidnapping into a fight club ordeal.

And then, out of nowhere, Lenny had that damn microphone again. "Ladies and Gentlemen, we have a fantastic surprise for you this evening! In addition to the bout you have just witnessed, the first time our audience has ever been exposed to a vampire's speed, grace and evil power, we have another first for you here at Fright Night—a *Battle Royal!*"

"Now this isn't the watered-down excuse for a Battle Royal that your silly 'sports entertainment' programs will show you. This is a true battle, where only the strong survive! Two teams will enter the cage, the great Warrior Trolls versus the forces of the evil vampires, and only one team will emerge victorious! But first, please step away from the cage. We need a little more room for this performance."

With that, he waved his hands in the air over his head, and the cage grew. And it didn't just expand outward, it got taller, too. What had been a fifteen-foot square with maybe ten-foot walls, was now a cage the size of half a basketball court with walls a good twenty feet high. And Lenny had transported all of us inside the cage. The spectators were outside, but Sabrina, Greg, Stephen, Mike, Alex and I were in the cage along with a bunch of terrified faeries, a bartender, a baker's dozen of trolls and one faerie magician.

I looked over at Greg. "I've got a bad feeling about this."

He nodded. "Help me, Obi-wan Kenobi. You're my only hope."

Chapter 30

We were still unarmed, and even more outnumbered than when it was just me one-on-one with a troll. I ran to the side of the cage and picked up the axe that Gorton had dropped when I felled him. He was still lying there, holding his elbow tight to his body and glaring at me, but he obviously wasn't going to be a problem. I just hoped we could end this thing before he healed and came after me. When Lenny had made the cage bigger, the other axe ended up on the inside of it with us, so I grabbed it too. I sprinted back to my friends and handed one axe to Greg.

"I figure we've got a few seconds before they figure out a plan and come after us. Sabrina, George—stay here and protect the humans. Greg, Stephen, come with me." I snapped the head off the axe and gave Sabrina the handle. It made for about a four-foot bo staff, but it was the best thing I could come up with.

I grabbed the axe just behind the head and looked over at Greg. "Fastball special?"

He looked at me and shook his head. "You read too many comic books, dude. That'll never work."

"You got a better idea?" I asked.

"No. Lie down on your stomach."

I did, and Greg grabbed my ankles and started to spin around in a circle. I held the axe head out in front of me and picked up speed with every rotation.

"I should try the hammer toss at the Ren Faire next year," Greg yelled as he let go of my feet.

I flew across the cage at the massed rank of trolls, axe-first. I hit the first one head-on with the blade, cleaving the top of his head right off. For such a stupid creature, he had a lot of brains to splatter all over the place. I kept flying into the second troll, and managed to take his head off as well before the axe handle became too slick with blood to hold.

By then Greg and Stephen had caught up with me and were picking up the weapons dropped by the dead monsters. Stephen grabbed a troll short sword that fit him like a claymore, and started laying about like a madman. I had to duck to keep him from lopping off my ears. I grabbed a fallen sword of my own. Greg had squared off against an axe-wielding troll, and was trying to chip enough important pieces off him to get him to stay down.

Sabrina, George and Mike had formed a phalanx in front of the huddled mass of frightened faeries, until a troll got too close. Once one came within a few feet of their defensive stance, a pair of men vaulted over their heads and launched themselves at the troll with a flurry of kicks and punches. These guys obviously remembered their last trip to the cage and had a score to settle. I remembered Alex's words to me earlier and grinned as I muttered "faeries, not pansies" to myself. At least for now, Sabrina, Mike and the others were safe.

I heard air whistling behind me and dropped to the ground just in time to avoid a gigantic clawed hand that would have ripped my lungs out. I lashed out with my sword, cutting the troll's Achilles tendon, and he dropped to the floor beside me. Through it all, I heard the crowd screaming for blood. Ours or the trolls, I couldn't tell.

I danced around as best I could, slicing out with my sword whenever I saw an opening, all the while trying to get back to where Greg and Stephen stood surrounded by trolls. I dove between one beast's legs, stabbing upwards through his torso as I came up, and snatched his axe out of the air as he fell backwards, dead before he hit the floor.

"How many left?" I asked Greg.

"I got two." He replied. "Stephen?"

"This one makes two for me. What about you?"

"I got three plus one incapacitated. So that leaves seven plus Lenny."

I looked around but couldn't see the faerie anywhere. It was about that time when I heard Sabrina swearing loudly. I looked over to where I had left them, only to see a troll lift her up and throw her out of the cage altogether. She landed in the crowd, and looked around for an entrance to get back in and help as the troll waded into the sea of humans and faeries, laying about with his huge fists, seemingly oblivious to the punches he was taking.

"Crap. Hold these guys," I yelled to Greg.

He nodded, and I took off across the cage with a roar that seemed to come from my toes.

The troll going after the captives didn't even look at me, just flicked out a huge fist and smashed me to the floor. I blacked out for a second or two, then came to just as the troll was swinging a sword at my head. I rolled to one side and leapt to my feet. Bad idea. I was dizzy from the punch in the head, and the troll saw it. He reared back and kicked me in the chest with one green-tinged foot. I felt a couple of ribs break, and flew about six feet before I landed flat on my back in the center of the cage.

The troll turned his attention back to the humans, and I staggered to my feet. He had just grabbed Mike around the throat and was rearing back to cave in his face with the other hand when I hurled my sword like a spear, right through the monster's back.

His hand tightened for a second around Mike's neck, and I saw his face go purple. I limped over and pried the troll's dead fingers off of him, and Mike drew a deep, raspy breath.

"Thank you, James," he said hoarsely.

"Pray for me, buddy." I shook my head to clear my vision.

Then I made my way back to the fight and tried to assess our odds. Stephen and Greg had taken out another couple of trolls, so the numbers were slowly evening up. The problem was, the remaining four trolls were in pretty good shape, and we were starting to look the worse for wear. I had a few broken ribs and probably a concussion. Greg had one arm that he couldn't move, and Stephen had a serious limp and blood pouring from a scalp wound. Plus we had the humans to watch out for.

I stepped up beside my two friends and we squared off with the remaining four trolls. They had an array of weapons to make the biggest *Dungeons & Dragons* geek envious. We had two swords, one axe, and a spectacular array of bruises.

"Ready boys?" I asked.

"Nope," Greg said.

"Not even a little bit," Stephen added.

"Good. So since none of us are stupid, what's the plan?" I asked.

"How about we kill the green guys, then we take turns cutting on the greasy faerie, and I collect my winnings," Greg replied.

"Winnings?" I looked over at him with one eyebrow raised. Apparently I can do it, but only if I'm so beaten up that half my face doesn't move.

"Yeah, I bet all my cash on you to win your match. Lenny owes me fifty grand."

"Fifty grand? How much did you bet?" I yelped.

"Two thousand. You were a pretty heavy underdog."

"No wonder he wants us dead. He doesn't want to pay you off."

"Probably," Greg agreed. "Should we start the killing now?"

"Yeah, may as well. Go for the legs if you can, the joints are the only weak spots that I've found."

"Well, that and their golf game," Stephen quipped.

"I'm the funny one," I said. "Stay off my turf, faerie."

"Bite me, vampire." He grinned and wiped a little green blood off his face.

"Tease. What would Alex say?" Then I charged, more to ensure that I got the last word than out of any real bravery.

I turned and ran straight at the nearest troll, pouring on the vamp-speed. Instead of taking another shot to the ribs, I jumped high into the air and came down behind the trolls. I cut backward through his left leg, and he fell backward onto the canvas. I sliced off his head and turned to see how the others were doing.

Greg had tangled with the biggest troll of them all, and wasn't doing so well. The troll held a huge sword in one hand, and a shield in the other, and was blocking all of Greg's axe blows with his shield, then lazily feinting at him with his sword. I didn't want to know what was going to happen when he got serious.

Stephen wasn't faring any better with two trolls all his own. One held a standard short sword, and the other a nine-foot metal-tipped quarterstaff. Stephen was fast enough to keep from getting his head crushed, but not trained enough to make headway against two opponents.

I slid in on Stephen's left and engaged the troll with the staff. He immediately caught me on the chin with his stick, and my eyes crossed again. I kept my feet, and kept moving enough not to get my head bashed in, but all I really accomplished was getting him off Stephen's back so he could fight the other monster.

Out of the corner of my eye I saw the big troll smash Greg square in the face with his shield, and my portly partner's eyes rolled back in his head as he slumped to the canvas. The troll lifted his huge sword over his head, and brought it down to chop Greg's head off in the middle of the ring.

Chapter 31

The sword met steel with an enormous bell tone, and I turned my head to see Gorton standing over Greg's unconscious body, an axe in his good hand. The other troll looked up at him in astonishment, and said something in a guttural language that I didn't understand. Gorton shook his head and barked something nasty at the larger troll, who stepped back from Greg into the center of the cage.

There was something oddly formal in the way the two trolls circled each other, then stopped, saluted with their weapons and rushed together with a clash of steel and a sweaty thump of green-hued flesh.

The monsters traded massive blows in the middle of the ring for several minutes, neither able to gain an advantage. Gorton was the better fighter, but his wounded arm evened the scale for the bigger troll, who had strength and health on his side. After three or four long minutes, it became obvious that Gorton couldn't win. He was just buying us time.

I looked over at Stephen, who had stopped fighting his troll to watch the duel just like I had. I jerked a thumb at the green brute behind him, and in unison we turned to the trolls next to us and lopped off their heads while they concentrated on the two combatants in the center of the ring.

The big troll saw what we did and flew into a rage, redoubling his attacks on Gorton. The smaller troll went down on one knee, and I rushed in to try to help him, only to run smack into an invisible wall.

Lenny floated down out of the air and said, "No interference, vampire. This is an honor match."

"I'm not really that honorable, Lenny, so get out of my way." Did I mention I hate magic? Well, I do.

"I don't think so. Be still."

He waved his arms at me and I was suddenly trapped, unable to move or lift my hands. Well, if I learned nothing else tonight, at least now I knew who was throwing around heavy-duty magic on this end of town, for all the good that would do me.

I turned my attention back to the fight just in time to see the bigger troll batter down Gorton's defenses. Gorton's axe head dropped to the floor, and the other troll reached out with one huge foot and stomped through the handle. Gorton looked up at him with a bloody smile, and the larger troll swept his head from his shoulders with one stroke. The body fell in the opposite direction from the head, blood pouring from the neck stump.

The big troll turned to me and grinned, starting to stomp my way waving his sword from side to side in a low arc. I couldn't move because of Lenny's spell. Greg was still out cold, and Stephen could barely move, he was so beat up.

I looked into the green-skinned face of my doom, and thought *this is not how I wanted to go out. Salma Hayek is not anywhere in the building.*

I closed my eyes as the troll got closer, and just as I thought I could feel its nasty breath on my face, I realized the spell was beginning to wear off. I could move, after a fashion.

I opened my eyes to see the troll standing stock still in front of me with a foot of steel sticking out of its chest. It started to fall forward, and I got out of the way the best I could. I heard a very startled Lenny mutter something very unpleasant under his breath, and looked up to see a golden-tinged dragon-man in full battle armor standing in front of me.

"Tivernius?" I gasped, baffled but grateful.

"Hello, James. Otto sent word that you had been attacked by trolls again, so Her Majesty asked me to protect her friends and her subjects."

He eyed Lenny like he was something smelly he'd stepped in. Maybe troll spleen. There was a lot of that lying around.

"Leothandron, fancy meeting you here. I thought you were banished to this realm and under strict orders to never touch magic." The dragon turned warrior put on a fake smile worthy of Joan Rivers on Oscar night. "Now what is the penalty for disobeying Her Majesty? Oh yes, I recall. Death."

With the last word, the dragon's face went cold and he closed on Lenny, sword flashing.

Lenny wasn't exactly defenseless. He conjured a pair of slim short swords out of thin air and easily parried the dragon's strokes.

"Your little bitch-queen has no authority over me here, and she knows it. If she could do anything to me she'd be here in person instead of sending her pet lizard."

Lenny slashed furiously at Tivernius' face, but the dragon saw the obvious attempt at misdirection and easily batted away the thrust that came at his midsection. He had a tougher time beating aside the next attack, which came straight at his head from both swords.

I stood there, not wanting to distract Tivernius. Besides he didn't need me. I mean, the guy was thousands of years old. He had to have learned a thing or two about sword fights, right? That comforting thought went out of my head when I saw Lenny open up a broad slash across the dragon's mailed stomach.

Lenny's black blades glowed red with blood, and the faerie smiled coldly. "You were never much of a challenge in human shape, lizard. You are only a threat in your true form, and you cannot transform in such a small building. Too bad, really. I'd love for all these people to see me beat a real dragon, instead of just another wizard."

Lenny kept fighting while he talked, a feat I had grudging admiration for. I can usually manage a one-liner or two, but this guy was positively Shakespearean.

The one thing he couldn't do was keep me bound by his magic while he fought and talked. My magical restraints vanished, and I quickly cut through the cage and got everybody out of there that wasn't already dead. Stephen protested, but I shoved him through the chain link and Alex took over from there.

I stayed to make sure Tivernius finished the job. The last thing we needed was Lenny getting away and going after his victims all over again. Plus, he'd *shot* me.

Tivernius was fast, almost faster than me, but he wasn't quite as ruthless as Lenny. The dark-haired faerie took every cheap shot he could, kicking, gouging, throwing random troll bits into the dragon's eyes, whatever he could think of to gain any advantage. It became clear after a few seconds that the combatants were pretty evenly matched, and it was all going to come down to who made the first mistake.

I couldn't get involved, because I was afraid of distracting Tivernius and getting him killed. Greg couldn't do anything, because as soon as he got everybody out of the cage, Mike and Stephen started working on his head injury. Sabrina stood beside me, coming back into the cage after reclaiming her gun. She handed me my sword belt, and I strapped on Milandra's sword. I felt a little ridiculous, but she didn't bring me my Glock.

The mistake was small when it came, just a tiny slip of a foot in a pool of blood, but it was Tivernius who made it. He lunged at Lenny after a blinding parry, and his front foot slid just a little. But that overbalanced him, and he couldn't get back in time to get his guard set.

The faerie saw it and launched a whirling counterattack that kept Tivernius off balance and backpedaling. I saw what was happening too late to do anything, as Lenny steered the dragon into the center of the cage, right where Gorton and I had finished our first scuffle.

Tivernius stepped back to avoid a slash at his throat, and put his foot right in the hole that I had made in the ring's floor. He went down clutching his knee, and his sword went flying across the cage. Lenny smiled a wicked smile and leapt up into the air, both swords flashing as he came down in a deadly strike aimed at Tivernius' sprawled form.

He never got there. As soon as I saw the opening, I launched myself at the flying faerie. Like I said, I'm fast. I was never going to make the varsity football team when I was alive, but add my vamp-strength to my ridiculous speed, and I hit Lenny in the midsection like an NFL linebacker with a bad attitude. We flew across the cage to crash into the wall, and I heard Lenny's swords clatter to the floor well behind us.

I hopped up to see the faerie already on his feet, and quickly got my head out of the way of his oncoming fist. I grabbed that wrist with one hand and threw a series of fast punches into his ribs with the other. He took my best punches without flinching, and I knew I was in trouble.

Okay, I knew I was in trouble when he took out the thousand-year-old dragon and conjured swords out of thin air, but I knew I was in real trouble when I didn't even faze him with my body shots. He did wobble a little when Sabrina put three rounds in the center of his back, but even that didn't slow him down. He quickly regained his focus. I heard Sabrina swearing from all the way across the cage. I understood the feeling.

Lenny backed away from me and squared himself up. I could almost see the wheels turning in his devious little head, and the second his hands started to wave I lashed out with a spinning kick at his head. He ducked easily, but I had disrupted his spell, so all I had to worry about was the counterattack. That was a punch to the groin that I blocked because, knowing what a dirty fighter he was, I expected the low blow. I didn't expect his other hand to stab at my eyes, but I managed to dodge back quickly enough to save my sight and my jewels.

"Nice shot. You learn to fight like that in the faerie prison?" I snarled.

He just smirked at me and flung himself at my knees. I jumped over his dive easily, and then cursed my stupidity as I saw him come out of a forward roll with a sword in his hand.

"I am the greatest swordsman the House Armelion has ever produced, vampire. You cannot best me in single combat. I will take your head, slaughter your scaled friend and your human allies and return to my homeland to wrest the throne from that lizard-loving bitch!" He advanced, his sword moving so fast the blade became a black blur whirling at my face.

"Wow, you've got some serious anger management issues. Good thing I brought backup," I said, and dove to one side.

Sabrina emptied her clip into the pissed-off faerie, which only served to distract him for a second. But a second was all I needed to come up with my sword drawn and set myself for the fight of my life.

I became a lot less set for the fight when Lenny turned to face me. His eyes were completely black, and the smile across his face was colder and crueler than anything I'd ever seen. The voice that came from his mouth was pure evil, a slithering, writhing sound that swirled around my ears and sent icicles down my spine.

"You expect to defeat me, little vampire? Do you really think you can best the greatest of the Fae? You can't touch me, fool. I was drinking babies' blood when your ancestors were crawling out of the mud and growing legs. I have waded through the gore of a thousand battles and eaten the hearts of kings. I have destroyed entire civilizations and crushed the souls of generations of men. What are you to me?"

"Well, I beat *Call of Duty 3* on Veteran. Does that count for anything? Oh yeah, and I once helped banish an Archduke of Hell. But enough about me." I lunged at him, a clumsy strike that he easily parried into a wicked slice towards my eyes.

The fight escalated into a blindingly fast exchange of thrusts, parries, slashes, dodges and curses as we both tried to grab any advantage. Sweat poured off my forehead after just a couple of minutes, and then I had the added irritation of blood in my eyes on top of fighting a more skilled opponent possessed by an undying evil spirit too evil for Hell. I called on the memory of every Saturday afternoon kung-fu triple feature just to stay alive.

After a series of whirling slashes, I saw out of the corner of my eye what Lenny was doing. He was trying his best to steer me over to the same hole he had dropped Tivernius in. The wounded dragon had managed to drag himself over to one side of the cage, leaving the hole conveniently vacant.

I spun sideways around a savage thrust and rolled forward, getting us turned around so Lenny's back was to the hole, and by the ferocity that he thrust and slashed to get us turned back around, I could tell that I was right. But try as I might to stop him, he maneuvered me around again.

If I went into the hole, nobody was left to bail me out. Sabrina was out of ammo, and everybody else was either human or injured, so I was on my own this time. I looked from side to side, frantically trying to find a way out, when Lenny caught me with a kick high in the midsection.

I screamed from the pain in my already broken ribs, and flailed my arms around like pinwheels as I stepped into the hole in the ring and went down on my back, just like Tivernius had.

Lenny grinned an evil grin and leapt into the air, just like he had over the fallen dragon. He came down with his sword ready to remove my head from my shoulders with extreme prejudice.

Except for the part where I wasn't lying there anymore. Since I knew what he was doing, I never put any weight on the leg in the hole. Instead I lowered myself backward onto the canvas in a fake fall worthy of any WrestleMania main event. When Lenny jumped, so did I, and by the time he came back down, his sword hit nothing but canvas and wood, burying itself a good foot into the floor of the ring.

Lenny looked around, startled, and his eyes got huge for a split second before I buried my fangs in the side of his neck. His blood spurted cleanly into my mouth, and I drank deep. The coppery taste of blood was mixed with the earthy taste of moss, pine trees, fresh-cut grass and late night rain in a spring wood. There was even a hint of something like mesquite before I got down to the nasty bits of Lenny, the hot anger that tasted like burned meat, spoiled cheese and a touch of churned grave dirt and tears.

I drank, and felt his hands hammer on my head and shoulders. He pounded on me like they were sledgehammers, but the more I drank, the stronger I got. His blows grew weaker and weaker. My cuts and bruises faded, and I felt my ribs begin to knit back together. Just before I took the last of his blood and turned him, I found the willpower to pull away from him, and that was the hardest thing I'd done in a long time.

I pulled back and he fell to his knees in front of me in the cage. And with him looking up at me from the brink of death and possible rebirth, I took my sword and cut his head off with one big looping stroke.

Lenny's head hit the canvas, and a black cloud of smoke billowed forth from his neck, shrieking loud enough to drive me to my knees. When I was able to open my eyes again, the body was nothing but a desiccated husk, a mummy in the middle of the cage.

Chapter 32

I closed my eyes for a long moment and let the blood flow through me, healing the hurts of my body and leaving a few more unpleasant scars on my soul. Taking in the dirtier pieces of Lenny's life force literally left a bad taste in my mouth to counterbalance the flush of healing energy I got from his faerie blood.

Sometimes I understand why Greg doesn't drink from the source anymore. Not often, but sometimes.

I looked around at the carnage and counted better than a dozen dead trolls, an unconscious vampire, a dragon with a broken leg, a bloodstained blonde faerie, a decapitated brown-haired bad guy faerie and about a dozen wary and blood-soaked humans.

Then there was me, a freshly fed monster with my opponent's blood dripping off my chin and fangs overlapping my bottom lip. The crowd stood frozen in silence for just a second after Lenny's corpse hit the canvas, then erupted in wild cheers like they had all hit the lottery.

In a way, I suppose they had, since they stormed the two trolls manning (trolling?) the betting windows and beat them with chairs, purses and whatever else they could find until the less-than-jolly green giants just threw all the money into the crowd and slunk off into the night.

I limped over to Sabrina and the others and slid down to sit in the cage with my back to the chain link. "That sucked," I said.

"Didn't look like much fun from here," she replied.

"Good. Wouldn't want you to romanticize it or anything."

"Don't worry, Jimmy. When I watch you fight, romance is the last thing on my mind."

"Yeah? Well, what does come to mind when you watch me fight, Detective?"

"The scarecrow from The Wizard of Oz on crystal meth," Greg said from where he lay on the canvas with a black bandage wrapped around his head.

"Nice. Where'd the bandage come from?" I asked.

"That would be me, James."

I looked over at Mike, who had on his priest's collar, but was now lacking the shirt that usually went with it. I couldn't help it, I started to laugh. Mike looked down at where his belly was poking out over his belt, and he laughed too. Then we were all laughing, slapping legs and the whole bit.

After a few minutes of silliness we calmed down, and looked around the empty warehouse. A few scattered dollar bills were all that was left of the cash wagered on the fight, and I swore loudly.

"What's wrong with you?" Sabrina asked.

"Lenny owed us fifty large for the first fight," I said.

She raised an eyebrow at me. "I don't think there's that much lying around."

"That's why I was cussing," I said, holding my not-quite healed ribs.

"Dude," Greg said from behind us. "I got it covered."

"How do you have it covered?" I asked.

"Lenny didn't trust all his money to the betting windows. I just grabbed about thirty grand off his dead body."

That's my partner. He might claim that I'm the money-grubber, but he's the one that'll bleed you dry. Figuratively, of course.

"Nice work, bro."

I turned to head for the exit, but stopped as the roll-up door slowly rose and a figure on a sleek black motorcycle rode in. The bike rolled up to us almost silently, and the rider pulled off her helmet as she got off and strode over to Greg.

Lilith, one-time mate to Adam the Father of Man, one-time outcast from the Garden of Eden, one-time servant to the fallen angel Zepheril and current proprietrix of the biggest and fanciest topless bar in North Carolina, strutted across the concrete like she owned the place. She was pure sex on two legs, with her leather jacket unzipped enough to make you wonder if there was anything under there, and leather pants tight enough to let you know there wasn't anything on under *there*.

"I'll take that." Lilith held out one hand for the cash.

"And why exactly would we give you my money?" I stepped in front of her. "And what are you doing here?"

"The answer to those questions should be obvious, little vampire. I'm here because this is my establishment. You'll give me the money because I now have a great deal of cleanup to do, not to mention more trolls to recruit after this debacle. Besides, you trashed my club. The money will cancel your debts to me." The immortal strip club owner held out her hand again, and I couldn't help but laugh.

"What ever happened to 'I don't know anything about the attacks you're investigating?'"

"I lied. As the scorpion said to the turtle, 'it's in my nature.'"

I got my laughter under control and said "Let me explain a couple of things, Lilith. One—we are not giving you any money. Greg won a bet, and your guys lost a fight. When that happens, you don't get paid."

She started to say something, but I reached out and put one finger across her delicious-looking lips. Lilith's lips are the reason mortal women take Botox—they're trying to catch up to what she has naturally. Too bad she knows it.

"Two—you're closed. For good. And three—"

I stopped talking because she had grabbed my finger and slid up against me, pressing herself along my body and looking up at me with a heat that I felt even without a heartbeat. She ran a finger over my lips, and I forgot how to breathe for a minute. Good thing for me it's more a force of habit than anything that keeps me alive.

Lilith looked up at me and purred "But Jimmy, I don't want to close. That would make me unhappy." She gave a little pout that made me want to give her my firstborn, my kidneys, Greg—anything to make her smile again. "And you'd much rather make me happy, wouldn't you?"

She stood up on tiptoes and licked along my jawline. I could almost feel my IQ drop into the single digits.

Suddenly Lilith flew backward and landed on her leather-clad rump, kicking up a little poof of concrete dust. I shook my head to clear it and saw a very angry Sabrina standing over Lilith with her finger in the immortal woman's face. "Look here, slut. In case you're hard of hearing as well as low on morals, the man said 'you're closed.' And I'm saying it again. You're. Closed. Any questions?"

"Oh, I understand you perfectly, Detective. But do you understand yourself?"

I've never seen anyone slink to their feet before, but Lilith moved with a liquid grace that was at the same time seductive and unnerving. Watching her walk made me wonder who was really the serpent in the Garden of Eden.

"I understand all I need to, you antique hag."

Lilith spun on her heel and stared at Sabrina like she'd been slapped.

"Yeah, I know who you are," Sabrina said. "And I know another thing—if you ever lay a finger on my cousin, or any other person in this city under my protection, I will personally end your ridiculously long life." Sabrina stood with her arms folded across her chest, almost daring Lilith to make a move.

"You can't kill me, Detective. Better women than you have tried." She turned those lethal eyelashes on me and batted them slowly. "Well, Jimmy, I could use a vampire like you. You have potential. What do you think? Money, power, and all the me you can drink? Sounds good, doesn't it?"

"Sounds yummy, except for the part where your last employee had an immortal hitchhiker wrapped around his soul. I think I'll keep my free will free, thanks. Besides, I don't go for older women," I said, stepping back from her.

I didn't know if she had anything to do with the *sluagh* infecting Lenny or not, but she didn't look surprised at the news.

Keeping Lilith at greater than arm's length was looking like a very good idea.

"Now get out of here, Lilith, and keep your nose clean. I owe you for helping us with the Belial thing, but after this, we're square. Your little fight club is out of business. Go back to running a strip bar. It's legal at least."

"Little vampire, you have no idea what forces you are setting in motion against you." Lilith stood ramrod straight, fire spitting from her eyes.

Obviously this was a woman unaccustomed to rejection. Especially from dead video game nerds.

"I do not take this insolence lightly. You will pay for the damages done here, one way or another. And you'll find that I collect my interest with extreme prejudice." Then she hopped on her bike and roared out into the night, her raven hair flying out behind her.

I heard Greg let out a long breath behind me and realized that I was holding mine as well.

"That is one scary chick," he said.

"Yeah," I agreed. "You think she knows helmets aren't optional in North Carolina?"

Chapter 33

An hour later, I was sitting on the floor of my den, leaning against a wall with a beer in my hand, looking at my friends scattered around the room and smiling. Sabrina was sitting on the floor next to me, her shoulder warm against mine. I could feel her heartbeat through her skin, pulsing along merrily. She was wearing another one of my T-shirts, her clothes having been splattered with troll blood. I was in a pair of sweats and a T-shirt, my hair still damp from a shower. I'd been covered with so much gore that I almost had to ride on the roof of my own car to get home.

Greg was in a chair pulled in from the kitchen, sipping a bag of blood from the crisper and looking better every minute. He hadn't bothered to change yet, since he was still a little dizzy from his head injury, and I told him in no uncertain terms that if he fell in the shower, he was just going to have to lay there naked until he healed, water bill be damned.

Stephen and Alex were sitting on the couch holding hands. Now that things had calmed down and no one was trying to kill any of us, Alex had a lot of questions about vampires, faeries and dragons. Stephen had more than a few questions about Faerieland for Tivernius, who sat in our lone armchair explaining what he could.

The dragon had waved his arms and all his clothes were sparkling clean again. I asked why he couldn't do that for us, and he went into a long-winded explanation that I cut off with "it's magic, you just can't." Mike walked in from the kitchen in a Batman T-shirt with a priest's collar holding a scotch for himself and one for the gimpy dragon, and sat in another kitchen chair.

"If this keeps up we're going to have to get more furniture," I said across the circle of people to Greg.

"Yeah, well, we can afford it now." He laughed, pointing over his shoulder at the pile of cash on the table.

We all chuckled, and Tivernius sipped his scotch, savoring the smoky flavor.

"I do wish we had this concoction in the lands of House Armelion," the dragon murmured.

"No scotch in Faerieland?" I asked.

"No, James, there are no fermented beverages at all in the lands of the Fae," he said.

"Well it's good to know the place isn't all purple puffy clouds, perfect weather and unicorns that poop glitter," I said.

"Unicorns do not defecate glitter, James. Whatever gave you that idea?" Tivernius asked.

"Just something I read on the Internet, pal." I laughed. Then a thought occurred to me. "Hey, Tivernius?"

"Yes, James?"

"How did you just happen to show up in the middle of the cage at just the right moment? Not that I mind, but it seemed a little more than lucky, if you get my drift."

If you've never seen a dragon blush, it's a sight to behold. Because of his normally golden skin tone, Tivernius actually turned a little orange before he spoke.

"After your departure, we interrogated the surviving members of Darkoni's retinue. They told us of his arrangement supplying trolls to the traitor Leothandron, and my queen conjured a portal by which we could observe Leothandron's activities."

"So you guys were sitting there in Faerieland watching the whole thing while we were getting our asses kicked?" I was a little pissed with that mental image.

"Oh, quit your whining and have another beer," Sabrina said. "At least he showed up in time to save your ass."

"I'll drink to that." I clinked my beer bottle to Tivernius' glass.

And I did just that. We sat, and drank, and sat and drank, until finally we had polished off the bottle of scotch as well as a twelve-pack of Miller Lite. When he finished the last of his drink, Tivernius stood, a little unsteadily, and waved a cheery farewell to all of us. He walked to the center of the room, waved his arms, and after a couple of unsuccessful attempts, conjured a portal in the air to take him home.

"I have enjoyed your company this night, and am proud to have fought alongside you. Be well, my friends." And with a wave and a smile, he stepped through the hole in the air, and vanished.

"I will never get used to seeing somebody do that," Sabrina said.

"You probably won't need to, babe. I'm kinda hoping there's not much need for portals to Faerieland in my living room," I said.

"Babe?" she asked, that one eyebrow shooting north.

I tried to return the eyebrow, but without having my face pulverized I could only move them two at a time.

She looked at me trying and laughed. "Call me whatever you want, Jimmy, but for tonight, call me a cab. I'm done."

"Take my bed. The sheets are clean," I said.

"No, I couldn't. I'll cab it home," Sabrina protested.

"Then have to cab it all the way back here tomorrow for your car? That's silly. Go to bed. I'll be fine on the couch. I don't really sleep anyway, remember?"

She started to argue more, then caught sight of Alex and Stephen watching us with smiles on their faces.

"What?" she asked dangerously.

"Nothing, cousin dear. We just think it's cute," Stephen said.

"Think what's cute?" Sabrina asked, voice dripping with danger.

I pretended to be busy getting a blanket out of the linen closet because I didn't need to be around if she shot them. Greg took that opportunity to mutter a quiet "good night" to everyone and run into his room, slamming the door behind him. I guess he'd seen enough bloodshed and brutality for one night.

"You two have never even kissed, and you're acting like an old married couple." Alex laughed while he said it, which might be the only thing that kept him from certain death.

He crossed to Sabrina and gave her a big hug. In the face of his hug and big grin she couldn't even pretend to stay mad. "Cousin, it was wonderful to finally meet you. Now I'm going to take my husband home and put him to bed. Good night everyone, and thank you."

"Yeah, guys. We can't thank you enough," Stephen agreed.

"That's okay, Lenny thanked us plenty," I said, pointing at the cash on the table.

We all laughed again, and the guys headed toward the stairs and into the dawning light. Mike went with them, counting on his clergy bumper sticker to get him out of a Breathalyzer test. Besides, his church was close.

Sabrina and Stephen took a moment at the bottom of the stairs, heads close together, talking softly. When they finished, he headed upstairs with Alex, and she walked back toward me, wiping at her eyes.

"Wanna talk about it?" I asked, holding out a bottle of beer.

"Not really. Family stuff. I thought you were out of beer?"

"We were out of guest beer. We were not out of my private stash." I smiled as I carried my blanket over to the couch.

Sabrina stood at the doorway into my bedroom and looked over at me, holding up her bottle. "I get to drink from the private stash?"

She raised that eyebrow at me again, and I knew it was going to take me a long time to get to sleep.

"Detective, you can drink from whatever you want," I said with a grin.

"Maybe if you play your cards right, I'll tell you the same thing someday," Sabrina said, grinning right back at me.

She turned, walked into my bedroom and closed the door.

Book 3:

Knight Moves

Dedication

To Suzy,
my continual source of inspiration

Chapter 1

I narrowed my focus, giving all my attention to my unmoving target. He stood there, a little more than sixty feet away, almost mocking me in how little fear he showed. My heightened senses took in everything around me, the flickering fluorescent lights overhead, the smell of stale beer and garlic from the fat man just a few feet to my left, the touch of lavender shampoo on the woman behind me, the squeak of feet on hardwood, the crash of wood on wood all around me.

Vampire speed and strength were no good to me now. This situation demanded all my concentration and probably more grace than I had at my disposal. I drew back, took careful aim, stepped forward and released.

"Gutter ball!" Detective Sabrina Law raised her hands in victory as my last chance to pick up the spare and redeem my god-awful bowling game plummeted into the gutter and left the seven pin standing without so much as a wobble. It mocked me with its lacquered maple arrogance.

"You win," I said, collapsing into one of the spinning plastic chairs as Sabrina recorded our final scores.

She beat me solidly, but I made a good rally in that final game and was within one spare of a tie.

"Nice try, Black, but you can't be expected to compete with a woman who bowls for the Police Championship League every year." Sabrina sipped her beer with a smile. "The sweet taste of victory."

"Ringer," I grumbled, reaching into my pocket for a twenty to cover the beer and slices we'd consumed while playing. Well, the slices *she'd* consumed. I'd been on a liquid diet ever since dying in the late '90s, so it was just beer for me. That little detail also explained my choice of bowling at Charlotte's only twenty-four-hour bowling alley.

I returned to our lane and started taking off my rented shoes. The disinfectant spray couldn't hide all the assorted smells from my heightened senses, so I drank more beer to keep from thinking about all the feet that had been in those shoes before me.

"So . . . Jimmy," Sabrina said after a minute or two of silence.

"Yeah?"

"Why here?"

"Well, look, we've been working together for a while now, and hanging out, so I thought it would be nice to commemorate the date with a visit back to the place where we first met."

"That's sweet. You mean the first place I ever handcuffed you to a plastic chair, don't you?" She pointed to a broken seat at a nearby table. Six months had passed, and they still hadn't replaced the chair. That case ended up with us battling an Archduke of Hell and saving a bunch of kidnapped children. Sabrina had been a fairly regular fixture in my life since then.

"Yeah, that's what I meant." I raised my cup of domestic beer, and she clunked hers to it. "Cheers."

We sat in silence for a minute, drinking our beer and changing into street shoes.

"So—" I said.

At the same time Sabrina leaned forward and said, "Well—"

"You first," I said.

"No, you go ahead." She pointed back at me.

"It's getting late, and I'm kinda done with bowling. You wanna get out of here?" I asked.

She gave me a teasing grin. "What did you have in mind?"

She was going to force me into making the first move, and I didn't know which moves were going to get me shot, and which moves might lead to something much better. Sabrina and I had been dancing around each other for months, ever since coming home from Faerieland, and I was still as clueless as ever. If given the choice between facing another Archduke of Hell or trying to figure out a woman's mind, I'd take the cage match in Hades every single time.

A new voice from behind me butted in. "Why don't we try solving a murder?"

I had never been so grateful and furious at my partner as in that moment. I turned around, and there was Greg Knightwood, the other half of Black Knight Investigations. He held my cell phone in one hand and my duster in the other.

"You forgot something when you went out tonight," he said, thrusting the phone at me.

I stood, took the phone, and put on my coat. "No I didn't. I left it at home. That doesn't mean I forgot it. Why didn't you call Sabrina?"

"I did. Apparently she left her phone somewhere as well."

I glanced over at Sabrina, who was very studiously not looking my partner in the eye. Well, maybe my night had been going to be better than I thought. Until now, of course.

My duster felt heavy, and I checked the pockets. Greg had loaded my Glock 17 into one pocket, and my Ruger LCP backup gun into another. I had loops and sheaths sewn into the lining that held a couple of knives and four stakes, and they were all full, too. I raised an eyebrow at him, but he shook his head.

"Well, let's roll, then." I slipped my phone into my jeans pocket and held my hand out to Sabrina.

She stood without my help, and pulled her phone out of her purse. "Crap. Five missed calls," she muttered.

"Three of those are from me," Greg said.

"That means two are from my Lieutenant. Lovely. Well, Jimmy, I guess the date's over. Sorry about that. Let me check messages and see where we're headed."

"The university. Construction site for the new football field. There was a body found a couple hours ago. Coed, twentyish, blonde. Body seems completely drained of blood," Greg said.

I froze in the act of clearing the cups off the table. "Did I hear you right?" I said very quietly.

"Preliminary examinations are showing that the body was completely drained of blood. So yes, you heard me right." All the teasing was gone from Greg's voice now. He knew what a big deal this could be.

"Time of death?" I asked.

"Site closed at 5 P.M., it's now five in the morning. So at most twelve hours ago."

"No, not that long. Sunset was at 7:30, so figure time of death for eightish at the earliest. That's still eight or nine hours. We gotta move." I might have shoved a couple of people out of the way in my rush, but I don't think any of them fell too hard.

Greg and Sabrina hurried to catch up. We got to the parking lot, and I looked at Sabrina. "Do you have any kind of portable LED flasher that I can put on my car?"

"Yeah, in my purse." She started to reach for it, but I was already moving down the aisle of cars to where I'd left my Honda.

"Greg, follow me tight with your flashers on," I said, counting on his vamp-hearing to save me from shouting.

He was moving fast toward his car, but I knew he'd heard me. Sabrina was almost running to keep up with my fastest walk, but I didn't slow down.

I got to the car and flung the door open. I slid behind the wheel and pulled out into the aisle. Sabrina slid into the passenger seat, rolled down the window and put a small square box on the dash. She pressed a button, and flashing blue lights strobed out. I jammed the car into gear and peeled rubber in the Concord Mills parking lot.

"I didn't know you could burn rubber in a Civic," Sabrina said.

"We don't have a lot of time. Can you call ahead and get us added to the case. Tell them Greg's an exsanguination expert or something. But we *have* to get to that body before it's moved." I took a left out of the parking lot, taking the back way to campus from the big mall.

"Why?" Sabrina asked.

"Because I only know of one thing that drains the body completely of blood, and that's a vampire. And what happens when a vampire completely drains a victim?" I didn't take my eyes off the road. We took a curve at eighty, and I managed to keep all four wheels on the ground. Barely.

Realization flashed across Sabrina's face. "Oh, shit."

"Yep, if we don't chop off the victim's head in time, there's going to be a new vampire in town."

Chapter 2

We pulled into the crime/construction scene just as our friend Bobby, the assistant coroner, was loading the body into an ambulance. I pulled the car over and sprinted toward the police line, only to come up short as a skinny young cop too new to even have creases in his uniform held up one hand and put another on the butt of his gun.

"Stop right there, sir."

I was impressed. His voice barely shook. I stopped, and was about to drop the mojo on him when I heard Sabrina's boots on the gravel behind me.

She held up her badge and said, "It's okay, Officer, he's with me."

"Lieutenant McDaniel said no one but CMPD personnel inside, Detective. I'm sorry, but your friend will have to stay out—"

"These are not the droids you're looking for. Move along," I said, locking eyes with the young officer. "You don't see me or the fat guy behind me. Detective Law came on the scene alone. And you hate the taste of doughnuts."

"Good luck down there, Detective. It's pretty bad," the young cop said, ignoring me completely as he lifted the yellow crime scene tape for Sabrina to duck under. I threw one long leg over the tape and moved to intercept Bobby, but the guard dog with a badge had slowed me up too much, and Bobby was already pulling away.

I looked over at Greg and waved him down toward the crime scene. "Go see what you can find out down there. I'll meet you back at our place after I take care of this."

He nodded and started down the hill.

I tossed my keys to Sabrina. "You drive. Let's roll."

"Where are we going?"

"We're going to chase down an ambulance and cut the head off a dead girl," I said in as casual a tone as I could muster as we ran back up the hill to my car, trying to keep another vampire from being born in Charlotte.

Bobby didn't have much of a lead on us, so we were able to catch up to the ambulance right before he pulled onto the interstate.

"How do you want to do this?" I asked, as we pulled up tight behind the emergency vehicle. As with the norm for dead passengers, Bobby ran with his lights on, but no siren, and obeyed the speed limit. After all, his cargo wasn't in any hurry for anything. At least as far as he knew.

"I thought I'd pull them over, and you'd mojo him into oblivion, then we'd figure out what to do about the girl."

I already knew what we had to do about the girl, but Sabrina obviously wasn't quite ready to talk openly about it.

"Well, it sounds like as much of a plan as we ever have. Let's do this."

She nodded and pulled around the ambulance, the little blue dashboard light glaring bright in the darkness. She waved the ambulance driver over to the side of the road, and we both got out.

Bobby rolled down his window but didn't get out. "What's going on?"

"Turn off the vehicle. We need to talk to you," Sabrina yelled over the noise of the engines. Bobby complied and joined us behind Sabrina's car.

"Oh," he said, as he caught sight of me. "It's you." His tone was flat, a little angry.

"What's with the attitude, Bobby?" I asked.

"I saw what happened to that girl. I know what you are. And I'm not stupid. I put two and two together, and I got you killing this chick. And that ain't right, man."

I tried to interrupt, but he was obviously on a roll. Bobby went right on talking over me, and that doesn't happen often. "Regardless of our business arrangement, and the fact that I might feel a little betrayed to think you're dissing the service I provide and taking your meals on the hoof these days, I don't hold with killing. Especially not with killing *cute* chicks."

Sabrina arched an eyebrow. "But it's okay to kill ugly girls?"

"There's a surplus of ugly in the world, Detective, but a finite number of hotties. It doesn't do to be taking them out of circulation."

I jumped in before things went from absurd to downright bloody. "Okay, Bobby, I get your point. But we've got two problems here. One, I didn't kill that girl. So get off your high horse. That means there's another vampire in town that none of us knew about before tonight."

At my mention of another vampire, Bobby suddenly looked a lot less sure of himself. "What's the second problem?"

"Your cargo was drained completely. That means she's going to wake up a vampire. A very hungry vampire. I don't think you want to be the first thing she lays eyes on when that happens."

"Oh, crap."

"*Oh, crap* is right. Now get in the car with Sabrina. And find some way to bloody your nose."

"Huh? Why?"

"Because I'm going to take care of this, and that means you need to get hijacked. This is just more guessing on my part, but I don't think you want me punching you in the face any more than you want to be Blood-Bank-Barbie's first meal." And of course, I heard it—the unmistakable sound of an industrial-strength zipper opening inside the ambulance.

"Bobby?"

"Yeah?"

"You want to be running now." I grabbed his arm and spun him toward Sabrina. She shot me a startled look, but I just growled, "Get out of here. I can't deal with her and keep you safe."

Sabrina and Bobby ran for her car just as the ambulance's rear door flew open from the inside.

Bobby was right. The girl had been beautiful in life. She was blonde, looked to be about twenty, and built to break hearts. She wore a bloodstained UNCC 49ers sweatshirt and strategically torn blue jeans, with a pair of boots that should have been registered as lethal weapons.

She dragged pieces of the body bag behind her as she came out of the ambulance, and her face showed nothing more than hunger and insanity. It had been a long time since I'd seen a newly awakened vampire, and while she was cuter than Greg at his coming-out party, she was no less raving. Her fangs were fully extended, and her eyes rolled in their sockets, as if they wouldn't focus. Then, suddenly, they did. She locked her eyes onto me like a pit bull on a sirloin and leapt out of the ambulance.

If I'd still been alive, I would have died. Since I'd been dead a lot longer than she had, and had taken a few judo classes, I was able to roll with her and throw her to the pavement. I glanced up to see Sabrina's taillights peeling back into traffic and caught a fist right on the chin for my trouble.

"Ow!" I yelled. "Cut that out!"

The newly dead vamp didn't answer, just jumped at me again, jaws snapping on air as I spun out of her path. I had a flashback to Greg's first morning as a vampire, and that memory didn't help me focus on the fight. Not to mention, the chick was super-fast. Like faster than me fast, and I was no slouch in the speed department. She must have been in really good shape when she was alive or something.

Fortunately for me she was completely, animal-growling, bite-the-dirt insane, or I would have been toast. Since she couldn't focus on anything for more than a couple of seconds, I was able to come up with a plan that seemed only somewhat ridiculous. The next time she lunged, I grabbed her arm and flung her back into the ambulance. As she crashed into the meat wagon, I reached to the side to slam the door shut on her.

Except . . . she bent the door beyond repair when she kicked it open. I still held the half-closed door when the new vampire launched herself out of the back of the ambulance once more, taking me down and latching her teeth onto my shoulder. Between banging my head on the asphalt and getting holes in my favorite Spider Jerusalem T-shirt, it was not shaping up to be a very good night.

I grabbed her by the hair and tried to pull her off me, but she was stuck tighter than a tick in July. I lurched to my feet, but she just wrapped her legs around my middle and kept drinking. Was this what the folks in *Alien* felt when the face-huggers got them? I felt my strength start to fade. The more she drank, the stronger she got. The stronger she got, the weaker I got. I was really starting to hate the merry-go-round.

I knew I had to do something fast, so I rammed her into the back bumper of the ambulance. I heard ribs crack, and she opened her mouth to scream. The second her teeth pulled out of my flesh, I shoved my left arm under her chin to keep those teeth at bay while I punched her in the side of the head with my right fist. After three or four solid shots to the temple, her legs relaxed from around my waist, and she slumped to the ground. I sagged down to sit on the bumper and drew my Glock, leveling it at her forehead.

The Glock was loaded with hollow points, so I was pretty sure I could decapitate her, or at least do enough damage to keep her dead, but something froze me before I pulled the trigger. I thought back to Greg on his first night as a vampire, how out of control he had been. This kid was just like that, probably just like I had been when I attacked my best friend and accidentally turned him. My finger tightened on the trigger again, but I couldn't do it.

It wasn't my fault she had been turned, but it wasn't my place to kill her, either. As of this moment, she was innocent. She hadn't hurt anyone, at least not anyone alive, and she didn't deserve to die because of what had been done to her. If I ever found out who turned her, that would be a different story. I put the Glock back in my shoulder holster and reached out to touch her shoulder.

She shook her head and growled as her eyes came into focus. "Who the hell are you?" she asked, wiping my blood off her lips with the back of one hand. "And where am I?"

"I think you're going to have a lot more questions in about an hour, but, for now, let me give you the basics. My name is Jimmy Black, and I'm a private investigator. I work with the police on some . . . special cases. You're on the side of North Tryon Street at almost six in the morning. You've been turned into a vampire. I'm one, too, and we have about half an hour to get inside before we both end up like my last attempt at a Thanksgiving turkey. And trust me, that wasn't pretty."

"Are you high or something?"

"Or something. For now, like they say in the movies, 'come with me if you want to live.'" I limped around to the front of the ambulance, got in and started the engine.

The girl sat on the pavement looking confused. And bloody. And cute. Which made for a terrible combination, especially since it was my blood.

I rolled down the passenger window. "You coming? Or dying?"

"Why should I believe you? What if you're a nutjob serial killer?" She reached into her pocket, where she probably carried pepper spray before the world and a hungry vamp made sure she'd never need pepper spray again.

"I haven't killed you yet, have I? And I'm the one with the gun. If I wanted you dead, you'd be dead." A little stretch on my part, because she was already dead, and I hadn't wanted it. I hadn't really wanted her to wake up, either. But I couldn't change that, so I had to be responsible for her. Greg was going to love this. He'd wanted a puppy for years, and I kept saying no. Now I was going to bring home a pet vampire.

She stared at me distrustfully.

I looked at the brightening horizon, and said, "Look, Pumpkin, time's a-wasting. You can either come with me and maybe die, or stay here and definitely die. But I'm leaving. Now."

She stared at me for a second or two longer, then got up in a ridiculously fluid motion and was at the passenger door in less time than it took me to blink twice. She got in and buckled up, and I headed off into the sunrise, trying the whole way to figure out where I was going to park an ambulance in our cemetery.

Yeah, Greg was gonna *love* this.

Chapter 3

"You did what?" Greg stood gaping in the middle of our den, a forgotten game of *Left 4 Dead 2* on the big screen behind him.

"Are you insane?" Sabrina demanded from where she stood, back to a wall and service pistol pointed at the girl's head.

"What was I supposed to do?" I shielded the girl from Sabrina's aim with my body. "She bit me and drank enough to become aware. I couldn't kill her then."

"Wait a minute!" The girl stepped out from behind me. "You were going to kill me? And now you say you were rescuing me? What the hell? I'm out of here."

She turned on her heel and headed toward the stairs, only to run into my oldest living friend Mike Maloney, who was on the way down to our apartment. I hadn't seen Mike in a couple of weeks, but I called him in to help calm down our new addition.

"James, why is there an ambulance under a blue tarp in your front yard? And where might you be going, my child?" Mike put out an arm to stop her, but she brushed past him with ease. A little too much ease, in fact, since Mike went flying across the room. I intercepted him before he crashed into anything structural and put him down gently.

"Sorry, Dad. She doesn't know her own strength yet," I said.

"Obviously." Mike's hands shook as he made his way to the armchair and sat down heavily.

He looked thin, and he smelled funny. Not funny ha-ha, but bad funny. Humans wouldn't be able to smell it, but it was obvious to me. I filed it away to ask him about later and turned my attention to the crisis at hand.

The girl made it to the top of the stairs. I heard the front door open, then slam shut an instant later. Just as quick, it opened again, and she dashed back down the stairs, smoke pouring from her clothes, her skin flaking like the worst sunburn you've ever seen.

Greg and I shared a look and both shrugged. I headed to the fridge. I reached into the crisper, got four of our last five bags of blood and a couple of beers, then walked over to where the girl paced and cursed around at the bottom of the stairs.

I handed her a bag of blood. "Drink this."

"You have got to be kidding me." She threw it back at me, obviously disgusted.

"Shut up and drink it. It'll heal the burns, and you didn't drink much from me. You need to feed, and there aren't any willing donors here." I threw it back at her and sank my teeth into a bag of my own.

She watched me drink for a few seconds, then turned around and tore open her bag. I heard weird slurping sounds, then realized that she didn't know how to use her fangs yet.

"You know you've got fangs, right? They make that a lot easier. It's kinda like a juice box, only you carry your straw with you."

She flipped me off over her shoulder, and I watched the skin on her hand return to a more normal deathly pallor. She finished her bag quickly, and I handed her another as soon as she turned around. I dove into my own second bag, trying to replace what she'd taken from me, and handed her a Miller Lite when she was finished.

"You trying to get me drunk?" she asked with a saucy little smirk. Her burns were already healing, so the blood was working.

This one was going to be trouble. I could tell. The last thing I needed in my life was a sex-kitten vampire half my age running around my apartment. I glanced over at Sabrina to try to gauge her reaction to this new development, but got nothing.

"I couldn't get you drunk if I wanted to. Not with beer, anyway. It just cuts the aftertaste of the anticoagulants. Now, why don't we start with the easy stuff. What's your name?"

"Abigail Lahey. Pleased to meet you."

She held out her hand, and I stared at it for a minute before I burst out laughing. The ridiculousness of the whole night caught up with me right there. I had gone from a very promising date with a very intriguing detective to becoming the adoptive undead father figure to a coed vampire. It was a lot to take in. I had to reach for a barstool to hold myself up, and that got Greg going, which got Sabrina going, which got Abigail going, until the only one not rolling with laughter was Mike, who looked at us like we'd all been possessed or finally gone insane. Either option was about equally likely, I supposed.

After a few minutes of hysterical laughter, we all settled down in the den. Mike, ever the gentleman, gave up the comfy armchair to Abigail. I grabbed a few more beers for everybody, and a Scotch for Mike, then sat on the couch. Sabrina gave a little shrug and sat beside me. Mike brought a straight chair in from the kitchen, while Greg lounged in his bizarre purple beanbag game chair with speakers in the butt region. When everyone was seated, I looked Abigail in the eyes. She had pretty eyes. They were a very deep blue. I felt a pang of regret at all the things she was going to miss out on.

"Now do you believe me? About the whole vampire thing?" I asked gently.

"I think so. I mean, I kinda remember biting you, and I did just drink a couple of pints of blood. That was nasty, by the way."

"That's why I gave you the beer."

"Then there was the whole burning in the sunlight thing, so I guess I believe you. I just . . ."

"Just what, my child?" Mike asked softly.

He had a way of getting people to talk to him. He would have been a good interrogator, but right now he was a pretty good priest, and that was what we needed.

"I keep waiting to wake up, you know?"

"I know," Greg said, a shadow over his expression that was way too familiar. "Believe me, I know."

"Well, unfortunately, you're not going to wake up. This is the new reality for you, Abby. No more sunbathing, no more silver earrings and a liquid diet forever." I tried to lighten the maudlin mood falling over everyone, to no avail. "But look on the bright side. You're stronger, faster and cooler than anyone you've ever met. You don't really turn into a bat, which is good, and you aren't required to wear all black and lurk in alleys. It's not all nancy-boy hair gel and soul-searching, no matter what you've seen on *Angel* reruns."

I got a little smile in response. "I've always kinda liked staying up late," she said, obviously trying to find a bright side.

"That's the spirit," I said in my best hearty voice. "But you might want to head to the bathroom now."

"Why? I feel fine."

"That will last for probably another five minutes. Then you're gonna puke. A lot. I'll have another beer here waiting for you when you're done. But we don't process food anymore, and your body is going to want to be rid of—" I stopped speaking as Abby jumped up off the couch and ran toward the bathroom.

Greg pointed the way, and she slammed the door shut.

Sabrina stood to go after her, but I grabbed her arm. "You don't want to do that."

"Why not, Jimmy? The poor girl's obviously in pain."

"She is, but not the kind you're thinking of."

"What are you babbling about now?"

"She's going to want to be alone for a little while as she finishes shuffling off the mortal coil."

"Is there an echo in here? Oh, wait, it's me. *What* are you babbling about?"

"She's gotta puke. A lot. Among other unpleasantries. We don't eat. We don't process food. Do you get the rather disgusting picture? She's barfing up everything she's eaten in recent memory and, even if you guys were friends, that's not something you're going to hold somebody's hair back for."

"Oh." Sabrina sat back down on the couch, and we waited for Abigail to finish in the bathroom.

After a few minutes, Sabrina pulled out her cell phone and checked in with the crime scene techs. When she hung up, she looked over at me and said, "The scene has been processed, but I managed to get them to keep it secure until I gave them the word, in case you guys want to get back out there after dark."

"Good deal," I said. "Since I never got to walk the scene, it would be nice to get a little alone time with the murder scene before it gets covered in a few tons of concrete."

About ten minutes later, Abby came out of the bathroom, drained her beer in one long swallow and got a glass of water from the kitchen.

She walked over to stand in front of the armchair, then looked from Greg to me and back again. Her eyes were red, but there were no tears in evidence, and it looked like she might have even touched up her makeup while she was in the bathroom. I noticed the square bulge of an eye shadow in one pocket that confirmed my suspicions.

"All right, which one of you did this to me? And why? Did you pervs think I'd sleep with you if you made me your little vampire slave? Is that it? Well, let me tell you something, it is *not* going to be like that. I'm not that kind of girl. Um, vampire. Uh . . . vampiress. You know what I mean. So just fess up so I can kick your ass, and we can settle that once and for all."

I looked over at Greg and mouthed "perv"?

He shrugged and looked over at Abigail. "Yeah, that's part of the problem. We didn't turn you. And we don't know any other vampires in Charlotte. So we don't know who turned you. Or why. That's why we were at your murder scene, to investigate. It's what we do."

Abby looked confused, so I stood up and passed her one of my business cards. It had my name, cell phone number and Black Knight Investigations, the name of our firm, on the front. "I'm Jimmy, the round one is Greg, and that's Sabrina Law. She's a detective with the CMPD."

Mike stood and held out his hand. "And I am Father Michael Maloney, of the Diocese of Charlotte. James and Greg have been friends for a very long time, and I didn't see any reason to sever our relationship because of their unfortunate demise." He gave her a warm smile and sat back down.

Greg stood and started to pace around our very small den, made all the smaller by a vampire of his girth pacing through it. "Can I ask you a few questions?" Abby nodded. "Did you see who attacked you? Do you remember anything about the assault?"

"I don't remember anything after leaving my chemistry lab. I was walking home and cut through the woods like I always do, making sure to keep my pepper spray handy."

"Yeah," I put in, "safety first."

Abigail shot me a hurt look, and Greg stopped his pacing to glare at me.

"Sorry," I muttered. I motioned for him to go ahead. It was his turn to do some of the heavy lifting on this case. After all, I'd fought the crazy new vampire and hijacked the ambulance.

"Anyway, the next thing I remember is you with a gun to my head. I don't remember anyone biting me, and I don't remember biting you. Sorry about that, by the way." She looked down, embarrassed.

"No worries. Better me than someone living. At least I managed to fight you off. And the best part is you don't remember it, so I don't even have to apologize for punching you in the head." Abby's head snapped up. "But I am sorry about that."

"Don't be. Stuff happens. Now, how do we find the guy that bit me?" she asked, eyes bright with anger.

"How do you know it was a guy?" Greg asked. "Did you remember something?"

"Well, no, but are there other girl vampires around here?" Abigail replied with a shrug.

"Abigail, we haven't met *any* other vampires, male or female. But they're obviously around. So we need to be open to all possibilities," Sabrina said. "Now, are you sure you don't remember anything after leaving class?"

"No, I really don't. I left class, waved goodnight to this cute guy and turned to go into the woods. Then everything turns gray and hazy."

"She was mojo'd." Mike had been uncharacteristically quiet since getting tossed across the room, but now he interjected his opinion with certainty.

"How do you know?" Sabrina asked. "I mean, it makes sense, but how can you be sure?"

"When the boys first revealed themselves to me, as they were learning about their abilities, they used their power of mental domination on me a few times. It was purely experimental, and consensual on all our parts, just to see what the limits were." Mike quickly put that last bit in when he saw Sabrina about to hit me. I gave him a grin and motioned for him to continue. "When they ordered me to forget things, it went exactly as Miss Lahey described. Everything went gray around the edges, and my memory just stopped. Then, it picked up later, like an old movie with the middle reel missing."

"So we've got a vamp with mojo. Yeah, that narrows it down." I was getting grumpy, so I stood up and started pacing opposite Greg. The already cramped living room felt downright claustrophobic with my long legs and Greg's jiggly belly vying for space. We took turns almost tripping over the coffee table for a couple minutes until something hit me. "Abby, come here."

She walked over to where I stood in the middle of the living room a little hesitantly, so I said, "Calm down, I've already decided not to kill you. Now, stand still."

I leaned over to study the bite marks on her neck. Those marks were the last scars she'd ever get. I had found out the hard way that anything up to and including a bullet through the heart would heal without a mark, but the scars that turned us were a reminder of what we used to be. I slid in to within a hair's breadth of her neck and inhaled deeply, trying to get all of her scent into my nostrils.

Greg usually had the stronger sniffer, but not for this. Not this scent. I breathed in rose-tinged perfume, a hint of my blood, a little sour smell of vomit, the three beers she'd had since waking and the deep rich smell of the blood I'd given her to feed on. But underneath all those smells, woven into the complex scent of Abby, was another smell, darker, older and somehow warmer than the others. I knew it was the scent of the vampire who had turned her, and that I'd be able to follow that scent anywhere.

I took a step back, fulfilling my evening's destiny and falling over the coffee table onto my butt. As I lay sprawled over the table, I flashed back to the last time I'd smelled that very same vampire's scent—the night she had turned me.

I met her at a bar, and she laughed at my jokes. That didn't happen much in the '90s, so I bought her a drink. Then, I bought her another drink. Then, she bought me a drink. Then we danced, which went better than normal. Better than normal meant that I didn't step on her toes too often or fall down on the dance floor. A slow song came on, and the world went away as I buried my face in her neck. I nibbled her earlobe, kissed the side of her neck and closed my eyes as the scent of fresh flowers filled my nose. She smelled like all the greatest things in the world, all layered over with a hint of sweat and promise.

We left the bar and made our drunken way back to my apartment. The den was in its normal state of disaster, but she ignored all that. She just stood there between the thrift-store sofa and the cheap Zenith television and kissed me.

When her lips touched mine for the first time, I felt it all the way down to my toes. I heard trumpets, saw fireworks and lost control of my extremities. She followed me down as I collapsed on the couch, and we made love right there on the living room sofa. She sank her fangs into me as we joined together and she killed me with my pants around my ankles and a Rolling Stone magazine stuck to my butt.

Her scent charged out of the past and knocked me nearly unconscious fifteen years later in the middle of another messy living room.

We had a *problem*.

Chapter 4

"What is it?" Sabrina asked, reaching to help me up.

I shook my head and marched over to the liquor shelf in the kitchenette. I poured a double scotch into a tumbler, looked at it, and turned up the bottle. The peaty amber liquid burned as it went down, and tears sprang to my eyes. I grabbed two beers from the fridge and downed one of them in a long pull. I held the other one to my forehead for a second as I leaned back against the refrigerator. I wasn't flushed. That hadn't happened since Clinton was President but, in times of stress, I sometimes flash back to reflexes from when I was alive.

When I felt I could move without stumbling or twitching like a junkie on day three of withdrawal, I went back over to where the others alternated between aiming panicked looks at me and throwing threatening glares at Abigail. "It's not her," I said, drawing a shaky breath. "Or more to the point, it's not anything she knows about."

"Then what is it, bro?" Greg sounded as solemn as I'd ever heard him and, when I looked, all hints of my dorky, harmless roommate were gone. He had a KA-BAR knife in one hand and a Glock in the other. He didn't turn his attention to Abigail when he spoke to me, and I noticed for the first time how scary Greg could be when he wanted to be.

"It's her sire. Or dam, or whatever the right word is. It's the scent of the vamp that turned her. I recognize it."

"But you've only ever met two other vamps before tonight, and I'm one of them. And if I didn't turn her . . . sonofabitch." Greg turned away from me and crossed to the door at the bottom of the stairs. He threw the heavy steel door closed and dropped an iron bar across it. Mike and Sabrina shared a concerned look, but said nothing.

"I don't know that we need all that, buddy, but it's not a bad idea." I sat back down on the couch, took a swig of my fresh beer, and put my head in my hands.

"You want to clue the rest of us in on what's got you so freaked out, Jimmy?" Sabrina asked softly. She leaned away a little, as if afraid I might not be in control of myself. That was probably a pretty good guess.

"The vamp that turned Abigail. She was the vamp that turned me," I said, looking at the floor.

My mind kept going back to that night, a girl way out of my league wanting to dance with me, wanting to leave with me, wanting to go back to my apartment. It was one of the high points of my less than illustrious post-college life, and it ended with her killing me on my couch, and me murdering my best friend.

"I'll never forget the smell of her. She smelled like magnolias, and incense and just a little bit of sweat. It was the best thing I'd ever smelled in my life . . ." Then, I was off the couch and headed for the bathroom. I crouched in front of the toilet and noisily revisited the beer, scotch and a couple of pints of blood. I sat on the tiles retching for a long minute or two before a hand reached in and passed me a glass of water.

I looked up at Mike's face, the face I'd known since we were in elementary school, and wondered where all that gray hair had come from. I took a good look at my friend for the first time in months and saw the yellow tint around his eyes, the sunken cheeks and the clean-shaven look so different from the neat beard he'd sported since our senior year of high school. Suddenly, everything clicked into place as I sat with the linoleum making flower patterns on my butt and the cool porcelain pressed against my side.

"Were you planning on telling me anytime soon?" I whispered low enough that not even Greg could eavesdrop.

Mike twitched a wry smile, and his lips barely moved as he breathed his answer. "I've been trying to figure out the right time."

"What is it? Lung? I know it's not brain. You lack the requisite organ."

He punched me lightly on the arm. "Esophagus. I thought it was acid reflux brought on by chasing you two idiots around all night but, apparently, it was a tumor. The radiation finished up last week, and I'm scheduled for surgery tomorrow. I was actually coming over here to tell you both about it."

"I would hope so," Greg interjected from the doorway, "because I was not looking forward to outing you." I looked up at Greg, his face solemn. When I gazed pointedly at the living room, he said, "Don't worry, I told the girls it was a private discussion, and I don't think Abigail has figured out that she has bat-ears yet."

"How long have you known?" Mike asked him.

"Since your first treatment. I do the cancer ward thing, remember?"

"What cancer ward thing?" I asked. Apparently, there were all sorts of things going on with my friends that I wasn't aware of.

"I volunteer a couple nights a week hanging with the cancer kids. It's something The Guys got me into."

"I wouldn't have thought those dorks would know there was a world outside their comic shop." I didn't have a very high opinion of the comic shop nerds Greg called The Guys, but they had been useful on a couple of occasions in the past.

"Well, you know Mark, the owner of the shop?" he asked. After my nod, he went on, "Mark's kid brother had leukemia, so I got to know some of the nurses. It was kind of a crappy place, so I took in some games, got them a decent TV, and I go in sometimes and play Xbox with them. You know, let the kids feel like kids for a little while instead of pincushions."

"Wow, Greg. That's . . . amazing. I didn't know anything about it. You never said."

"I dunno why. It's just something I do."

I looked at my best friend, trying to think of something to say. A therapist would probably say something about him trying to compensate for having to drink life by helping the sick or something like that. But I had bailed on the only psychology class I ever took, and Greg looked embarrassed, so I decided to let it drop.

Mike reached over and put a hand on Greg's arm. "I'm sure it helps them quite a bit, my friend. Quite a bit. Now, before the obvious questions arise about a Catholic priest and two vampires in one small room, shall we rejoin the ladies?" We all laughed, and just for a second, it was like we were kids again. Then reality came back.

I grabbed Mike's hand for help getting off the bathroom floor. "We'll talk about this a little more, right?" I didn't really mean it as a question.

"Yes. I'll give you all the gory details. And when this is all over, I'll have a nice set of neck scars all my own." He grinned lopsidedly and almost managed to hide the fear in his eyes.

I looked at Greg and could almost read the thoughts printed across his face. Mike was our oldest friend, our Third Musketeer, and neither of us wanted to know what the world was like without Mike in it. I'd already watched from the trees, smoldering through my jacket as I watched them lower my dad into the ground, and learned firsthand how hard it was to lose someone you couldn't say good-bye to properly. I knew if anything happened to Mike we wouldn't be able to attend any of the services. Even if they were evening visitations, it wouldn't do for the deceased two best friends to suddenly come back from the dead to give him a good send-off. Sometimes being dead sucks.

I turned away, but out of the corner of my eye I saw Greg wiping away a pale pink tear when he thought I couldn't see. I knew exactly how he felt.

Chapter 5

Sabrina and Abigail were watching the news when we made our way back to the den. Abigail's face smiled down larger than life from the flat screen on the wall.

"Looks like the news has broken," I said, taking my spot on the sofa next to Sabrina.

"Yeah, what are we going to do about it?" Abigail asked. "My parents think I'm dead! They've already been interviewed about finding my body. I want to call them, but she took my cell phone." She glared at Sabrina, who looked pretty unfazed by the girl's anger.

"Good move," I told Sabrina. "Look, pumpkin, I've got a news flash you're not gonna find on WCNC—in every way that matters, you *are* dead. You can't call your parents, or your roommate, or your boyfriend, or anyone. They need to move on without you because you're going to have to move on without them. You're a *vampire*. You burn in the sunlight, don't like silver jewelry, have issues with true believers and have a very, *very* strict liquid diet. If you don't get that through that pretty little head of yours, you will be dead again, this time forever. *Comprende?*" I realized suddenly that I was shouting, and stood there for a minute, working to bring myself back under control.

Abigail sat there, staring up at me angrily, then threw her beer bottle at my head and made a dash for the door. Fortunately for her, Greg was really fast for a fat vampire, and he grabbed her after about three steps. I could see his eyes go wide as she fought against him, surprise written all over his face at her strength. She almost wriggled free before I stepped between her and the door with my Glock pointed at her head.

Abigail froze.

"Behave," I said. She drew back to hit me, and I pulled the hammer back on the Glock. "Sit. Down. I'm tired, I'm hungry, I'm not crazy about having another vampire standing in my den, and I'm getting a little testy about the whole night. So if you don't want to learn the hard way about regenerating from gunshot wounds, I'd really suggest you sit down."

She didn't budge, so I nodded at Greg. He picked her up from behind, and carried her into his bedroom. I motioned for Mike to follow, heard a muffled *thump* as Greg dropped the girl on the bed and then came out, closing Mike in there with her.

"Is that safe?" Sabrina asked. "Leaving Mike in there with her? She seemed pretty mad."

"Safer than having her out here where Jimmy could stake her," Greg said, grabbing a beer and picking up the wireless mouse and keyboard he kept on the desk in the den. He switched the TV over to computer monitor mode and started surfing the web. "I'm going to spend a little time trying to track our mystery vamp while you two figure out what to do about the ambulance parked behind our house."

I looked over at Sabrina, who looked back at me. "How long do we have before they really start looking for the ambulance? I took off the plates, but I think that might be of limited use, given the conspicuous nature of the vehicle."

"The APB went out right after Bobby made it to the hospital with his story of being carjacked. It helps that we're on the other side of town, and in a cemetery, but we've got to make that thing disappear today."

"How was Bobby?"

"A little shaken up, but also pretty excited. He thinks all this crap is cool."

"We are cool, babe. You know, studly stalkers of the night, protectors of the innocent, sexy predators that all men want to be and all women want to be with." I went for my best rakish look, but Sabrina had burst out laughing at "sexy predators."

"Yeah, whatever. You got any clients that run chop shops?"

"No. You got any old informants that owe you a favor?"

"No. So if we're out of the stereotypical ideas, what's next?"

"I sent her an email," Greg said over his shoulder. "She's sending a guy over. I'll get ten grand out of the safe and put it on the driver's seat. It'll be taken care of in an hour."

"Uh, two questions, buddy. One, we have a safe? And two, who are you talking about?" I watched as Greg got up from his goofy little game chair and went over to the fridge. He pulled it away from the wall to reveal a safe set into the floor underneath it. He dialed a combination and pulled out a wrapped stack of hundred-dollar bills.

He shoved the fridge back into place, dropped the cash in a paper bag and handed it to Sabrina. "Now, do you really have to ask that second question? Who is the one person we know with fingers into almost every illegal pie in Charlotte?"

Sabrina and I looked at each other and said, "Lilith."

The immortal seductress had insinuated herself into all sorts of unsavory operations since coming to town as an indentured servant to a fallen angel. When the angel had suddenly became un-fallen, Lilith was stuck here running his operation, and she was not happy about it. She was pretty pissed off at us the last time I saw her, but apparently ten grand bought a lot of tolerance these days.

"So where the hell did you get ten grand?" I asked.

Greg looked at Sabrina, then back at me, then shrugged. "I play a lot of online poker."

"I thought that was illegal." I clapped my hand over my mouth as soon as I said it, but the damage was done.

Greg glared at me. "Actually, playing poker on the Internet is perfectly legal. It's against the law to process payment transactions, or to accept wagers from American players."

"Do I even want to know?" I asked.

"Probably not, but since we're this far in I may as well finish. The server in the coat closet is mirrored with one I own in Costa Rica, and I bounce my signal between them to play."

"I have no idea what that means," I admitted.

"It means that the poker site thinks I'm in Costa Rica, so it's legal for me to play."

"I was right. I didn't want to know."

Sabrina took the cash upstairs and deposited it on the seat of the ambulance. While she took care of that, I cleaned my guns while Greg started his online investigation. The vampiric blast from my past had kicked my normal paranoia into high gear, and I wanted to make sure all my weapons were in tip-top shape. A few minutes later Greg called me over to the computer.

"Check this out," he whispered, clicking through a series of web pages faster than I could see them, much less read anything. Ten seconds of that, and I snatched the mouse away from him. I clicked through the tabs more slowly and saw that he'd called up the *Charlotte Observer* online archives as well as somehow gotten into the paper's internal document storage. I looked through the articles on missing students, then swung Greg's other monitor over. On that screen, he'd hacked into the Charlotte-Mecklenburg Police Department case file database, and he had called up a good dozen or more missing persons cases.

"Anything look familiar?" he whispered.

"Why are you whispering?" Sabrina asked from over my shoulder, making us both jump.

"Look at this." Greg pointed, drawing our attention to the screens. "Fifteen students missing over the past eighty years. All seniors or juniors ready to graduate early. All missing after a night class, and no bodies ever found. Sound familiar?"

"Yeah, it sounds like Little Mary Sunshine in there is just the latest in a whole string of vampire kills on campus." I pointed to the case file screen again. "But something's wrong. The last missing person was just six months ago. None of the other attacks have happened within three years of each other."

"So our vampire got careless," Sabrina said.

"Careless vampires don't live very long. And they certainly don't live most of a century in one location and then make a stupid mistake like turning someone too close to the last victim. Besides, look at this case." I clicked on one of the older files and pointed at the date.

"What about it?" she asked.

"I know two things for a fact. One, the vampire that turned Abby was the same vampire that turned me. I'd know that smell anywhere. And two, I know that she was not in Charlotte when this murder was reported."

"What makes you so sure? I mean, I believe that it smelled like her, but don't some people smell alike?"

Greg and I didn't even hesitate, we both just said, "No."

My partner, ever the more educational type, explained a little. "Scents are like fingerprints, at least in our experience. No one smells just like someone else. There are a lot of things that go into a person's scent—their ethnicity, their blood type, their geography, their occupation, their diet, their drug uses and abuses, even whether or not they drink regular coffee or decaf. The odds of two people having the exact same scent is so astronomical as to be impossible."

Sabrina's eyes were wide. "I didn't know you got that much out of someone's smell." She looked at me pointedly.

"It can get a little personal if we're not careful, so we don't talk about it. But trust me, when a vampire says he likes the way you smell, it's a pretty huge compliment."

She blushed and looked away. After a minute she asked, "And how do you know the vampire that turned you wasn't in Charlotte that particular night?"

"Because that's the night she killed me in Clemson, almost three hours from here. She didn't have time to do both." I didn't elaborate, and didn't intend to.

Greg moved me out of the way and reclaimed his rightful position as master of the mouse. "Then we have two vampires working here. The original vampire, who's been hunting on the campus for a long time, and your sire, who has just stepped all over his hunting ground tonight."

"Dam," I said quietly.

"What's wrong?" Sabrina asked.

"Nothing, but she's not a sire. Sires are male. She's a dam."

"Like a horse?"

"You know it, missy." I grinned at her and waggled my eyebrows.

I opened my mouth, probably to put my foot in it with a lame innuendo, but Mike saved me by opening the door to the bedroom and walking out. *He's at least moving under his own power. That's always good.* Abigail followed meekly behind him, apologizing to all of us as she went to the fridge, grabbed the last bag of blood and joined us around the big screen.

"So what's the plan?" Abigail asked, slurping on the blood. Sabrina looked a little pale, and I reached over with a paper towel and wiped a thin line of blood off the kid's chin.

"You missed a spot."

"Sorry."

"It's okay. You get the technique down over time. For the first few days, though, it's easier to use a straw."

"Huh. Never thought of that."

"Neither did I. Greg came up with it."

"Easy to see who's the brains of the operation, huh?" The kid leaned in a little closer than I was comfortable with, and Sabrina kicked me under the table.

"What?" I asked, sitting up straight.

"Oh, nothing." That woman had an uncanny ability to lower the temperature of a room with just a couple of syllables.

"All right, then. If it's *nothing*, then let's get back to the business at hand. Namely, the sudden increase in the known vampire population of Charlotte," I said, standing up and starting to pace. "Here's what we know. First, Abigail here was turned by the same vampire that turned me fifteen years ago in a bar outside Greenville, South Carolina. Second, we know there's another vampire that's been turning UNCC students for a lot of years, and has been very discrete about it. So, maybe the vamp that turned me and Abby is working with this local vamp?"

"That doesn't work," Sabrina said. "From what you've said, the vampire that turned you is anything but discrete. She picked you up from a populated area and took you back to your apartment without any regard for who else might be home, then left you there on the couch."

I turned away a little at the memory. It wasn't the best night of my life, waking up dead with my boxers around my ankles while my best friend screamed at my corpse. Then there was the part where I killed him. That was a buzzkill, too.

Sabrina went on. "That, coupled with the way she posed Abigail's body after she drained her, tells us that she has no compunction against killing and leaving her victims where they could easily be found. There's no way she's been in Charlotte all this time without us knowing about it."

"I agree," Greg added. "The third thing we know is that we know very little else. She killed Abigail sometime between 11 P.M. and two in the morning, and she could have been anywhere from around the corner to Nashville in the time between committing the murder and sunrise."

"She's still here," Abigail said suddenly.

"What do you mean?" I asked.

"I can feel her. She's still close."

"What, like some kind of vampiric radar? Like you're tied to your sire or something?" Greg asked.

I didn't bother correcting him this time.

"I dunno," the girl said. "I just know she's still close. Like she's not finished with me."

"Maybe she mojo'd you before she killed you so you'd know she was close," Sabrina chimed in.

"Can we stop saying she killed me?" Abigail pleaded. "I'm right here, after all."

"Just being precise, dear. You are now part of the walking dead, after all." Sabrina had a snippy tone I'd never heard from her before.

Before the girls escalated things into an all-out catfight, I said, "Why don't we all just get a little sleep and go back to the crime scene tonight? We should still be able to pick up any scents or clues then, and with decidedly less risk of spontaneous combustion. Besides, I'm sure the humans in the room aren't the only ones who are starting to drag. Between bowling, fighting a newborn and hijacking an ambulance, it's been a long night."

Sabrina started to gather her things to leave. "Good idea, Jimmy. I'll meet you guys back here around eight tonight. We can figure out where this vamp-factory is hiding out, stake her and then your little sister can be on her merry way." She pulled on her jacket and holster as I gaped at her.

"Little *sister?*"

"Well, yeah. After all, you two were made by the same vamp, so doesn't that make her your sister?" She flashed me a vicious grin and headed up the stairs.

The more I hung out with her, the more confused I was as to exactly which one of us had the fangs.

Greg rolled in his chair a little until she leaned back around the stairs and said, "So what does that make her to you, Greg? Your aunt?"

He fell out of his chair with a thwack, like a side of beef hitting the carpet, kind of wet and fleshy. Mike smiled and followed Sabrina up the stairs.

"If you two comedians are done, I'm going to bed," I said, heading toward my room.

"Uh, where am I supposed to sleep? Should I have a coffin or something?" Abigail stood in the middle of the den looking confused and a little scared.

"Nah, there's an air mattress in the coat closet, and the couch pulls out," Greg said, demonstrating the convertible sofa. "You've seen the shape of my room, and Jimmy's is much, much worse, so trust me when I say this is the safest place for you to sleep."

"But what if somebody comes in and tries to stake me in my sleep?"

She was starting to shake a little, and I felt something I hardly ever felt—sympathy. The first few times I went to sleep I dreamed a lot. And they were all dreams of being alive, which made waking up really rough when I realized I'd never see my mom or dad, or anyone I'd ever known, again. I didn't envy her the next few nights.

"Okay, look," I said. "We'll all camp out in here for the night. It'll be fine." I dragged my mattress onto the floor and plopped it down between the stairs and the couch. I went to the coat closet for my shotgun and deposited it on the floor beside the mattress. "There. Now anything coming in the door will have to get through me, and my little friend." My best Pacino impression was pretty bad, but it got a smile out of her.

Greg dropped his mattress on the other side of the couch, between the den and the kitchen, effectively barricading our guest in the general vicinity of the sofa.

She looked around at the arrangement and settled in on the couch. "Thanks, guys. I'm just a little scared, you know?"

"I know," Greg answered from the floor. "It's been a while, but I remember what it's like to wake up a vampire. It's a scary thing, but we're here for you."

"Just in case," Abigail said, as I turned off the last of the lights and settled in for a quick snooze, "Can I have a gun?"

"No!" Greg and I shouted in unison.

Chapter 6

I awoke with a tickling sensation under my nose and resisted the urge to sneeze. I shook my head, trying to figure out what it was. I pried one eye open, saw a veil of yellow across my vision and became even more confused. I took a deep breath and stretched, or tried to. I realized that my face was covered in hair, and there was something lying on my arm. A half-second later, I realized that the some*thing* was a some*one*, and exactly who it was.

"Oh, crap," I whispered, as I sat bolt upright, dumping Abigail off my arm, off the mattress and onto the floor. I looked around the room and saw Sabrina sitting in the armchair drinking a soda and staring at me with eyes full of hurt.

"This isn't what you're thinking," I blurted, trying to disentangle myself from the blankets and the blonde. I eventually stumbled to my feet.

"And what am I thinking, James? Are you suddenly psychic on top of your other *gifts*? And what business is it of mine if you fall into bed with the first cold body that comes along? After all, I have no claim on you. So what do I care?" Her tone of voice said she was unconcerned and didn't have a care in the world, but her pounding heartbeat said she was a hair's breadth away from shooting me in the face.

Greg had woken up at the noise, and in a fuzzy sleep-haze, was looking between Sabrina, me and the blonde lump on the floor that was Abigail. "What's going on?"

"Shut up," Sabrina and I said in unison.

"Oh," Abigail said from the floor. "Sorry. I got scared in the middle of the day and crawled in bed with you. I hope that's okay." She stretched, doing that languid movement that only really attractive women can do first thing in the morning, and I just sighed.

I stalked over to Sabrina in my T-shirt and boxers, hair haystacked all over the place like a porcupine on a bender, and pulled her to her feet. I looked the furious detective square in the face and said, "I don't know exactly what's going on between us, and I don't think you do, either. But I know this—you matter to me. You matter more to me than any person has since I've been dead, and I will not do anything to screw that up. I don't have a whole lot going for me. I'm skinny with bad hair and a big nose. I've been dead since you were in middle school, and I can't ever go on long walks in the sunlight with anyone again. I can't write poetry or play music, and I have dietary restrictions that make veganism look easy. But I am one thing above all else—I am loyal. I don't have many friends, or whatever we are, in my life, and I will fight past death to keep the ones that I have. So if you're pissed at me, fine. Be pissed. I earn that a couple dozen times a day. But if you think for one second that I would ever do anything to hurt you, then you better think again, Detective."

Then I kissed her. I grabbed her face in both my hands and I kissed her like my life depended on it. She stiffened at first, but after a second, she put an arm around me and kissed me back, and it was the greatest feeling I'd had in all the years I'd been dead. After a long minute, she pulled back, and I saw one tear rolling down her right cheek. I reached up with my index finger and wiped it away.

"No more of that." I pulled her to me for a tight hug. I could have sworn in that moment that I felt some of her warmth leach into me and push away the cold for just a second.

"Well, then," Sabrina said. "I suppose we'll talk more later. But we've got a few things to do first. One, put some clothes on. We've got a crime scene to check out."

"What's two?" Greg asked, heading toward his room and a shower.

"Two is this." Sabrina walked over to Abigail and leaned in very close. She whispered too low for even Greg and me to eavesdrop, but I saw Abigail turn a couple of shades paler as she listened. After a long moment, the dark-haired detective leaned back and looked deep into the blonde vampire's eyes. Abigail looked back, swallowed deeply and nodded. Just to make things even more surreal, Abigail then threw her arms around Sabrina's neck and hugged her fiercely before getting to her feet and running to the bathroom.

"What was all that?" I asked, as Sabrina came back to my side.

"The facts of life. I don't think she's ever had very many girlfriends, so I explained the way the world works."

"Is that all?"

"That and I told her if I ever found her playing all snuggly with you again that I'd stake her and leave her in the middle of Panthers Stadium to watch the sunrise." She gave me a little kiss on the cheek, and said, "Now, go get cleaned up. We've got work to do."

A quick shower later, we were back at the big hole on campus. According to Sabrina, she'd gotten a ton of pressure from the upper floors of the Charlotte-Mecklenburg Police Department to release the crime scene so that the city's latest construction jewel could move forward, but she had managed to buy us one more night to poke around. That meant anything we wanted to collect had to be gathered right now because any trace evidence would be gone come sunrise.

"I don't get it," Abigail said, as we got out of Sabrina's unmarked car at the crime scene. "Weren't the CSI guys or whatever here already?"

"They were," I answered. "But we have a few resources they're lacking."

"Like what?"

"Like a super-sniffer that knows what it's looking for," Greg replied, jumping down into the foundation where the police found Abigail's body less than twenty-four hours before.

I followed him down the vampire way and grinned a little at Abigail and Sabrina carefully picking their way through the red dirt and rocks.

"You could jump, you know. I'll catch you," I yelled up at them.

Sabrina looked up and shot me the finger, while Abigail responded, "You'd enjoy it too much."

A few minutes later, we congregated in the bottom of the construction site. Greg took Abigail off to one side to give her a lesson on her newly enhanced senses, and to get her away from the place where we had found her corpse, while I started sniffing around the actual crime scene. It took a few moments to separate the scents of diesel fuel, mud and hydraulic fluid, but after I zeroed in on the location where she had been drained, I found the trail almost immediately. The spot was a couple of yards away from where the body had been, and there was just one tiny drop of blood in the dirt to mark it. I stood still, breathing deeply.

A second later, the scent of *her* flooded my nostrils and set me on fire like cheap moonshine, burning away everything else. I smelled lilacs, swamp water and a hint of rot under the hot scent of fresh blood and vamp saliva. The hair on the back of my neck stood as I locked onto the trail and followed it up the steepest part of the excavation. When I got to the top of the pit, I turned and looked back, taking advantage of the perfect image below. The slab of concrete where we had found Abigail was beautifully lit by the full moon, just like it would have been last night. I closed my eyes and imagined the girl lying there, posed as if she looked up at where I now stood.

"Sacrifice," I murmured.

Greg's head popped up. "What?" he whispered back to me across a hundred yards of construction debris.

"She was an offering to something. I don't know what, but she wasn't just turned and left here. She was meant as an offering."

"Interesting theory, little vampire. However did you get so smart?" purred a low voice from directly behind me.

I jumped a little and pinwheeled my arms to keep from going head over heels back into the pit. I whirled around once I'd caught my balance to find a short woman in leather pants and a sheer black top standing behind me smirking. Her dark hair was pulled back in a severe ponytail, and a spiked leather collar and thigh-high boots completed the dominatrix look perfectly. I didn't need super-senses to know she wasn't wearing anything under that top, and the patent leather pants were so tight she must have had more super-powers than I'd known about to get into them. That image, coupled with a scent somewhere between cinnamon, sex and cotton candy swirled together to make me more cautious than usual whenever the oldest hottie in the known universe was around.

"What are you doing here, Lilith?" I growled.

"The same thing you are. Trying to find out why there's suddenly another vampire running around in my city," she said calmly.

"Your city? Aren't you still the new demoness on the block?" I asked.

"I live here now, so this interloper concerns me. I wouldn't want anything *else* interfering with my business."

I was pretty sure the "else" she was referring to was the mess I made of her strip club a little while back. There was a dustup with a gargoyle that ended with a lot of broken furniture. And a few broken people.

"Which business is that, Lilith? The strip club or the illegal fight ring? Or have you gotten involved in something even more lucrative, like snuff films?" I hid my dislike for Lilith about as well as she hid her disdain for me. We weren't exactly the mutual admiration society.

"So defensive, little vampire. And after I helped you with your little ambulance problem, too." She stepped closer, and even my dead heart sped up a little. Lilith was sexy before a word even existed for it, and she made me seriously uncomfortable. After all, anyone who could answer 'boxers or briefs' about the original Adam had some serious magic.

"Yeah . . . um, thanks for that. Now what do you know about this new vamp?" I circled around Lilith to put her back to the big hole in the ground. I figured it best to limit my obvious threats to one at a time. I could usually avoid falling in big holes, or I could avoid getting into a fight with immortal hotties, but I wasn't sure about my ability to do both at the same time.

"I *know* even less than you do, Mr. Black, and I promise you those are words I never thought I would hear myself say." Lilith took a step over the edge and floated down into the pit to stand beside the concrete altar where Abigail had been sacrificed.

"Nice trick," I said, jumping down to land beside her in a puff of gray concrete dust. The others joined us, Sabrina leading the way. Lilith acknowledged her arrival with a nod, the way two gunfighters nod at each other in old western movies. I knew they'd rather throw down than talk, but they put that aside for the moment.

"Okay," I went on. "Let's move on from what you *know*. I'll settle for what you sense. Or even guess."

Lilith walked up to Abigail and sniffed around her for a few seconds, looking carefully at the scars on her throat. She even leaned in and licked the side of the girl's neck, which I was sure sent Greg to a happy place, but it just creeped me out a little.

"I sense nothing out of the ordinary," she said. "I know nothing about the vampire who made this new one at all, except that she made both of you."

I didn't give her the satisfaction of asking her how she knew. I just nodded for her to go on.

"In the ancient days when monsters were entering the territory of another, stronger beast they would leave a peace offering where it would be easy to find. A sacrifice, if you will, to request safe passage. Perhaps that is what you were, my dear."

"I was an offering?" Abigail sputtered, outraged.

"Looks like it, kiddo. Now we need to find out to who," I said.

"To whom, little vampire, to whom. And while I would normally suggest that I would be the logical choice, this is not the place to make a sacrifice to my authority. And I have little use for the Sanguine. So I suspect that you are looking for someone else as the intended recipient of your lovely sister."

"Don't you mean *we* are looking for someone else, Lilith?" I asked.

"Oh no, little vampire. There is no *we*, royal or otherwise, in this equation. Now that I am fairly certain that this involved me not at all, I shall remove myself from the fray. If you require my assistance at any point, you know where to find me. You'll find my prices *very* reasonable." Lilith stroked a hand down my chest, grinned at Sabrina, then floated back up to the lip of the construction site and walked away. A few seconds later, I heard a motorcycle rev up and drive off.

I wondered for a second why I hadn't heard her drive up until Greg said, "She was waiting for us, bro."

"Huh?" I grunted, studiously not looking at where Lilith had just gone and even more studiously trying not to think about how *warm* her hand had been on my chest. That woman made me more uncomfortable than most, and that's saying something.

"I didn't hear her drive up, and I was paying attention. She was waiting for us. I'd guess she came out here during the day, got whatever information she was going to get, and waited for us to show up to tell us it wasn't her deal."

Abigail actually raised her hand. "Um . . . for the new kid, who was that?"

Greg put on his best professor tone for his answer, and I could have sworn he actually got a little taller while pontificating. "That was Lilith. Rumored to be the first wife of Adam. Yeah, that Adam. She was banished for wanting to be on top, and Eve came along afterward. Theoretically, she was made from the same dirt Adam was, thus had the silly idea that men and women should be equals. That led to the whole thing about creating Eve from a rib so women would forever be subservient to men, and we see how well *that's* worked out for everyone. So Lilith is an immortal, and there are rumors about her being a succubus, a demoness, and a host of other unpleasant things. And she's kinda the Kingpin of Charlotte, if you've read enough *Daredevil* comics to get the reference."

"I saw that really crappy movie with Ben Affleck, if that's what you mean," Abby said. "But I get it. What does she do?"

"Owns a strip club, launders money, runs hookers, kidnaps innocent people and forces them to fight to the death in underground cage matches, disposes of stolen ambulances, whatever pays the bills," Sabrina added, distaste dripping off her tongue.

"And you guys don't like her?" Abigail asked.

"*Despise* is a better word," Sabrina answered.

"Yeah, despise works," Greg said quickly.

"Not me, I'm just afraid of her," I said. Abigail looked at me until I clarified. "I'm afraid of anyone and anything I can't kill. And Lilith tops the list in Charlotte, so I'm scared shitless by her. I try not to let it get in the way of occasionally having to work with her, though."

"She tried to have us all killed a few months ago for interfering with one of her illegal operations. That's not something I've managed to forgive yet," Sabrina said.

"And the lovely Detective Law has been looking for an excuse to try out Lilith's famed immortality ever since," I added.

"I don't get it," Abigail went on. "Why did she come out here just to tell us that she wasn't responsible for . . . turning me?"

Greg ticked off the points on his fingers as he spoke. "Lilith is above all else a businesswoman. She loves few things in this world, but money is high on the list. And if we go in and start wrecking her club again, that costs her money. She knows we'll probably believe her if she tells us the truth, so that saves her money and saves us time. It's a win-win. And I did just give her ten grand for a five grand disposal job, so she probably looks at this little info-dump as keeping her books square."

I looked at my conniving little partner with respect.

"Well, if Abby wasn't a sacrifice to Lilith, then to whom?" Sabrina asked.

"That's why we're detectives, I guess. Our job to find out. I lost the scent of the vamp when she got into a car at the top of the pit, but I caught something else odd up there. Greg, come with me. You two keep checking for physical evidence. Abby, this will be a good test for your vamp-vision."

"What am I supposed to do?" Sabrina asked.

"I dunno, Detective. Teach her to detect?" With that, I turned around and bounded up the side of the pit in a couple of jumps, my pudgy partner right on my heels.

Chapter 7

"What are we looking for?" Greg asked at the top of the hole.

"Take a good whiff." I gestured to the woods near the site.

Greg walked over to the trees separating the stadium site from the apartments just off campus and took a deep breath. He doubled over, coughing with the intensity of the smell. Sometimes I forgot that Greg's sense of smell was much stronger than mine. This wasn't one of those times. I'd just really wanted to hit him over the head with my discovery.

"Holy crap!" he gasped when he was able to speak again.

"Yeah. Now what is it?"

"What are *they*, to be precise. There are two distinct scents here, both from last night."

"Okay," I said, trying to keep my patience. "What. Are. They?"

"Well, there's the scent of vamp, a bunch of them, and at least one of them is really old."

"How can you tell?" I sniffed the air experimentally, but couldn't find anything that told me if any vamp was old or young.

"You know how blood smells after it's been sitting on the counter for a few days?"

"Boy, do I, and I've been meaning to talk to you about taking out the trash a little quicker."

Greg cut me off with a wave of his hand. "Later. Well, this is the same thing. Abby smells like fresh blood because she's a new vamp. You and I don't. Lilith smells way older, even though she's not a vamp. I think it's got something to do with the tissue, or how we maintain our life force or something."

"Anyway," I threw in quickly before Greg got too far down the rabbit hole with his theorizing. "So several vamps, at least one old one. What's the other thing? That thing that smells like a cross between cheap cigars and wet dog?"

"I have no idea, man. I've never smelled anything like it." He edged further into the woods and sniffed deeply.

"Like what?" Sabrina asked from behind me.

I jumped about seven feet in the air and whirled around on her. "I swear I'm going to put a bell on your neck."

"Try it. We'll see where that bell ends up. Never smelled anything like what?"

"We don't know," Greg said from the woods.

"Well, what about all these vampires I smell?" Abigail asked, causing me to jump again.

"Dammit, would you two cut that out!" After I calmed down, I said, "I don't know what we're going to do about the vamps, but we can't do it tonight."

"Why not?" Sabrina asked.

"Not enough guns and too many potential appetizers in the party." I gave her my best don't-argue-with-me look. She took the hint, which kind of amazed me.

"Fine," she said. "Then you should at least reconnoiter their location so we can get back there when we're better prepared. It's supposed to rain tomorrow, and that'll wash away any scents they've left behind."

"How do you know that?" I asked. "It's not like you have a super-sniffer of your own." Of course, with her being mojo-proof and able to sneak up on a vampire, I shouldn't be surprised if she did turn out to have some kind of super-powers.

"There are these miraculous creatures, Jimmy, called dogs. We in the police department sometimes work with these creatures to apprehend bad people called criminals. So we spend a lot of time in a great place of learning called the Academy, so we can study these creatures and how best to use them." She spoke very slowly, as if to a particularly stupid child, which I supposed was somewhat fair.

Abigail covered her mouth with one hand, but Greg didn't even bother to hide his belly laughs. I shot them both the finger and walked off into the woods to follow the vamps' scent.

I motioned for Greg to stay behind because he's about as stealthy as an epileptic rhinoceros. I also hoped that he'd be able to keep Abigail back there as well. If I was going to go stalking a nest of vampires, I didn't need a rookie looking over my shoulder. I lost the scent a couple of times, but had watched enough bad survival movies to track in concentric circles until I picked it up again.

The UNCC campus was built on the outskirts of Charlotte, and over the years the city has grown out to meet the college, creating a whole suburb in the area. Developers hadn't gotten to everything, though, so there were big chunks of wooded land surrounding the campus. I was traipsing through one of those in a general northwesterly direction, my less stealthy tendencies masked by the carpet of pine needles on the ground. The scent of honeysuckle was heavy as the undergrowth thickened, slowing my progress and reminding me that spring was definitely in the air.

After sneaking through the woods for about half an hour, I came to a tall fence around a Victorian-style house complete with porch pillars. It looked like a cross between *The Amityville Horror* and the frat house from *Animal House*, with peeling paint, loose shutters and a parking lot full of stereotypical college beaters in the front. The scent trails ran up to and over the fence line, so the vampires must have gone into the house. I had to admit, if I wanted to prey on college kids, this would be about the perfect place to live. Isolated, secure, and by the looks of the overgrown driveway, largely forgotten. Between the scents and the footprints, I figured there had to be at least a dozen vamps in there. I decided I didn't want to take on that many vampires by myself, so I settled for watching the house instead.

I eyeballed the place for about fifteen minutes and saw no hint of movement inside. Nothing flickering past a window, no glow of a TV, no sounds of rampant teenage fornication, nothing. What I did see was a lot of windows with heavy curtains to block light, bars to keep out unwanted visitors, and the telltale extra wire running along the top of the fence that told me it could be electrified with the flip of a switch. Pretty heavy security for a frat house.

I marked the house's location on my phone's GPS, took a couple of grainy pictures and crept back to the others.

"Well?" Sabrina asked. They'd finished up their crime scene investigation and were waiting on me at the car.

"Deep subject," I replied. "Let's go get something to eat, and I'll tell you all about it."

"You don't eat," she shot back.

"Yeah, I do, and the cupboard's pretty bare. So let's go visit Bobby and do a little grocery shopping. I'll fill you in on the way to the hospital."

"Bobby's out sick today. Stress from last night's *attack* and all. What's your Plan B for dinner? Because I am *not* interested in donating."

"I wasn't going to ask. Take Greg home. Abby and I will catch a ride." I got out of the car.

"Oh, no," Greg said. "She comes with me. I am not going to have you teaching her how to hunt. Not this early. So we need a better plan."

"We don't have a choice. She hunts, or you do. The fridge is *empty*. Miss Impetuous here drank us dry after her little trip outside this morning. Now you can keep your morality, or you can keep Abby all lily-white, but you can't do both. Abby, how do you feel about takeout?"

Greg wasn't ready to give up yet. "I am not okay with this. We don't have to be monsters, Abby. We can find another way. There's a guy in the ER down at Mercy South that I've used once or twice. We can call him."

I took a deep breath, counted to ten, then counted to ten again in Spanish. Then I spoke. "Greg, that dude knows about *you*. And he's only ever been able to come up with three or four pints at a time. It's going to take double that to keep all three of us moving and sane until we can hook up with Bobby tomorrow."

"I'll call him. I'll see what he can come up with. Maybe he can do better," Greg said.

I took another breath. "Call him. Then go see him. Get as much blood as he can give you. We'll meet you back at the house in an hour."

"You don't have to do this, Abby." Greg wasn't quite pleading with the girl, but he was close.

"Well . . ." The girl looked down at her feet for a second, then back up at me with a grin. "We are the top of the food chain, right? I guess I should learn to act like it."

"Exactly." I looked at Greg and Sabrina, who looked respectively disappointed and disturbed.

"Fine, but while you're off raiding the campus buffet, I'm going to grab a computer and look up property records on that house you found. We do have a murder to solve, remember?" Sabrina said.

"I think I'll remember," Abby replied. "After all, it's *my* murder."

I moved closer to Sabrina, and said quietly, "I'll see you at our place. Okay?"

She gave me a long, steady look, but finally nodded.

"Don't worry. He knows how much this means to you. He'll take care of her," I heard Sabrina say to my partner as they walked to his car. She looked over her shoulder at me, and I nodded to let her know I'd gotten the message.

I looked at Abigail, the very image of youth and innocence, and actually felt a twinge of guilt before I put my conscience back into its lead-lined box and said, "All right, kiddo. You ready to learn how to be a vampire? The best thing about a college campus is the variety. It's like a buffet for vampires, if you look at it in the right way. You've got young, old, boy, girl, all the ethnicities and dietary preferences. And all of those things affect the taste of the blood," I explained in a whisper as we walked. We weren't even walking together, more like twenty feet apart but, thanks to our vamp senses, Abigail had no trouble hearing me. "Personally, I prefer my snacks to be a little on the heavy side, because they seem to have a shorter recovery time, and over legal drinking age because I don't like biting children. I also shoot for the healthy-looking meals, but nothing that smells like a vegan. I didn't care much for carrot juice when I was alive, so it's not really on my menu nowadays. Now I'll feed first, and you can watch how it's done. Then, it'll be your turn."

"O-okay," Abigail whispered.

"I usually use a little mojo first. It takes away the normal fight or flight instinct. It's really hard to enjoy a meal when your entrée is fighting you every step of the way. So first we lock eyes with our target and push our will out at them. You overwhelm their mind with yours, and then you're in the driver's seat."

I felt the tension coming off of her even from a few yards away. I thought back to my early days as a vampire. It sure would've been nice to have had somebody with a little experience to show me the ropes, instead of having to figure it all out with Greg, who only had his Anne Rice library and a string of bad movies to draw from. There had been a lot of mistakes along the way, ranging from hilarious to downright terrifying, and I was determined to make things a little easier on Abby.

I realized with a start that I was beginning to feel protective of her, like she really was my little sister, even though I was technically old enough to be her father. I shuddered and pushed *that* thought way, way down in the dark recesses of my mind.

I spotted my dinner coming out of the theatre building, one of my favorite spots on any college campus. The tech students were generally there until all hours. They usually started off pretty pale and had a predilection for turtlenecks that made my life a lot simpler. I picked a girl of about twenty with long, dark hair and blue eyes. She was tapping away on her iPhone when I stepped out of the shadows. She whipped up her little can of pepper spray lightning-quick, but locked eyes with me before she started spraying. That was her last mistake of the night.

"Put that away." I put the force of my will behind my words. Her eyes glazed over, and the pepper spray went back into her purse.

"Come with me," I continued, and she followed me into the woods between the theatre building and the visitors parking deck.

I led her off the path a couple of yards and had her sit with her back to a tree. She wasn't beautiful by any stretch, but had a striking air about her. I sat next to her and chatted idly about the weather for a moment before I leaned into her and bit deeply into her carotid artery. Hot blood splashed the back of my throat, and my eyes rolled back in my head. The coppery taste was so much better from the source than from a bag, but it was the sensation of life pouring down my throat that I'd never been able to explain.

It was like everything about the person was flowing into me, like I was drinking their dreams, their hopes, their very soul. It was a better rush than anything I ever felt while alive. Every time I took a victim, I understood a little better why some vampires went nuts and did it all the time. But I also understood why Greg tried so hard to stay off the vein, because it was harder to go back to the bag after every fresh meal.

I knelt there, letting the visceral pleasure of drinking from the source wash over me for a couple of seconds before I forced myself back to reality. I drank for several minutes, taking about three pints from the girl before I felt like I could sustain myself for a night or two. When finished, I took a moment to lick the last drops from her neck and watch as the vamp saliva healed the puncture wounds almost immediately.

I looked in her eyes, and she stared back at me glassily. I'd drained her just to the brink of unconsciousness and felt a twinge of guilt about that. I'd fed more than usual, but the past couple of nights had taken a lot out of me. I'd had more close calls in twenty-four hours than I usually had in a week, leaving me with a distinct sense that my life wasn't going to get any less complicated in the near future. "When you wake up, you won't remember me. You'll remember drinking too much and lying down here to rest for just a minute. Now sleep." She obediently rolled onto her side and began to breathe evenly among the pine needles.

"Will she be okay out here all night?" Abigail asked.

"I checked the weather. It's supposed to be unseasonably warm tonight. Lows in the sixties, so yeah, she'll be fine. No one will notice her out here, and she'll wake up in the morning a little dizzy and maybe a touch embarrassed, but none the worse for wear. Now, let's find you some dinner."

We wandered the campus for almost another hour before Abigail found somebody she wanted to bite. It was like taking a picky eater to an all-you-can-eat Chinese buffet and having them order chicken fingers. I mean, really, what was the point?

She finally found a guy she liked in a parking deck over by the student center and mojo'd him into the back seat of his Suburban, although I wasn't sure if she needed any mojo for that. She was pretty cute, after all. She even made out with the guy for a few minutes before he made some comment about cold hands, and then she bit him. I watched her back stiffen when she got her first intentional taste of fresh blood, and it was almost like her hair stood on end. She drank from the guy for a minute or two, before I reached in and tapped her on the shoulder.

No response. I grabbed her shoulder and shook her. Still nothing. I leaned into the back seat with a growl and grabbed a fistful of her blonde hair. I yanked, and she finally came free, glaring at me with fangs bared.

"Hungry!" she demanded, voice low and threatening.

"Stupid," I replied, my own voice very calm and very flat. Either my word or my tone registered with her, and reason came back into her feral eyes.

"Is it always like that?" she asked quietly.

"Yeah, every time. It gets easier to know when to say when, though. And sometimes you'll find someone who ate something that disagrees with you, but most of the time it's pretty awesome."

"So why do you drink out of the bag? That stuff tastes like crap. I can't imagine drinking that plastic-tasting junk after what I just had."

"We drink out of the bag because we can't hunt every night, or even every couple of nights, and stay hidden. And staying hidden is pretty important when you're as allergic to sunlight as we are." I didn't go into all the moral implications with her. It didn't feel like the right time.

"And you're afraid you'll like it too much and turn into the monster you think you are?"

I hated perceptive women, and now fate had dropped another one into my life. "Something like that. Now clean up and juice him into forgetfulness. We've gotta get home." I talked her through the process again, and she mojo'd the guy to sleep.

She wiped the blood off her chin, and then looked around, confused. "How exactly are we going to do that? You sent Sabrina and Greg off with the car."

"You're in a car, aren't you?"

"Yeah, but he's out like a light."

"Then he won't mind if we borrow it, will he?" I reached into the guy's pocket, grabbed his keys and got behind the wheel.

"What about when he wakes up in a cemetery?" Boy, she was just full of questions.

"I think we might be better off parking at the CVS across the street and walking a couple of blocks home, don't you?" I answered her question with a question, like all my best and most irritating teachers always did to me.

"Probably. I guess you've kinda got this down, huh?"

"I haven't stayed undead this long by coasting on my looks, kiddo. Stick with me and you might learn a thing or two." I grinned at her as I turned the monstrous SUV around and headed home.

Chapter 8

It was almost dawn by the time we ditched the car a couple blocks from the cemetery, got home and caught everyone up on the vamp nest I'd found. There was an email waiting from Mike, demanding that we keep him in the loop no matter his upcoming surgery. So I emailed him a summary of the night's discoveries and asked him to meet us at our place after sundown, figuring if there were a lot of vampires around, a priest and a cop were about the only flavor of humans we were willing to take in with us. Sabrina headed home for a couple hours' sleep, and the rest of us trundled off to our respective rooms, with the sofa for Abby.

I felt the sun setting as I awoke. The odor of wet dog and cheap cigar filled my room and I lay perfectly still, my senses painting a picture of the room around me. There was only one of them, so I wasn't too worried. It wasn't daylight anymore, so my guest was either a really bad vampire hunter, or he didn't want to kill me. I felt a pressure on my mattress, then smelled gun oil. I felt the barrel press against my temple and heard my intruder take a breath before he spoke.

I didn't bother opening my eyes, just took a deep breath and said, "You stink. It was bad enough when it was scattered all over a murder scene, but it's really over the top in my bedroom."

I finally opened my eyes to see a large hairy man who smelled of cheap cigars holding a pistol to my temple and leaning far too close to my face for comfort.

"Give me one good reason not to splatter your brains all over the comforter, you bloodsucking parasite," he growled, and I got a much better look at his slightly pointed canines than I needed.

"Because I'm a bloodsucking contributing member of society? I mean, really, I pay taxes and everything."

He growled again, and I heard the cocking of the pistol.

"Okay," I tried again. "How about because I have a Glock 17 pointed at your testicles and can pull the trigger at least once before you can get a round through my head?"

"Won't kill me, bloodsucker. Unless you're packing silver rounds, which I doubt." He leaned back a little, though, and looked down to see that I did in fact have a pistol aimed straight at his most prized possessions.

"I don't think I care, pal. You ever had to regrow your balls? I bet it hurts like the devil. And it's really about the suffering when you're shooting somebody's nuts off, anyway. So why don't you get off me, go wait in the den and I'll come join you for a beer after I take a leak?"

"You're awfully calm for somebody with a gun in his face." He hadn't moved yet, but I was pretty sure he was about to, which was good, because he was heavy and making me have to pee. And I was really starting to dislike the smell of wet fur.

"That's because," came Greg's voice from the doorway, "he knows I've got you covered, and my shotgun *is* loaded with silver slugs. Now, get up, and let's go to the den." The guy got off me, holstered his pistol and left my bedroom under my partner's watchful eye. I headed to the bathroom thinking about the new security system we were totally going to have to install.

I took care of nature's rather urgent call and joined Greg and our unexpected guest in the den. They were standing over the couch, looking down at Abigail's sleeping form. She had her hands folded across her chest in a funereal pose, and a placid expression on her face. "All she's missing is a lily in her hands," I said, as I grabbed the back of the couch.

"Wake up, Sleeping Beauty!" I tipped the couch far enough to dump the kid onto the floor. Her pink panty-clad rump with "Tuesday" written on it in purple letters pointed up at the sky for a few seconds before she whirled the blankets around herself and shot into the bathroom at top vamp speed. Laughing, I sat down on the sofa and tossed a beer at our guest.

He raised his monobrow briefly before twisting off the top and plopping down in the armchair. "Thanks," he grumbled. He was obviously a little put out at my lack of fear, but I wasn't giving him any answers until he gave me a few first.

Greg took up his post in the game chair and glared at the intruder drinking our best domestic swill. "Okay, now would you like to explain who you are and what you're doing here?"

"I'd rather not, but that's probably not an option at this point, is it?" tall, dark and hirsute answered.

"Probably not, furball," I replied before Greg could get a word in.

That eyebrow shot up again, and he tipped his beer at me. "So you know."

"I do, but I don't think Greg does."

"How?"

"You're not the only one with a nose that works."

"Know what?" my behind-the-times partner asked.

"See?" I said.

"I do," the werewolf in my den answered. "My name is Kyle King. I'm a private investigator working on a series of odd murders all over the Southeastern U.S. I followed the trail of bodies to Charlotte and picked it up last night at the university. That trail led me to you two, and here I am."

"Wow," I pronounced grandly. "That is a true marvel of understatement, Mr. King. Shall I point out just a few of the things that you may have neglected to mention? There was the fact that the trail you followed here didn't exactly lead to us, but rather to the very mobile young lady in our bathroom. There's the fact that murders are investigated by the police, you know, people with actual authority and jurisdiction? Then there's the fact that you didn't follow our trail by any ordinary means, but rather by your prodigious sniffer. And last, but not least, there's the fact that you couldn't come visit us last night because you were too busy scratching fleas and chasing cars under the full moon to focus on anything else. Isn't that right, Mr. King?"

"I don't chase cars. And I don't have fleas, bloodsucker." He stood up from his chair and stalked over to me. I stood up at the same time and got in his face, while Greg sat in his little purple chair ticking off the new ideas on his fingers. So much for him being the smart one.

"Wait a minute." Greg bounced up and interposed his gut between King and me. "You're a *werewolf*?"

"Yeah," King muttered, sitting back down.

"That is so *cool*!" Greg did that annoying thing where he bounced up and down on his heels again, so I took the opportunity to go get another couple of beers. Abigail came out of the bathroom while I was at the fridge, and I waved her back into my bedroom.

"Bite me. I want my pants," she said in the tone of a pretty girl who was used to all the guys gawking when she walked across the room. I felt an odd anger rising in my chest when I saw the interest in Greg's eyes, and I felt a sudden urge to punch King right between his furry eyebrows. It was weird, kinda like she *was* my little sister, or my kid. *Note to self*, I thought. *Get her some more clothes. Like burlap.*

As she was pulling on her pants and giving Greg the closest thing to heart palpitations he'd felt in a decade and a half, King looked her up and down one more time, drawing that strange red mist across my vision once more, and asked, "Are you Abigail Lahey?"

"Yep." She held out her hand. "Pleased to meet you. And you are?"

He stood and shook her hand. "Kyle King. I was informed that you were dead. Apparently, someone was mistaken."

"Not really. I'm pretty dead. Feel how cold my hands are." She laughed as King jerked his hand back. "What's the matter? You were perfectly willing to accept that the boys were vampires, so why not me?"

"I saw you. I mean, you were at the college."

Abigail had done exactly what I'd hoped she would do; she'd rattled King into giving us more information than he intended. I decided that it was time for me to jump in.

"Yeah, about that," I said, head still in the fridge. "Was that before or after she was left as a peace offering to the local vamp warren?" One of these days, I was going to have to figure out the correct name for a group of vamps. Were we a pride? A nest? A clutch? Who even knew those things?

"She was dead when I got there, bloodsucker. I don't kill people." King settled back in the chair.

"No, you don't. You just hump their legs and pee on their tires." I tossed beers to Abigail and Greg and sat back down on the couch next to Abigail. "Are you old enough to drink, Abby?"

"I'm dead. I think it's okay. And yes, I'm twenty-one." She flicked the bottle cap at me. I caught it and tossed it in the general vicinity of the trash can.

"Twenty-one forever. I can think of worse fates," King said.

Greg and I just stared at him with flat looks.

"So, King. Why are you here?" King started to say something, but I cut him off. "Yeah, yeah, I know the whole line about murders and chasing the killers, but why are you *here*? Or if you want to get real specific about it, why are you here instead of hunting down the vamp that killed Abby? Or at least chasing down the coven of vampires at the school?" Still having trouble with the group designation, I just decided to run through all of them until I figured out the best name for a bunch of vampires.

"I saw you at the crime scene and did a little research. Sounds like you lumps are actually pretty good at what you do, no matter how stupid you look."

I let that pass, but Greg got an indignant look on his face. I'd warned him about the spandex for years, but sometimes he just had to hear it from somebody outside the family.

"I can't take this vampire chick on my own. I've tried. And if I can't take out one vamp, there's no way I can take out the dozen or so that are hanging around campus. I checked with a couple of folks around town, and everybody says you're square. So I came here for help."

"You've got a peculiar way of asking, buddy. And who did you talk to, anyway?" I wasn't quite ready to let go of the whole waking-up-with-a-gun-in-my-face thing.

"I jumped to a couple of different conclusions when I saw Miss Lahey lying on your couch. Sorry about the gun. And if I went around giving up my sources I wouldn't have sources for very long, would I?" He actually looked a little contrite, so I figured I'd give him the benefit of the doubt.

"Fine. Sorry about threatening to shoot off your junk." I leaned over, and we clinked beer bottles, sealing the apology according to the guy code.

"You threatened to shoot off his . . . you know?" Abigail suppressed a giggle.

"Yeah, I've had a couple of unusual awakenings this week, so I've taken to sleeping with a pistol. I heard Chief Howls-at-Moon here when he came through the door upstairs, so I was ready for him when he got to my room."

"Why didn't you just stop him in the den?" she asked.

"I wanted to control the situation, and the smaller room worked in my favor. I'm better in close quarters because I'm skinny and can navigate better than he can. Plus, I know where all the crap on the floor is in my room, and there's no telling where Greg left an Xbox controller in the den for me to trip on."

"Good point. I found three buried in the couch, along with an Apple TV remote."

"I've been looking for that." Greg jumped up to grab the slim silver cylinder from her.

"Well, King, you found us, but I'm not feeling too helpful just yet. Why don't you tell me the real reason a PI is chasing a murderer across state lines, and we'll see if we want to help you," I said.

"It's personal," King growled.

"So is breaking into someone's home with a gun. And I've never had werewolf for breakfast, so why don't you cut the crap and tell me a story, Papa Wolf?" I finished my beer and set it on the table, then leaned back with my hands behind my head. I wanted to make it very clear that he wasn't getting any help until he answered a few questions.

Apparently it worked, because he looked me in the eye, then drained his beer in one long swig. He took another deep breath, like he was working himself up to telling me his story, then said, "She murdered my wife."

I wasn't expecting that. I leaned forward. "Who?"

"Her name is Krysta. She's been a vampire for at least a century, and she's a psycho. She turns people for fun, and kills anybody who gets in her way. I got in her way, so she decided to turn my wife to teach me a lesson. But lycanthropy and vampirism don't mix, so . . . my wife didn't rise. She just stayed dead."

For once, I didn't say anything. I just sat there, watching the big man struggle to keep his emotions in check. His shoulders tensed, and I feared for the structural integrity of the beer bottle he was holding. He took a deep breath, held it, took another one, then let it out in an explosive rush and relaxed his grip on the bottle's neck. After a long pause, he continued.

"The same woman who turned you killed my wife. I can smell her on you like cheap perfume. I've chased her for ten years, and this is the closest I've ever been. So I'm going after her, and I'm going to kill her. And if this nest of vampires you found is protecting her, I'm going to kill them too. Any questions?"

Nobody answered for a long moment, then I said, "Okay, King. You want to kill the vamp that turned Abigail. I get that. And I've got a little beef with her myself. But what's the plan? And do you want to just ignore the fact that there's a frat house full of vampires that have been snacking on coeds for the past century? I don't think so. Not in my town."

"You can do whatever you like, fangboy. I'm going to find Krysta, cut her head off and stick it on a fencepost facing east. Then I'm going to light up one of my hand-rolled Cubans and watch the sun rise." King set his beer bottle down on the coffee table and leaned back with a satisfied smile.

"I hate to burst your bubble, Mr. King, but didn't you just say that you can't take this vampire?" Abby's voice shook a little as the big werewolf growled at her, but she held her ground. "You need us, Mr. King. And we might need your help, too. If Jimmy's right, there are a lot of vampires in that house, and they've been killing people for a long time. So we can work together. If you're willing to work *with* us."

I stared at our newest addition, wondering what kind of classes she'd been taking before she got eaten by my vamp-mom.

"So, yeah. What she said. Now, do you have a plan other than 'Hulk Smash'? 'Cause I'd love to hear it." Even though I figured I'd probably hate it.

Chapter 9

I was right, I hated the plan from the second King started with, "We should split up to cover more ground."

"Seriously?" I asked, shocked right out of my fangs. "You're a werewolf, and you've never even seen a horror movie? Do you know what happens when the good guys split up? Nothing good, that's what."

"I hate to agree with my partner, but it is kinda typical of the genre. The good guys split up and no matter who the camera follows, they end up needing exactly the item or skill that's with the other team," Greg said, nodding.

"Yeah, it's one of the cardinal rules of horror flicks. There's a monster hiding right where the cat just jumped out from, the virgin always lives and you never, ever split up. So we stick together," I said with finality.

"Then how do you expect to gather intel on the operations of the vampires at the school while we chase down your sire and separate her head from her body?" King asked.

"We do one, then the other. The college vamps have been there for a long time and, if they're anything like the college kids I knew, they're probably stoned. So they'll still be there, with the munchies, when we get back," I said.

Of course, there was nothing to say that they *were* anything like the college kids I'd known. Abby certainly wasn't, and that thought was enough to give me a moment's pause. Then I thought about just how long it had been since I was a college kid, and how different Mike was from those days. Greg and I weren't. It's like when we were turned we fell into stasis and never changed. Until recently.

I snapped back to the conversation when the door opened. My subconscious must have registered her footsteps or her scent coming down the stairs, because for once I wasn't surprised by Sabrina's entrance.

"Back from where?" the lovely detective said as she came down the stairs. She was wearing a pair of jeans with a scoop-necked blouse and a light jacket to ward off the evening chill. Even in late spring it was still cold late at night. She walked across the living room, gave me a quick kiss on the cheek and sat on the arm of the couch next to me.

"Wasn't expecting you here this early," I greeted her. "You get any sleep?"

"I'll sleep when I'm dead." She tossed an empty energy drink can into my recycle bin.

"Not from what I'm experiencing," Abigail said. "Looks like tonight we chase more dead people, but this time we get to bring a bloodhound."

"I'm not a bloodhound," the surly werewolf groused.

"Detective Sabrina Law, meet Kyle King. He's another private investigator looking into a string of murders all over the South. Abby here seems to be the latest victim." I made the best introductions I could as Sabrina shook hands with King.

"And he's a werewolf," chirped Greg, still bouncing with excitement. Sabrina raised an eyebrow at King, who bared a couple of teeth in response.

"Another PI, huh? And who are you working for, Mr. King? This might be something peculiar to North Carolina, but here the police investigate murders, not private investigators."

"Like your boyfriend here?"

"He's a consultant. They work for me. And you didn't answer the question."

"The vampire I'm chasing killed my wife. I guess you'd say this one's pro bono." King raised a corner of his mouth in a snarl as he leaned back.

"Long canines don't do much for me anymore, Mr. King. Got any other tricks?" She seemed unimpressed. I guess when you'd hung out with vampires, battled demons and had a cousin who was a ballet-dancing faerie, you got to be a little blasé about those things.

"Yeah, but I don't think your little boyfriend here would appreciate me showing them to you."

"Unless you want to reenact *Dracula versus Wolfman* in my living room, that's probably a good choice," I said.

"So," Sabrina said. "If you two are done measuring things no one else is interested in seeing, what's the plan for the evening? Are we going after the chick who killed you and Abby before she makes another little 'peace offering,' or are we rousting a bunch of frat-boy vamps at the college before they take offense at the new predator in town and start a vampire gang fight in my city? Because I'd love it if Charlotte didn't become ground zero in a vampire turf war."

"King wants us to split up and go after both groups of vamps, but Greg and I said no." I pulled a chair in from the kitchen for Sabrina and looked around for a place to sit. If we kept adding supernatural associates to our little Junior Justice League, we were totally going to need a satellite. Or at least a real office.

"Why not?" Sabrina asked.

"Yeah, Jimmy, why not?" King said in a mocking singsong.

"It's one of the first rules of horror movies, babe. Never split up."

"One of the first rules of hanging out with women who carry firearms is never call them *babe*, babe." Sabrina glared at me. "And that's dumb. We should totally split up. That way we can gather intel on the nest and keep you three from getting ambushed while you deal with the threat from out of town. Abby and I will stake out the frat-vamps, while you three go deal with your sire. Or mom, or whatever you call her."

"I'm going with you?" Abigail asked, a little nervously.

"Of course, you are. We can bond. And find a twenty-four-hour Walmart and pick you up a few things. You've been wearing the same outfit for a few days now. I'm sure it's a little ripe."

"Yeah, these jeans are about ready to walk themselves to the washing machine. I'm with Cop-Girl." Abigail walked over to Greg and leaned down, putting an inordinate amount of girl-flesh in his immediate vicinity. "Greggy, can I have some cash? I need to buy a few things."

My poor partner didn't even bat an eye, just walked over to his little hidey-hole under the fridge and got her a pile of cash. She threw her arms around his neck and kissed him on the cheek.

I watched with no small discomfort as a flash of cleavage bent Greg's will all the way around Abby's little finger. I'd never really liked girls who thought all they needed to get what they wanted in life was to flash a little leg and a smile. Now I had one sleeping on my couch. With super-powers, no less.

"Ta!" she yelled over a shoulder and headed up the steps with Sabrina in tow.

I reached out and grabbed Sabrina's wrist. "Be careful," I said in a low voice. I knew Abby could hear me, but I was counting on her being distracted by the wad of cash Greg had just handed her.

"I know. She's a little flighty, but if I can keep up with you two, she should be no trouble."

"That's not what I mean. King says there are at least a dozen vamps in that house, and they've been in town for a long time. They've probably got pretty good security and, if they're any good at all, you won't know about them until it's too late. Make Abby pay attention. Her senses are the only thing you've got going for you."

"Well, not the only thing. I still have my silver stake." She smiled wryly and patted a jacket pocket.

"Yeah, but only the one. Just . . . be careful, okay?" I leaned in even closer and whispered into her hair. "I really don't want to lose you."

She pulled back and gave me a firm look, eye to eye. "You won't." Then she kissed me, quick and fierce, before following Abigail up the stairs.

I stood there for a minute thinking of the old saying, *I hate to see her go, but I love to watch her leave.*

I turned back to amused glances from Greg and King. "You got something to say?" I growled.

"Yeah," Greg said. "Where do you go to kill a vampire from out of town?"

Chapter 10

King had tracked my sire to a new luxury hotel downtown, right next to the basketball arena. It looked like a good hunting ground, lots of out-of-towners who could be nibbled on without being missed. The Bobcats' season was over, but there was a concert at the arena, so the sidewalks were full of people going in and out and generally milling about. Add in the traffic to downtown watering holes, and the whole area was full of people oblivious to the predators in their midst on a mild Tuesday night. We rolled into downtown in King's truck, because he decided he wanted to be all alpha dog and drive. Plus, it appealed to the Clemson grad in me to ride around in a Silverado King Cab with the windows down and Hank Williams III blaring.

"There," King said, pulling his truck into a parking lot and pointing toward a rooftop lounge. "If I know her at all, she's up there."

"And how well do you know her, King?" My spidey-sense was going off like fireworks, but I couldn't tell if it was anything real or just nerves at seeing the vamp who had turned me after all these years.

I wasn't sure whether I wanted to kill her or thank her. I supposed it was like seeing the girl from high school who dumped you right before prom, but you ended up going to prom with your future wife—except I'd never had a date to a prom, not even one that dumped me for giggles. I went to all my proms stag with Greg and Mike, and we stood against the bleachers in the gym, mocking the couples and pretending like we weren't choking on our own envy.

"I've never laid eyes on her. I've just followed the trail of bodies." He got a distant look in his eyes, and I knew he was thinking about his wife. I decided to let sleeping dogs lie for a change.

We walked into the lobby, and I had to shield my eyes against all the highly polished wood and chrome. The place looked like a piece of LA had been dropped into the middle of Charlotte, just a little too shiny for the city I knew. Greg and King made a beeline for the elevators, but I hung back, scoping out the stunning girls behind the front desk, and the boys gazing at them in futility. After standing helplessly in the elevator for a few moments, Greg and King came over to where I waited.

"You need a key to get up to the rooftop lounge," King growled. Werewolf or not, the guy always sounded like he had something stuck in his throat.

"I figured as much. Wait here." I walked over to the front desk and almost had to cover my eyes again from the dazzling smile the woman behind the counter gave me. Her smile dropped a degree or two when she got a good look at me, but she recovered well. One downside to being turned into a vampire when you're just out of college is that people in fancy hotels never take you seriously, no matter how old you really are.

"May I help you?" she asked brightly.

Her nametag told me that her name was Miranda and that she was from St. Louis. That wasn't surprising. No one in Charlotte was actually from there. She had probably relocated when her dad was moved by a bank or something.

"I sure hope so, Miranda. I went out for a few drinks with the guys from the convention, and it looks like I left my key in my room. Can you run me a new one real quick?" I gave her my best harmless Southern-boy accent and waited just a second until she looked back up at me.

"Sure, can I just have your room number, Mr. . . . ?" When our eyes locked, I threw my will into my eyes and wrapped her head in my mojo.

"It doesn't matter. Just make me a key that will get me into the rooftop lounge. Then forget you ever saw me. And have a nice night." I kept my voice low and a smile on my face for the security cameras I was sure were watching.

"Yes, sir." She put a key card into the magnetic coding machine, pushed a couple of buttons, then handed it to me. "Here you go. Don't forget that you have to leave the key in the slot while you press the button for your floor." She smiled again, and I walked toward the elevators.

The boys caught up to me halfway across the lobby. King asked, "What did you do to her?"

"A little mojo," I said with a smirk. I put the key into the slot and pushed the button for the roof. As the elevator doors slid closed, I saw King's eyes narrow a little. "Don't worry," I went on. "It's harmless. And I'm pretty sure it only works on humans."

"At least it's never worked on any non-human we've ever tried it on," Greg added. "And I really don't suggest attempting to mojo a dragon."

"Yeah," I agreed. "They get testy about that stuff."

"And it's no good on zombies, either." My partner seemed determined to drag out all our failures for our newfound furry friend.

"Yeah, and demons and faeries are right out, too. Come to think of it, it doesn't even work on all humans. So you probably don't have anything to worry about," I said, needling the big guy a little.

"I'm not worried. Try that crap with me, and I'll rip out your heart and eat it. Then, I might change shape to finish you off." He gave me a frigid grin, and the elevator doors dinged open just in time.

The doors opened onto a nicely appointed rooftop terrace with several dozen well-dressed business types milling about. There was a pool with a few people swimming languidly in the underwater lights, and they were definitely the type of women who were at home wandering through a black-tie party in a bikini. A black marble-topped bar dominated one corner of the roof, with the building to the bartender's back, and the low outer wall of the patio looked out over the skyline. I admired the lighted buildings, the arena and the fantastical architecture of the children's theatre building just a couple blocks away.

"Where is she?" Greg asked, jostling my elbow. "Do you see her?"

I motioned for him to be quiet as I peered through the crowd, trying to find anyone familiar in the suits and party dresses. A loud group of guys wearing the oxford shirt, khaki pants and flip-flops uniform of off-duty bank employees cheered as they downed their tequila shots over by the ledge. As their group parted and meandered back to the bar, I saw her standing alone, watching me.

Her eyes locked with mine, and my borrowed blood ran cold when I saw a smile crawl across her lips. The smile never touched her eyes, which stayed as blue and cold as iceberg chips. She held out a hand, curling a finger in an unmistakable "come hither" gesture. I had taken a good half-dozen steps before I ran face-first into King's chest, breaking the spell and almost breaking my nose in the process. I shook my head and stepped to the side, but King put a heavy hand on my shoulder.

"I think that might be a bad idea, Junior," the werewolf said, carefully not looking straight at the vampire, who pouted beautifully at me for a second, then smiled and laughed as a man in a very expensive suit brought her a glass filled with what looked like red wine. It looked like wine at first glance, but I smelled the blood all the way across the terrace. When I looked back to where the man had come from, I saw one of the banker-boys leaning heavily on his friends, looking for all the world like a broker who'd had a little too much to drink a little too early.

"Holy crap," I whispered to Greg. "He drained that guy right here in front of everybody. And it's like nobody even noticed."

I was shocked at the new guy's actions, but even more shocked when he looked up at me and smiled a raptor smile. *He'd heard me.* With my whisper, not even a vampire should have heard me from more than a few feet away, but this guy had heard me from fifty feet. I was starting to think we might be a little out of our league.

That thought barely had time to form when the new guy smiled a little wider, showing a gleaming set of razor-sharp fangs, then whispered, "They noticed, little vampire, but they don't mind. After all, they all belong to me. These are all my people." His eyes went from emerald-green to pupil-less black in a blink, and the patio fell completely silent. I turned around slowly and saw that every single eye was focused on me and my traveling buddies, and none of them seemed happy to see us.

"Be cool," I muttered to Greg and King, who had both reached for weapons when the crowd of beautiful people suddenly turned ugly. "They're human."

"Exactly." New Guy was suddenly right in front of me. I'd never even seen him start to move, and judging by the sharp intakes of breath I heard behind me, neither had the other guys. "Now, why don't we all sit down like civilized beings and discuss the impasse at which we find ourselves?"

"And what impasse would that be?" I looked anywhere but at the new vamp. I didn't think he could mojo me, but this guy was the strongest vampire I'd ever seen, so I didn't want to take chances.

"You would like to kill Krysta. I do not want you to. That leaves us at an impasse, wouldn't you say?" New Guy was now sitting at a table with five chairs halfway across the patio, the vamp chick beside him.

"I assume Krysta is your date's name?" I asked, showing off a little super-speed of my own by crossing the patio in the blink of an eye, then taking a seat. "I didn't catch it the last time we saw each other."

The vamp who killed me threw her head back and laughed, a silvery peal of mirth that made me want to rip her lungs out through her nose. "I had other things I was looking for that night, Mr. Black. You'll have to forgive my rudeness. I hope you've been well in the years since our last encounter. I've thought of you . . . often."

"Yeah, and the Easter Bunny craps jelly beans," I snarled. "You killed me and left me on my sofa. Then I woke up and murdered my best friend. All because of you, you evil, bloodsucking bitch."

I hadn't realized how angry I was until Greg put a hand on my shoulder and murmured appropriate calming noises, trying to get me to take my seat again.

"Well done, Mr. Knightwood. After all, we wouldn't want to ruin our lovely evening with unnecessary bloodshed, would we? Now, would anyone like a bite to eat? I find business discussions go so much better on a full stomach," New Guy said smoothly.

"Don't worry," Greg said flatly, suddenly standing right behind me. "Any bloodshed will be absolutely necessary, I promise."

I glanced over at my partner and shivered a little at the look on his face. He was seriously pissed, the likes of which I hadn't seen since high school when the center for the football team used his *X-Men* collection for toilet paper. Suddenly, it looked like the werewolf was going to be the voice of reason at the party, and I had a really bad feeling about that.

"So who are you, how do you know Krysta, and why exactly shouldn't I rip out her heart and eat it?" I asked, leaning back in my chair and waving one of New Guy's human minions over. The guy came over, knelt beside my chair, and rolled up his sleeve as if it were something he did every weekend for kicks. For all I knew, it was. With bravado I didn't feel, I sank my teeth into his wrist and took a big drink, my eyes never leaving Krysta. She smiled a slow smile as she watched me drink, and the hair on the back of my neck went up again. Something about this whole scene wasn't right, and New Guy's next words told me how unfortunately correct I was.

Chapter 11

"My name is Gordon Tiram, and this is my city." New Guy looked over the patio like a feudal lord, which I supposed he had just declared himself. I dropped the arm of the human I was munching on and gaped up at the vampire who had just declared himself my new boss.

"What do you mean, *your* city?" Greg sneered, despite my trying to wave him to silence. Usually running off at the mouth was my shtick, but apparently Greg had appointed himself Dumb Question Guy for the evening. I was starting to see just how annoying my habit could be to an observer.

"I mean, Mr. Knightwood, that I am the Master of Charlotte. All vampiric activity within the metropolitan area falls under my dominion. Krysta here has paid appropriate tribute as a visitor to my territory, and I have given her my protection. That extends to all my subjects, including yourself and Mr. Black. So you will not harm her without my permission, which I will not give. Do I make myself clear?"

Greg started to answer, and I gave up on trying to subtly shush him. Instead, I reached over and poked him in the gut. He let out an *oof* and shot me a nasty look, but I ignored it and started talking fast and thinking faster. If I didn't come up with something pretty quick, we were going to end up in a big fight with two seriously powerful vampires and a couple dozen humans. I wasn't at all sure we could win, and I knew we couldn't win without making a lot of well-dressed corpses.

"So," I began, "is Master of the City a city-only position, or is it like most things around here, a city-county collective? I mean, are you the Master of Charlotte, or are you the Charlotte-Mecklenburg Master of the City? I just wanna know if I have to ask permission just within the city limits, or does your control reach all the suburbs, too? And what about neighboring counties? Are you more like the Master of the Greater Charlotte Viewing Area, because I don't watch much TV, and that might be tough. And did we enlist in your little army, or were we drafted? Because our mail service has been really spotty for the last fifteen years or so, and I think I might have eaten the guy who brought me the certified letter telling me that I work for you." I paused to take a breath and check for reactions, but Tiram just sat there smiling what he probably considered an enigmatic smile. I guessed it was, since I had no idea what it meant, but I wasn't about to admit to that.

"I have heard of your legendary wit, Mr. Black. Now I see that those reports are at best half-true." I put on my best wounded expression, but he went on, "I am the Master of the City, and my territory extends to all vampires living, if you'll pardon the term, within the region. There is another Master in Atlanta, and one in Washington. But you only need concern yourself with me. And you do need to be concerned with me, Mr. Black. Because you are correct, you cannot defeat me. You cannot even hope to survive a moment of my displeasure. So please, sit." He laid a lot of mojo on the last word, and my butt was in the chair before the sound died on his lips.

"Now," he said, "I understand that you feel you have an unresolved disagreement with Krysta, and that Mr. King here has convinced you she is an evil creature, murdering willy-nilly all across the country. But I assure you that she is not, and that Mr. King here is mistaken. And you gentlemen would like nothing better than to forget all about this unpleasant encounter and go back to your ridiculously boring existence."

I felt the weight of his words, and he made a lot of sense. I mean, why would a vampire like Krysta, obviously someone of good breeding, run around killing random people? It just didn't make sense.

I was halfway out of my chair when Greg spoke up. "Are you done playing Boggle with his brain yet? Because it's not working on me or Jo-Jo the Dog-Faced Boy, and I really hate to see Jimmy so confused all the time."

I shook my head to clear it and realized that Tiram had put the mojo on me something fierce. Greg and King were apparently immune to the effects, but I'd bought it—hook, line and sinker. I was totally going to have to take up yoga or some of that other meditation crap Sabrina kept yammering about.

"Interesting. My words had no effect on you at all?" Tiram asked Greg.

"Yeah, they annoyed me. You're a pompous ass, and your girlfriend is a mass murderer. And we're going to kill her. Now how many of your walking hors d'oeuvres are you willing to sacrifice to protect her?" Greg got to his feet, a samurai sword coming from under his long coat to end up in one hand, and a pistol in his other.

"Fascinating. Your mind is so much stronger than your friend's," the Master of the City mused.

"That sets the bar pretty low, pal. Now, can we get back to the question at hand? Namely, are you going to get out of the way so we can off your arm ornament, or is this going to get ugly?" Greg was pretty intense, and King looked as if he were ready for a fight, but I was still having a hard time clearing my head.

Everything got very clear very quickly when Krysta reached out and grabbed a pretty waitress by the throat. "Put away the sword, fat boy. I'll happily kill this human and leave the mess for you to deal with." She held out her other hand, claw-like, and I could see her ripping the girl's throat in my mind.

"Okay, kids, let's everybody calm down." I stepped forward with both hands out, trying to defuse the situation a little. "Nobody wants to hurt anybody here. We just want to talk."

"Actually, Mr. Black, I'm pretty sure we all want to kill each other," Tiram said, his eyes never leaving my partner.

"I know that. I just didn't have anything better to say, and I needed to get a little closer."

"Closer?" he parroted.

"Yeah, so I could do this." I drew my Glock and shot Krysta in the wrist, shattering both bones in her forearm and causing her to drop the waitress.

I grabbed the human girl before she hit the floor and looked her in the eyes. "Run," I said, my voice low and heavy with mojo.

She took off as if the hounds of hell were on her heels, and when I turned around, I thought she might have been right. King had obviously taken my hint to get ready for a fight, because where a tall guy with a monobrow had stood seconds before there was now a seven-foot-tall wolf-man with claws like razorblades and a seriously grumpy look on his face. Or muzzle. Or whatever.

Greg and I got shoulder to shoulder with the wolf-man and squared off to face Tiram, but he hadn't moved.

"Do you three really think you can defeat us?" he asked with a cold smile.

"Not really," I answered honestly. "But I think we can take one of you. And I bet neither one of you selfish chumps wants to be the one we take."

I leveled my pistol at Krysta's face, and Greg lined up his sword on Tiram. King growled low in his throat and bunched his muscles to leap into the fray.

Chapter 12

Just as our wolf-man was about to pounce, I felt a huge impact on the side of my head and was knocked to the patio. I broke my fall with my hands, but my gun went skittering across the concrete and right into the swimming pool. Contrary to popular fiction, a good pistol will fire even when wet, but I hated swimming, and I was wearing my favorite pants. I had just about enough time to realize all of this before I felt a rush of air toward my head.

I rolled over in time to see a spiked heel slam down right where my temple had been half a second before. I looked up to see a beautiful human woman in a very short skirt trying to stomp me to death. I had no time to enjoy the view because she quickly lined up for a second stab with her stiletto heels. I clambered to my feet with all the grace a scrawny vampire could muster, which wasn't much, and caught her fist as it flew toward my eye.

"Sleep," I said as we locked eyes.

Nothing.

I heard Tiram chuckle behind me and chanced a glance over my shoulder. He was leaning against the bar sipping a drink with an umbrella and smirking at me while the babe in the miniskirt landed a solid punch on my cheek.

All right, I thought, *the hard way it is.* I took the shot to the face while still holding her other hand, and as she drew back again, I reached out and slapped her to the ground. I felt bad about it for about half a second, but when she kicked up and caught me in the shin with a heel, all remorse went out the window. I ducked under a punch thrown by another blank-eyed yuppie in party clothes and picked up the first chick by the collar and one leg. I lifted her easily over my head and threw her into the pool, taking out a waiter and a tray of drinks in the process.

I looked around, and Greg and King were similarly occupied with mesmerized bankers and their tarted-up girls *du jour*. One guy jumped on King's fuzzy back and beat him in the head with a Blackberry, while Greg used his sword to deflect glassware hurled at him by two women near the bar. Another mortal rushed at me, head down and feet churning. All I needed was a red cape and some tight pants to complete the picture of me as matador and the idiot as bull. I dodged, picked him up by the scruff of the neck and his belt as he passed and pitched him into the pool on top of the first girl, who was just climbing out.

King flipped the guy off his back, and I looked on in horror as he wrapped a huge furry fist around the human's throat. He leaned in, fangs bared and eyes narrowed, and drew back his other hand for the killing stroke. Just before he ripped the man's face off, Greg ducked under a flying highball glass, which caught King a solid blow to the temple. His yellow eyes rolled back in his head, and the giant wolf-man collapsed on top of the human he'd been about to eviscerate.

"Nice timing!" I yelled to Greg.

"Thanks!" he shouted back. "You got any bright ideas?"

"Yeah, don't kill the humans!"

"Got it!" He shattered two martini glasses with a swipe of his sword.

I heard the squeak of a leather shoe behind me and ducked under a punch that would have knocked me into the middle of next week. I looked up, and up, and up to the largest human I'd ever seen up close. Almost seven feet tall and wider than most doorways, he stood over me like a very grumpy bald mountain with a goatee and more tattoos than the entire lineup of Mötley Crüe. He drew back a fist that looked bigger than Rhode Island and swung for my head. Fortunately, he was almost as slow as I'd hoped, and I ducked his punch easily. Unfortunately, he wasn't as stupid as I'd hoped, and by ducking under his haymaker, I put my face right in front of the uppercut he threw behind it. It felt like a lead-lined Christmas ham hit me right on the point of my jaw, and I staggered back a good five feet before crashing into a glass and metal patio table. Steel bent, glass shattered, and one undernourished vampire got wrapped up in lawn furniture like a grievously wounded pretzel.

The walking mountain came at me again. I tried to stand, but I was too tangled in table parts. He helped me to my feet, if by *helped* one could refer to picking me up, table and all, over his head, and throwing me twenty feet into the swimming pool. I sank to the bottom instantly and would have drowned in seconds except for my one little advantage—I breathed out of habit, not necessity. I felt a little like Br'er Rabbit in the middle of the briar patch down where it was cooler and no one was trying to crush my head. I took a few seconds to disengage from the mangled table and looked around for my pistol while I was down there. No luck. I figured it had been sucked into a drain or something. I made my way as stealthily as possible to a ladder and climbed out of the pool on the side away from the fracas.

Greg seemed to be holding his own, swatting glassware out of the air like Luke Skywalker in Lightsaber 101. Every once in a while, one of the minions would get brave and dart in for a punch, but Greg always smacked them back with the flat of his blade.

I was actually impressed, which might explain how I missed the dripping wet minx in the miniskirt aiming my gun at my best friend's back and pulling the trigger half a dozen times. Before I could react, Greg was down with a tight grouping of new orifices in his back, and the mesmerized woman had turned the gun in my direction. There was most of a patio and a swimming pool separating us, but I covered the entire distance in one very pissed-off leap. I landed in front of her and knocked the gun out of her hand before she got off a round. I punched her in the jaw and had the small satisfaction of seeing her eyes roll back into her head as she collapsed to the deck.

The noise of the gunshots had shaken the mojo out of some of the revelers, and they were looking around in bewilderment. Then one guy looked down at Greg, saw the bullet holes, and screamed like a seventh-grade girl at a Justin Bieber concert. That sparked a stampede for the elevators, and I found myself swimming upstream trying to get to my partner's side.

I finally reached him, but about two seconds too late. Krysta had Greg by the throat, and I was even more impressed by her strength when she casually lifted his bulk into the air with one hand. She was a tall woman, so getting him off the ground wasn't an issue, but Greg had never been what anyone would call svelte. She smiled at me, then looked over at King, who was just now regaining consciousness, albeit in human form.

"Now, dear son of mine," Krysta said, with a smile that made my blood run cold. Or maybe that was just from my dip in the pool. Either way, it was getting chilly. "Whatever shall I do with this sack of meat? He's no good for a plaything. He's much too homely. You were bad enough, but I took pity on you and shared of myself. But this?" She gave Greg's limp body a shake. "This thing isn't even worth keeping around." She finished insulting my manhood and my friend, then casually tossed my partner over the side of the patio to the sidewalk some sixteen stories below.

I ran to the edge and looked over, seeing just the last second of his fall before Greg hit the unforgiving concrete with a wet thwack.

I spun around, my vision completely red, but Krysta and Tiram were nowhere to be seen. I was alone on a patio with a half-dressed, semi-conscious werewolf, five comatose partygoers, and one very nervous security guard, who had just gotten off the elevator. I threw King over my shoulder, nodded to the guard, and got in the elevator.

I pushed the *L* button, while the guard stared at me, dismayed. "Lightweight," I said, nodding to King's incoherent, and very heavy, carcass. Then, the doors slid shut, and I went down to try and scrape my partner off the sidewalk before the cops showed up.

Chapter 13

Through a combination of insults and slaps to the head, I managed to get King ambulatory by the time we reached the lobby. We walked quickly toward the doors, ignoring the frightened looks we got from the humans. A crowd had started to gather around Greg's inert form by the time I got there, and I had to push my way to his side. It was tough going for the first few feet before people noticed I had a giant wolf-guy in tow. Then the crowd parted like grease in a Dawn commercial.

I knelt by Greg's side and pretended to feel for a pulse, while I tried to inconspicuously shake him awake. "Play dead," I whispered.

"I am dead," I heard him mutter back.

A huge weight lifted off my shoulders when I realized that "being thrown off a building" had moved onto the Will-Not-Kill-Vampires list, and I went ahead with my plan. I reached down and grabbed one arm, pulling him carelessly to his feet.

"Hey, watch out!" I heard somebody yell from the crowd. A few other onlookers shouted concern for his well-being, and I turned to address the crowd.

"What? Don't you people read the paper? This is a stunt dummy. A prop. See, I can poke my finger inside the fake bullet holes." That was nasty. "We're shooting outtakes for the new Will Smith movie. The cameras are in the van over there." I pointed at a parking lot across the street. "This isn't even a person. Here, feel the skin. Cold as the grave, right?" I held Greg's arm out to the nearest old lady, and she shrieked appropriately.

I hefted Greg into a fireman's carry across my shoulders and started making my slow way to the car. The crowd parted, disappointed no one had died. Three guys slipped me business cards and told me they were stuntmen or extras. I thought about telling them King was really Vin Diesel, but decided we didn't need autograph seekers.

King backed his truck out of its parking space, and I tossed Greg into the back, then hopped in beside him. King pulled onto the street, his tires barking and laying a stinking strip of rubber behind us. Greg let out a feeble groan when we hit a set of railroad tracks, and I grabbed his head to hold it steady. I wasn't sure if he'd broken his neck, or if we could live through that. I banged on the cab. "Slow down."

King slowed as we headed out of town toward our cemetery. I pulled out my pocketknife and opened up my wrist. I held Greg's head higher and pressed my wrist to his mouth so he could regain a little strength.

He latched onto my arm like a drowning man grabbing for a rubber ducky, and I felt the blood flow from my wrist into his mouth. I let him feed for a minute or two before I felt my strength start to ebb, then I pried him off. He'd gotten a bit of color back and was able to sit up a little.

I looked down into his moon face and blinked back a tear. After all we'd been through, there was no way that bitch was going to get away with throwing my best friend off a building. We'd gone through puberty together, died together, fought demons together, gone to Faerieland together and laughed our way through all the *Twilight* movies together. Even with Abby on the scene, with whatever was happening with Sabrina, with Mike getting sick, with all that, Greg was my constant. He was my best friend, and Krysta was going to answer for this.

He coughed a little and spit out a mouthful of blood.

"You okay?" I asked.

"Now I know how that coyote felt in the cartoons."

"I would hit you for that, but I'm afraid it might kill you."

"Yeah, me too." He closed his eyes and leaned back against the cab of the truck. "I thought I was done for, man. I thought she was going to break my neck right there and twist my head off. I haven't been that scared in a long time." He kept his eyes closed, but even in the flickering streetlights I saw a hint of moisture around the lids.

I put a hand on his shoulder. "Me too, bro. Me too. I'm just glad you've got a little bounce to you. I'd hate to train a new partner after all these years."

"Yeah, I don't think Abby's ready for the pistol range just yet." He chuckled softly, and I felt him pull back from the edge. Greg's always taken things a lot harder than me. Even back in middle school when the jocks shoved us in lockers and flew our underwear up the flagpole, he took it to heart. Me, I just shrugged it off and put sugar in their gas tanks.

We got clear of downtown, and I banged on the cab again to get King to pull over.

He pulled into a fast-food restaurant parking lot and got out of the truck. "Look, bloodsucker, if you dent my cab, there's gonna be hell to pay."

He'd shifted back into human form, but apparently whatever magic made him change didn't make his clothes change, too. The only things that had survived the shift were his boxer briefs, and it looked like he'd stretched some of the elastic to the limit, judging by how he held them up with one hand. I smirked a little, and he reached behind the seat for a suitcase.

"Congratulations, King, you really are a redneck." I complimented the baffled werewolf as he unpacked a Lynyrd Skynyrd T-shirt and a tattered pair of jeans.

"We went to Clemson. He knows a redneck when he sees one," Greg affirmed.

"Good, you're not dead," King said to my battered partner.

"Well, technically . . . ," I started, but gave up. "I need to get something to eat. Wait here with Greg 'til I get back." I started walking, but stopped short when I realized King was following me.

"What are you doing?" I asked.

"I'm hungry, too. I burned a lot of calories shifting, and getting the crap knocked out of me didn't help."

"I'm not exactly going in to order off the dollar menu. I gotta get my nutrients a little closer to the source, if you get my drift. I'll just top off the tank, then you can go get a Happy Meal. Cool?"

King nodded and stayed by the truck while I headed off in search of dinner.

I took a position beside the kitchen door and only had to wait about five minutes before a grumpy Latino kid came out for a smoke break. He tapped a cigarette out of a pack from his shirt pocket, and then almost jumped out of his Reeboks as I spoke up behind him.

"You know that stuff'll stunt your growth."

"*Dios mio*! What the hell are you doing there, man? You trying to scare somebody to death?" The kid picked his lit cigarette up off the ground and looked up at me.

Our eyes locked, and I pushed my will into his head, taking him over in the blink of an eye.

"Stand up." He did. "When this is over, you will remember nothing. You went out for a smoke, it wasn't very good and you decided to quit. You will never smoke again. You'll finish school and go to college. You will study hard and work hard and make a good career for yourself."

I tried to lay as much positive reinforcement on him as possible in the few seconds I had, then I grabbed the kid by the shirt and pulled him close to me. I bent his head to the side and bit deep into his neck. I felt his blood against the back of my throat like a hot crimson fountain. I could almost taste his heartbeat through the rush of blood into my mouth. My body gulped it down, starving to replace what I'd given Greg and what I'd burned up in the fight.

The kid moaned a little as I drank, and I heard my own throat echo him. He sagged, and I put my other arm around his back to support him. I drank deeper than I'd intended and felt his heart falter a touch before I gave myself a mental shake and pulled back from him. I held him gently as he collapsed to the ground, then I leaned him up against the wall in a seated position. I ran a finger over his throat and used the tail of my T-shirt to wipe away the blood seeping from the already closed wounds.

I stood up, a little dizzy from the influx of new blood and the nicotine in the kid's system, and made my wobbly way back to the truck. King was sitting on the tailgate eating a sack full of cheeseburgers, and Greg shot me a disappointed look as I hopped into the bed of the truck.

I said nothing, just reached over and took a long slurp of King's super-sized coke. "Too much cola's bad for you," I said as he snatched his drink away from me.

"Yeah, and drinking my cola's bad for *you*," he snarled, setting the drink well out of my reach. He wiped at the straw where I'd left a little red stain behind and looked at me quizzically.

"You don't want to know," I said.

"Then I already know."

"Then you don't need to ask, so same difference. We can go whenever you're ready."

"And where are we going, exactly?" King asked, finishing off the last of what looked like a dozen cheeseburgers. He walked a few feet to throw the bag in a nearby garbage can.

"Home. We need to plan some more before we go after Krysta and her boyfriend. And Greg needs a place to heal up. And I could use a beer. Or seven."

"Sounds good enough. Let's roll." King hopped back behind the wheel, and Greg grabbed shotgun, then promptly passed out cold. I was stuck in the backseat trying to find a comfortable place to put my feet among several weeks' worth of fast-food wrappers, soda bottles and dirty clothes.

Chapter 14

All thoughts of our housekeeping skills went out the window the second we pulled into the cemetery, because it was pretty obvious we wouldn't be keeping house there anymore. A pillar of black smoke reached for the sky, and flames leapt a good twenty feet into the air as we parked in front of what used to be our caretaker's cottage and underground lair. I jumped out of the truck and ran toward the house, but King grabbed me before I covered any real ground.

"It's gone, man." He held me off the ground, my feet churning like a cartoon character. "There's nothing in there that survived."

I relaxed in his arms with the realization that he was right. Everything we owned was gone. Just as I was starting to mourn the loss of my comic collection, I heard a girl's voice rising above the flames in a tortured scream.

"Abby!" I twisted free of King's grasp and fell to the turf. My hands and feet clawed the ground uselessly for a couple of precious seconds as I tried frantically to get everything working together. Finally, I heaved myself off the grass and bolted into the burning house, yelling for Abby the whole way.

For the second time in one night, it was very handy that I only needed to breathe to make my vocal chords work, because the smoke poured from our underground apartment in thick black tendrils. I leapt down the stairs, crashing through the last few and gashing open my left leg. I fell face-first with my hands in a puddle of blue-tinged flame, then hastily beat out my burning sleeves as I fought to disengage from the splintered wood. I took a quick look around at an apartment fully engulfed in fire. Our furniture had been piled together in the center of the den to make a pyre, and something had obviously been poured around the whole room to make it burn like that.

I pulled myself loose from the steps with a sick sound of tearing flesh, and yelled again for Abby. I doubled over coughing as I drew in smoky air to shout again, but I was able to get low enough to see her feet dangling from the far wall.

I got down on my hands and knees and pulled open the door to the coat closet at the bottom of the stairs. I yanked my leather duster off a hanger and covered my head and shoulders with it so my hair wouldn't catch fire. I blew out as much foul smoke as I could get from my scalded lungs and commando-crawled across the floor to where I had seen Abby's feet. I got to her with vamp-speed, but lost a few precious seconds trying to figure out how she was floating on the wall. By the time I got to my feet, the fire had surrounded us, and I had no clear path back to the stairs.

I turned back to Abby, and it finally sank in why she was still in the apartment with all that fire—she'd been nailed to the wall and couldn't pull herself free. Thick silver stakes pierced her forearms just behind the wrist. They had been driven into the wall, holding her a good foot off the ground. Over her head, left as an unmistakable message for me, were spray-painted the same three Greek letters I had seen on the vamp lair. I decided in a heartbeat that I was going to kill a whole mess of frat boys before this was all over.

Abby moaned and tried to pull away when I shook her shoulder to bring her around. I grabbed one of the stakes and tried to pull it from the wall, but it only wiggled between the bones of her arm, making her scream in agony. I yelled a little too because the hot silver burned my hand, then yelled again when I noticed the back of my duster coated with flames. I ripped off the coat and beat out the fire in a semicircle a few feet around us, then reached back up to grab the stake again.

"Abby," I said, trying to get her attention on my face instead of the pain in her arm. "We're gonna do this on three, okay?"

She nodded weakly, and I started to count.

"One, two," and on "two" I yanked with every ounce of strength in me.

The stake came free, and Abby sagged onto me, howling. She screamed and thrashed around, clawing my arm and shoulder to ribbons where I tried to hold her up and beat back the fire at the same time. I reached over and yanked her other arm free, but this time the spike stayed stuck in her arm as they both came free from the wall. *I'll take what I can get,* I thought as I turned back to where my stairs used to be.

There was nothing there, just a pillar of fire reaching out into the cemetery. Abby was fighting like a crazed animal, so I set her down on her feet. She whirled on me and went for my throat, fangs out, but I was ready. I put one wrist in her mouth, effectively blocking her, then punched her in the side of the head with enough force to crush a human's skull like an egg. Fortunately, vampires don't get concussions, and with her stake wounds and burns, I didn't think she'd even notice when she woke up. I tossed her over my shoulder and turned for the exit.

I stomped out the last shreds of my duster and covered Abby's face with it, then ran and jumped my way across the minefield my apartment had become. I reached the hole under where the stairs used to be and gathered all my strength for a vertical leap.

I heard the crackling sounds of walls collapsing above and jumped for all I was worth for clean air and sky. I hurtled up through the fire like a scrawny, retarded phoenix, landing just long enough for my pants to catch fire, then executed another jump that would have made Jordan retire out of pure jealousy. With solid ground under me, I hotfooted—pun intended—it back to the truck where Greg and King were waiting.

King pulled a small fire extinguisher from his rolling garbage dump of a vehicle and sprayed us down. I dumped Abby into the bed of the truck and hopped in beside her.

"Get us the hell out of here," I yelled, then fell to my knees as King floored the gas pedal.

I had just enough time to make it to the side of the truck before the contents of my stomach and lungs came up. Black bits of ash mixed with blood and beer as King shifted into high gear and booked it out of the cemetery as the emergency vehicles started rolling in. I reached into my pocket for my phone to text Sabrina.

Then, suddenly, the really bad news hit me. Despite the fact that my shoes were still smoldering, I got goose bumps and started to shake uncontrollably.

"What's wrong with you?" King asked through the rear window of the truck.

"Sabrina wasn't in there."

"That's good, right?"

"They've got her," I clarified, staring at the lightening horizon.

"Are you sure?" King asked.

"She wasn't in the apartment. Even through all the smoke I would have smelled her. They took Sabrina," I said. "And it's almost sunrise."

"So you can't go after them, if you even knew who 'them' was," he replied.

"I've got a pretty good idea," I said. I told them about the letters painted on the wall over Abby's head.

"Sounds like pretty solid evidence to me, but we still need to get you three indoors before you catch fire. Again," King said. "So, where to?"

"Only one place we can go when all hope is lost." I pointed him toward a left turn.

"A bar?"

"Church."

Chapter 15

The sky was getting light when we pulled into St. Patrick's. I directed King around to the rectory. I beat on the door for what felt like an hour until a sleepy young priest finally opened it.

"Can I help you?" he mumbled, tugging his shirt around to get the collar just right.

"Where's Mike?" I demanded.

"I'm sorry, sir. Father Mike is on medical leave for a few weeks. He's having surgery today. Is there something I can help you with?"

Oh, crap. I'd forgotten about Mike's surgery in all the fighting, shooting and burning. "No, thanks, Father. It's personal with Mike and me. We go way back."

I saw the humor in his eyes and remembered that I had stopped aging at twenty-three. Mike and I were the same age, but he looked a lot older than his almost-forty, while I still got carded from time to time when buying booze. Good thing for me I usually stole my booze from my dinner dates.

The young priest asked again if I needed any help, and while help was exactly what I needed, or at least near the top of the list, I couldn't ask for help or blood from an unsuspecting clergyman. I thanked him again and limped back to the truck. My back and neck were really starting to sting from the fire, and I just hoped that I could heal burns, or Abby and I weren't going to be nearly so attractive anymore. Greater loss for her than for me, but I'd grown accustomed to my face, as the song went, and I didn't want it to be all melty for the rest of eternity.

"What's wrong?" King asked, as I got back in the truck.

"My contact at the church, who happens to be one of my very best friends in the world, is in the hospital having a tumor the size of a golf ball removed from his esophagus today. I'd completely forgotten about this relatively important event because my house was just burned down. Or up, since it was a basement. My best friend and business partner is riding around in a werewolf's pickup truck trying to heal from being thrown off a roof, and my new protégé is in the bed of said pickup while she tries not to scream in agony from being staked to a wall and set on fire. Add the fact that I just got my ass kicked by the Master of the City, a vampire I never even knew existed, and I'm having a pretty crappy night. Oh, yeah, and the closest thing I've had to a girlfriend since 1993 was just kidnapped by a group of stoner vampires, and I can't do anything about it because the sun is coming up. So as far as 'what's wrong' goes, did I leave anything out?" My voice might have gotten a little shrill by the end of my recitation, and the possibility existed that I bared a little more fang than I really intended, but those things could happen.

"Nah, I think you covered it," King replied. "So what are you gonna do about it?"

"Thanks to this little issue I have with the sun, which is quickly rising, I'm going to do the only thing I can—namely, call in some reinforcements that don't share my sunburn problem."

"Sounds like a fair plan."

"I'm so glad you approve. Now, do you have anywhere we can crash, preferably with a supply of B-negative in the fridge?"

"Nope, after our little run-in with Krysta last night my hotel is probably being watched, and it has too many windows, anyway."

"All righty then, Plan D it is." I opened the door and dropped the tailgate.

"Plan D?" The werewolf asked, as I tossed Abby over my shoulder and started walking into the cemetery behind the church.

"Yeah, grab Greg and follow me," I called over my shoulder.

"Follow you where?" he asked, but he did as I said.

Where was a sizable crypt Greg and I had used on a few occasions when we were having issues with hallowed ground. It turned out that was all a psychological thing, not a mystical thing, but it never hurt to have a few extra hideouts up your sleeve. Or in your armpits if your sleeves had been burned off. The crypt was one of those old family ones that were more common in New Orleans than North Carolina, and there were no dates more recent than 1910, so we'd used it from time to time to crash. There was a big open space in the middle, a couple of benches on one wall and about two dozen plaques on another wall where the coffins were stored. I dropped Abby onto one of the benches, and King settled Greg on the floor along the wall with the plaques.

When we had the wounded settled as comfortably as possible, I sagged against the wall furthest from the door and pulled out my cell phone. It was wrecked. The screen was shattered, and all that happened when I pushed the buttons was kind of a sad clicking sound. I rolled Greg over and grabbed his phone. Of course, even after falling off a building, his shock-resistant, water-resistant, fall-proof, titanium-coated cell phone cover kept his smartphone from getting busted. I scrolled through his contact list for a minute until I came to the name I was looking for, then dialed.

"What do you want?" Anna's voice crackled across the telephone wires. Anna was a local witch and good friend of Mike's who had helped us out once or twice in the past. She kinda hated my guts, but I was hoping that she'd do a little tracking spell for me on Sabrina's behalf. Strong women working together, that kind of thing.

"Hi Anna, how are you?" I put a fake pleasantness into my voice whenever I spoke to her. I didn't really have anything against the woman, but she really, really didn't like vampires.

"I'm fine, Black. What do you want?" she repeated.

"I need your help."

"No." She hung up. I stared at the phone for a minute, then dialed her again.

She answered. "I said no."

"Wait! It's for Sabrina," I shouted into the phone.

"Why didn't you say so?" Anna answered in a much more pleasant tone.

"You didn't give me a chance. You hung up on me."

"I don't like you. I thought that was a perfectly reasonable response to receiving a phone call from someone I don't like while sitting in the hospital waiting room as someone I *do* like is undergoing surgery for a potentially life-threatening cancer. You did remember about that little event, didn't you?"

Shit. She was with Mike. Where I should have been, if I wasn't trapped in a crypt with two vampires and a werewolf waiting for sundown.

"Yes, Anna, I remember Mike's surgery, and I will get there to visit him as soon as I can. Please tell him that for me."

I guess she heard something in my voice that flipped her bitch switch to the "off" position for a few seconds, because her answer was surprisingly gentle. "I will. I promise. Now what do you need?"

"Sabrina was kidnapped by vampires. I think they've got her at a house near the college, but I need some daytime intelligence gathering. Can you help?"

"Yes. Do you have anything of hers that I can use for a locator spell?" I did, but it all got burned up with my apartment. Then I remembered, and reached for my wallet. I opened the tattered leather bifold, and there, tucked in the folds behind a couple of twenties and my membership card to an upscale strip joint, was a little white rectangle.

"I've got her business card. Will that work?"

"That'll do in a pinch. Mike's in surgery now, so I'll come over, do the spell, and be back here before he's out of recovery. Where are you?"

I gave her directions, she muttered something about stereotypes, and told me she'd be there in twenty minutes.

I paced until the knock came at the door, and Anna came through, looking much more civilized than the rest of us. Of course, in our defense, she hadn't been thrown off a building, fought a couple of über-vampires or spent any time in a burning building in the past twelve hours, so she could still look nice in a long rust-colored pleated skirt and white top. She looked around the crypt like she didn't want to touch anything, and I didn't really blame her.

"Who are all these people? And what the hell happened to that poor child?" She moved toward Abby with an outstretched hand, but I stepped in front of her. Her eyes widened at my speed, and she staggered back a step.

"Sorry," I said, taking her arm to steady her. "That's Abby. She just got turned, then staked to a wall and set on fire. Probably better to let her sleep right now, if you don't fancy being her breakfast."

"I'm Kyle King. I kill vampires," King said from where he sat on the floor with his back to a wall. He didn't get up, just offered a lazy wave.

"A profession I approve of wholeheartedly," Anna said.

One of these days I was going to dig into why she hated vamps so much, but this wasn't it. "Abby got set on fire, King and I got our asses kicked, and Greg got thrown off a building. And Sabrina was kidnapped. So it's been a night. Can you help us find Sabrina?" I asked.

Anna held out her hand and I gave her the business card. "Yes, I can feel her. There's a connection with this. It's weak, but enough to cast a locator spell and to scry her briefly."

"Scry her?" I asked.

"I can cast a spell that will allow you to see her. You will see her as she is right now, and you will see whatever is happening to her. You will not be able to communicate with her, and there will be no sound, only images."

"Do it," I said. Anna looked at me, not the "look at this idiot" looks she usually gave me, but a sharp look with a little fear in it. I didn't care. She wasn't going to be the only person afraid of me before this was through.

Anna cleared off the top of a big sarcophagus in the center of the room, then drew a circle in the dust on top. Around the inside of the circle she drew symbols, all kinds of squiggly lines and geometric shapes. She set the business card in the center of the circle and murmured an incantation. The business card began to glow, then flared with a bright white light that made me turn away. When I looked back, the card was glowing with a pale blue light.

Anna reached into the circle and took the card. She handed it to me. "This will lead you to Sabrina. You will feel a tug in the direction you should go. It is not precise, and the object may have formed a stronger bond with other objects in her possession than with the detective herself, but as long as they are together, this should locate her."

"Thanks," I said. I handed the card to King. "Can you take this and go to campus? Between this and your nose, you should be able to pick up her trail. When the sun goes down, we'll head out there together."

"Yeah, I can do that. I'll even wait for you to start the staking party." King left, and I heard the sound of his big pickup roaring to life.

I turned back to Anna. "You said something about scrying?"

"Yes. I can do this, but just for a moment. Stand back." She waved her hands over the circle again, and murmured more Latin or whatever. The surface of the stone coffin shimmered, then transformed into an image of Sabrina tied to a chair in a lush apartment somewhere. She had a black eye, and a split lip and her clothes were torn, but it looked like no serious damage had been done.

A big vampire was drinking from her when the image swam into view, and I stood there, frozen. I couldn't turn away, but I knew there was nothing I could do, either. The vamp, a linebacker-sized white guy with a crew cut, drank a little, then pulled back and waved another vampire over. The next guy came at Sabrina from the front, earning himself a headbutt for his troubles. She hit him square in the face with her forehead, and I laughed a little as he spun back. I could tell he was swearing even without the audio track.

The big guy cuffed her in the back of the head. I stared hard at the image, fixing him in my mind's eye. *That one dies slow.*

"I can't hold the image much longer," Anna said, her voice shaky.

"It's fine. She's okay for now. Thank you, Anna." I turned away from the scrying and went to the door, taking a self-indulgent moment to kick it and swear before I turned back to the witch.

"How's Mike?" I asked when I had myself back under control.

"Scared. This is a bad type of cancer, James. I don't know how much he's told you, but it's bad."

"Are there good kinds?" I asked.

She gave me a pitying little smile. "There are certainly kinds with higher survival rates."

Once again I was forced to think about the possibility of a world without Mike in it. Then the obvious solution came to mind, and I shoved it aside. I could no more turn Mike than I could turn Sabrina. Besides, his religion was kinda founded on a resurrection of a different flavor.

My eyes met Anna's again. "No," she said. Her mouth was a tight little line. "Don't even think it. He'd never let you. And I'd kill you if you tried."

I looked down at the witch and said, "Lady, I'll put up with a lot. Threats are fine. Insults are just peachy. But you try and come between me and my best friend when he's sick and I will end you. I won't bother turning you. I'll just shoot your ass. Mike's one of my oldest and best friends. I'd do anything for that man. But I am not bringing another vampire into this world, not even for him." We stared at each other for a long time, almost daring each other to look away.

Finally Anna nodded once and said, "Good. I believe you. Now what are you going to do about your lady friend?"

"As soon as King gets back with a location, I'm going to make a plan.

Then when the sun goes down, I'm going to get her back and leave a lot of dead vampires in my wake."

"Sounds good. I'm going back to the hospital. You can call me later for word on Mike's condition."

"I'll do that. Thanks."

She left, and I was stuck in a crypt pacing a hole in the floor waiting on King to come back. Greg and Abby were still out cold, and I left them that way. With the injuries they'd sustained, there was nothing I could do for them. Rest was the best solution. Too bad I couldn't get any.

Fortunately for my nerves, King got back less than an hour after Anna left.

"What's the deal?" I asked as soon as he got the door closed.

"The little locator thingy led me back to the house, but I couldn't see anything inside. There were some serious blackout shades over all the windows, and the doors were all locked tight. I decided breaking in was probably not the stealthy approach we were looking for, so I came back here."

"So she's there." I cracked my knuckles.

"Or at least her stuff is there. Remember, the witch said—"

"Yeah, I remember what she said. It's still the best lead we've got."

"Now what?" King asked.

I stared at the light under the crypt door. "Now we wait for the sun to go down, and then we go kill a lot of vampires."

Chapter 16

King sat with his back blocking the door, just in case anyone got too enterprising during the day, and we tried to get a few hours' rest before I went off to tear a pack of vampires into little bat-shaped pieces.

That whole thing about us passing out as soon as the sun came up was a myth, like so much of what people had written about us over the years, but the second I sat down, the events of the night caught up with me, and all the anger, fear and pain washed over me like a tidal wave. I went crashing down into a deep sleep for the next three hours or so.

I woke up with a stiff neck and a bad attitude. Greg and Abby were still out of it, both looking terrible. King's eyes snapped open the second I stirred, and by the time I had my feet under me, he was standing with a hand under his jacket.

"Relax," I said. "Nothing going on, just me."

The werewolf relaxed and sat back down against the door. I leaned over to Greg and shook him awake.

"Where are we?" he asked, rubbing his head and wincing at the new bruises he'd accumulated in his fall. He'd been out cold when I dragged him inside, and he looked around in confusion for a minute.

"Crypt behind Mike's place," I muttered.

"What's on fire?" He took a couple of deep breaths and tried to get up, but he was still too beat up to stand for more than a few seconds.

"Nothing now. The college vamps burned our place down."

"Burned?" Greg asked in a small voice.

I watched him processing the things lost in the fire—his video games, his computers, comic-book collection, probably some exotic porn that I didn't really want to think about. "Yeah, burned. And they kidnapped Sabrina and tried pretty hard to kill Abby in the process."

"And let me tell you, I'm pissed about that," Abby said in a weak voice. "Now is there anybody to drink in this . . . where are we?" She tried to stand and failed, so she slumped back down on the wall opposite me.

"Sorry, kiddo. All my reserves went to Captain Sidewalk Pizza over there last night. I got nothing left. And as to where, we're in a crypt behind a church."

"Did you say they kidnapped Sabrina?" Greg interrupted.

"Yeah."

"Do we know where they took her?" he asked.

"Yeah." I wasn't quite at the point where I could talk about that in more than one syllable.

"Are we going to do a lot of shooting and stabbing tonight?"

"Oh, yeah."

"Then we're gonna need dinner. I couldn't fight my way out of a wet paper bag right now."

"Here, take a little. But let go when I tell you to, or I'll break your fangs off." King knelt in front of Abby and Greg with his sleeves rolled up. Abby locked onto the proffered arm with gusto, but Greg held back.

"C'mon, bro, you gotta eat something or you won't even be able to walk, much less help me find Sabrina," I cajoled.

"Just drink, kid. It's the full moon, so I heal even faster than usual. I'll be back to normal in a couple of hours, even if you two were to drain me almost dry. And I ain't letting that happen." King stuck his arm back under Greg's nose.

My vegan partner stared at it for a few seconds, then the pain of his wounds and his hunger won out, and he bit into the werewolf's arm and started to drink. I sat against the wall, mouthwatering, while my partner and our protégé drank enough from King to heal most of their wounds. It only took a few minutes before he shook them off his wrists and pulled a dirty bandana out of his back pocket.

I went over to him, tore the rag in half and bound the wounds. "You know they'll heal almost instantly, right?"

"Werewolf physiology is a little different. Those wounds will seep longer on me than on a human. Something to do with a symbiotic and subservient relationship weres are supposed to have with vampires."

"I've never heard anything about that," I said.

"I've been on the road for a while. I've talked to a lot of people about lycanthropy and other critters that go bump in the night. So I'd like to keep any blood covered while the two starved vampires get their wits about them."

"You're pretty smart for a Labrador." I tied off the last knot and ducked as he took a swing at me.

"Thanks. And you're not half-bad for a soulless bloodsucking parasite."

"One does what one can. How are you?" I asked, looking over at my partner.

"I'm fine," Greg answered irritably, swatting my hand aside when I tried to check his pupils.

"You must be fine if you're grumpy." I went over to Abigail. She still looked pretty rough, and she sat with her back to the crypt, none of her normal attitude in evidence. "How about you?"

"I'm okay," she said in a blank voice that told me she was anything but.

She sat staring at nothing, rubbing her wrists where the stakes had been driven through.

"It's understandable if you're scared. They really did a number on you. I don't—"

She cut me off with a look. Her eyes were cold, almost completely soulless. The only thing they reminded me of was the way the Master of the City had looked—completely predatory.

"I'm fine. They're the ones you should be worried about. When do we leave?" She stood up, but wobbled a bit, still unsteady on her feet.

"*We* aren't going anywhere. You two are staying here with the furry blood bank, at least for tonight." I held up my hand at their protests. "Come on. You both know you're too weak, and it's the peak of the full moon, so I can't take Fluffy here with me anywhere. You guys might as well stay here, take the occasional nibble from the regenerating fountain of youth, while I go get some help and generally do what I do."

"And what is it that you do, exactly?" a dizzy King grumbled from his spot on the floor.

"I hit things and make huge messes."

I headed out to do just that.

Chapter 17

The last rays of sunlight made me squint and gave my skin that nice rosy tint that either said, "vampire got out of bed too early," or "ginger kid stayed at the beach too long." I wasn't really angry when I left the crypt, but I wasn't ready to sing campfire songs, either. Everywhere I looked I saw Sabrina's face, and every smell on the air reminded me of her. Thinking of her tied to a chair with a vampire gnawing on her gave me a cold feeling in the pit of my stomach, that feeling a person gets when they know they are going to do a large number of very bad things to people before the night's work is finished.

It wasn't a good feeling, but that was where I was when I got into King's Silverado and headed down to Wilkinson Boulevard. Wilkinson was home to all the porn stores, strip clubs and pawnshops one could ask for, with a gigantic country bar thrown in for good measure. Since I wasn't in the mood for line dancing, and all my guns had just been turned to slag, my internal compass led me straight to the biggest pawnshop in town. I walked in just as the clerk was trying to lock the front door.

"Sorry, man. We closed. You gotta come back tomorrow." He was six foot six and three hundred pounds of large black dude with no hair and enough gold around his neck to give Mr. T a chubby. He put his hand on my chest and tried to push me back toward the door.

That didn't go so well for him. I broke his arm below the elbow, so he'd only have to wear the short cast, but that was the only consideration I gave him.

He was tough, though. He went for his gun with his left hand. I picked him up by his belt and held him over my head for a few seconds, just staring at him. I couldn't get my head on straight enough to mojo him, but apparently, being hoisted into the air by a skinny white kid with fangs made him decide that this was not the time to be a hero. He dropped the gun, and I set him down.

"I don't want no trouble, man. Lemme go, and you can have whatever you want." He sank to his knees in front of me, and big tears started to roll down his round face.

"Open the safe."

"I don't know the combination, man. You got to believe me." He was really crying at this point, but his eyes kept flicking behind me to the door, as if expecting somebody. I heard soft footsteps and the sound of somebody trying very quietly to cock a revolver, and I was on the move.

I jumped one of the shelves with an easy hop and ran around behind my new attacker. A kid, barely sixteen, stood in the aisle looking very confused and holding a .38. I tapped him on the shoulder, and said, "Boo," when he turned around. The kid jumped and yelled a little, and the gun went off, the bullet ricocheting off the floor into a shelf. I quickly snatched the gun from him and slapped him across the face.

"That's why children shouldn't play with guns. Now get out of here." He looked in my eyes for about half a second before he decided to take my advice. He ran like hell itself was behind him, and I turned my attention back to the sobbing mountain of humanity on the floor.

"Open. The. Safe." I leaned in, showing my fangs, and the fat guy nodded. He went around behind the counter, and when he knelt down to open the safe, I continued, "If you do anything with the gun in there except hand it over quietly, I'll eat your spleen and make you watch."

I don't even really know what a spleen looked like, or where it was in the body, but it sounded good. Tiny pulled a couple of stacks of cash out of the safe, along with a Glock 19.

"I'm gonna go out on a limb here and guess that gun mysteriously doesn't have any serial numbers on it," I said quietly.

"I don't know nothing about that, man. I just work here. You broke the shit out of my arm. Why you gotta do that?"

"Seemed like a good idea at the time. Now, do you want to open the gun cases, or should I break the glass?"

"I guess I'll get in less trouble with the boss if you break the glass, so go ahead."

So I did. I broke into the display cases and loaded up with another pair of Glocks, half a dozen magazines and three boxes of ammunition. A short-barreled pump shotgun with a bandolier on the stock completed my arsenal. I pocketed the cash and looked up at Tiny.

"Sorry about this, Tiny, but I'm a little peckish." I had settled down enough to mojo him a little, so I made him knee-walk out into the main aisle. I bit into him just below the left ear and was rewarded with a rush of blood and stimulants I'd rarely felt in my life. Whatever Tiny was on, it was more than just a five-hour energy drink. I felt my muscles sing. I had to admit I liked it. I drank until I was full, then paused for a second, burped loudly and took one last sip.

"That's truly disgusting," a voice from behind me said.

I whirled around, bringing the shotgun to bear on the intruder.

Greg leaned against the store's front door, a disapproving look on his face. "Couldn't just rob the joint, could you? You had to trash the place, too?"

"Yes, I did, *Mother.* Tiny here thinks he'll get in less trouble with his boss the more mess I leave behind. Looks like he fought more. How did you get here? And how did you find me?" I wiped my mouth on Tiny's sleeve and walked over to Greg. "Help yourself. If you're coming with me you're gonna need guns."

"We could have bought this stuff. I have cash in a fireproof safe back at our place."

"Back at what used to be our place. The place that got incinerated, remember? Look Mother Teresa, we're the goddamn apex predators, okay? We're the top of the mother-loving food chain, and it's about time you sack up and act like it. Now either gear up, or go home. They've got Sabrina, they've started feeding on her, and I've got a lot of vampires to kill and not a lot of time to kill them in."

He stared at me for a long time and I could almost hear the bitchy things he wanted to say. Finally he decided that there would be a better time to discuss comparative morality, and started picking pistols out of cases. "Finding you was simple, doofus. You've got my phone, remember?"

"Yeah, and . . . ?" I had no idea what he was babbling about.

"For such a nerd, you are technologically stuck in 1998. I tracked my phone online using King's tablet computer. Then I caught the bus over here."

"You can do that? Track a phone, I mean? And how'd you catch a bus? You don't have any cash."

"Any idiot can track a cell phone. And hello, mojo? Do you ever have a plan?"

"You know my favorite plan. I punch things. I think you like to refer to that as the tactical solution. Now we need to get our tactics the hell out of here before the cops show up. So top off the tank on Tiny here. He's on something good."

"You know I don't do drugs. Or humans," Greg said with distaste.

"Drink. I need you at full strength. Or more."

He caught the look on my face and drank a little bit from Tiny just to shut me up. A couple of minutes later, Tiny was mojo'd into thinking there had been five of us driving motorcycles, and my partner and I were headed for the parking lot.

"What was that guy on? I feel amazing," Greg said, then looked down like he hated admitting that.

"I dunno, but I got a feeling we're going to need a lot of amazing before the sun comes up."

Chapter 18

We loaded the backseat of King's pickup with guns, covering them with a layer of fast-food wrappers, and rolled north toward where we'd last seen the frat-boy vampires. I had a big pickup truck full of guns and ammo, my best friend riding shotgun, literally, and a belly full of blood. I felt pretty good about my chances for pulling this off and getting Sabrina back in good shape.

"What's the plan?" Greg asked.

We stopped just inside the tree line, and the house loomed about fifty yards in front of us. It was just like it had looked on my scouting run, except all the crappy college-kid cars were all gone. When we got closer, I saw the Greek letters over the door proclaiming it as the Beta Beta Beta house, and I chuckled a little.

"What?" Greg whispered.

"The sign. I was so preoccupied before, with the whole trying not to burn to death thing, I didn't catch it. Bunch of smartasses," I said.

He still looked puzzled, so I took my moment to be the smart one. It didn't happen often, so I tried not to let those opportunities pass me by. "The Greek alphabet doesn't really have a *V*, so the Beta is as close as it gets for ancient Greek. By calling themselves Beta Beta Beta, they're saying, *VVV*. Basically they're hanging a sign out saying 'Vampire.' I admire that kind of audacity, even if I plan to gut every one of them."

"You're a weird dude."

"Says the guy with the utility belt."

"Touché. Now, what's the plan?"

I looked over the front of the building and saw no lights on anywhere. "Hard and fast. I go through the front door first and take the upstairs. These old houses usually have a big staircase in the foyer, so I'll head up while you clear the main floor. If you finish the ground floor before I finish the second, you leapfrog me to the third. If everything's clear, we meet in the main foyer to go downstairs together. If everything's not clear, we converge on the trouble and make it dead. Fast."

"Yeah, but why do we wait to go downstairs together?"

"Because that's where I think they'll be if they're home, and there are a bunch of them. We probably can't take them alone, so we should go together. But I don't want to go into the boss fight until we've cleared the rest of the level. Make sense?"

"Yeah, when you make everything sound like *Legend of Zelda*, it makes perfect sense." He chambered a round into his shotgun.

I made sure I had a pistol in each hand cocked and locked, and we bolted for the front door. I blew through the door as if it were made of tissue paper and made it up the main staircase in about three long steps. I heard Greg on the first floor, knocking doors off hinges and stomping through rooms. I found myself in a long hallway with doors on both sides, like a scene from a French farce, or a horror movie. There was one door at the end of the hall, and I went for it first, smashing through the old wood like it was nothing.

You know the drill, it's always the door at the end of the hall. The hero spends all that time checking the rooms on the sides, and there's nothing there. Then he gets to the door at the end of the hall and that's where the bad guy is. Or the girl tied to a chair. Or a bomb. Or, in my case, an empty bathroom. A really disgusting fraternity bathroom at that. By the smell of things in the bathroom, Sabrina had never been there. Neither had bleach. The fixtures were all disgusting, and something in the sink smelled like Ebola, or what one would think Ebola would smell like if one could smell a virus, which I could, and had a morbid curiosity about whether or not one could catch hemorrhagic fevers, which I couldn't.

The other rooms on the second floor were all similarly gross, and all showed the same lack of sexy police detective presence. They were typical dorm rooms, mostly, except with a lot of discarded blood bags and no pizza boxes. The bongs and Bob Marley posters were still present in about the same ratio, as well as black-light posters and a ridiculous number of porn DVDs. Hadn't those guys discovered the Internet yet?

One whole room was devoted to a small marijuana-growing operation, just a dozen or so four-foot plants, but enough to make me wonder why they'd never been raided by campus police. It also made me wonder if we could get high the normal way. I'd only ever gotten a buzz from booze or stoner's blood, so I had no idea, but was willing to try. I was just going into the last room when I heard Greg's footsteps on the stairs.

"Ground floor's clear," he whispered as he passed my floor.

I opened the last door and found a room very different from all the others. It was neatly decorated in modern chrome and black leather, with no pipes, bongs or rolling papers to be seen. A laptop sat in the center of an IKEA desk, the only personal touch in the room.

The screensaver caught my eye as soon as I crossed the threshold. On the screen was a picture of Abby staked to the wall in what used to be our house. Three goofy vampires posed in front of her making obscene hand gestures and stupid faces. I sat down in the chair and tapped the touchpad to wake up the computer.

The laptop flickered to life, and a document appeared on the screen. It was a note, addressed to "BusyBody Investigations, Inc." I assumed that was us, so I read it.

"Dear nosy boys, if you're reading this, then you must have gotten our little message at your home last night. She was cute, but a little noisy. Her screams as the silver went into her veins were particularly shrill. If she survived our little barbecue, I do hope you work with her on her wailing. A lower pitch would be much more appealing to the ear. If she didn't, then my condolences. It can be so hard to lose a sibling."

"As for the snack, we thank you. We accept your peace offering of the lovely detective, and will agree to cease all hostilities between our organizations as long as tributes of this quality continue to arrive on a quarterly basis. You can leave them here in the house for us, and we won't cause you boys any additional harm. There need be no further contact between our organizations as long as you fulfill your duties to us like good vassals. If you refuse, that is, of course, your choice. But please understand that any refusal will be met with my extreme displeasure and may have unfortunate repercussions on certain clerical associates of yours."

It was signed, "Sincerely, Professor Wideham."

I sat there for a long moment trying to keep my cool, then gave up. I picked up the desk chair and threw it through the wall into the next room. I flipped the bed, tossed a couple of other small pieces of furniture and ripped the door off the hinges. Greg came running in like a bat out of hell, but paused at the door when he saw I was alone.

"Dude, is there like some invisible monster in there?" he asked from the hall.

"No."

"Then would you like to explain what's going on?"

"No. Read it yourself." I pointed to the computer.

He came in, giving me a wide berth as I stood holding the two halves of the door, shoulders heaving with the effort of not going *completely* nuts. He read the letter, chuckled a little, and closed the lid on the laptop. "What a douche," he said. "Now we're totally going to kill all these assholes, right?"

"Totally."

"Okay, then. Third floor's clear. I got a new laptop out of this deal, so let's go into the basement and kill a whole lot of bad guys." He led the way out of the room, then looked back at where I still stood trying to get my temper under control.

"Hey!" Greg yelled.

My head snapped up, and I glared at him.

"Hulk smash down here." He pointed down the stairs, and I followed him to the basement and my chance to hurt a lot of vampires who were trying to eat my girlfriend.

Chapter 19

Except there weren't a lot of vampires in the basement. In fact, there wasn't a lot of anything in the basement, except for the ubiquitous red plastic cups found at every college party in the world. The basement had long since been turned from any lair-type use into a rec room, complete with a pool table, a foosball table, three plasma TVs on the walls, an old Pac-Man game in one corner and a full bar along one wall. A huge open space, it was littered with couches, chairs and futons, all covered in magazines and empty blood bags. I did spot a couple of *Rolling Stone* and *High Times* magazines amidst the porn, but those pinnacles of literacy were few. The only concession to lairdom was a thick metal door with bolts driven through the frame into the concrete foundation of the house. Once that door was locked from the inside, nobody would get in without a wrecking ball.

Greg glanced around the room and immediately started tapping on walls, looking for hollow areas behind them. I tried the more direct approach. I walked over behind the bar and started flipping light switches on the wall. One turned on a blender, resulting in a spray of some truly nasty concoction that for all the world smelled like an O-negative margarita. Another, mundanely enough, turned off the lights, causing Greg to trip over an ottoman and swear at me. I enjoyed that so much I did it a couple more times just for fun.

The third switch was the charm. As soon as I flipped it, servos in the door swung it shut and automatically locked the bolts. All the lights in the room went red, making it very difficult for humans to see, but no problem for those of us with undead eyes. The Pac-Man game dropped into the floor on an invisible lift, and a tunnel was revealed behind it.

"I think we should go that way," I said, leaning carefully on the bar to avoid getting my elbows in the grossness there.

"Show-off," Greg muttered, unclipping a flashlight from his utility belt.

"You're the one with a utility belt, but I'm the show-off?" I followed him into the tunnel.

"If the fangs fit, pal."

"That doesn't even make any sense. Sorry, I'm worried, and I'm being a dick."

"I'm used to it. You're always kind of a dick. But I forgive you," Greg said.

I crossed into the tunnel, then froze as the wall slid shut behind me. I looked around for a few seconds, but couldn't find a switch to open the door again.

Greg and I exchanged a look.

I shrugged. "Onward and downward?"

My partner, decidedly more grumpy with our escape route cut off, nodded tersely and started down the tunnel.

"Wait!" I hissed.

Greg stopped cold. "What?"

"What if there are booby traps?" I was suddenly very interested in the walls and floor of the tunnel.

"What makes you think there are booby traps?"

"These guys have lived up to every stereotype we've been able to think of so far, right?"

"Yeah. So what?"

"Okay, think about it. Can you imagine having a secret lair with tunnels underneath it?"

The look on his face told me I'd just tapped into the pleasure centers of his brain.

"Okay, now imagine you have a lair with tunnels. Got that image?" From his little smile, his tunnels were full of Playboy Bunnies. "Now, can you imagine any scenario in which you would *not* booby-trap those tunnels?"

His smile dropped like Enron stock.

"We gotta be careful. There's no way these tunnels aren't booby-trapped," he said, just as if it had been his idea. He moved forward, slower this time, playing his flashlight along the walls and floor.

I shook my head and followed. I wasn't a huge fan of small spaces, which was why I'd never been much for the coffin stereotype. Give me a California King bed and a vaulted ceiling any day. Skulking along an old tunnel with a ceiling just barely high enough for me to stand upright was nowhere on my list of fun things to do.

The tunnel was dry, at least, and there weren't any apparent spiders. I wasn't afraid of them. I just didn't like them. What did anything need that many legs for, anyway?

It was dark, but Greg had a couple of those snap-and-shake glow sticks in his utility belt. He handed me one, so we each had some light. The floor was packed red clay and looked old, like it had been there a lot longer than the house. I ran my fingers along the rough brickwork and tried to figure out what the place had been before the stoners had made it into their lair.

As if he'd read my mind, Greg whispered, "Underground Railroad."

It made perfect sense to me. There were abandoned cellars and passageways all through the South left over from the Civil War, or the War of Northern Aggression, as my redneck Uncle Morris called it. Morris was one of those guys who still used racial epithets in casual conversation and had a confederate flag flying in front of his trailer. He wasn't my favorite uncle by any stretch, but as the saying went, you could pick your nose, but you couldn't pick your family. I was wondering what had ever happened to Uncle Morris when Greg froze in front of me, one hand up, fist closed in a "stop" gesture.

"You realize you were never in the army, right?" I whispered.

"I watched a lot of *Stargate: SG-1*. Now shut up and be still. There's a trap here."

I looked down and didn't see anything. I was about to say so when I caught a glimpse of it out of the corner of my eye. A thin monofilament line had been stretched across the passageway, going from a hook in one wall to an eyelet mounted opposite. I couldn't see where the line went after it passed through the eyebolt, but I was betting it wasn't attached to anything pleasant.

"You going to disarm that?" I asked.

"This isn't Dungeons & Dragons, dude. Just because I'm wearing black doesn't mean I have the Find & Remove Traps skill."

"Besides, you haven't passed a Dexterity check in this millennium." I chuckled softly when he flipped me off. "What's the plan?"

"I thought we'd try to not break the trip wire. How does that sound?"

"Sounds good to me. After you." I gestured grandly down the hall, and he took one exaggerated step over the trip wire.

I saw the disturbed soil on the other side of the wire just a hair too late to keep him from stepping on it, then I heard a solid click from the ceiling. I felt a whoosh of air and reached forward to shove Greg to the ground. He sprawled facedown on the dirt, breaking the trip wire with his back foot. Nothing happened there, of course. He'd already triggered the trap when he stepped on the pressure plate on the other side of the dummy trip wire.

I whirled to the left with blinding speed, but I still wasn't fast enough to save Greg and get out of the way. Being a good friend and hero to the downtrodden, I chose to shove him to the dirt and hope that I survived the booby trap. Then the pole swung out of the ceiling and caught me square in the gut with a foot-long wooden stake.

Chapter 20

I stood for a long moment staring straight ahead at where my partner lay in the dirt. The stake had passed over his head by a hair and embedded itself about three inches below my solar plexus. I didn't feel anything at first except the impact, but then the pain of the wound started in, and it took all the restraint in the world not to scream bloody murder. A ball of fire exploded in my stomach, and I sagged on the rod that held the stake.

"Greg," I croaked.

"Yeah, what was that all about?" He rolled over angrily, but his eyes went very big when he saw the stake sticking all the way through my skinny frame.

"Would you be a pal and pull this thing out of my stomach?"

He nodded and reached up. The stake hung up on a rib, and he had to stand up to get enough leverage. Eventually, he put one foot on my chest and pulled, exertion making his face scrunch up and his forehead bead with pinkish sweat. With the grinding sound of wood on bone, which I felt as much as heard, he slowly pulled the stake from my midsection. After what felt like a year, but was probably only a couple of seconds, he got the booby trap out of me, and I collapsed to the tunnel floor.

I lay in the dirt for a few minutes trying to recover as Greg examined the trap. "It's really ingenious, you know," he said, as he swung the pendulum that mere moments before had been embedded in my guts. "The fake trap concealing the real trap. That's some serious Indiana Jones stuff there. And to use a stake on a stick? Genius, I tell you."

I wasn't in a mood to really appreciate the brilliance of the trap that had impaled me, but as I stood, I put a hand on Greg's shoulder, and said, "You're welcome."

"What are you talking about? I saw it coming. I dove out of the way just in time. And besides, the stake got you just under the rib cage. It didn't cause any major damage."

When I was finally able to stand up straight, he noticed that the hole in my shirt was level with his heart. Greg sometimes forgot that he was better than half a foot shorter than I was. He looked from my stomach to his chest, gulped deeply, and said, "Thanks," in a very small voice.

We continued down the tunnel, disarming a couple of other traps along the way. They were minor inconveniences, nothing really suited to taking out a vampire—a few poison darts, a couple of spears poking up out of the floor—standard adventure-movie gimmicks. After about half an hour of wandering around underground, the tunnel started to widen and light began to stream in from ahead. The tunnel ended at a high-tech-looking door set into the antique stone walls. A completely anachronistic digital keypad was set into the wall to the right of the door, and what looked like a retinal scanner was right above it.

I tapped for a few minutes, trying out various combinations of UNC-Charlotte important dates on the keypad. Basically, that meant typing every variation of forty-nine I could come up with, since all I really knew about the college was their prospecting mascot, the 49er. I didn't even know if it had anything to do with gold or with the fact that NC Highway 49 ran right past campus. Given the originality of my home state, I'd put my money on the latter. After watching me for a little while, Greg pulled out his cell phone and a funny cable, pushed me aside, and started his geek-fu on the keypad. He got at least as far as I did, but, five minutes later, we were still on the wrong side of the door.

"Scoot back." Greg's frustration made him growl a little. I thought I even saw a hint of fang.

"For what?" I asked, moving back into the tunnel a couple of feet.

"For Plan B." He grabbed the doorframe in both hands and pulled.

Greg was really strong, like drop-a-bus-on-your-head strong, but even so, it was all he could manage to pull that door out of the frame. After healing my stake wound, it was all I could manage to stand upright, so I just stood back and watched as the veins popped out in his neck and he turned a couple of really odd shades of red. He got a little movement in the frame, let go, bent his knees to get a lower grip, and wrenched the door out of the wall and over one shoulder. The door turned out to be about eight inches thick and solid metal. It was the wall around it that finally gave way, not the door, and two-hundred-year-old bricks fell in all around us as the tunnel shook from Greg's efforts. He dropped the door off to one side, and I was almost bounced off my feet from the concussion.

"Color me impressed," I said, peering past him into the room beyond the doorway.

"Color me herniated," he gasped, both hands on his knees. "If you see something round on the floor, it's my O-ring. I want that back."

"You're disgusting. Give me your flashlight." The doorway led into a chilly room dimly lit by wall sconces, but the dust from the door's destruction made it hard to see. After a few minutes, I stepped into the room to get a better look. The room was big, with high ceilings. Shelves lined every wall and made aisles all through the room. Every shelf was full of bottles, and when I pulled one from a rack, I realized where we were.

"Greg?" I asked.

"Yeah, what?"

"We're in a wine cellar." Then I took a better look at the bottle in my hand. Instead of a vineyard logo and a year, the label had a name and a photograph of a college-aged girl taped to it. Apparently, I held a bottle of Stephanie, 1963. I took out the cork and sniffed. Sure enough, we were in what had to be Professor Wideham's blood cellar. The blood smelled pretty good, especially for a vintage from the Kennedy era, so I tipped the bottle and took a swig.

It was blood, but it was blood cut with red wine to make it last. Apparently, Wideham had figured out how to mix fermented grape spirits with fresh human spirits to make a pretty tasty treat. It wasn't something I thought would catch on at the local supermarket, but it had a nice bouquet. I drank about half the bottle, then passed it to Greg.

"Top off the tank," I said. He took the bottle and sipped cautiously. "What?" I asked. "I drank it and thought it was fine."

"Yeah," he replied, "but you drink Miller Lite by choice." He finally turned up the bottle and drained it dry, licking his lips afterward.

"Not bad, huh?" I asked.

"Not bad at all. Maybe we'll ask this Professor Wideham, or whatever his name is, how he makes it."

"Before we cut off his head?"

"I think we've got a better shot at an answer if we do it before."

"Good point. So let's find him, get his secret recipe and cut off his head." I started moving through the stacks of bottled blood wine toward a staircase. Greg followed close behind, and we took the stairs up, pausing at the door atop the staircase.

"What if he's not up there?" Greg whispered.

"Then I eat whoever is up there and make them tell me where to find Wideham."

"Not necessarily in that order," Greg corrected.

"Good point. I get the info, then I eat them. Plan?"

He looked like he wanted to pick apart the finer points of my plan, like the eating people part, but finally just sighed and said, "Plan."

With his approval, I turned the knob and stepped out into a very busy restaurant kitchen, surprising two dishwashers and three cooks and making one poor waitress faint dead away.

Greg and I stood stock-still for just a moment, then he pushed past me, pulling his long coat closed over his utility belt and holding his wallet in the air and shouting the one word guaranteed to empty most restaurant kitchens: "*Inmigración! Inmigración!*" He walked through the kitchen masquerading as an ICE agent, and the employees scurried like vampires at a tanning bed convention. In about thirteen seconds, we were alone with the unconscious waitress and one very angry head chef.

The chef picked up a big knife and looked like he was about to part Greg's hair with it. I tapped him on the shoulder. He whirled around, looked into my eyes and froze as I mojo'd him into pliability. "Sleep," I said, and he collapsed like a balding sack of potatoes.

"I think we took a wrong turn at Albuquerque, doc," Greg said in his best Bugs Bunny voice.

"Yeah, me too. And we need to get out of here before whoever owns this restaurant shows up. Because if they knew about that little wine cellar, they're tied to Wideham. And they might be more than we can handle on our own. This isn't a new setup, and it hasn't happened without some people with some juice knowing about it."

"Yeah, and the last time we tangled with anybody packing that kinda juice, I got thrown off a building."

I turned to look for an exit. "Then it's fortunate for both of you that this restaurant is on the ground floor," the Master of the City said from right behind me.

Chapter 21

"Really?" I said to the air. "This is really happening?"

"What is really happening, Mr. Black?" Tiram asked, obviously not happy to see me in his kitchen.

The Master Vampire was impeccably turned out again in a suit that cost more than my car, complete with Italian leather shoes and a pocket square. I didn't even know they still made suits with pocket squares. Of course, he might have had that suit for a generation or two.

"What is happening is that in fifteen years of living here and being what I am, I had no idea you existed. Now I've run into you twice in thirty-six hours, and I'm *not* happy about it."

Greg slunk around behind me, putting as much distance between himself and Tiram as possible. I didn't blame him. It might not have been Tiram who tossed him off a roof, but he certainly had the power to do us serious harm, and I wasn't convinced that Greg had completely healed.

"Somehow, I believe that I may even be less thrilled with our recent level of contact than you are, Mr. Black. Now, why are you here? What were you doing in my wine cellar?" He motioned to the door behind me.

"We were looking for a vampire calling himself Professor Wideham. We followed the tunnels from his lair to your cellar, and came up the stairs hoping to find him here." I figured there was no point in lying about it. It wasn't like we could have come from anywhere else.

"And why are you looking for the professor? I would have thought that the antics of his group would not appeal to you."

"They don't. He and his rejects from *Lost Boys II* torched our home, almost killed one friend of ours, and kidnapped a police officer. We intend to get her back and get a little revenge." I showed a little fang and let my eyes go black around the edges.

Tiram's eyes widened when I mentioned Sabrina's abduction. "That was not authorized, I assure you. Feel free to mete out whatever punishment you feel appropriate under the circumstances." He turned to go into the restaurant. "Now, if you'll excuse me, I have impatient customers that I will now be forced to bespell into thinking they had a delicious meal, and it seems I need to find new kitchen staff as well."

"Hold up there, Spanky." I grabbed his elbow before he got too far away.

I heard a sharp intake of breath from Greg, and Tiram turned back to look at me. The little smile that had played across his face since he first caught us in the kitchen was gone, and I felt a little bit of the will of a real Master Vampire hammer at my mind. I pushed past it, throwing him out of my head, and saw his eyes widen.

"Is there something else I can do for you?" he asked after a second.

I let go of his arm. "You said the attack on us wasn't authorized. But something was. What was authorized, and by who?"

"By whom, Mr. Black. Everything that happens in this city is authorized by me, of course. And when Professor Wideham told me you had been spying on him, I granted him permission to destroy your lair. I did not authorize an attempt on the life of a fledgling vampire, nor did I give my blessing to Detective Law's abduction. Now, if you'll excuse me?" He made to turn around again, but I dashed around him, blocking his path.

"How did you know the friend they almost killed was a vampire? And how did you know they took Sabrina?" I got very close to Tiram's face to watch his reaction, but it wasn't at all what I expected.

He threw back his head and laughed like I'd told a really funny joke for once. "Mr. Black, until very recently you have had only three friends in all the world. Mr. Knightwood is here with you. Miss Law is a detective, so it reasons that she was the kidnap victim, and poor Father Maloney is in the hospital. How is the good father, by the way? Please tell him I inquired about his health, won't you? So, given that information, the only person left that you could have possibly stretched to consider a friend is young Miss Lahey, so newly turned by my lovely Krysta. Now that I've proven that I do indeed know more about you than you know about me, or will ever find out about me, may I go on about my business? Or must we have another unpleasant encounter?"

He looked up at me without any mojo, without anger and without the slightest hint of fear. He just stood there, supremely confident that, if there was an "unpleasant encounter," he would come out ahead.

I figured he was right, so I got out of his way.

"We're not finished, Tiram," I said to his shoulders as he went out into the restaurant.

"Oh, no, Mr. Black. We've only just begun." The swinging door closed behind him.

I turned to Greg and found him leaning heavily on one of the long metal prep tables. He looked paler than normal, and I saw his hands shaking a little as he tried to get himself under control.

"You all right, pal? Everything's okay. We didn't have to kill the big bad guy. It's cool." I tried my best to reassure him, and after a long minute or two, he got himself together.

"Yeah, I'm okay. But Jimmy?" He raised his eyes to mine, and I hadn't seen him that scared since we slipped the video camera into the girls' locker room in seventh grade and caught the gym teachers doing the deed in the showers.

"Yeah, bro. What's up?"

"I don't ever want to mess with that guy again. He scares the crap out of me."

"Me too, Greggy. But I've got a really bad feeling that we're not going to be able to avoid him forever."

"Yeah, I feel it, too. But let's give it a shot, huh?"

"Will do. Now, you got any great ideas about how to find Wideham and his goofballs?"

"Yeah, I've got two. But you're gonna hate both of them." He looked at the floor, and I was pretty sure by his words that I knew what was coming.

"Really?" I asked with a sigh.

"Anna and The Guys have the best sense of what's weird in town, man. Between the four of them, they should have some ideas about where to start looking." Greg still wouldn't look at me, but he had the little smirk bouncing around on his face that I really hated.

"You're probably right." I groaned. "One meeting with Anna in a day is too many for me. You deal with Her High Priestess-ness, and I'll meet you at the comic shop around eleven. That should give them time to get the civilians safely to bed, right?"

"I doubt it. This is Game Night, so there'll be people there all night. But on the plus side, that means that all three of the guys will be there." He didn't mention that he'd get to try out his new *Magic: The Gathering* decks, or whatever he played nowadays. I'd always been a nerd, but my partner's geekitude truly knew no boundaries.

"Great. Just what I need after a long week—a dive headfirst into the great unwashed horde of Dorkdom." I turned and headed into the restaurant.

I stopped cold at the scene before me. The restaurant was full and gorgeously decorated in a classically elegant style. There were lots of high-backed booths for privacy, marble floors and leather chairs, and not a screaming kid anywhere in sight. The clientele was as high-tone as the decor, Charlotte's version of the glitterati out for a gourmet meal, and by all appearances, everyone was having a grand old time—eating, drinking, laughing and chatting like all was normal. I even saw a waiter bringing a check to one table, as a man in a tailored dress shirt and tie folded his napkin onto his plate.

His empty plate. His clean, fresh-from-the-kitchen empty plate. What made the scene so bizarre was that there was no food anywhere. The plates were all empty, not a crumb or splash of sauce dirtying up the joint. And all the customers seemed full, or at least seemed to think they were full. I made my way over to where Tiram stood at the host stand near the front door, greeting people and telling them that the restaurant unfortunately was fully committed for the weekend.

"And honestly, we are booked solid for the rest of the month. If you would like to make a reservation for a weekday evening, I believe we have some openings next month. Our weekends are committed until summer, I hate to say." He wore a look that told everyone he didn't really hate to say it at all.

"And how hungry will your clientele be by then?" I mused as I stood next to him.

"If someone hadn't terrorized my entire kitchen staff, tonight's guests would be dining on grand American cuisine rather than simply thinking they were getting their money's worth," he replied, shooting me a dirty look. "Now, please leave my restaurant. You don't meet the dress code."

"Good point. Since I don't meet the dress code, and the amount of human blood in your wine doesn't meet the health code, why don't you loan me an American Express card or two so Greg and I can replenish our wardrobes?" I held out my hand.

The Master of the City gave me a condescending look, then broke into peals of laughter. "You idiot. You actually pay for things? Just take whatever you want, then tell the cashier you've paid for it. I haven't dealt with currency in three hundred years. We don't need money, child, we have power. Now, shoo." He waved us out into the night with a peremptory gesture, and we left.

Greg and I stepped out onto the sidewalk. Apparently, we'd covered a couple of miles underground because the restaurant was in an upscale retail development south of the college, complete with high-rise condos, a man-made lake and a towering Hilton hotel.

I looked over at Greg, and said, "Okay, then. Plan stays the same. You go talk with the Wicked Witch of the New South, and I'll meet you at the comic shop."

"How am I supposed to get there?" Greg asked.

"Well, you can either eat a cabbie or steal a car. I'm going to steal a car. Over there." I pointed toward the hotel parking lot. "You steal yours somewhere else."

"When did we become thieves?" Greg asked, a little whiny.

"*I* became a thief shortly after I became dead. *You* became a thief when the really bad guys burned down our house with all the money in it, kidnapped our friend and blew up our cars." I was getting tired of explaining things as I felt the seconds tick by. Even if Sabrina had made it through the night alive, there was no guarantee that she'd survive another one. We had to find the Professor and his students, and soon.

"What do you mean blew up our cars?" Greg was pretty attached to his car, so I'd been holding that tidbit back until he regained a little more strength.

"Yeah, when they burned up our place, they torched the garage, too. Your ride is a goner. Sorry." I shrugged.

"Now, I'm pissed. Your car?"

"My car was a piece of crap. Of course, it melted. But I didn't have a decent ride, anyway. I plan to correct that in the immediate future." I started walking toward the Hilton lot.

"Hey, Jimmy?" Greg called after me.

"What?"

"What are we gonna do about King's truck? He'd be pretty pissed if you left it there."

All visions of swiping a nice Mercedes or Lexus faded from my mind. "I'll get a cab back to the truck."

The night was getting nothing but worse. Not only did I have to drive a pickup full of guns to a comic-book store, I still had no idea where Sabrina was being held. But I was damn sure about to find out, if I had to eat every comic-book nerd in Charlotte to do it.

Chapter 22

I pulled into the parking lot beside the comic shop a little after eleven o'clock, and found Greg leaning on the hood of a Porsche convertible. He'd obviously taken the MoC's advice about upgrading his ride to heart, but he didn't seem proud of his wheels. When I got closer, I could tell by the look on his face that Anna had told him about Mike's prognosis, so I did something I never, ever did. I walked up to him, didn't say a word and gave him a big hug. He and I held each other for a long moment before he pulled away, and we stood there wiping at our eyes.

"If I hear a single gay vampire joke out of you right now, I swear to God, I'll stake you in your sleep," I said once we had our crap relatively together.

"Deal." Greg's voice was still a little thick with emotion.

I gestured to the back door of the comic shop. "How do you want to do this?"

"Dude, we're not talking about a SWAT entry. We're going into a comic-book store on all-night Game Night to talk to some nerds who happen to be friends of mine. I think we can just walk in."

Then, he did just that, pulling the door open and walking in to thunderous cries of nerd appreciation. It was kinda like when Norm walked into the bar on *Cheers*, only with no beer and lots of Red Bull. I followed him into the brightly lit back room, where about a dozen folding tables were spread out with all kinds of table, role-playing and collectible games in progress. There were nerds of all shapes and sizes scattered around the room, from your classic forty-year-old Star Trek geek who lived in his mother's basement to the preteen nerdlets playing Yu-Gi-Oh! or some other unpronounceable card game.

The three guys we needed to talk to were at the head table, moving little lead figurines around in a complicated-looking game. My particular nerddom was always focused in a different genre, so I had no idea what they were up to, but Greg fit right in. He was almost a hero to some of the youngest dorklings, having once won the weekly *Magic: The Gathering* tournament for four months straight. His streak probably would never have been broken, but we had a zombie thing come up one night, and he missed that week's game. I wasn't sure he'd forgiven me for that yet.

Nick, the shop owner, sat at the head of the table surrounded by books, dice and a laminated, colorful dungeon master's screen. His screen looked like it was from the original '70s set, and knowing Nick, it might have been. Nick was pushing fifty, having started the shop back in the eighties in a desperate attempt to avoid getting a real job. Now, thirty years later, the guy with the ponytail and a T-shirt with D&D dice on the front was a successful businessman, although much of that credit belonged to the clean-cut guy beside him.

Trey was the business guy of the operation, and the one who looked the most out of place in a comic shop. He actually wore shirts with collars most days, but he'd succumbed to the casual-Friday atmosphere and wore a Naval Academy T-shirt.

Dusty was . . . well, Dusty was an institution more than an employee. He was that skinny guy with the cactus-looking chin beard and an encyclopedic knowledge of comics that was a little creepy in the depth and breadth of it. He knew as much about R. Crumb and *Maus* as he did about *Captain America* and *Green Lantern*, and would happily go for hours on the difference in artistic styles between John Byrne and Neal Adams. Dusty was always working on a project of his own, talking about leaving the store to make his own art, but he still showed up for work every day.

These were the guys on whom we had pinned our hopes of finding Sabrina. I felt the ball of dread in my stomach grow with every step closer to their gaming table, and it didn't shrink at all when Nick looked up over his DM screen and shouted, "Greg! Come for my rematch? We're in the middle of an adventure right now, but go ahead and warm up on the vermin, and I'll get to you in a couple hours."

I was pretty sure he included me in the "vermin" remark, but he'd waved his arm over to where a bunch of kids were playing cards.

"Nick, I need your help," Greg said quietly, and the buzz of conversation halted immediately.

Every head in the place turned to Greg and Nick, as the two superstars of this little universe got ready for a team-up. It was like a real-life crossover issue for Charlotte's nerd set.

Nick leaned back in his chair, affecting a Godfather posture, and said, "What can I do for you, Greg? Whatever it is, I'm sure we can come to some sort of an . . . arrangement." He smiled a slow smile, and I remembered Greg mentioning that Nick had been after a few of his more prized comics for the last few years.

"We don't have time for this," I muttered to Greg, keeping my voice out of the range of human hearing.

Out of the corner of my eye, I did notice one teenager jump a little at the words he shouldn't have been able to hear. I looked at him, and he ducked his head and started throwing decks of cards into a backpack. *Wonder what he is?* I thought, and filed his face away for future reference.

"Be cool. If it looks like he's going to be a real ass about helping us, you can eat him. But let me try to talk first," Greg whispered back.

"Fine, but talk fast. We're running out of moonlight, and I'm finishing this tonight no matter who I have to kill to do it."

"So what do you need, Gregory? I'm in the middle of a new *Rogue Mage* campaign here." Nick always used full names when he was being a jerk. I never got it.

"Is there somewhere we can speak privately?" I asked.

Nick turned on me what he obviously thought of as his best demeaning stare, the kind of look that made preteen boys quail with fear when questioning the valuation of a comic. It didn't have a lot of effect on me. Face certain death enough times, especially if you really did end up dead, and normal mortal intimidation techniques just don't work like they used to.

"Anything you have to say to me, you may say in front of my minions and my legions of adoring admirers." Nick made what I was sure looked like a grand gesture in the movie in his mind, but in real life looked like he swung a scrawny arm around his head in a spastic flurry of motion.

"We'd really rather do this in private," I insisted.

"Greg, tell your rude friend that I'm not leaving my game." Nick folded his arms in front of his equally skinny chest.

"Okay, pal. Your disaster." I moved to the front of the room where everyone could see me clearly. "Hey, everybody!" I clapped my hands.

Every head in the place swiveled around, and all eyes were on me. Über-geeks weren't that accustomed to being addressed, so when given the opportunity for some attention, they got a little deer-in-the-headlights look about them. I noticed that I felt stronger, like it was less of a strain to mojo that many people. *Hmmm, maybe eating faeries and immortal succubi has its privileges.*

When I had everyone's attention, I said, "You will sleep for the next thirty minutes. You will not notice the loss of time. When you wake up, you will swear off chocolate and drink lots of water for the next six months. Soda will taste like cardboard, and you will have no appetite for sweets or fried food. Except for you three." I waved my arm at Dusty, Trey and Nick. "You three are off the hook. Now sleep."

Every head except for the Three Stooges dropped to the gaming tables with a sound like so many unripe watermelons dropped from a bridge onto a passing truck. I actually knew exactly what that sounded like from a past experience.

Nick and his cohorts were still awake and aware, and a little freaked out.

"What was that, some kind of mass hypnosis?" Trey asked.

"Yeah, something like that," I said.

"What was the bit about chocolate and fried food?" Dusty asked.

"I figured if I had the chance to help these poor schmucks get a date for once in their lives, may as well take it," I replied. "Now, guys, we need your help. I don't know exactly what Greg has told you about us, and I don't care. For tonight, we're in a hurry. An actual life is at risk."

They looked back at me blankly, giving me their best ignorant stares, so I knew Greg had spilled the beans.

"Go ahead, fellas, he knows the deal," Greg said, and the nerd brigade sprang into their own strange brand of action.

Nick ran into the store and came back with a backpack and a huge flashlight. Trey whipped out a laptop and fired up a browser window, while Dusty just sat there looking a little confused.

"I'm ready, team!" Nick announced, brandishing his flashlight like a lightsaber.

"I think right now we need a little more of Trey's kind of help and a little less charging blindly into the fight," Greg said gently.

Nick looked crestfallen and put his flashlight through his belt.

I patted Nick on a shoulder. "Don't sweat it. That's my first instinct, too. Unfortunately, that's kinda what got us into this mess."

"What am I looking for?" Trey asked, fingers twitching over the keys.

"We're looking for a vampire who calls himself Professor Wideham and his gang of bloodsuckers over by the college. We went to their main lair tonight, but it was abandoned. So we need to figure out this guy's identity and where he might be hiding out," Greg said, leaning over Trey's shoulder.

"Oh, is that all?" Dusty said, coming out of his semi-trance and looking around.

"What do you mean, is that all?" I asked him. Talking to Dusty was always a little like talking to Rain Man. I never knew whether what came out was going to be pure gold or pure crap, and it usually took a long time to figure out which.

"I know Dr. Wideham. That guy's got one of the best Gold and Silver Age collections in the state. He used to come in here all the time on Game Night, but he never played anything, just looked through the back issues for hours. Said it was the only time he could make it into the store. He knows everything there is to know about Silver Age Justice League, and Flash in particular." Dusty looked pleased with himself, kind of like the look a cat would have when he dropped a dead mouse at his owner's feet.

"That's great, D. But do you know where to find him? Like we said, the frat house was empty." Greg spoke softly, so as not to spook the savant.

"Yeah, man. He hasn't lived there in years, since one of the guys messed up his Justice League Number 77. Took him like three years to replace that book, so he took all his stuff and moved into a place of his own." Dusty's gaze fogged with recollections of Silver Age Justice League issues, and Greg had to snap his fingers to bring him back.

"Sorry, man," Dusty apologized.

"It's okay, D. Where does he live now?" I asked.

"Who?" Dusty looked confused again, and I was afraid I was going to eat him if we didn't get to the point sometime soon.

"Dr. Wideham. Where does the Professor live, Dusty?" I spoke slowly, using small words.

"Oh, I don't know off the top of my head, man. Somewhere up near the university, but not with the other guys anymore. Not since they—"

I cut him off. "Ruined his Justice League Number 77, we know. But how would you get in touch with him if you found a rare comic that you thought he'd want to see or maybe buy?" I thought if I used his terms, maybe that would get Dusty down out of the clouds for a couple of precious seconds.

"Oh. I've got his address in the computer, man. Why didn't you ask?" He wandered off toward the computer at the front of the store, shaking his head.

"Go with him. Make sure he doesn't get lost," I told Greg with my face in my palm. He came back a few minutes later with a slip of paper.

"Got it. Two known addresses for Dr. Wideham, who sometimes uses the name John Jones for anonymous auction-type stuff." He grinned when he said the name, like I should recognize it.

"I give up. Who is John Jones?"

"The secret identity of The Martian Manhunter, J'onn J'onnz, dude! This guy is a *total* Justice League nerd." Greg used a tone that said I needed to turn in my nerd card for not knowing that one.

I still didn't get it, but I nodded enough to get him to leave. We were almost to the back door of the shop when I heard Dusty's voice coming from the cash register. "Hey, man, if you like, exterminate him, can I have his comics?"

Chapter 23

I grabbed the scrap of paper with Wideham's addresses on it from Greg as we walked to the car. Then I stopped cold.

He kept going for a couple of seconds before he noticed I wasn't with him anymore. "What's up?" he asked, jogging back to where I stood.

"Well, we don't have to worry about which address he'll be at." I pointed to the paper.

"Why's that?" Greg asked.

"Nothing about this address looks familiar to you?" I asked, waving the paper in front of his face.

"Not at that speed, no." He grabbed it from me and looked closely at the numbers Dusty had scrawled. After a couple of seconds, it hit him. "Oh, crap."

"Yeah. Oh, crap is right. Think it's a coincidence that this Professor character has an apartment in the same building the Master of the City has a fancy restaurant?" I took the paper from him and threw it over my shoulder.

"Not so much. So, what do we do?" Greg didn't look too keen on any more run-ins with the Master, and truth be told, I wasn't thrilled with the idea either. But Sabrina needed my help, so I swallowed hard, got in the truck and cranked the engine.

"We don't do anything tonight. We've only got a couple hours left until dawn, and I'd bet anything that Tiram has told Professor Wideham all about our little visit by now. We need to hole up someplace and make a plan. And I know just the place." I pulled the truck into traffic and started back toward the campus. Greg looked at me quizzically, but I just smiled and dug out the phone I'd swiped from Tiny back at the pawn shop.

King answered after a couple of rings. "I almost didn't answer, but I figured not knowing the number doesn't mean much around here."

"Yeah, sorry about that. I'm tough on cell phones. This one's a loaner."

"Does the owner have any use for a cell phone anymore?" the werewolf asked.

I stared at the phone for a minute in confusion, then the meaning of his words sunk in. "Dude! I did not kill the last guy that had this number. Seriously. Now meet us at the back entrance to the church in ten minutes. I've got the address. Greg wants to grab a few toys out of the safe at our old place, then we're going to go be very, very violent."

It took more like five minutes to get to the church, and we loaded everyone into the pickup. Abby and I took the back seat, and we headed for what used to be our apartment.

We drove right through the yellow police tape, and Greg hopped out, running straight to the burned-out shell of the garage. His boots kicked up little puffs of ash as he ran, and I looked around the desolation that used to be a decent apartment, albeit an underground lair type of apartment. Greg let out a wail of anguish and fury when he got to his car. His beloved 1967 GTO was nothing but a frame on melted tires, barely enough left to recognize it for the badass muscle car it had once been.

I left him to his grief and jumped down into the remnants of the apartment to poke around. Not much was left standing, just the major support beams and a couple of walls. The cheapo desk Greg's computer had lived on had made it out almost unscathed, confirming my belief that particle board was made of magical components to reduce cost and increase weight. I wandered dumbly through the den and kitchen that had been my home for more than a dozen years, thinking about the good times we'd had there. I made my way into what used to be my bedroom, kicking debris out of the way, until I saw a glint of metal. I reached down and picked up the sword that had come back from Faerieland with me, still in its leather scabbard. The scabbard and sword belt seemed none the worse for wear, and when I drew the sword, the blade gleamed just as brightly as when I had used it to fight trolls in the castle of the Faerie Queen.

Before climbing out of the hole, I paused by what used to be our kitchen and kicked over the refrigerator. The door fell open, spilling exploded beer bottles and bags of boiled blood onto the ground. Our safe was intact, so I yelled up to Greg for the combination. I didn't understand why he picked 11-10-60, and didn't care, because when I pulled the door open, there were stacks of cash and a bag full of fake IDs and credit cards for both of us. I stuffed whatever would fit into my pockets and carried the rest up to the truck.

"Nice haul," King said.

"Well, you always forget something when you go on a trip, right?"

"Yeah, but it's not always a hundred grand and half a dozen passports."

"Boy Scout motto is be prepared."

"You were no Boy Scout," Abby said from the backseat.

"Yeah, but I've drunk a couple of Eagle Scouts in my day. Besides, most of this is Greg's." I gave Greg another moment or two to mourn his car, then waved him back into the truck.

"What's the plan?" Greg asked, as he slid into the backseat of the pickup.

I looked back at him. "We go get our friend back. And kill anything that tries to get in our way. Agreed?"

"Agreed. And maybe get a little revenge for what they did to Maybellene."

"You called your car Maybelline? Like the makeup?" Abby asked.

"No, like the old song, you know?"

"No. I don't. And why do guys have this obsession with naming things, anyway?"

"We are so not having this conversation." Greg turned to look out the window, and we rode the rest of the way in silence.

That sucked for me because I didn't need more time to think about what they might be doing to Sabrina. Or to worry about Abby's role.

I wasn't crazy about bringing Abby in if we were going to fight a bunch of vamps, but we'd seen how well leaving her behind had worked. We parked at the far end of the front parking lot, and I gathered everybody in to explain what little plan I'd devised.

"Here's the deal. We're going in blind, with no idea what's in there waiting for us. Judging from the traps laid out around the frat house, it seems like our friend is a wee bit security-conscious, as well he should be. So we don't know if Sabrina's in there, or where she's being held or how many bad guys we might have to face to get to her."

"So, it's hopeless?" Abby asked.

"Well, if we weren't already dead, I wouldn't have a lot of confidence in our coming out of this alive. But since that matters less to us than to a lot of people, I think we'll be okay." I didn't think anything of the sort, and I could tell from the nod King gave me that he knew it. But Abby was scared enough, so there was no point in giving her anything else to worry about. "Now, we have enough firepower here to seriously ruin a vampire's day, but you have to know what you're doing."

"I've never even held a gun before, but cool!" Abby struck a pose straight out of *Tomb Raider*. *Just what I needed, a psycho gun-nut cheerleader coed to raise as if it were my very own. Next time I'm totally getting a cactus.*

"That's why you're on the shotgun. Point, pull the trigger and rack the slide. Lather, rinse, repeat. Anything in front of you will have a tough time getting through all the lead you'll be slinging." I handed her a twelve-gauge and a couple of boxes of ammo. "When you're out, put shells in here. If you run out of time, use it like a baseball bat."

King was already neck-deep in the stack of guns I'd swiped from the pawnshop. He grabbed an AR-15 and a pair of 9mm handguns.

"I don't know if I have ammo for that rifle, King," I protested.

"I do." He reached into a toolbox bolted to the bed of the truck and pulled out a box of rifle shells.

"But you don't carry a gun?" Abby asked.

"Ammo isn't illegal anywhere, darlin'. Guns are a different story. It's not usually a big deal to pick one up wherever I am, but it's not something I want to have in the truck if I get pulled over by a nervous state trooper." He took a few magazines, then put one in the gun and the others in his back pockets.

Greg got out of the truck and helped himself to a couple of pistols and a shotgun. I took another AR-15 and started loading my own clips. After a few minutes, we were as ready as we were going to get.

I looked at my motley crew. "I don't know if we'll find anything. Might be all that happens is we scare the crap out of a few bankers and move on to the next house on our list. Or we might find a nest of vamps ready to kill us all. But . . ." I ran out of words trying to let them know how important it was to go in and get Sabrina to safety.

Greg stepped up and put a hand on my shoulder. "Let's go get her back."

We all nodded and headed toward the front door, bristling with fangs, firearms and bad attitude.

The entrance to the restaurant was separate from the apartment lobby, so we had at least a passing chance of getting upstairs without the Master knowing about it. I walked in the front door and strode to the security desk as if I owned the place.

"Can I help you, sir?" This came from a polite blond kid with a crew cut and some fierce acne.

I leaned my elbows on the counter and locked eyes with him. "Everything is normal. Nothing out of the ordinary has happened tonight. You lost your security badge somewhere." I reached out and snatched the magnetic ID card from around his neck. "You never saw anyone except residents and guests."

The mesmerized guard nodded slowly, and King took a second to strip down to his undies before shifting into his tall, dark and furry form. I thought I saw Abby lick her lips at the werewolf's trim form, but pushed any comment aside for later as we got in the elevator.

"We know his apartment number, so that's the easy part. King and I will go in first. Greg, you follow five seconds later with Abby." They all nodded, and I took a deep, and completely unnecessary, breath as the elevator dinged at the penthouse level. We crossed the foyer to Wideham's door, King on my heels and the others about twenty feet behind.

"What's the plan?" he whispered.

"I'm making it up as I go along. Can you hear anything?"

"No, but gimme a second." He put his nose to the hinge side of the door and sniffed deeply. He bent over and repeated the process at the bottom of the door, then stood back up. "There are at least two vampires on the other side of the door, both packing."

"How—" I started to ask, but he waved me off.

"Stale blood and gunpowder. How do we go?"

"Fast. I've got the left."

King reared back with one huge foot and kicked the door off its hinges. He and I were the first ones through, and what we saw in there made us both stop cold. There were about a dozen vampires in various states of undress, sleepwear and drug-induced stupor.

But my eyes locked on Sabrina. She was tied to a straight-backed kitchen chair with a skinny vampire standing over her. He didn't look like any professor I'd ever seen, and he didn't exude that sense of power over the other vampires that would make me think he was their creator, so I pegged him for just another punk bloodsucker in a Widespread Panic T-shirt.

"Make another move, and I'll drain her before you can blink," the vamp said. "She's pretty empty already, what with my boys here snacking on her for the past couple of days. It shouldn't take more than another nibble or two, and she'll never need sunscreen again. So put down your weapons, and let's pretend to be civilized."

I knelt and laid my rifle on the carpet. As he smirked at me, I reached behind my back, grabbed the .357 revolver I had tucked into my belt and shot him once in each eye.

Chapter 24

The vampires reacted to stress a lot like humans, especially the ones that hadn't been dead for very long. It wasn't surprising, since we started off as human, and no one gave us a vampire behavior manual when we were turned. So it wasn't unexpected when about a third of the vamps took off at a dead run once the shooting started, because that was what about a third of humans would do. Another third sat there like morons and screamed, which made them particularly easy to dispatch, but the final third presented a little more trouble.

I shot the three screamers in their foreheads. The large-caliber bullets wouldn't kill them since they weren't silver, but they weren't going to be any threat for the rest of the night. I tossed the pistol aside and bent down to pick up my rifle again. Before I could raise it, I heard the roar of a shotgun and felt the breeze as pellets flew over my back. I dropped flat onto my stomach and rolled over to see Abby standing over me, barrel smoking. Her eyes were huge, and I followed her gaze to where a vampire lay in two pieces on the tattered rug. A twelve-gauge at eight feet made a big mess, and Abby had gotten the guy full in the gut.

"I think that counts as decapitation," I said from the floor, and reached a hand up to Abby. I looked over at Sabrina, who had closed her eyes against the splatter of guts, but none of the pellets had so much as scratched her.

Abby helped me stand, and we looked around the room. Of the four vampires who had attacked when I shot the first guy, all but one was down. Greg had emptied a 9mm magazine in one guy's face, King had ripped one vampire's throat out with his bare hands, and a third poor bastard was standing there looking at us with a kitchen cleaver in his hand.

I took one step toward him, raised my AR-15 and said, "Did you touch her?"

He stared at me blankly.

I repeated myself. "The girl. Did. You. Touch. Her?"

He shook his head frantically. "N-no."

"Then I don't have to kill you." He stood there, staring at the barrel of my gun. "You should run now."

He apparently thought that was good advice because he dropped the cleaver and ran straight through the living room window. His legs never stopped moving, and I wondered idly if he'd learn how to fly before he hit the ground. I looked out at where he lay crumpled on the hood of a burgundy Jetta. *Nope. Guess not.*

Greg was already at Sabrina's side, kneeling by her legs and untying her. She looked up at me, still bleeding a little from a bite on her neck and splattered with blood and vampire bits and said, "You're late. The movie started at nine."

Then she gave me a little grin, and I felt blood flow to places I barely remembered were places.

"Traffic was a bitch," I said, kneeling beside her chair and cutting her bonds.

"Who's the Wookie?" She nodded at King, who was still seven feet of hair and bloody claws.

"Remember that PI you met last night? This is his work uniform," I said.

"Don't you have any normal friends?"

"Do you count?"

"Not since I met you."

"Then no."

She looked around the room at the dead and writhing vampires, and then looked back at me.

"You made a mess of this place. The cops will probably be here soon." She wiped her eyes, obviously trying to regain her composure.

"I doubt that sincerely, Ms. Law. As a matter of fact, they will not be responding to any calls in this part of town for the next several hours."

Sabrina leapt to her feet and snatched the AR-15 from my hands. She checked the chamber and slammed the gun into her shoulder, ready to fire.

A tall, well-dressed vampire stood in the remains of the doorway. He exuded class and breeding, things I'd read about in books but never really seen much of. His long brown hair was pulled back into a neat ponytail, and he picked his way through the debris as he came toward me, careful not to soil the cuffs of his suit pants. I hated him on sight.

"Professor Wideham, I presume?" I stepped forward, getting between him and Sabrina, and held out my hand. I wanted him dead, didn't really care if I killed him or Sabrina did, but I needed information first. *And once again, the bloodsucking fiend is thrust into playing the voice of reason. This keeps up, people are going to tell me I'm acting my age.*

He shook my hand and nodded. "Precisely."

I decided if he called me "my dear Watson," I'd just rip his head off and skip the banter.

"To what do I owe the unique pleasure of your company this evening?" he asked.

"We're here to retrieve our friend. Oh, and to cut off your head and crap down your neck. That's all," Greg said from beside me. He was pretty fast for a fat dude.

"I don't think that will be necessary, Mr. Knightwood. After all, we have such mutual affection for one of my students. Come in, my dear. Say hello to your big brother." He waved an arm and a pretty young girl, about the right age for a college senior, came into the room.

I heard a sharp intake of breath from beside me and decided as soon as the girl came into view that this guy was coming down with a bad case of dead. Tonight. I expected it to be terminal. And permanent.

Emily had been six when we were turned. She was the cutest little kid—smart, funny, sweet, and Greg had doted on her. She was the little sister I never had. Letting her believe we were dead had been the hardest thing Greg had to do since being turned, and now there she stood. She stopped beside the elder vamp, her eyes glazed.

"Let her go. She's got nothing to do with this." Greg's voice was low and dangerous.

When I looked over at him, I saw a pain in his eyes I hadn't seen since a cheerleader pranked him at our junior prom. I swore that night nobody was ever going to hurt my friends like that again. Now this asshole trots Emily out like a goddamn show pony? After burning down my house and kidnapping my girlfriend? Oh, it was *on*.

"Oh, but she has everything to do with this, Mr. Knightwood. After all, she's missed you terribly. She talks about her dearly departed brother in all of our advising sessions. She's really very bright, you know. It would be such a waste if anything were to happen to her."

He put a hand on her shoulder, but all I saw was how close it was to her neck. There was no way any of us could get to her before the monster snapped it like a twig.

A heavy silence fell over the room. I almost heard us all thinking, trying to come up with a plan that didn't end with Emily dead, or worse. After an eternity or two, I said, "What do you want?"

"Well, I seem to be in need of a new door, for starters," Wideham said calmly.

"And we're short a place to live. I think we're probably even on that count, Teach." I sat down on the remains of the sofa and put my feet up on the coffee table.

Sabrina lowered the rifle and moved over behind the sofa, putting the furniture between herself and the supernatural creatures. It seemed like he was more into talking than fighting at that moment, and anything I could do to ratchet the tension down a hair was probably a good move.

"Yes, well, that was unfortunate. But you did initiate the hostilities." He flipped an armchair upright and sat in it. Emily knelt at his side like an obedient pet.

I caught Greg's eye and gave him what I hoped he took for a "chill out,

I have an idea" look. But for all I knew, it just looked like I had to sneeze. Either way, he backed up a step, and so did King.

"What are you talking about? We didn't even know you existed until I caught your scent where Krysta killed Abby." I leaned forward, really confused.

Oddly enough, that was a little comforting. When you spent as much time confused as I did, it became kind of your status quo. Without a clue what was going on, I felt a lot more normal.

"You mean, where Krysta left young Abigail as an offering to me. A gracious gift in exchange for passage through my territory."

"Your territory? I didn't realize this was your city?" I might not be the most socially-adept vampire in the world, but I was beginning to see the picture.

"It's not my city, but I have an arrangement by which the University area is my domain."

Suddenly, it made a lot more sense.

"I get it now. Krysta hunted on your turf, so she had to make it right. And the way to do that was to give you Abby."

Out of the corner of my eye I saw Sabrina's gun start to inch up, ever so slowly. King started to ease off to the left to flank Wideham as he fell into the soliloquy trap. Everybody knows the way to beat a bad guy—give him a chance to talk about his plan. And Wideham was more than happy to play all leather-elbowed lecturer. All he needed was a pipe and a poncey accent to complete the image.

I leaned back again, waving at Abby to be quiet. Her twenty-something college student idealist feminist sensibilities had been offended, so I looked up at her. "It's got nothing to do with you being a girl, sweetheart. It's more about the fact that you were a meal. Krysta turned you, and the Prof here was supposed to find you and make you part of his little posse."

"Exactly, Mr. Black. Perhaps you aren't as much an idiot as you appear," Wideham said, smiling as he played with Emily's hair.

"I'm not enough of an idiot to keep putting my hands on Greg's sister with both of us in the room, that's for sure."

His hand froze, and his eyes flicked over to Greg. Greg hadn't moved, but that was all the distraction I needed.

I kicked the coffee table up into the air, and yelled, "Grab her!" to King.

The big werewolf was almost vamp-fast, and had been waiting for my signal. He snatched Emily up and bolted for the door. A young vampire came in from the hallway to intercept him and found himself suddenly with a face full of lead courtesy of Sabrina and her AR-15. The last thing he saw was a .223 round punching through his eyeball. King got Emily out of the room and didn't stop moving as Greg, Abby and I encircled the older vamp.

"Very well played, children. But now it's time for the grown-ups to be in charge again. So *sleep*."

I felt the mojo in his words roll over me, and I watched Sabrina sag bonelessly to the floor. Abby fought it, but she was no match for the older vampire's mind. The couple of Wideham's minions that had managed to regain their feet went out as well, and Greg and I were left alone with the professor-turned-vampire.

Chapter 25

"Should we do this the easy way," I asked Greg, "or the hard way?"

"I vote the hard way," my partner said, as he cracked his knuckles.

I drew the faerie sword and passed it over to him. He had a lot more *Lord of the Rings* fetish than I did. I just wanted to punch the bad guy's heart out through his spine, but I figured Greg wanted to do things with a little more flair.

"Boys, do you really think you can match my power, my intellect, my experience?" Wideham was trying to maneuver us so we had our backs to the shattered window, but I didn't budge. Greg didn't either, and that was a lot of bulk to move.

"Nope," I said. "But I think we've got you crushed on witty banter and dashing good looks."

I launched myself at the vampire, but he dodged easily. Of course, when he did, he dodged right into Greg's meaty fist. I heard a sound like a lot of bubblewrap popping all at once.

I winced. "And the good-looks gulf just gets wider. I'm pretty sure that's the sound of a crushed nose."

The Professor let out a snarl and dove for me, almost taking flight in his rage. I easily sidestepped, then caught one arm as he went past. It wasn't exactly judo, more the product of watching a lot of Saturday afternoon Bruce Lee movies, but it was enough to toss him into a wall. More drywall dust filled the room, and Wideham pulled himself out of the shattered wall. He turned to us, holding up both hands in a placating gesture.

"Now, boys, why can't we be friends? You can join my fraternity, live in our house with us. I hear you need a place to live. We could hunt together, pick up college girls together. Dine together." I heard a creak of the ruined floor and dropped straight down, just barely avoiding the machete swinging at my throat from behind. Greg wasn't as quick, but he didn't have to be. The difference in our heights once again proved his salvation, as the blade whistled right over his head and buried itself into a wall.

I stood up and found myself face-to-face with maybe the single largest vampire I had ever seen. Six foot ten if he was an inch, the bearded blond behemoth looked every bit of a *Thor* stunt double, only with fangs and über-white skin. He looked down at me, something that almost never happened to me, and grinned.

That was twice in one week I'd been the short guy in a fight, and I didn't like it one bit. I smiled a sickly smile, and mumbled, "Nice giant, don't eat the skinny one."

Thor punched me in the gut, and I folded like an origami swan. I heard a couple of floating ribs crack and dropped to one knee. Thor smiled and reared back to kick me in the face. That's when Sabrina came up from behind the sofa with her rifle and put five rounds in the big vampire's back. Thor howled in pain and whirled on my grinning girlfriend.

"How?" I croaked.

"I don't mojo, remember?"

She emptied her clip into the big vampire, but he never stopped. Thor charged, and Sabrina swung the rifle like a bat. She connected with one forearm, but Thor backhanded her into Dreamland.

I came to my feet with a pistol in each hand and a lopsided grin on my face. "That was my girlfriend, asshole," I said.

Thor just looked at me and laughed as he pulled a shotgun out of the back of his pants. Seriously, the dude had a sawed-off shotgun in the waistband of his pants as if it were a .38. He pointed it at my face, and said, "You're right, dipshit. She *was* your girlfriend. Now she's my next snack." He flashed a vicious grin and pulled the trigger.

The shotgun boomed loud in the small apartment, and buckshot blew out even more glass, but I was out of the way long before Thor pulled the trigger. I was fast—crazy fast. I tapped the behemoth on the shoulder, and when he turned around, there was a 9mm pistol pressed against each cheekbone.

"Now put the gun down, and jump out the window, or I'm repainting this place in Giant Brain Gray."

Thor did as I told him, and I heard a sickening crash from below as he landed on a vehicle and blew every piece of glass out of the frames.

I turned to where Wideham stood in the middle of the room. He hadn't budged through my whole encounter with his bruiser, just stood there watching. Greg had a gun in his non-sword hand, but something told me he wasn't going to have any more luck shooting the Professor than Thor had shooting me.

"Well played, gentlemen, well played," Wideham said, stepping forward with a smile.

Greg pulled back the hammer on his pistol, but then the older vampire's hand blurred, and the gun simply wasn't there anymore. I heard another small crash outside, and then heard the gun go off down in the parking lot.

"I thought I was fast," I said, looking at the master vamp with new respect.

"You are, for one so young. But I have been haunting institutions of higher learning since I entered Cambridge with little Francis Bacon. I have, as you say, learned a thing or two along the way. And one of those things is that gentlemen, true men of letters, never sully their hands in a confrontation with the lesser classes."

With that, he bolted for the open door, only to find Greg standing there. I never even saw my partner move, he was just *there*. Wideham looked at Greg's stony face, then at the golden sword and stepped backward into the room. He turned to make a dash for the open window, but I blocked his escape.

"I don't want to fight you boys. It's dreadfully uncivilized." The Professor held up his hands as his eyes scanned the room for another way out.

Greg tested the edge of Milandra's sword on his thumb, licking the thin line of blood that appeared. I never understood how that sword stayed so sharp. I only ever used it in sparring, but it never got dull. That might be a very good thing before the night was over.

"I think you're right, Professor. Somebody's going to get hurt." Greg's eyes were flat, a slight tremor in his hands the only hint at the rage he fought to hold back.

The old vampire looked over at me, pleading. "Mr. Black, please restrain your friend. There is no need for further violence, is there? I can leave town, never return. Find a new place to hunt, a new university in which to lecture. I give you my word I shall never return to Charlotte."

"You're right," Greg said, "You won't." And in a blinding lunge, he thrust the sword through Wideham's heart.

The sword wasn't wood or silver, but it seemed to have the desired effect anyway. The blade slid out the back of the elder vampire's chest, and then the whole thing started to glow with a bright purple light. The Professor's body glowed in turn, and the same purple light came flooding out of his eyes, ears, nose and mouth. In a matter of seconds, his entire body was consumed with blinding lavender light, and then, quicker than a blink, the light was gone.

And so was Dr. Wideham. There was a small pile of clothing covered in purple dust on the floor where he had stood, and the sword in Greg's hand was just an ordinary, if very sharp and ridiculously magical, blade again.

I reached out carefully, took the sword from him and slid it back into the sheath on my hip. He looked at the pile of dust on the floor, raised a foot and kicked it all over the rug. "Nobody messes with my baby sister."

Then he turned and walked slowly toward the door. I stood there like a moron watching him go, then shook myself and helped get Sabrina and Abby awake.

"Come on," I said to Sabrina. "We should get out of here before the police show up."

"The police are the least of your worries, Mr. Black," a familiar voice said from the hallway.

The lack of a door was really starting to get on my nerves. I looked up to see the Master of the City standing in the doorway. Greg backed up a lot faster than he'd been walking forward, but at least he didn't run away.

"People have got to quit calling me that. It makes me think my dad has shown up all of a sudden, and that would not be cool." I tried to look a lot less terrified than I actually was. I took a step in front of Sabrina, and Greg motioned for Abby to get behind him.

"I apologize for any respect I may have granted you then, James. Now, what in the world are we to do about you? This makes twice in one evening where I have been forced to mesmerize an entire restaurant full of patrons. I simply cannot allow this type of behavior to continue." He stepped into the room and surveyed the damage. "And where shall I send the bill for this cleaning? I understand you are between addresses at the moment."

It wasn't my finest moment. I should have kept my mouth shut in front of the vampire who'd already beaten me to a pulp once that week.

But I wasn't known for my discretion. I crossed my arms and said, "We would have been done with this hours ago if you'd bothered to tell us that this douche-rocket was here in your building, instead of making us run all over town looking for him. Then we would only have inconvenienced you for one meal, not two."

Tiram looked up at me, eyes wide. He obviously wasn't accustomed to being called out, at least not by anything that wanted to keep living. We stood there, almost nose to chin for the longest few seconds in recent memory, then he did the last thing I expected.

He laughed. The Master of the City threw back his head and laughed as if I'd just told the funniest joke since Bill Cosby retired from stand-up.

"Well said, James, well said. You are correct, of course. Had I not been protecting the 'douche-rocket,' as you so eloquently put it, we would not be in this predicament now. But I don't believe that is the point."

"You're damn right that's not the point, you pointy-toothed son of a bitch," Sabrina said. She pushed her way past me and got right up in the Master's face. She looked up at the boss vampire with a set jaw and gleam in her eye that said she really, really wanted to stake something.

"Have I done something to offend you, Detective?" Tiram said with a raised eyebrow.

"You mean other than aid and abet a kidnapping, harbor a fugitive and assist in the assault of a CMPD detective? I'm sure I can come up with something else, but that sounds like a good start to me. Now why don't you come clean about what you really wanted out of this mess and quit yanking our chains before I haul your ass five blocks south and stick you in an east-facing cell?"

Tiram glared at Sabrina, then looked back at me. "Can't you keep your human under control?"

"I'm not even stupid enough to try, pal. She carries a gun and a stake, and knows how to use them both." I held up both hands and tried not to smile at Tiram's discomfort.

"And he knows exactly where I'd shove that stake if he or anybody else ever tried to control me, asshole. Now spill. What was this all about?"

I put a hand on Sabrina's shoulder. "Stand down, Wyatt Earp. It was all a play to get us to kill Wideham. Or Wideham to kill us. I don't know which, and I really don't think the Master here really cared one way or the other."

"Well said, James. You're absolutely correct. I had no real preference which group survived this encounter, as long as one of you did not."

"Why?" Sabrina asked.

She looked around the room and I could see the sheer carnage start to sink in. There was blood thicker than the paint in some places, and the carpeting was so sodden it squished under our feet. There were pieces of vampire *everywhere*, and the stink of blood was enough to make a slaughterhouse smell like a rose garden.

"Because now we can't band together to overthrow him," I said, looking at Tiram.

He nodded. "Wideham's group was stupid, but numerous. You are few in number, but you have amassed some very powerful allies in a short period of time and have proven resourceful. I did not want you to join forces with Wideham against me. I could easily slaughter one of you, but not both."

"And now, with Wideham turned to so much crud on the carpet, Tiram's power base is solid again. Because we don't want to run things, and even if we did, we couldn't take him without a lot of help," I said.

"And thus status quo is restored," Tiram said with a little bow.

Sabrina looked at the Master and smiled. "Fair enough. Stalemate. We aren't strong enough to beat you in a fight, and you don't have enough muscle to kill us off, not to mention that there's a lot of interest from local authorities when a police officer is killed. But remember one thing, *Master*. These guys do have friends with a lot of juice in this town. And I'm one of them. So you screw with them, and I'll hurt you in ways you can't even imagine."

"I have a very vivid imagination, Detective." Tiram looked at her with a leer.

I grabbed the front of his shirt and picked him up. "You ever look at her again, and I will rip your head off and drink you dry from the inside out. Do you understand me?"

Tiram nodded, a little smirk playing across his face. "You can try, James. You can try."

I saw a shadow flicker across his eyes, and I flashed back to a couple of possessed faeries I'd killed recently. I started to have a sneaking suspicion that Tiram might have a hitchhiker in his psyche, but I wasn't going to go after him tonight. I was tired, hungry and not at all sure I could beat him on my best day. I set him down, deciding to find a better day to take on the Master of the City.

"I am so glad we have reached a peaceful conclusion. But what shall we do about all of this?" He gestured to the mess, including the puddles of dissolving vampire strewn around the apartment.

"Call a cleanup crew and mojo your way out of the bill?" I suggested with a shrug.

Tiram cocked his head to the side and laughed again. "Well, of course. But I was referring to them." He pointed more specifically to the vampires we didn't kill. There were a good five or six of them in various states of disrepair, but they'd all heal with enough blood and time out of the sun.

"I don't really care. We didn't kill them, but that's as far ahead as we thought. There were other things we had to take care of, if you know what I mean." I waved a hand at Sabrina, and the Master nodded.

"Well, I am short on kitchen help, and they should be able to wash a dish if nothing else. All of you!" He clapped his hands, and the recuperating vamps all came to attention, or at least managed to stand. "Go downstairs and hide in the walk-in freezer. It has a bolt on the inside of the door, and a five-gallon bucket of blood labeled 'pig testicles' on the top shelf. Try not to spill too much."

The survivors made their shuffling way out of the apartment, giving Greg and me wide berth as they did. I didn't blame them. After all, we had kind of shot them just about an hour before.

"Okay, then," I said, "What are we all waiting for? Let's go home. Maybe get a little sleep."

"And a shower," Sabrina said, looking at the brains and blood splattered all over her clothes.

"Need help washing your back?" I asked.

She glared at me, and I gave her my best innocent smile, which was hampered by the fact that my fangs were still extended. Hey, I was hungry. Really.

"As soon as I do, Jimmy, you'll be the first to know." She smiled a little at me as we all walked down the hall to the elevator.

Chapter 26

It was a little surreal riding in an elevator with the Master of the City. This was the same guy who'd stood by as Krysta tossed my best friend off a roof, the same guy who hid the Professor from us while Sabrina was his captive. Every instinct in my body told me I needed to kill him. Well, every instinct except the ones that were screaming to run away as fast as my size elevens would carry me.

For his part, Tiram just stood in the elevator like anyone else, watching the numbers change and whistling a little tune.

"So, how did you become the Master of the City?" I asked in a feeble attempt at small talk.

"I killed my predecessor," Tiram said simply.

Greg shot me a look that said, *Do not piss off the badass super-vamp.*

I didn't take the hint. "Why? Just to run Charlotte? Or did he do something to you?"

"He was the Master. I wanted to be. It was impossible for me to become Master while he yet lived, so I solved the problem. And now, gentlemen, I bid you adieu." He bowed gracefully to Sabrina as the doors slid open behind him. "Detective," he said, making a grand gesture for her to exit the elevator. She ignored him and pushed her way out of the elevator.

That gesture froze in mid-swoop as he caught sight of King and Krysta squaring off in the lobby. In the middle of a giant atrium of marble and glass, the werewolf and my vampire mommy looked like a couple of prizefighters circling, looking for the right moment to strike. Krysta had the lobby guard by the throat, using his body as a shield, and King was circling her, trying to get a good shot. He had his AR-15 at his shoulder, and the assault rifle looked like a toy in the hands of the seven-foot werewolf.

"It seems your friend has found his quarry, Black," Tiram said from beside me. "Unfortunately for him, she is under my protection as a visiting vampire to our fair city. Should she come to any harm, I would be forced to respond with extreme retribution."

"In English, please. It's been a long damn night."

"According to the ancient treaties of vampiric territory and hospitality, if your wolf friend kills Krysta while she's under my protection, I'll be forced to kill him and anyone that tries to help him."

"Yeah, that's what I thought you said," I said, heading toward King.

"Greg, get Emily out of here. Abby, go find us some transportation. It needs to seat at least six. Sabrina, cover me. Tiram—"

"I will do as I will, Mr. Black," the Master Vampire snapped.

"Fine, just don't get in my way while I clean up your mess. Let me deal with King." I turned to face the Master, and he held up both hands with a slight smile on his face. I knew there was more going on here than he was admitting to where Krysta was concerned, and it was really pissing me off. Out of the corner of one eye, I saw Greg pull Emily from behind the guard's desk and hustle her out the front doors. Abby was long gone, and with Greg keeping Emily safe, I could concentrate on the big furry problem at hand.

"I wouldn't dream of interfering." Tiram leaned against the wall beside the elevators, arms folded, as I headed toward King.

"King, what's going on?" I asked, as I came into his peripheral vision.

"What does it look like, Jimmy? I'm going to kill this bloodsucking bitch." He never took his eyes off Krysta, who kept an equally sharp focus on King.

The guard looked at me as if I were Santa Claus, the Tooth Faerie, and Jesus Christ all rolled into one. Yet he was the one I was least likely to save. At least he wasn't likely to have to live with the disappointment.

"I can't let you kill her, King. She's under the Master's protection."

"So you're working for the Chief High Bloodsucker now? Can't say as I'm surprised. All you bloodsucking assholes stick together anyway."

"I'm not working for him, you dick. I'm trying to save your life. If you kill her, Tiram kills you. And I don't let my friends die on my watch."

"Then don't worry about me. I'm not your friend."

"Fine, but I'm still not going to let you get yourself killed on my watch." I stepped directly into the line of fire and held up both hands so he'd see that I was unarmed.

I didn't expect him to believe it, of course, but not holding a weapon at that second was the closest he was going to come to me being unarmed. I had a Glock 17 in the back waistband of my pants and a magical sword hanging off my belt. I wasn't sure I'd be able to take King if it really came down to it. I knew I didn't have any silver ammo, but I wasn't sure what he'd loaded up with, and I didn't want to think about the damage he could do with the bowie knife on his belt. In my hands, it would be a short sword. In King's, it was more like a toothpick. But the rifle was my first concern, mostly because it was pointed right at my face.

King took a couple of steps forward. I took a couple in the other direction to counter, but I heard Krysta whisper from behind me. "Don't get too close, or he'll shoot through you to kill me."

"Stop right there, Kyle. I don't want to hurt you. But I'm not going to let you murder her."

He lowered the rifle an inch or two and looked at me as if I were nuts.

That seemed to be the look I was getting the most this week.

"Putting that monster down won't be murder, Jimmy. It'll be public service." He raised the gun again as he spoke.

I drew my pistol and aimed it at his left knee. "I don't have any ammo that will kill you, Kyle, but I bet putting a round through that kneecap won't be much fun if it's silver or lead. Now lower the weapon."

He lowered it, but asked, "Why are you protecting her? You just shot, slashed, and stomped your way through a bloodbath of biblical proportions, and now you've got a conscience? Is this some kind of vampire unity thing? Am I going to have to kill you, too? Because she dies tonight. Or I do. There's no third option."

"There's always another option, King."

"Not for me. She killed my wife. She dies. End of story."

"Is this what your wife would want you to be doing? Come on, man. Let's go get a beer, talk about women and forget this crazy bitch."

"You go get a beer. I've got killing to do."

I looked up into his yellow eyes and saw the pain there. Tears welled up, and he reached one paw over to dash them away. I snatched away the rifle, bent the barrel and tossed it across the lobby. King's hand flew to his bowie knife, but I caught his wrist before he drew it.

"No," I said. "You know it's worth your life if you hurt her while she's under Tiram's protection."

King looked down at me with a face full of anguish. I could almost see his dead wife's face in his eyes. "You act like I care, boy. You don't know loss. You don't know pain. You don't know anything. Now get out of my way."

"I know I'm not letting a good man kill himself for revenge. I know you miss her, but this is not the way. Now pull in the fangs. We're leaving. Now."

"I'm not," King said through clenched teeth. Then he punched me in the gut with his other hand, and I flew a good three feet before I hit the floor.

I shook my head to clear the cobwebs then stood up, facing King. "Ouch. Look. There is no more killing people tonight, no matter how much they deserve it. And if you have a problem with that, then we should deal with it right now." I pulled a pair of knives from my arm sheaths.

"So be it, Jimmy. Hate it had to go this way, but that bitch dies tonight, and anyone in my way dies with her." He drew that massive bowie knife and let out a roar that shook the windows.

We charged.

Everything I knew about knife fights I had learned watching Jackie Chan movies and *Deadliest Warrior* reruns. By the way he swung his giant toothpick at my head, King had a little more practical experience. So I figured I'd have to do what I always did when I was outclassed in a fight—cheat. As the werewolf charged, I did the most counterintuitive thing in the world. I threw away one of my weapons. Of course, I threw it right at King, so there was a point to it.

Pun totally intended. The knife sank hilt-deep into the werewolf's shoulder, and he paused for about half a step to yank it out and toss it aside. I waited until he was almost on top of me, then jumped straight up into the air, using my height and vamp-strength to my advantage. King slashed at my feet, but I was a dozen feet in the air and climbing by the time he got to me. I twisted around in midair and came down behind the wolf-man, who ignored me and kept charging straight for Krysta.

Krysta responded just as I expected, by throwing the guard at King and running for the hills. "Way to help yourself out, lady!"

"I don't fight dogs!" Krysta yelled back at me from her new hiding place behind an ATM.

I tossed my other knife at King's furry back, and he drew up short as the new blade sank to the hilt in his muscled flesh. King caught the guard and set him down before turning to deal with me.

"I guess we're going to have to resolve this little disagreement before I move on to the main event," he growled.

"Gotta get through the undercard first, Rocky." I drew my sword and hoped it wouldn't turn King to dust if I cut him with it.

"I don't want to hurt you, Jimmy."

I'd noticed that people only said things like that when they intended to hurt me quite badly. "And I don't want to get hurt, so why don't we just call this off and grab a beer?" I gestured toward the street outside. "There's a great brewery just a couple blocks from here. You'd have to de-fur, though. I think they have a no pets rule."

King just snarled and charged me again, leaping the last ten feet to block my jump. I stood there, waiting for him to land, then stepped to the side as soon as he got to me, slashing toward his right hamstring with my sword. He twisted at the last second and caught my blade on his, twisting my sword aside and leaving me open. With his left hand, he landed a shot to my jaw that spun me completely around and made my ears ring. I recovered quickly enough to drop to the ground and slash at his ankles, but he hopped over my attack easily and kicked me in the jaw on the way up.

I flopped onto my back and sprawled on the cold marble floor, dropping my sword in the process.

King landed nimbly in front of me and sneered down at me. "Not used to fighting someone who's as fast and strong as you are, vampire?"

"Not used to fighting someone who smells like a wet cocker spaniel, furball." I spat a little blood out along with the wisecrack, then quickly scrambled out of the way as the big bowie knife slammed into the floor where I'd been lying. I picked up my sword as I rolled over it, came up behind King and drove the mystical blade through the back of one leg. He howled in pain and swept a huge furred arm across my chest. I flew about eight feet before landing flat on my back again, this time cracking my skull on the floor.

After a couple of seconds, the stars cleared from my vision enough for me to see King limping toward me, bowie knife in one hand and my sword in the other. Sabrina stepped out from behind a desk by the elevators and fired three quick shots at the wolf-man, but he just winced and staggered. He didn't fall. I tried to stand, but a wave of dizziness took over, and I went back down on one knee.

King got to where I was kneeling and tossed my sword aside to snatch me up by the collar of my jacket. The sudden motion made the room spin again as he held me high over his head and drew back for a finishing blow with his bowie knife. The combination of the spinning room and the pain from my other injuries left me with only one move, so I used it.

Just as King slashed forward to gut me with his pig-sticker, I puked square in his face. A fountain of blood from dinner earlier cascaded into his eyes, nose and open mouth. The werewolf dropped me straight down onto my face as he tried to wipe the blood from his eyes. I lay there for a second or two listening to the werewolf curse before I got enough equilibrium back to stand up fast. I landed an uppercut to King's testicles on the way.

The big wolf collapsed, wiping his face with one paw and holding his crushed groin with the other. As he went down, I put my right kneecap through his nose. His head hit the stone with a sickening crack, and his eyes rolled back in his head. The bowie knife skittered across the lobby. After a couple of seconds, I heard a slow, sarcastic clapping and looked up to see Tiram walking slowly toward me.

"Well done, James. I thought the part where you vomited on your opponent was truly inspired." He offered me a handkerchief. I wiped the blood from my lips and passed it back to him. "Keep it," he said with a small hand gesture.

"Thanks. I came up with that move all on my own. We gonna fight now? 'Cause if so, you win."

I put the handkerchief in a back pocket and walked over to where Krysta had been watching the fight. She'd obviously decided that hanging around the superior firepower was a good move, because I found her holed up behind the guard station with Sabrina and all the guns.

"My hero," she gushed, throwing her arms around my neck in mock gratitude.

I pushed her away, in not mock disgust. "Lay off. I hooked up with you before. It didn't end well. Why didn't you run?"

"It needed to end, one way or the other. Now that you've beaten him, I'll drain him, and we'll be done with this silliness once and for all."

She started toward where King lay helpless, and I caught her arm. She struggled for a minute until Sabrina tapped her on the shoulder with a shotgun and raised one eyebrow meaningfully. Apparently, there had been a conversation while all the fighting was going on.

"I said nobody else dies tonight, and I meant it. Now, we're leaving, and you're leaving town. If I ever see you again, or even hear about you turning anyone else in my city, you're dust." I held out a hand for Sabrina, and we started for the door.

"Your city, James?" Tiram asked. "If I didn't know better, I'd think that sounded like a power play on your part."

Chapter 27

I turned and walked over to the Master of the City, picking up my sword along the way. The faerie blade glowed with a blue-white light as I approached Tiram, and I saw that flicker in his eyes again.

"I don't care how it sounds, Tiram. This is the deal. She has until midnight tomorrow night to get the hell out of Charlotte. After that, if I ever see her, smell her or hear rumor of her anywhere near this town, I'll stake her myself. This is a one-time pass, a limited-time offer. And if you don't like that, we can dance right now."

I was bluffing, of course. Tiram could take me on my best day, and my best day would always be one that didn't include a fistfight with a werewolf. The only real card I had was the sword in my hand, and by the way Tiram was focused on the glow coming from it, it was the ace I needed.

The Master looked at me with a little smile, the way a parent looks at their ten-year-old who's just made a perfectly logical argument for having ice cream for breakfast. He stared at me for a long moment, then surveyed the lobby. King was starting to come around, Sabrina was still packing a shotgun and at least one pistol, and Greg had come back into the building once it was safe for Emily.

Krysta shot the Master a look of appeal, but he shrugged and finally said, "As you wish, James. Krysta, my hospitality is hereby revoked. You are forbidden to remain in my city past midnight tomorrow, and you may never return under pain of death." He looked back at me. "Happy?"

"Thrilled. And Tiram? Next time you bring somebody in from outside the territory to settle your scores for you, don't make it be Krysta." I replied, turning and heading back to the door.

"Well done, James. You figured it out. I brought Krysta in to start the fight with Wideham because I knew you'd find her, and you couldn't resist if she were involved. Nice work. You may grow up to be a detective yet."

I sketched a little bow, came up with one finger pointed to the sky in Tiram's direction and turned for the door.

I made it about halfway across the lobby before Krysta got up the nerve to charge me, screaming like a banshee. I braced for another fight, but before I had a chance to slug my maker in the face a few times, she was tackled by a blonde streak that moved faster than any vampire I'd ever seen, including Tiram.

Abby drove a shoulder into Krysta's gut and kept right on going, running full speed into an elevator with the elder vampire taking all the force of the impact. Then, she unleashed a savage beating on her vamp-mother. It was no hair-pulling, eye-gouging chick fight. It was vampire claws, fangs and superhuman speed. Krysta looked like a frog in a blender as Abby rained punch after punch on her face, then commenced to banging her head against the polished marble floor. Less than a minute into the fight, Krysta was out cold, and Abby was up and headed to where King had rolled to one side to watch the carnage.

"Move," she snarled at the werewolf, and he scooted quickly out of her way. She picked up the bowie knife where King had dropped it, and raced back to where Krysta lay moaning, both legs broken and probably her skull as well.

I dashed to intercept Abby, but she stiff-armed me into a wall, and I sat down hard, seeing little birds and stars for about the fifth time that night.

Abby stalked over to Krysta, stood over her and said, "This is where Jimmy would say something annoying, but I don't care enough to come up with a joke."

She grabbed the vampiress by the hair with her left hand, pulled her into a sitting position and cut off her head. A black mist billowed out of her neck wound like a cloud of angry insects, coalescing around Abby for a moment before dissipating through the air.

Son of a bitch. My vamp-mom was possessed by a Sluagh.

Abby dropped the head a couple of feet away from the body, tossed the knife to land near King and walked toward the front door.

"I have an Escalade. It seats seven. Let's go."

She didn't look back at any of us as she headed out the door, and we all just watched her go. After a couple of seconds, Greg and Emily followed her wordlessly out to the waiting car, leaving me alone in the lobby with my almost-girlfriend, the Master of the City, and a werewolf that I'd beaten half to death. I wasn't sure which one of them I was more afraid of.

Sabrina came over to where I lay on my back on the marble floor and knelt down. "You okay?"

I got almost all the way up into a sitting position, then winced as I felt something slide back into its original anatomical location. "No. I mean, yeah. I mean . . . crap. Lemme try that again. Nothing's seriously broken, but the cold marble feels really good on all the hurt spots. You know what I mean?"

"Yeah. Where does it hurt?"

"I don't think my left pinky toe hurts. And my lips. And my right ear. Everything else is pretty well beat to shit."

She leaned in and kissed me, and I felt a lot better. "I knew you'd come for me."

"I always will. You're . . . I . . . I suck at this, sorry."

"You haven't had a whole lot of practice." She smiled a little. "Neither have I."

"Can we figure it out together? Might be a lot of fun trying."

"It might at that." She pulled back and looked at me.

I tensed, waiting for it. This was *that* moment. The one where the girl says something nonsensical and gentle and then walks out of the hero's life forever. But she didn't do that.

She let out a deep breath and said, "I really did. I knew you'd come for me. I've never had anybody I could trust like that. Not family, not a partner on the force, nobody."

"You've got somebody now," I said, and pulled her back in for another kiss. "Now help me up. That wolf-man really kicked my ass."

Sabrina stood, then held out a hand for me. I groaned as I got to my feet, then looked over at Tiram. I gestured to Krysta's rapidly dissolving corpse. "We're not going to have any problems between us after this, are we?"

"She was no longer protected by my hospitality. I care nothing for what happened to her."

"And the Professor?" If the guy was going to come after me, I wanted to know about it.

"Wideham and his band of morons had become an annoyance. By destroying them, you performed a service. That service almost balances the cost of the mess you created. Almost. I will not seek redress for the money you have cost me, and you are free to live in Professor Wideham's house, but the apartment here reverts to me. And I expect you to stay out of my wine cellar."

"Most days," I promised.

"Fair enough." He pressed a button for the elevator and got in as I turned to face King.

The big wolf-man had regained his feet and sheathed his bowie knife. He was human again, mostly naked, covered in blood and puke. He stood over Krysta's body, watching her turn to dust and slowly stroking the gold band on his left ring finger.

"We good?" I asked.

"Yeah, we're good."

"Thanks for your help tonight."

"Don't sweat it."

"Sorry I kicked your ass."

"Sorry I kicked yours."

We stood there for a long minute before the last bits of Krysta disappeared into a pile on the stone floor.

"What's next for you?" I asked.

"Go home. See about putting my life back together. Stay the hell away from vampires." He held out a hand.

I looked at it for a second, then gave it a shake.

"You're not bad for a soulless bloodsucking fiend, Black," he said, as we walked out the front door.

He turned left to where his truck was parked at an expired meter, tore up the tickets under his windshield wiper and got in. He fired up the truck and pulled a U-turn in the middle of the busy street, peeling rubber as he headed off to start over.

"You're not bad, either, King. For an overgrown Peekapoo," I murmured as I got into the passenger seat of the Escalade.

We'd gone about a mile before my curiosity overwhelmed me, and I looked over at Abby. "Where'd the car come from?"

"It's on loan from the bank. Or I guess it's on loan from a banker. He let me borrow it for a week while he's on vacation." She giggled a little.

"Where did he go?" I asked, my head full of visions of dead bankers littering downtown.

"Nowhere. But he's going to think he went to Aruba and let me borrow his car. Don't worry, Jimmy, I didn't kill him. Just mojo'd him a little." She reached over and patted my leg. "I know how testy you get about killing the entrées."

"I get testy about killing everyone, Abby. So you want to explain why you beat Krysta into paste?" I looked over at her, and her face had gone grave and very still. It looked as though she was getting the hang of being a vampire.

I wasn't sure I liked that.

"She killed me. I killed her back. Sounds fair to me," she said, not looking at me.

I stared at her for another mile or two, and she finally cracked. I'd had more time to practice the stony vampire stare, and she wilted under my impassive gaze.

"Please don't hate me, Jimmy," she whispered, a pale pink tear rolling down her cheek. "I lost it. I saw her coming at you, and I just lost it. I couldn't stand the thought of her hurting you, and then I couldn't stand the thought of her hurting anyone else. I had her down, she was beaten, but she looked up at me at the end and smirked at me, as though nothing I did mattered. That's what did it. I had to wipe that smirk off her stupid face." Abby pulled the SUV into a parking space near our new house and sat there, head on the steering wheel, shoulders shaking.

I reached over and clumsily patted her on the shoulder for a second or two. She glanced up at me, smiling like she'd just won the lottery or something.

"Gotcha!" Abby yelled, peals of laughter filling the cab of the Escalade.

"Seriously, Jimmy, did you really buy all that navel-gazing crap? I was *pissed*. Sure, I didn't want her hurting you, but the bottom line is, that bitch killed me, so I returned the favor. Now let's go have a beer. We won this one!" She got out of the truck and slammed the door behind her.

I looked back at Sabrina and saw the furrowed brow and worried look on her face that mirrored my own. I couldn't be sure, but I thought I'd seen a familiar shadow flicker through Abby's eyes.

"We'll take care of this later," I said, opening my own door. "For now, a beer sounds really good."

Chapter 28

I sat on the steps of the frat house, cold beer in my hand and Sabrina by my side, as we stared at the stolen Escalade across the parking lot. Greg and his sister sat on the tailgate for a long time before they got up. He hugged her for a long moment, then I saw him stare into her eyes and walk back to the frat house. Emily walked across the lot, got into a newish Prius and drove off without seeming to notice we were there.

"You all right?" I asked Greg as I handed him a beer.

"Nope." He twisted off the cap and flicked it into the distance.

"You want to talk about it?" Sabrina asked, leaning around me to stare at my partner. Her brown hair fell in front of her furrowed brow, and I absently reached over to tuck it behind her ear. She caught my hand as I brought it back down and held it while she watched for Greg's response.

"Nope." He drained his beer and reached for another.

I passed him one from the cooler behind Sabrina and watched as he sucked it down, too. It wasn't as though he could get drunk off a few beers, or even a whole lot of beers, but drinking as an Olympic event was more my speed than Greg's.

We sat there in silence looking up at the stars for a long time. Okay, we were doing more airplane-watching than star-gazing, since we were still in the city, but it was still pretty nice to sit still after the week we'd had. I was enjoying the quiet and the warmth of Sabrina's hand in mine when Greg spoke again.

"I mojo'd her," he murmured.

"You had to," I said.

"I know, but it sucks."

"Yeah, but it sucks less than her waking up tomorrow and knowing the truth. That doesn't do anybody any good." I put a hand on his shoulder, but he shrugged me off.

"I hate this, you know? This whole thing. I hate it. I know you think it's cool, being a detective, playing superhero. But it's not. There's nothing cool about this. We're just doing what we can to make it suck as little as possible, and maybe help somebody else out along the way. That's all we've got. We don't get to grow up. We don't get to have families. We just get to play video games and run around in stolen cars and watch our friends die. And I hate it. And I hate you for doing this to me." Greg never looked at me. He just stared straight ahead and let the heat in his voice carry through the whispered words.

I stared at him, not knowing what to say. After a minute that stretched into hours, all I came up with was a whispered, "I'm sorry."

"I know," he said. "And most days, that's enough. Most days, I can deal with being twenty-two and fat forever, with never being able to meet a girl who might actually like me, with never going to the beach with my kids someday like my parents did with me. Most days, I'm okay with it. But today's not that day. Today, I want to meet my little sister's fiancé. Today, I want to see her graduate in May. Today, I want to be the big brother that looks out for her all the time, not just at night. Today . . . I want to kill your sorry ass." He stood up and went into the house.

A few seconds later, I heard a door slam in the basement and knew that he had locked himself in a room.

"He'll be okay," Sabrina said.

"Yeah."

"He didn't mean that."

"Yeah, he did. Today he did. And he's right. I did this to him. I lost control and killed my best friend, and now he's got to put up with my mistake forever."

"You didn't know. You couldn't know."

"Doesn't matter, does it? It's done. I took everything away from him. He didn't deserve that. Nobody does."

"Life sucks, wear a helmet," Sabrina replied in a steely voice.

I whipped my head around to stare at her, openmouthed. After a second of doing my best fish out of water impression, I asked, "What?"

"Life's hard, Jimmy. You can wallow in it, or you can move on. No, it's not fair that you got turned into a vampire right out of college. It's not fair that you went nuts and drained your best friend, and now you guys are stuck in a bizarro *Friends* episode forever. It's not fair that Mike has cancer, or that Abby got turned before she graduated, or that my gay cousin is really a changeling from Faerieland or that my boyfriend is an undead monster. But this is the hand we were dealt. You made a choice. You chose to help people. You could have decided to be a psycho like Krysta, or a cold-blooded ass like Tiram, but you decided to take all your crap and do some good with it. So quit whining and play the game."

She reached into the cooler, got two more beers and handed one to me.

I sat there staring at her for another minute, then twisted the top off my beer. "Boyfriend?"

"That's what you got from what I said?"

"Yep. It was either that or undead monster."

"Shut up and kiss me, you idiot."

So I did.

For a long time.

Acknowledgments

As always, this book would not have been possible without the love and support of my amazing wife, Suzy. There are a few other folks I'd like to take a moment to mention here.

I've got to give a big shout out to my buddy Curtis Krumel for suggesting the name of the book. It's fairly obvious that I'm working on a theme here, and Curtis gave me this title.

Thanks to Valerie Huffman for the initial beta-read, I appreciate her help in letting me know if I was too far off track with the book. And thanks to everyone who has read the first few books and become friends with Jimmy, Greg, Sabrina and Mike. I love these characters, and it makes a poor author feel fantastic to know that you guys do too.

As always, you can find me online at johnhartness.com, and you can email me at johnhartness@gmail.com.

Thanks!

John G. Hartness
August 5, 2011

About the Author

John G. Hartness is a recovering theatre geek who likes loud music, fried pickles and cold beer. He's also an award-winning poet, lighting designer and theatre producer whose work has been translated into over twenty-five languages and read worldwide. John lives in North Carolina with his lovely wife Suzy and writes full-time.

CPSIA information can be obtained at www.ICGtesting.com
Printed in the USA
BVOW081401300912

301609BV00002B/1/P